Above The Law

By

C. P. Lamont

Text copyright © 2014 C P Lamont

All Rights Reserved.

This is a work of fiction. Names, characters, businesses, places, events,
And incidents are either the products of the author's imagination or used
in a fictitious manner. Any resemblance to actual persons, living or dead,
or actual events is purely coincidental.
No part of this publication may be reproduced, stored in a retrieval
system or transmitted in any form or by any means including
photocopying, electronic, recording or otherwise, without prior
written permission of the rights holder, application of which must be made through the publisher.

Dedicated to

The Dundee Volunteers of the International Brigade

CHAPTER ONE

He approached the solicitor's office in Reform Street in Dundee in a furtive mode; he looked up and saw that the building was in complete darkness. His dress sense was unusual for someone in their mid-thirties. He was wearing the uniform of the youth of today. The pristine white trainers and the baseball cap had all been purchased from the same trader. He was assured by the trader that all were genuine. Where else could you pick up a Lacoste leisure suit in "Winter Colours" for twenty pounds? All in all his youth's uniform had cost him less than fifty pounds. He knew that the baseball cap was also genuine; he didn't need to ask the stall holder why it only cost eight pounds. No need. But that was all in late October, now it is one week before Christmas, the season of Peace and Goodwill for the many; for the few it would be the month of mayhem and more. He casually looked up and down the street, making mental notes of the throng of Christmas shoppers and workers making their way home past the Counting House pub. This is a time when the 'credit crunch' and 'insolvent banks' were not in everyday lexicon. Two thousand and seven seemed like a normal year people were living for the day and participating in a spending frenzy; personal debt seemed to be a badge of honour. When he first walked up the street he noticed that the Counting House was jam-packed, but that the other pub on the opposite side of the street is less than full. He continued on his way to Commercial Street; took a right on to High Street then completed the circle back onto Reform Street. That was where he checked for any text messages, there were none.

The appointment had been made a week earlier. A woman had called the solicitors office and had tearfully explained that her son, Francis, had been caught shoplifting.

'That was not a problem; Mr Williams had many clients like your son, would next Friday at 4.30 be okay'? That was to be the final appointment as the office was to be refurbished.

'Fine Mr Williams will see Francis Forbes on Friday; tell him he must be on time, if he's a minute late Mr Williams will not see him.'

***

Ian Williams is in his forties, he grew up in Fintry, a Council estate, his dad unemployed and unemployable, due to his love affair with the bottle. His mum was brought up in the wealthy suburb of Broughty Ferry, she was a teacher, but gave up her profession, when she too was seduced by the bottle. Ian had always pledged to himself since that day he came home from Linlathen High School, and had seen his parents lying prostate on the filthy carpet, surrounded by wine bottles and beer cans, that he would study hard, commence a career and abstain from alcohol.

He achieved all that and more. He had earned more than a million pounds in Legal Aid fees, from the disaffected youths, junkies and hardened criminals. He had become one of the nouveau riche, the Legal Profession didn't like it one bit. There had been numerous complaints to the Law Society in Edinburgh, from his learned friends in Dundee and surrounding areas. They said he had been touting for business around the sink estates of Dundee. They said he had people at the District and Sheriff Courts press ganged into being represented by Mr Williams. Ian had refuted these wild and inaccurate allegations and put it down to professional jealousy. The Law Society acquiesced with Ian. Five years earlier he had purchased a block of apartments on a golf course in Spain.

One of the first occupants for a two week holiday had been an old friend from the time he had studied with him at St. Andrew's university. He had given him use of the apartment free of charge. His father was and still is in charge of the complaints at the Law Society.

One event that surpassed his elation at the degree ceremony; was that both his parents were there and both were sober. He never thought he would have another rush of happiness like that. But he was wrong, so wrong. His parents had been alcohol free for more than a year. Every month he had taken them to various pubs in Broughty Ferry for lunch, Jolly's, The Royal Arch, and their favourite, The Tay Inn, which looked proudly onto the Tay. They loved the breath-taking views, and after lunch they loved the walk along the beach.

Today would be different. He picked them up as usual on a Thursday at 2.30pm. He never went *into that* house that he was raised in. He *never* called it home. As usual, both parents were glad to see him. His mum had explained that their whole house had been decorated, and would he like to see it? He explained that he was too busy, but one day, if he had time he would cast his professional critical eye over it. His dad looked at his mother as if to say I told you so. She cut the silence by asking how the refurbishing of his office was going. He told her wearily, that the plans were passed but work would not commence till maybe next year, if lucky in November or December.

   He drove onto the Kingsway then into Broughty Ferry; he looked into the rear mirror he could see in his mother's eyes' the happy memories flooding through her mind. After all this was her Heaven and she had been to Hell. That day he had not parked the BMW in the car park in Broughty Ferry Road. He continued on and turned into Camphill Road and stopped at the beautiful stone house. His mum looked surprised when he got out of the car and opened her door. She just sat in the seat looking up at him. 'Are you going to sit there all day? Or are you coming in for lunch?'
'I don't understand?' His dad was confused   'It's yours,' he said. His mum got out the seat like a new born foal. She stared at him. 'Do you mean...?'
'C'mon dad, out the car, they're all waiting.' His mum is staring at the imposing windows' of the house. '
'Who's waiting?'
'Peter and James… your two sons, they're waiting in *your* house.'
His dad got out the car and followed his wife and Ian up the path to the house. She stopped half-way up the path and told Ian that this was her parents' house a long time ago.

   He waited on his dad to catch up with them. When his dad had caught his breath he told him that he had bought his mother's former house. He also explained that his two younger brothers that had been taken into care then adopted; had returned to Dundee from Wales. They wanted to meet their natural parents. 'Today they would, if you agree?'
Margaret looked at Thomas would this be the moment that she had silently hoped and prayed for?
'Everything will be all right,' Thomas reassured his wife. 'Let's move into the house.'
Margaret approached the door with apprehension; she noticed the two faces at the bay window she couldn't tell whether they were smiling or otherwise. She pressed the old- -fashioned brass bell, it was the original bell that she last pressed over forty- years ago.
'You don't have to do that mum it's your house. 'Turn the handle the door is open.'
   This she did and entered the long- hall with confident strides; she then took a right turn into the spacious lounge. Thomas is amazed at his wife's turn of speed; he followed her not knowing what awaited him in the lounge. Ian let his parents enter the lounge then he halted at the open lounge door. The wails of anguish that had built up in Margaret's heart; were let loose.
'Forgive me, forgive me', she sobbed as she threw her arms around her two sons' that she had not seen for fifteen years.
'Everything is okay mam,' James said in a Welsh accent, tears coming down his cheek. 'We are altogether now, a family said Peter.
'Da, come over here and join us.'
Thomas was always the strong silent type but he was reduced to babbling, and begging forgiveness.
   Ian watched all this with bitter- sweet memories flashing through his mind. He knew what events triggered his latent anger at his parents, but now he was trained not to let the negative thoughts enter his head. A flood of positive thoughts came to him, and self- satisfaction took hold. His mother caught Ian smiling at them, and gracefully broke away from the reunion. She flung her arms around him in a protective way and thanked him.
'Would it be okay if I could show the rest of the family around the house?
It was good to hear her say the rest of the family. 'Well you know the house better than anyone here, you take the lead, and the family will follow you.'

A nice warm feeling ran through him when he mentioned the family. He would remember that word when depression descended upon him. She garnered them altogether telling them that this was her family home before she met Thomas. Thomas is looking forward to the tour of the house, because this is the first time he had been in the house. Margaret's parents had not approved of Thomas.

They were schoolteachers and decided Thomas was not of the standard that their only daughter should marry. They were not impressed at his choice of employment either; he was a shipwright at the Caledon boat yard. They made it clear to Margaret that Thomas would not be welcome in their home. They told her that the workers' at the boat yard; were crude, ill-educated and hard drinkers, a recipe for disaster. Margaret took great pleasure in telling them that Thomas didn't drink or smoke, a feat in itself in Dundee in the nineteen- sixties. They pointed out that they didn't live in Dundee. They lived in Broughty Ferry. And so it went on and on. Petty arguments erupted till the day she left and married Thomas at the registrar office. Both sets of parents failed to attend. They set up home in a one- bed roomed flat with no bath or hot water and an outside toilet in Alexander Street, directly across the road from the noisy jute mill. She had given all this up for him. That was not the ultimate sacrifice, which had still to come.

'Does everyone agree that we should start from the top of the house and work down?'
She must have sounded like that when she was a schoolteacher at the High School of Dundee. Her voice sounded much younger, but it still carried authority. The family made their way up the twenty-four stairs, if Margaret remembered correctly. She is telling them about the cornice in the upstairs hall but at the same time counting the stairs. Twenty-four it is. She let out a sigh of relief.
'Is everything okay mam?' Peter enquired.
'Mam's just out of breath, she's not getting any younger,' said James teasingly. It was so good to hear her boys call her mum... even in a Welsh accent.

'There are four bedrooms up here, and one large bathroom,' she continued. 'The door furthest from the stairs was my bedroom; she pointed it out to them. Then next to our bedroom were my mother and father's bedroom. As I was an only child, the other rooms were used as a music room and a guest room.'
She walked with confidence towards her bedroom, her steps became haltingly painful. She instructed her family to keep up, but they all noticed how apprehensive she became as she came nearer to her bedroom door. Ian looked at her.
'Do you want time to yourself in your room mum?'
'Would it be okay?'
'No problem, take your time, I'll stick on the kettle.' The three sons galloped down the stairs like teenagers full of noise and happiness.
Thomas walked towards Margaret, smiling. 'Do you know what you said there?'
Margaret looked puzzled. 'You said our room. Are you going to show me the room then?'
She turned the handle and entered, the room is large but it was so modern, or so she thought. The original wooden floor is still there and looking majestic. She cast her eyes up to the ceiling; the rose and cornice were still in place. Her eyes darted to the original skirting. The bed is different as expected after all these years. But there is something missing?
What is it? She couldn't answer her thought. Contemporary mirrored wardrobes were the only addition, apart from the paint on the walls from the original bedroom. Then she saw a glimpse of it; the fireplace. It is there. She walked towards it, and bent down and touched it. The same black fireplace with the same Victorian tiles hidden behind chest of drawers. She stopped touching the tiles and stood upright. The tears' started to flow again. She moved towards Thomas, who met her and placed her head on his shoulder
'Everything will work out,' he whispered to her. She had to muffle her sobs.
'I don't know if God will forgive me, but will Peter and James ever?' She was inconsolable.

Thomas held her tightly and spoke quietly. 'Forgive us, not you. It was me, and me alone that destroyed this family. You did your best, but it was me, an alcoholic, that enticed you to drink. But what matters now is we have been given a second chance.'
'What must Peter and James think of us? Are they up visiting... will we ever see them again?'
'I wish I knew, I wish I knew... and let's not forget Ian, he has bought this house for us.
 And it's not just a beautiful house it was your mother and father's house; that must have taken some planning. I am too scared to ask him how much he paid for it.'
A knock is heard on the door. 'Is it okay to come in?' It was Ian.
'Come in Ian,' said Margaret.
Ian walks in and noticed his parents had been crying. 'Everything is okay... look I know what you have been thinking... about things that have happened in the past. I'm not even going to go there. The tea is ready in the kitchen, after we have our tea; mum you can continue with the tour.'
'I just want to say sorry Ian for all...'
Ian interjected. 'You have nothing to be sorry for, times were different then, not another word.'
Ian had to pinch himself for what he is saying, but it felt good.
'You as well mum, not another word.'
'We are so proud of you son, to be brought up in those horrible days, and forgive us...'
'Mum, give your face a wash, you as well dad then come downstairs to the kitchen, you know where it is mum,' he stands up. 'Don't be too long there's more news.'
Thomas looked worried. 'What kind of news?'
'Good news...' Ian noticed that he was worried. 'But until you both come down you'll never find out.' He smiled then left the room.
'I wonder what the news is,' said Margaret her eyes were red.
'Never mind that, that was the first time I have seen Ian smile, I mean naturally, not a forced smile.'
'I have never noticed that, I thought Ian always smiled.'
'Oh he does but that's part of his job, but that was a real, happy smile.'
'What do I say to the boys?' asked Margaret
'Let the words flow, but we won't know till we talk to them.'
   Margaret tries to compose herself outside the kitchen door Thomas places his hand on her shoulder and gives her a reassuring push then nods towards the door. She takes a deep breath, smiles and turns the handle and walks in smiling. All three of her sons stand up.
'Have a seat mam, what do you want in your tea,' enquired Peter
'Just milk please.'
James poured the strong tea. 'What about you da?'
'Just milk... son.' He said son, nervously. Margaret motions for Thomas to sit beside her. When he sits down he moves the farmhouse chair closer to her.
'This is all a shock to us as well mam; you can thank Ian for this. Too cut a long story short, he contacted my office and as usual came straight to the point. He asked how Peter and I would feel about meeting you and da again.'
Margaret sipped the tea praying that she would not cry again. Thomas pressed her shaking knee gently.
'I told Ian, I had hoped for this call for years, I wanted to tell you that I am an architect; and that Peter is a chartered surveyor, but I never knew if that call would ever come, that's why we are here, here to stay, if you'll have us?'
Margaret placed the cup on the table trying to look composed; she was trying to shepherd her racing thoughts. Thomas rose from the table.
   'We have never stopped loving you and Peter; we will carry the burden of placing you in care, to our graves. And you ask us if we will have the both of you? No, I ask you and Peter, will you have us as parents'? Ian started to feel very emotional; he had to say something before the ocean of tears that would come from his parents.

'Mum and Dad, this is your house now, James and Peter will be living here. They have given up their jobs in Cardiff. I have managed to secure an office for them, and I have work for them so don't worry on that score. The construction industry is booming in Dundee. I have a large land bank and James will be forwarding plans to obtain planning permission for three blocks of flats to the Council, in the next six to eight weeks. Once planning permission is granted, Peter will be ordering all the materials and will be overseeing the project, so they will be continuing with their careers.'
Margaret still looked troubled. 'I thought that would ease your mind ma?' said James.
'No, no, I'm pleased to hear what Ian said, but, what did your adoptive parents' say about you contacting us, never mind living with us as a family?
'Peter, I'll let you explain,' said James. 'Nothing would make us happier, that's what David and Mary said. They knew that this day would come. Mary said she would give you a call in the next two weeks, once you and da had settled in.'
'So mum, don't fret, and your house in Fintry will be going on the market next week, you should achieve ninety -thousand for it. That will be handy for your old age,' said Ian.
 'I am old now! In fact it's my birthday tomorrow I am sixty-six.
'And I am sixty-nine in March,' said Thomas.
'You've got years ahead of you, and tomorrow all of us including my wife Anne, will be in the Tay Inn to celebrate your birthday mum.'
Thomas and Margaret were taken aback at this because they had never seen, never mind met, Ian's wife. Their ship had come in and it was the QE2.
'I'm looking forward to that; how is she?'
'You'll have plenty of time to ask her yourself tomorrow dad.'
'What a wonderful day this has been.' Endorphins had rid her mind of depression.
'It's quite hard to take in… can I have another cup of tea James please.'
'Dad, do you fancy a breath of fresh air?'
'I was just thinking that.'
Margaret looked at him and Ian with concern.
'It's okay mum, I just want to run a few things by dad and get his opinion, if you don't mind?'
When Thomas heard this he felt more useful than he had been for years, Ian is going to ask him, his opinion. 'C'mon then son, let's go for a walk, how long will we be?'
'Half an hour tops.'
'Remember and take your coat Thomas, its November you know.' He looked at her smiling.
'I know that but it's a warm sunny day in my heart.
   Thomas and Ian left the house, Ian stood on the pavement looking at the house.
'What are you thinking son?'
Something is troubling Ian, he knew what it is, but is this the time to seek counsel from his dad? No. Today had been the day when all the sins of the past had been washed away. There is plenty of time to explain the conundrum. Thomas thought maybe he hadn't heard him.
'What are you thinking son?'
'I heard you the first time dad.' Do you not see what I see?'
Thomas stared at the house. 'What do you see… what am I looking for?'
'Never mind, I'll show you when we get back from our walk, which way do you want to go, up the hill or down?'
'Down towards the beach.' They moved in unison down the road Ian with his hands stuck firmly in the pockets of the long black winter coat.
'What's on your mind then?'
'You get straight to the point don't you?'
'I'm just worried about you.'
'Okay, replied Ian. What I am going to tell you is confidential, don't even mention or hint to mum.'
Thomas nodded.

'You realise that the docks are being gradually reduced from being a working port, into residential areas.'
'Yes, it's always on the news and in the newspapers.'
'Well, my company is proposing to buy a large swathe of land at the docks or which is now described as the waterfront. All the finance is in place, and this is where you come in. You worked at the boat yard for a long time, and you know all the area surrounding the boat yard.'
'I wouldn't say I knew all of it, but if I can help you, I will.'
'I know you would dad, but I think you have more knowledge than you realise.'
'After Christmas and New Year are out the way you and I will be going to the old area of the docks, to have a walkabout, that's if you don't mind.'
'I'm looking forward to it already, I can tell you many stories good and bad about the Caledon when I was young, they were the happiest days of my working life,' replied Thomas.
'That's what I want to hear *all* the stories, whether you think that they're relevant or not. But as I said don't mention this to mum, it's nothing illegal or anything like that, but the less people know about this the better.'

***

Margaret and her sons have moved into the lounge. She has been asking about their adoptive parents.' How they got on at school, university, and were they married?
A myriad of questions elicited from her energetic mouth. They explained that they had enjoyed their school days. The teachers' took a shine to them because of their Scottish vernacular, University was a natural progression. They were both single.
David moved to Wales because of his job he was at the forefront of developing computer programmes', back in the nineteen- eighties, computers were just being developed for the consumer market, and David was the software expert. It is Margaret's turn to explain her past and the events that resulted in her two sons being taken into care then adopted. She knew that this is going to be painful, but it would be easier because Thomas is not present.

James and Peter who had been unconsciously moving about the room looking at the paintings on the wall but are still listening attentively, sat together on the green Chesterfield sofa.
She shuffled herself into a more comfortable position. She explained that she had loving parents, and she was an only child but that they were strict they vetted her friends. But overall she had a happy childhood. She excelled at school, and went on successfully to Teachers Training College. She had met Thomas while she was browsing in a bookshop on the Perth Road near the university. Her parents never approved of Thomas. So she left home married Thomas then set up home in Alexander Street.

One of her friends, who was a teacher at High School of Dundee, told her that a position had become vacant at the High School. Her friend gave a glowing reference to the Headmaster.
When the Headmaster and Governors interviewed her, she explained that this is her first interview for a teacher's position, and that she could be an asset to the pupils and the school. She succeeded in securing the position as an English teacher.

Ian was born ten years into the marriage, by that time they had purchased a two bed -roomed flat in Dens Road, for the princely sum of six hundred pounds. It was a struggle, but the both of them were working and happy. They lived there for five years. They then moved to a semi-detached villa near the Stobswell ponds. And the reason that they were able to do this was that her mother made contact with her again; saw that Thomas was a hard -working family man, and she wanted to see her grandchild. They gradually built up a relationship again; and soon enough her mother and father became frequent visitors to their flat in Dens Road. Her father casually mentioned is it not time to move to another house that had a garden? He went on to explain that he knew an old friend was emigrating to Canada, and he was sure that if a good price is offered, it would be enough to make it theirs.

When Margaret is told where the house is, she rejected it out of hand.
'We couldn't afford a house like that,' she protested. Her father took them up to see the house; they were taken aback at the style and splendour of this house. Her father asked them if they liked the house, when they said that they loved the house, her father and his friend went into the study while we explored the expansive gardens with numerous fruit trees. When we went back to the house, everything had been agreed, the house would be ours, once all the legal work is completed. Two months later we moved in.

'That was one of the worst decisions that your dad and I had come to. Everything on the surface couldn't be better. My father had paid the full asking price for the house, we were mortgage -free. The proceeds from the flat in Dens Road, less the loan from the Building Society left us more than comfortable, as I said life couldn't have been better. Then your dad came home from the Caledon blazing drunk that warm July, it was the Dundee Trades Holiday. To say I was shocked was an understatement. He ended up hating the house.'
'Why was that?' asked Peter.
'It seemed,' she continued 'that he was being made a fool of because he lived in a wonderful house. His work mates were jealous, and your dad who was never confrontational, took it all badly. Instead of being proud and telling them where to get off, he let it build up inside of him. That was the Dundee mentality at the time. When there were redundancies at the Caledon, he used to have notes shoved in his locker saying it should be him to go, as he had a big house, and his wife is a teacher. And a lot more hurtful things that I do not wish to disclose. He came home drunk that July, to prove he was one of the boys, but he never was.

'He is an individual who is well –educated. He could have been a teacher and should have been. But he always classed himself as working- class, he used to supress his intelligence, in fact, he grew to be ashamed of it. He drank more frequently, took more days off and finally lost his job. He was not yet forty- years of age. Ian was ten at the time, and I fell pregnant with you two. After the birth, I never felt myself; I was bursting into tears for no reason. Back then it was called the' baby blues.' Today we are in more caring times it was Post Natal Depression. I started drinking for no reason, or so I thought... then I found it harder and harder to cope. I was advised by Social Services that I was able to cope with Ian, but not two babies.

'My father fell out with me again because your dad and I had lost our jobs and he lost two of his grandchildren. He saw the house deteriorating inside and out, he persuaded us to sell the house to him. We reluctantly agreed. We ended up in a council house in Fintry; it was a lovely house but was light years from Clepington Road. The money we made from the house, we gave it away or drank. I'm sorry... but that's the truth. I didn't see my mother and father again. I didn't know when they died, we were told once both of them had been buried. They didn't want us to embarrass them in death as we had in life.'

Peter and James moved closer to each side of the chair. They looked at this little fragile woman, with her head buried in her lap.
'Mam, we're here now, and we're not ashamed or embarrassed, we're so proud of you mam, so proud. You were ill at the time, but you, you and da have come through it. You're back in your old house, with your two sons, who don't blame you or da. Things were different then mam, you were ill. Da was driven to drink because of the mind set of workers.'
'Everything is fine just fine,' added Peter
She raised her head. 'I am truly blessed.'

***

Ian and Thomas stood at the railings overlooking the River Tay; once more the conversation had lulled. Thomas is looking at the supply boat that is making its way to the North Sea.
'Does the sea still have the same effect on you dad?'
'Oh, sorry, that's me drifting again, when you get to my age, you can't help but reminisce.'

'Do you fancy making our way home now, your starting to shiver,' Ian noticed somewhat alarmed.
'It's too early, we'll walk a little more,' they started to walk.
'How are you getting on with the golf?'
'I'm no really interested in it I just don't see the point in it.'
Thomas comes to a sudden halt. 'If you are not interested in golf, then why buy apartments on a golf course?'
'That's just part of my property portfolio, it's just an investment.'
'And how is the investment going then?'
'It's steady, I have people on the complex, a husband and wife who manage and clean the apartments for me.'
'How much do they charge for that?'
'Fifty- pounds they are good people, they meet- and-greet the golfers and make sure the apartments has the air- condition on at the correct temperature.'
'Sounds easy money to me, compared to the Caledon.'
'Oh right dad, he laughed, the Caledon had Spanish Practices.'
'It should never ever shut down; I loved that boat yard, loads of good men.'
There is bitterness in his voice.
'You could have done better dad.'
'Ian, I know that son, but working- class laddies in those days were expected to get a trade. Very few went to university.'
'It's still the same dad; there is still the old -boy network, when I take on a trainee solicitor I always peruse their CVs and... Why don't you and mum not spend the winter in Spain, the apartments' are nice?'
'Ian, no more please, we have had enough surprises for the day thank you.'
'Maybe next winter then… you promise?'
'We'll see, and I'm not dismissing that fabulous offer... but I don't think your mum could leave Peter and James… again.' The words trailed off.
'Dad, time to turn back now, I'm freezing.'
'It's the North Sea wind that cuts through you.'
   They make their way back to the house. As they are walking along the esplanade, Ian turns up the collar of his overcoat, his father looks at his watch it's over two hours' since they had left the house.
'You can't beat a good walk on a winter's day, Ian.'
'What time is it anyway?'
'Half past five, we've been out for more than two hours, do you fancy a coffee, before we make our way home?'
'I'm easy... where do you want to go?'
'The Tay Inn, if you don't mind.'
'The Tay Inn it is, and I can see what you're up to.'
'Oh aye. ' He stopped and looked at Ian. 'What am I up to then?'
'You're giving mum time to catch up with Peter and James's past.'
'Am I that obvious?'
'You should come back as a window in your next life. I can see right through you.' Ian smiled.
'Your hearts in the right place son.' They continued to walk.
'Dad, I want to ask you a question, and you don't have to answer, but if you do, I want the truth.'
'Fire away son.'
'When I take you and mum for lunch, into the Tay Inn or any other pubs, is it hard...do you get the urge to drink again?'
'God, that's an easy question, your mum and I slayed that dragon years' ago, you have no worries on that score. We love being sober, but we knew we were bad parents when we were alcoholics, we can't change the past, but we can look to the future with confidence, anything else on your mind?'

'No. It just troubled me, just now; it never crossed my mind before.'
'Could I ask you a question Ian?'
'Of course, what is it?'
'Your business, how is it doing?'
'What side of the business are you referring to?'
'You tell me?'
'Every aspect from the Legal side to the property side, everything is fine. If my plans come off, I will be forming a building company to build residential and commercial premises... is there something troubling you dad?'
'Well it's just that when your mum and I were in the Tay Inn we were having a high- tea in there a couple of weeks ago. Mum went to powder her nose I was looking at the menu, out of the corner of my eye I noticed two young men in their thirties sat at the next table. I just felt uncomfortable, for what reason I do not know. Then I overheard one of them say something about you.'
'Me!' He looked worried. 'What did they say?'
'They didn't actually mention you by name, but when you mentioned the docks and boatyard earlier it made sense. One of the men did all the talking, he said to the other man, 'he's normally in here, with his parents,' then he went on to say, 'nobody has ever been able to shake you down but he would have no option, as they had the security contract for the buildings at the docks.'
The one who was saying this went on to say. 'If he didn't hire the security firm; accidents do happen.' 'They started laughing.'
'Laughing?' Thomas nodded. 'The one who had remained silent then said like the new build flats that went on fire in the West End.' Ian, you must have seen that report about the fire in the evening paper?'
'Yes I did. But they are not talking about me. So don't worry.'
They were only about a hundred metres from the Tay Inn; the freezing gloom that engulfed the Tay had had an adverse effect on Ian. He looked visibly shaken; he couldn't hide it from his dad.
'When we go in here, try and remember where you were sitting, and if possible try and get the same seats.'
'Okay, but what good will that achieve?'
'I just want to think things out.' He motioned his dad to enter the bar first. The bar was sparsely occupied, but it still had that uplifting atmosphere at this time of day, all the office workers that had late lunches were back in their homes. Paul the owner; is behind the bar, he greeted them, and told them to have a seat and the waitress would be over.

    Paul is ever grateful to Ian. Five years' previous, it looked increasingly possible Paul was going to jail for VAT evasion. His solicitor advised him to plead guilty, that way he would only get three years' in prison instead of five. A 'no brainer' said his solicitor. Paul had mentioned this to a friend of a friend.

    The friend of the friend suggested he give Ian a call. That was the best twenty-pence that he spent in his life. Ian perused the Court documents meticulously, his solicitor had been correct it was an open and shut case...up to a critical but crucial legal point. Ian had spotted a flaw in the warrant, as well as minor faults in the way the warrant had been served. On the advice from Ian he thanked the solicitor for his time, ignored his advice and promptly paid him. Paul would be pleading not guilty. He then engaged Ian to defend him. At the beginning of the trial, Ian pointed out to the Court, that the warrant was flawed; it had the wrong middle name. Because of this error, his Lordship, a stickler for detail agreed with the Defence Counsel, that the warrant was not competent. Case dismissed. His Lordship vented his spleen on 'schoolboy errors, in preparing the case.'

    Paul did not bat an eye-lid when he was presented with the bill for Ian's services. The invoice was for sixty-four thousand pounds. The invoice had to be paid in twenty-eight days. He paid the invoice that day by electronic bank transfer. He wasn't going to jail. He managed to keep his businesses going

Paul acted on Ian's advice that he should have his accounts' taken over by a more professional firm. Ian's accountancy firm would be that firm. Paul didn't realise that Ian was involved in accountancy. Neither did Ian, he formed that Chartered Accounts Company the following day.

Since that day, if Paul needed any advice about his burgeoning business empire that included buying up pubs, shops and flats, he would go to the well- established firms, listen to them, and then go to Ian. He trusted Ian with his life. Paul always felt he owed Ian, not in monetary terms but in friendship. He thought long and hard. He thought he was on a winner. He had a cadre of business friends; he effortlessly guided them all without exception, from engaging long- established solicitors and chartered accountants to Ian.

Paul was not concerned Ian had no lineage from 'old money' or had not inherited a fortune from the long- dead but still despised Jute Barons. These new clients he guided to Ian were welcomed with open wallets, as far as Ian was concerned. However, the old guard of long –established professionals incubated antipathy towards Ian. From the Legal professions to the career criminals, they formed an unlikely alliance.

Ian is in no one's pocket he would be beholden to no one. Ian is one of the get rich quickly new breed of solicitors. He was one of the first solicitors in Dundee to advertise on television, no win no fee. He made nearly a million in less than two years in this embryonic new industry. He sold this part of the business to a blue chip solicitors company that covered the United Kingdom, two million it was rumoured. That was the rumour; three million was the reality.

Ian motioned his dad towards the table that he had sat at when he overheard the two men had this worrying conversation. His dad gestured for his son to join him, Ian gave him a reassuring nod, he held up two -fingers, at the same time mouthed silently 'two minutes.' Thomas looked around the bar; six people in. He took off his coat then sat down. The waitress came over with a tray that held a large coffee pot, two cups, milk, sugar and utensils. Quick service, thought Thomas.
Ian made his way towards the table.
   'What day did you say it was when you were in here with mum?'
'Let's think now...Tuesday afternoon, about three o clock...' he didn't have time to tell him, that he always left before three- thirty as they liked to get home so they could settle down for Countdown.
Ian returned to the bar and engaged in an animated conversation with Paul. He took a beer mat, tore it in two and wrote something on it. He then gave it to Paul. He went across to the table and sat down. His dad is disappointed that he didn't take his overcoat off. It would be a short stay.
'Have you not poured the coffee yet?'
The rare smile returned to his face. Ian looked a lot younger when he smiled.
I wish I smiled a lot more when I was younger thought Thomas. Then again he had very little to smile about. His conscience pricked him; he had plenty to smile about now.
'Will I be Mummy then?'
'I'll do it Ian, even on a bleak day; this is still a cheerful place to come.' He poured the black steaming coffee.
'I know...that day you were in here, Paul was working that day, he can recall the description of the two men. But if they come in again he'll let me know. And to put your mind at rest, they weren't talking about me, somebody else, but definitely not me.'
'I hope so, but how can you be so sure?'
Ian leaned over the table. 'Without breaching client confidentiality, there is a young solicitor who moved from Glasgow to Dundee because of problems. He is similar to me in stature. He can look after himself, but I'll mention the conversation you overheard to him.'
'Don't say it was me, Ian! You know how much I worry.'
'I'll pass it on through a friend; I'll say it is a passing acquaintance.'
Thomas sipped the steaming coffee. 'My mind is easy now.'
Ian knew that what he said to his dad was a lie. They were talking about him, he is convinced of that.

Paul mentioned it to him before he could ask if he recalled the two men. Paul told him that the men casually enquired that they heard that he came into the bar for lunch. One of them said that he is a partner in a construction firm, and he is looking to expand into the student accommodation market. He ran off an impressive array of figures, over forty- thousand students are currently studying in Dundee. He is looking to purpose build and renovate old Jute factories, to accommodate the burgeoning student population. That is the reason they needed a solicitor with extensive knowledge of the current Local Plan; someone to navigate and nullify any dissenters that objected to these proposals. They knew all about Ian; that is for sure. Paul observed the quieter of the two is his personal security. He rarely spoke a syllable, but he nodded a lot. Ian asked Paul if it were possible to take a look at the security camera video of last Tuesday. Paul acquiesced to this request. Ian gave him his *other* mobile telephone number this is the 'ongoing problem mobile.'

As soon as that mobile rang it had his utmost attention. He knew, the problem is exacerbating or it had been resolved. Luckily, he hadn't given out this number for a while. This would be the only problem, and he aimed to solve it quickly, whatever it is. He told Paul to call that number; and that number only if he wanted to talk to him regarding the two men. It was seared into his brain not to give this number out to anyone. He is acutely aware not to probe or ask what it was all about. If there were subliminal threats of any kind, or threats that manifested Ian could contact thugs, because that's what they undoubtedly were thugs, through a third party, of course, and he would be rid of that particular itch. Paul did notice Ian's facial expression change, when he alluded to the properties for exclusive use for students'. This is obviously news to Ian, or is this Ian feigning surprise? He knew not to ask.

***

Margaret is much more relaxed now. The reservoir of tears that she had built up over the years was gone. When her two boys were talking excitedly, sometimes finishing the others sentence she would smile. She was studying their faces as only a mother could. The conversation is only one-way. Today is a dream, a pleasant cosy dream, which she didn't want to wake up from. However, she knew this is cold stark reality. Her sins' had been forgiven from the sinned, but she couldn't forgive herself; ever.
'Would you like more tea mam?'
Margaret smiled, 'just what the doctor ordered James.' She raised herself from the chair and straightened her stiff back. 'Ah! That's better.' She noticed that darkness had descended outside. She made her way to the large bay windows Peter watched her move slowly.
'I hope your father is okay,' she glanced at her watch, the one that her father had given her when he came to their flat in Dens Road. She rubbed it tenderly. 'They have been gone a while.'
James came in with the tea. 'There we are help yourselves... enjoying the view?'
'Mam's concerned that da and Ian are enjoying themselves,' said Peter. She walked to the side of the bay window, and moved the heavy velvet curtain to the side and looked out expectantly.
'Come over here mam, and have your tea, they'll be home soon.'
    Her hand lovingly ran over the soft velvet material, the curtain automatically fell into its proper place as she gently released it; she heard voices as well as laughter; things must have gone well between them she thought.
'That's them now; I can hear them come up the path.' She made her way to the front- door she halted about six -feet from the door. She waited.
'I wager he's looking for his key, the old fool, the door is not locked.'
She had to contain the laughter pouring out of her.
She waited. Silence was beyond the door.
'I'll open the door myself,' she thought, she took two steps forward and turned the handle and pulled open the door. The winter chill came into the hall, no one was there
She took another step forward, and looked from side- to -side, they must be in the garden.

'Are you two coming in then, I know you are there!' The rose bushes swayed; no reply came back. She called out again telling them to come in she knew they are in the garden somewhere. Only the swish of the tree broke the unsettling silence. She stepped back into the warmth of the hall, turned around and her eyes stared into the darkness that engulfed the garden; then hurriedly closed the door. The old worries returned.

***

'That's a real good heat from the fire Ian, it's just a pity it isn't a real fire.'
Ian placed his cup back on the saucer, his finger methodically rubbing the rim in a circular motion.
'You thought it was real, until I mentioned it to you in the summer,' replied Ian teasingly.
Ian is smiling again; the smile is quickly replaced by a frown.
'The two business men... are you sure that it's not you that they're looking for?'
'Again without breaching any client confidentiality, and again this is between us. That solicitor that our two friends are looking for, well, he left not under a black cloud, but let's call it grey. He had clients' that were involved in criminal activity. Rumours were abound that, he was laundering money, but when the money came back it had shrunk a little. His clients were not too impressed by his washing technique, if you know what I mean. He had his offices raided by every Government Department you can think of. So, he had enough of this harassment and he moved to Dundee to start afresh, or so he thought.'
'But why are they men after him?'
'Unpaid bills of some kind? It could be the men that came in here were Debt Recovery Officers.'
'Is what they call them nowadays?'
'That's their official title now, but they employ the same methods as they did in your day, personal visits or recovery through the Courts. It's a billion pound industry. Assets can be seized cheaply and quickly, if they are acquired illegally.'
'Do you think the lawyer's life is in danger then?'
'Solicitor, dad, solicitor...it all depends what he has done, and what action or gesture he does to alleviate certain pressures. That could be by paying money or breaching certain confidences.'
'Have you ever had people like that, after you?'
He shook his head. 'I wouldn't get involved with anything like that; my company is doing fine, if a well- known criminal or a colourful businessman for example comes to my office, and I have a bad feeling about them or their particular problem that they need put right. I go with my gut instinct and decline.'
'But, what if they suggest that you do help them?'
'That's where Plan B comes in.'
'What is Plan B?'
'I pass them on to more unscrupulous solicitors. I have a list of them, in here.' He taps his head.
'I call so- and- so tell him I have so- and -so in the office, I'm up to my ears in work and as he is the specialist in that field would he be interested? As soon as I say 'specialist' that means he can inflate his normal fee by a considerable margin, but the client is well -known or he is tainted.
   The client goes to the other solicitor, the other solicitor can move house or order an extension and I have got rid of my problem. Everyone is content; the client has a solicitor, the solicitor has money he earns in one case instead of ten, and I don't have a troublesome client.'
'But, why would you turn down a lucrative case, if it's all above board?'
'Simple, I have a good reputation amongst the Police, VAT, and Council bodies, and I aim to maintain that respect. Other solicitors' thrive on representing well -known criminals, they love seeing their photograph in the local and national newspapers'. What they don't realise is, because they have convinced the Court that their client is innocent the client comes back to them again and again. Or worse still, friends of the client will come to them for representation.'

'But, I would have thought that would be a good thing, I mean that would mean more money surely?'

'That's the first mistake they make. I'll explain briefly what happens. After the client has been cleared, or charges have been dropped. Or serious charges have been replaced by lesser ones. The client is overcome by generosity; he'll tell the solicitor that he is very impressed by his legal skills. In addition to the fee that he paid promptly, in cash of course; and that he would accept a receipt showing thirty- thousand pounds instead of forty- thousand. The solicitor is ten- thousand pounds up on the deal, but that's not the end of it. The client has had background checks on the solicitor, he finds out if he's a keen racing fan would he fancy going to the Kentucky horse sales?

'Or if he is a keen golfer, would he care to take a trip to the US Masters, one of his friends has broken his leg, and there's a spare place. The hotel is a five- stars, of course. So the solicitor thinks all his birthdays' have come all at once, before he has had time to answer, the client's mobile rings, it is the travel agent. What name shall they put on the flight and hotel documents? They need to know in the next fifteen minutes? Could you hold on for ten seconds please', says the client. He turns to the solicitor, and apologises. 'Look I know it's very short notice, but things move quickly, if you can't manage because of cases, I'll understand'. The solicitor's mind is racing, I could be mixing with Tiger Woods, or if he is a racing buff, J.P. McManus at the Kentucky sales.

'No problem, I'll make it, I'm due time- off anyway. The client confirms the solicitor's name etc. If the solicitor has any second thoughts about the trip, they all evaporate when the tickets' arrive at his office. There are also one thousand dollars' as expenses. At Heaththrow airport... they never fly from Scotland to avoid Customs and Special Branch.'

'Ian, I am getting really scared now...I don't want to know anymore.'

'Dad you asked, so I am telling you, this will put your mind at rest. Where was I? I know...not only to avoid Customs and Special Branch but avoid a chance meeting of bumping into fellow- criminals. He is met by the client who gives him a ticket for the VIP lounge, when he enters, he is introduced by his client to two other associates; one is a business acquaintance or partner. The other is a corporate solicitor who manages the client's business concerns.

'They'll all have drinks for a few hours, then the client will move away to talk to his business partner, he apologises and says he'll be back in ten to fifteen minutes. Once they move away, the corporate solicitor will mention immediately, how impressed and more importantly, how his client is impressed, by his handling and outcome of the case.

'The stroking of his ego has begun in earnest. He would also say in the strictest confidence, that he can see more 'difficult' cases coming his way, that's if he feels he can give his full and ongoing attention to the cases. The corporate solicitor can understand if he wants to continue to represent the underclass, shoplifters and junkies. He also realises that he makes a good- living out of them. However, what age is he now, forty- eight? You look much younger, do you want to look back in ten years' time, and regret the opportunity that I have offered you? All this is too much for the solicitor who said, 'what opportunity?'

'Sorry, I was under the impression that, so- and -so had put the proposals to you.'

At this juncture, the solicitor looks mystified. 'No one has put any proposals to me? If you can elaborate, I would be grateful.'

'Bear with me, the corporate solicitor will say, he'll move from the table over to his other two colleagues.

'A throng of heads will be nodding and staring at the solicitor. After a few minutes all three will make their way back to the solicitor's table looking uncomfortable. They'll sit down, apologise for the misunderstanding. No problem, but these proposals, what are they?

The corporate solicitor explains to him. 'Our business is expanding, because of the vibrant property market; the company will be opening an office in the next six- months in Dundee. The company requires a diligent and respected solicitor to manage the office; that person is you. The office will have eight- solicitors; you will recruit them. The office as you expect will have the latest IT.

'Everything from the computers to the coffee machine to the water- coolers will be cutting edge technology. The office will deal only with property matters; conveyancing and property management. No criminal work. The company will be expanding all the way up the East Coast. We will have two offices in Aberdeen and two offices in Inverness. The company has many subsidiaries, from licensed premises, which range from beer and spirits delivery to public bars to night clubs. We have building merchants to building companies. This is why it is imperative to have the office for the East Coast in Dundee. The office is all kitted out and ready to go. We understand that you are a junior partner in your firm, and that you need to give six months' notice, or you pay an exit fee, which we understand, is one hundred -thousand pounds.

'On paying the hundred thousand pounds, you can leave immediately, with no restrictions. He takes an envelope from his briefcase and hands it to him, this is a standard contract, without the Latin phrases, you'll see the figures are north what you are being paid at the moment. You will also see the bonus is equal to your year's salary.

  'The solicitor is in a dream like trance, he quickly reads it over again, a top of the range Mercedes is part of the package. Yes! Yes! Yes! His mind is shouting, he starts to feel hot, he loosens his tie. The corporate solicitor, tells him not to make a decision immediately, enjoy the trip and wait till he arrives back in Dundee, where he can reflect; and come to an informed decision.'

'This is like the Mafia in New York!' exclaimed a worried Thomas. The waitress approaches, removes the empty coffee pot and cups' and replaces them with fresh coffee and cups.

'Thanks,' Ian said.

'Ian you seem to know an awful lot, of how they operate, do you mind me asking how you know?'

'The best man at my wedding was an old friend from my university days. His name was Daniel Fordyce his family came from Cambridge...'

'You said was, his name was...'

'If you let me finish...'

'Sorry,' said Thomas.

'That's all right dad. When he completed his law degree, he moved to a practice in Liverpool. We always kept in touch, he didn't like Liverpool, so his father pulled a few strings and he secured a position with one of the largest solicitors practice in Glasgow. He was with that company for five years. Then I contacted him about being best -man at my wedding. He was thrilled at the news that I'm getting married, then he asks who the lucky girl is and I tell him her name, he is less than pleased, the girl I married was his ex- fiancée. I tell him not to be immature he apologises. He tells me he's been married for three years, so we have a laugh talking about our student days. He comes through to the wedding, everything goes well, and then at the reception in the evening, he tells me that he's coming to work in Dundee for a new company and that he will be the senior- solicitor.

 'At this news, I'm a wee bit taken aback, he tells me where the office is going to be, and I can tell you that it's in a very expensive part of Dundee. He said to me that he heard on the grapevine that I'm not totally happy with my work. He offers me a position with his company there on the spot, the salary was double what I was currently earning at the time, which was just the appetiser, he mentions the company car. He's a little bit drunk at this stage. So I pump him for information, and he tells me about the client who is so impressed with the way he handled the case, he has a spare ticket for the US Masters, he was a scratch player himself; it's yours if you want it. He takes the bait. The office in Dundee opens, he's the senior solicitor, and the young solicitors are of the highest calibre. The two- trainee solicitors that are employed have progressed through their unique Graduates scheme. They were cherry- picked by their university tutors, and recommended to the company. They learn all the commercial aspects of property from the brightest young solicitors who are all in still in their twenties. A lot of firms transfer their accounts to them because the company has undercut all the well- established firms. You can imagine how the bad feeling was starting to swell up against these Young Turks. Danny was living and working in Dundee, I had been down to his Penthouse flat at the docks; he was always on edge. We lost touch for a while.'

'Why was he on edge then?' asked Thomas.
'I thought he was just overworked, maybe it was too much for him, I know he didn't like going to Glasgow for meetings. He phoned me about two years ago in an agitated state at three o clock in the morning, lucky I was up and I was enjoying a few days off work. He kept talking in the past tense how I was a great friend to him; how I was lucky to be working for myself. He kept repeating how stupid he was; and there was no escape from them he said that over and over again.'
'Was he drunk?' asked Thomas.
'He was stone cold sober, but he seemed frightened, scared. He apologised for disturbing me, then puts down the phone. About a month later I'm in my office, when Danny's dad calls, he said that there was some bad news. Daniel had had an accident in France skiing, he was dead. At the funeral, I spoke to an old friend from my university days; he was there when Danny was killed. He told me they were skiing when Danny went off- piste and just skied right over the edge of the mountain. He came to the difficult conclusion; it was suicide. He told the police that it was an accident; he told Danny's family the same thing, so they were shielded from the suicide, and Danny's wife would receive the insurance money. I told him to keep what he told me to himself.'
'Maybe the pressure of the work was too much for Danny?'
'Nah, if that was the case why didn't he just resign from that firm?'
'Maybe he needed the money?'
'Dad his family are millionaires, in fact Danny was a millionaire on his seventeenth - birthday, his great- grandfather had made his money in India. So it was not money that held him back from resigning.'
'What do you think drove him to suicide?' asked Thomas looking ashen.
'Something or someone in that company made him ski over that precipice in Chamonix, of that I'm certain.' He saw the worry take hold in his father's face.
'Or maybe I'm jumping to the wrong conclusion. Perhaps he had changed over the years, people do. I know I'm contradicting myself, but, there's something not right about this.' His finger was moving around the empty coffee cup.
'Do you want a top- up Ian?' He looked at his watch.
'No, no thanks. Do you want to head back home?'
'I was thinking that myself, but before we go, I'll nip into the toilet.'
'I'll wait here.' Thomas left the table, as he squeezed past his son, Ian noticed how old he is looking, but he still had a good gait about him. In fact, if you were a stranger, you would think he was an old soldier. Ian then noticed the bar had become busier. He cast his eyes around the bar; young couples were in groups of four or more. Only one table is occupied by a couple, Ian guessed they were in their late- thirties. They aren't looking content. They must be married.

   His mind cast back to the day when Paul came into his office. Bad enough he thought he was going to jail, but to lose this bar would have been a financial disaster. After Ian had had the case dismissed. Paul took him back to the bar. He told Ian that he had agreed in principle to sell the bar including stock to Robert Hughes, a businessman who had a litany of business failures behind him. But all his assets fortunately were in his wife's name. Unfortunately, these were beyond his creditors means. He assumed he was buying the Tay Inn and the ground beyond it, which would make a nice enclosed beer garden, or a valuable plot of land for a substantial house.

   The story that he was telling his friends or people that the thought were friends was this. He already had a buyer for the bar, which would have given him a one hundred per cent return on the purchase price. Omitted was the plot of land. His solicitor had redrawn the title deeds. The plot of land was now owned by Mearns Investments. Mearns Investments would be owned by his wife. She would also own the Tay Inn, that's if Paul was sent to jail. Ian asked Paul whether anything had been put in writing. Nothing was.
'Where did this meeting of minds take place, 'Hughes' office or his solicitor's office'?
'No, it took place here, standing at the bar.'

When the case was dismissed, Robert Hughes was in Court as support for Paul. He left the Court in a hurry. His solicitor drafted a letter and sent it to Paul by fax.

'Regarding the agreed bargain that his client had concluded with him, when would he like the money transferred to his account; when would it be convenient to discharge his right to the property? Please make an appointment soon as possible.'

Ian took care of that problem. He called the solicitor from his office.

'No conversation regarding sale of assets had been discussed. Moreover, as a recent bankrupt; if this conversation had taking place; and I reiterate, it didn't, does your client realise he was breaking the Law? And more serious if you, as his solicitor were aware of him being a bankrupt, you too would be breaking the Law. Lengthy prison sentences in the past for bankrupts' trying to circumvent the Law have been known to be administered from the Courts.'

The solicitor for Robert Hughes insipidly explained that his client had misunderstood the Law that requires bankrupts' to pass on income or monetary movements to the Appointed Trustee.

In fact, he was just in town and was seeking advice for his wife, the sole shareholder for Mearns Investments. I hope this clears up the misunderstanding. My client after much thought; now realises that he misunderstood the conversation. Pass on my apologies on behalf of my client, for any distress caused by this understanding.'

Paul was delighted at the outcome of this worrying episode. Paul asked him what would be the best course of action to develop the land, as a beer garden, sell the land or build a house and sell it. Ian told him he would give much thought to these proposals, and he would get back to him with his advice.

***

'Who was that at the door mam?' asked Peter.
'I thought it was your dad and Ian, I thought I heard voices coming up the path.' She looked worried.
'It was probably people passing outside the house, don't worry they'll be home soon,' said James.
'I noticed you touching the curtains there, were there memories coming back while you were at the window?'
'When I was young, we weren't allowed to look out the window, it was deemed to be rude. And if you ruffled the curtains, she sucked in air... then you were in big trouble. But enough about the old days, let's look to the future.'
'Well said mam, ever the optimist, we're looking forward to going into the town centre, Ian said it's changed a lot; has it changed for the better?'
'Peter, I'm the last person you should ask, your dad and I have not been in the City Centre for years and years. But we'll join you if you don't mind; it will be a nice day out for us as well.'
'That's tomorrow taken care of then, is the Deep Sea Restaurant still open?'
'I really don't know Peter! Imagine me not knowing that!'
'It will be an experience for all of us then,' replied Peter. Mam, you have a lot of living to catch- up on. If you have not been to the City Centre, you will notice a lot of changes. We shouldn't be shocked because we have been on the Internet and seen the town centre on the web- cam, do you know what a web- cam is mam?'
'Peter... we chose not to go into the town centre, because we are alcoholics; some part of our brain still functions, and we know that man has landed on the moon as well.'
'I'm sorry, I didn't know why I said that,' said Peter.
'You keep saying to me don't worry; now it's my turn, don't you worry.'
Peter nodded his head. Margaret continued, 'don't be afraid to ask us about our drinking problem, which we have overcome, I can assure both of you.'
'I'm sorry mam; I didn't mean to bring that up.'
'It was me that brought it up, so don't berate yourselves, I mean you as well James.'
'Mam, I know, I know... we are just glad to be here with you and da,' said James.

'This house, has so many bittersweet memories, I cannot believe at our time of life we are here; with our children. Your father would agree we could not have dreamt this could happen, being reunited with our sons' again; and miraculously in my former family home. It is just mind blowing. Ian is a very intelligent individual, but more important he is kind. He is very modest, but I see this as a good thing, there are a lot of individuals in the world who are very arrogant.'
'This is our dream come true as well mam, did Ian buy this house on the open market, or did he approach the owners?'
Margaret looked shocked. 'I have no idea! I don't think I will ask Ian. Maybe he has told your father when they have been on their walk. I don't think I will sleep tonight. Another thing on my mind; the furniture in the house, Ian must have taken a long time to source the various items, and have the house decorated from top to bottom. It's just a dream.'
James looked at her, time to tell her other news. 'Ian will dispose of the furniture from your old house, before he puts it up for sale.'

***

Thomas returned from the toilet. 'Are we ready to move then?'
'Sure, do you want me to order a taxi?'
'No, I enjoyed the walk down here I'm sure I can manage back, how about you?'
'I'm fine,' he stands up, he pulls out his wallet and leaves a ten -pound note under the coffee pot.
'Let's go then.' Thomas looks at the money under the coffee pot.
'Is that wise?'
'What do you mean?'
'That tenner under the pot, will it be safe?'
'I think so, do you want to stare at it or do we make our way home?'

Thomas shrugs his shoulders, leaves the table and moves towards the door, he smiles at Paul as he passes him, Ian says goodnight and continues on his way. As Thomas leaves the bar with Ian, a young man in a dark suit leaves his table and follows them out the door, he watches them move along the street, he follows them for a further ten minutes, until they reached the bottom of Camphill Road. He observed them starting to climb the steep incline of the road. He pulls out his mobile and talks for a few seconds, then places it back in the inside pocket of his suit jacket. He reaches into his outside pocket takes out a cigarette from the packet and lights it. He inhales deeply; he notices a police car moving slowly towards him, as it's about a hundred metres from him, the car cuts its speed he is eyeballing the two occupants of the car. The car stops. He takes the cigarette from his mouth, drops it on the pavement and crushes it in an aggressive circular movement.

He heard the engine of the police car start up and it move slowly towards him. The car is parallel to him the window winds down. He moves towards the open window.
'Are you looking for someone officer?
'Get in prick, the back door is open.' He enters and closes the door, the car moves off. The officer in the passenger seat looked at him with contempt. 'Did you make contact?
'What do you think..?'
'Pack it in you two,' the driver said clearly irritated He looks in the rear view mirror, he didn't welcome the passenger in the rear, but he and his partner are being remunerated well above the daily rate for a police officer. His partner still deluded himself that he is an incorruptible officer of the Law. He ceased to be when he accepted his offer of a golfing holiday to Spain.

That was the first time he had entered the spider's web. He was fifty, his colleague forty, both still constables but now called officers, they had observed younger colleagues whiz past them up the promotion ladder. The young ones' are now in the ascendency and he and his colleague are the old -school. Why should they be punished for not buying into this politically correct security force; he stopped believing this was the police force when they started recruiting midgets

Police officers at five feet .six, but with six foot egos', female officers' tipping the scales at twelve-stone, and standing with great pride at five –foot four with their hats on. And then, the final straw that broke the camel's back; the recruitment of Asians.

They were instructed not to charge any Asian or other ethnic minority involved in a domestic incident. When he queried if an Irishman beat his wife did the same policy apply?
If the Irishman is black he was told.   He questioned nothing else, while the older generation rebelled; they were marginalised and "promoted" to desk jobs, with the promise of an increase of salary. The officers who accepted this promotion; and applied for their salary to be reviewed, were retired on health grounds

Savvy police officers realised they were conned into the desk jobs; and had seen the consequences that befell their colleagues' who enquired where was their salary increase?
They either accepted they were pen- pushers working for the police, or, like the majority, they took early retirement on ill-health grounds, invariably; back problems. Those police doctors were a credit to medical science; they examined them for a maximum of two- minutes and decided they were unfit to continue their police careers. He was not prepared to sing- along with that song.
He enjoyed being out on patrol and the numerous perks; from fish suppers to cash bribes.
He felt no shame in accepting either, not in the slightest. He was still fighting crime; albeit in an unorthodox fashion. He had the drug dealers who regularly supplemented his salary; he would look out for them, as long as he received his monthly stipend. He helped the dealers' remove the 'competition.' They gave him the names of the new dealers; when they had an adequate stockpile, he would pass the names to his friend in the drugs squad. They in turn would raid the dealer; confiscate part of the drug stockpile, sell the surplus to the other dealer, and collect the money and a hefty bonus in return

They were instructed to pick- up the passenger at Camphill Road; male dressed in a black suit, average height, and he would be smoking. When the passenger saw the patrol car stop, and then crawl towards him he would throw the cigarette on the ground and stand on it. He would then climb into the rear of the police car. He would be then dropped off at the City Quay. No questions would be asked; by either parties. The journey should take ten- minutes. This was the one and only time they would see their arrogant cargo. The passenger had the air of supremacy as he sat in rear; he looked out the window for most of the short journey. The police officer who was eyeballing him every minute or so in the mirror, thought he was glancing at him in a contemptuous manner; with a fleeting momentary snigger. He was contemptuous of them all right. But they could be his safe passage out of here when the indenture had been successfully completed. His mind started to move to another matter as the car sped along Broughty Ferry Road towards his rental flat at the City Quay. He was hungry. He would have an Indian curry from Taza's the restaurant beside the small harbour.

A smile ran across his face, he had Becks in the fridge that would be the perfect accompaniment to the curry, later he would watch the football on Sky.   He liked the apartment, it was luxurious; the majestic vista of the Tay challenged his attention on a regular basis when he was watching the large LCD television on the wall. Reluctantly he had to activate the closure of the wall- to -ceiling curtains frequently. It was unfortunate but not unexpected he would have to cut- short his year- long lease, due to the impending commitment.

The booming property market had led him to establish an office in Dundee selling holiday homes in Bulgaria. He had shied away from the Costa's as the properties there had risen in value over the last few years.   It was his view a correction in the market was looming. On the television and in the newspapers over the last eighteen- months, holiday programmes and articles in newspapers were highlighting Bulgaria. The country was just developing tourist areas. One- bedroom flats could be bought for as little as fifteen -thousand pounds. A two- bedroom flat fully -furnished, of course with a forty- two inch plasma could be purchased for forty- thousand pounds, a villa for seventy- thousand. When potential buyers came in to the office, and were told the various prices they were disappointed that prices were more than they had imagined.

The sales rep easily explained they were buying the ultimate property. 'Of course you could buy cheaper from other companies. However, the properties that we are constructing would not be available for two years. You would be buying in at off- plan; and the buildings would be constructed using British Standards, even though Bulgarian building standards were good, they wouldn't be acceptable here. We realise that our properties are more expensive than other companies,' we use the best British best materials and British workers. No short-cuts with us. Here take the video home and view it, then if you want to ask me questions, please make an appointment and we will go over anything that you're not comfortable with. Fill out this form, with your age, salary etc. The form will speed things up if you require a mortgage.'

Inevitably, they would return, primarily to be reassured that this was a great investment. What did they expect to hear? 'The proprietor is a scam merchant, that video has been copied from a well - respected company and you're stupid to hand over fifty-per- cent of the purchase price. If the clients' wish to fly to Bulgaria and visit the location and the construction site that does not cause any problem. They were told: 'Flights are not as regular as Spain from the UK, but the company can arrange a flight and a hotel, or the client(s) can stay in one of the company's show -flats that would give them an idea of the property they had purchased.' They were blissfully unaware that the flat was owned by an innocent individual renting it out, same if it was a luxurious villa.

The scam company paid the rent up- front, usually six- months in advance.   If the scam was attracting clients who were handing over their credit cards with a grateful smile, they would then negotiate with the owner another advantageous six- months lease. When they had appropriated a large tranche of money, they would disappear from the face of the earth. The flat or villa owner would be left with the wrath of the client. The scam was bringing in a tsunami of money, his colleague in Bulgaria kept in touch by email, they rarely saw each other, it was better that way. As soon as the money came in it was wired to a bank in the Cayman Islands, later it would eventually arrive in Jersey, via several African countries. The bank manager in Jersey was very accommodating, when the Bulgarian operation had come to its natural conclusion, all bank transactions would be wiped clean from the hard drive of the bank's computer. He was patently aware the scam was in its last throes. The bank manager would be well- rewarded; his inflated invoice would be for financial advice.

The office in Dundee was attracting wealthy clients, and other professionals. The montage of properties in the window were attracting a regular clientele; it had not gone unnoticed that the values of the various properties had risen by twenty- per cent in two months. The clientele could no longer suppress the urge to enter the office rather than just observe, they felt a need for more information. This was the sprat that caught the shoal of mackerel. The clientele paid the hefty fifty per cent deposit, they did not want to miss out on the rapidly appreciating properties. In the weeks to come they would see the properties in the window for sale had risen in value. They felt an air of smugness, they were pleased to casually mention this to friends, family and if they were financial advisors; their clients. Which of course, they would charge them a hefty fee for this information. Primarily they were pleased to see their own investment appreciate so quickly. Thus the lucrative Ponzi scheme would be born. The clients would introduce friends who introduced other friends. The clients were visibly impressed with his office, with the contemporary surroundings and complementary drinks machine. Modern art paintings hung on the walls, by well- known Bulgarian artists. Brochures were strategically placed on the large coffee tables. He had installed software that made the phones ring, when a customer was present and was dithering whether to hand over their credit card or write a cheque, he would apologise to the customer and have the incoming call on speaker phone. It was the builder bringing good news or his agent saying that was the development sold out he was going to view a location where they could erect the next phase.He would apologise for this, and say sorry that he had nothing available at the present day prices but he would place them on the mailing list when Building Consent was granted.

These new apartments or villas would be more expensive than the previous development, but they would be built in a more prestigious location. As the potential new client knew her or his friend had bought at a much lower price, and their properties had risen in value, they didn't need any incentive to hand over by cheque for fifty thousand pounds, the fifty per cent required.

They were the first to purchase a hundred -thousand pound villa in Bulgaria. Or so they believed. They accepted that their villas would not be ready for two years. But they were comforted by the knowledge that their villas had greatly appreciated in value. The clients were purchasing off- plan, they would sell the properties when they were completed. He would be able to sell them on immediately; pension funds and hedge funds had seen the benefit of the boom in construction in Bulgaria and he would be the broker between the client and the pension fund or hedge fund. However, it would be beneficial to instruct the solicitor to sell the property immediately it was completed; thus reducing Capital Gains Tax. A reduced flat fee of five thousand pounds would take care of the Legal Fees. Did they wish to settle the Legal Fees' now?

Very few of the clients would offer any resistance to this legal tax avoidance measure when it was explained. The Capital Gains Tax would be based on property values, would it not be better to pay the Capital Gains Tax at the purchase price of one –hundred thousand pounds, rather than the value of the property in two years hence? When asked what the value would be then? He said he would be surprised if the value had not increased by at least fifty –per cent. The client's eye-brows would shoot north. The clients were spending their profits before a brick had been laid. Common sense would dictate that it was more tax efficient to pay Capital Gains Tax on one- hundred thousand than one hundred and fifty –thousand. The credit-card was zipped through the machine with alacrity. He would casually mention if they had an accountant, some UK taxes would be imposed on the profit returning to their UK bank account. However, if you inadvertently have a lapse of memory, and fail to advise your accountant, no taxes would be liable when the money arrives in your UK bank account. Then he would give that charming smile and escort the client to the door. Another five-grand into the company's coffers, a flicker of a reassuring smile would be projected onto the satisfied client who in turn would imbue the client with a sense of achievement.

The cold winter wind blew into the office as he stood at the office door and gave a confident wave of farewell to the client climbing into the top of the range BMW 4x4. The sign on the door advised the office would be closed for the forthcoming Christmas and New Year holidays. It would close on twentieth of December and reopen on eighth of January. Alas, it wouldn't. The Lease was paid in advance up till April, to avoid suspicion by the Landlord. The company had paid for the refurbishment of the offices; all the computers' were leased till April. The companies that supplied the office furniture, paintings and drink dispenser were paid in advance. The only losers would be the clients'. But at least they appreciated the coffee.

This scam had worked all over Europe for more than ten -years. All it needed to succeed was peoples' greed. On Christmas Eve all the money was electronically wired from the Bulgarian Property Company to his account. This was the last month the Bulgarian Property Company would be in existence. There would be no Press releases apportioning blame to' accounting irregularities' or 'difficult trading conditions.' The company would cease on Christmas Eve. He knew it but no one else did. He would come in before Christmas Eve and wipe the computers of all information, no information relating to the client data base; however innocuous, would be on any of the hard-drives. Experience had shown when the scam came to light and was highlighted in the local or national Press; some clients' were reluctant to air their grievances to the Press. Others kept quiet to save themselves from embarrassment and opprobrium. He was shaken out of these pleasant thoughts, by the car coming to an abrupt halt in City Quay. He left the car without saying anything. He smirked at the belligerent police officer; a contemptuous look was returned instantly; he left the car and closed the door carefully. It was a cold night but it was much colder at the City Quay, because of the icy wind coming off the River Tay. He stopped and lit a cigarette; he casually looked around him through habit.

Everything was in order. He would always take a longer circuitous route to his apartment block. Tonight would be the exception he would meander through the City Quay development, and then go to Taza's for his infrequent Indian curry. New apartments that had been built but were not occupied, he was surprised developers' had come to Dundee and built this 'wilderness by the sea' as some critics' had unfavourably dubbed it, in an economic recession. It didn't matter if they were sparsely occupied, when good times emerged from the recession, and good times were approaching this would be a prime –location, but presently it was unwelcoming and looked eerily menacing.

When he gazed out from his window during daylight hours he rarely saw anyone out walking. He had seen the occasional car pass. Someone made a killing here he was told by the postman. The land had lain derelict for years. But someone saw an opportunity, continued the postman. If only he knew. As he took the last puff on the cigarette he noticed that the stars were out in their hundreds, he stopped and gazed up at them in wonderment; he threw the cigarette away. The temperature was plummeting there was no doubt about that, he thrust his hands into his jacket pockets, and made his way to the Taza restaurant. He was observing the few occupied apartments with their lights on; he was struck by the lack of Christmas trees on display. It really was a soulless place. His spirit dipped at the bleak emptiness of the blocks of apartments that were devoid of any cheer and hope. Maybe that was a sign of the times he thought, secularity was in vogue and Christianity was on the wane. He walked across the wooden bridge that took him from the car park to the shopping and restaurant area. The Taza is on the left. He ordered his curry and Nan bread to take out. He was told it would be about fifteen minutes; he took a seat at a table so he could watch the television, a music channel was on mute, which he thought odd

Three tables in front of him are two young women in their twenties. They are animated and talking loud, very loud. He is flicking through the free classified ads newspaper to pass the time, he is so grateful to be in the warmth. His attention is drawn towards the blonde girl he had heard her say to her friend that her parents had bought a villa in Bulgaria, but it would not be ready for two years. It had risen in value by twenty-thousand already.
'But is Bulgaria not dodgy with the Mafia and con men,' commentated her friend.
'Some parts were, but where their villa is being built, it is in an area where the neighbours would be diplomats, ambassadors and government officials. So they would be okay.'
This is benign news to him. Even he knew not to resort to implausible hyperbole. However, he welcomed the parents of the blonde young woman, for adding another line to the sales pitch. It is amazing what the human condition can do to convince themselves that what they are doing is correct, and to reinforce this they have invented another reason to reinforce their original decision. He wondered how many of the clients' had been to his office because of this 'fact' that Diplomats and Government Officials had purchased their villas' in an exclusive enclave?

He smiled as the young woman is describing the area and amenities close by, and the exclusive hotel and ski-resort that would be built by Hilton, Marriot Hotels or Trump Hotels, she couldn't recall which hotel chain were rumoured to be financing the five star hotel and ski-resort.

He is slightly disappointed when he was told his order is now ready. Another couple of minutes would have been interesting listening. He folded the paper and placed it back in the rack. He hoped the young blond woman frequented this popular restaurant at the weekend. Her sales pitch was so convincing. He rose from the table and collected his curry paying by cash. Life had just got better. The good news that he had just heard made him immune to the mind-numbing cold that hit him as soon as he left the restaurant. He had a spring in his step, and a wide smile emanated from his face. Diplomats and government officials meant twenty-four- seven security, another reassuring tenet for purchasing in Bulgaria.

CHAPTER **TWO**

The police car was parked on Hill Street facing the Law (Hill.) The two officers were enjoying their steak rolls and cups of tea; perks of the job, courtesy of the owner of the all night cafe around the corner in Main Street. The owner had the utmost respect for these two police officers because they protected him, and his café from the yobs who had hurled racial abuse and smashed his window on the first night he opened his cafe.

When he first complained two young officers came to see him. It was so apparent that they didn't show any interest or compassion for his current plight. He was displeased by their *laissez- faire* manner; they obviously joined the police to catch bank robbers not deal with the day to day petty crime in the Hilltown area. Some of the public just accepted incidents like this as part of their environment and did not register it as a crime, the public just endured it. The bored officers did not attempt to disguise their disdain for the old man in his sixties. This was an exercise in utter futility as far as they were concerned. The officer took out his notebook and pen.

'What were the two youths wearing?'

'Tracksuits and baseball caps,' he replied. The officer taking the statement pushed back his cap with his pen and let out an audible sigh.

The café owner looked dismayed. 'What's the matter...?

The police officer told him he had just described the youth not only of the Hilltown, but of Dundee, if not the UK. The cafe owner threw his arms in the air 'Why do I bother!'

'Don't you have them on CCTV?' The police officer's colleague enquired

'Is this a joke?' the owner retorted, he was now getting agitated.

'Calm down sir, we're here to help.' The officer knew he did not sound convincing.

The exasperated cafe owner went behind the counter muttering in his mother tongue; he started to wipe the counter. The officer shifted from one foot to another.

'Do you have them on CCTV?'

The owner stopped cleaning and threw the cloth on the floor with disgust. He came marching from behind the counter, took the officer by the arm, reluctantly the officer allowed the old man to lead him outside of the cafe. 'There!' shouted the owner. The officer followed the line of the owner's outstretched arm he saw nothing.

He turned to his colleague 'Can you see what he's pointing at?' His colleague shrugged his shoulders and shook his head.

'Don't you understand?' The owner exasperated at their lack of vision. 'Someone stole the camera two weeks ago, didn't you know that?

They both shook their heads. 'Do you wish to make a complaint?'

'Against whom,' screeched the owner? The officer took rudimentary details, and told him they would be in touch.

Things were very different now for the cafe owner. The following Saturday night, the same feral youths came in and repeated their repertoire; drink and bravado are a heady mixture. They came out from the cafe unsteady on their feet shouting invective and kicking the door, but became instantly sober when they literally barged into the two older police officers. The officers' grabbed them and ushered them back inside the café. The officers emptied the shop of customers waiting for their orders, they offered no resistance. The owner explained to them that the youths had been the bane of his life. Threats and racial abuse were the norm from the youths.

The officers threw them against the counter and shouted at them to empty their pockets of everything. Unconvinced one of the officers searched them, while the other officer stood at the door to prevent a premature exit. The officer found some sachets of heroin on one of them; the officer stuck them in his pocket.

The officer told the owner that he wouldn't be seeing the youths ever again in his cafe. The youths repeated this with a little encouragement from the other officer. He told him that they were going to Police Headquarters.

After the youths had been charged and processed, the officers would return to see him. One of the youths protested that there were no witnesses' to the racial abuse. But before he could finish his diatribe, the other officer explained they had seen everything. However, that was the least of their worries, both of them, not one of them, had in their possession a Class A drug; Heroin. When they heard this they were ashen faced. Both were out on bail for previous drug offences.
'We will be back later to see you,' he repeated to the owner. The owner respected these police officers, they had seen nothing, but they were prepared to say that they had seen all the threats and racial abuse.

The officers took the youths to the car and invited them into the rear of the car. The youths' climbed in with leaden feet. The officers waved to the owner, entered the car and drove down the Hilltown. The youths were silent in the back both staring out blankly out of their respective windows. The silence was broken by the officer driving the car.
'Where did you get the smack?' Stony silence remained.
'Last life lads, where did you get the smack?' Stubborn silence was their considered reply.
'Well, he continued, no problem for us,' he pulled on latex gloves and then pulled out a half- kilo of brown powder wrapped in cling film from the glove compartment. The youths were puzzled by this; suddenly he threw the package on to the lap of the youth who looked scared witless
He panicked, and threw it away from him, it landed on his friend. He threw it back at the officer.
'Thanks lads, did you enjoy pass the parcel.' He took the brown powder and placed it strategically between his feet. The officer driving; casually remarked that their prints were all over the smack, this happened to be contaminated.

Earlier in the month the Drug Squad had interrupted a consignment of heroin in Glasgow that had taken the lives of eighteen junkies, it was cut with a toxic ingredient that caused sores which didn't heal, and then became festered and eventually poisoned the blood; septicaemia. Some of the heroin which was destined for the East Coast had got through.
'Two junkies who had lived in an Alexander Street multi- storey had died courtesy of the contaminated heroin…How would that go down with their chums and other bona -fide dealers if they saw in the newspapers' that they two were behind it? How long do you think that they would last on the streets?'
'You can't do that to us!'
'Do you want to bet?' The officer replied laughing. The police car went past the sub-station on the middle of the Hilltown. The youths were clearly flummoxed at this. Now they were getting worried.
'Are we going to Bell Street?
The youth enquired his voice going up an octave. His friend continued to look out the window, their options, if they had options in the first place had just diminished.
'This is too big for us, we'll have to hand you over to the Drug Squad, unless…'
'Unless, what!' The other youth shouted out, tears welling up in his eyes.
The car came slowly to a stop. 'Tell us who the main dealer is.'
'Tam Winston,' blurted out the youth.
'Try again, don't mention Sharon Thomas, Wullie Lewis, Carol Ingles, we know all the low- level dealers.' The youths looked at one another, who is going to say it, who is going to be the grass?
The officers knew they had them. They had to play it patiently. Tears were in one of the youth's eyes and his leg started to shake he put his hand on it to try to disguise the motion, he felt the increasing pressure building in his bladder. The officer looked both of them in the eyes.
'I'll make it easier for you both.' He turned back and rummaged in the glove compartment. He came out with a note pad and two pencils. He gave each of them a pencil. He gave the note pad to the one who had been crying. 'You write his first name, and your pal can write his surname. That way no one is a grass, and when the both of you have done his name, I'll give you this; he was holding a cigarette lighter, only when we see who it is, and then you can set it alight.'
They liked the sound of that.

'But it's not as simple as that,' said the tearful one.
'It's all right,' replied his mate whose knee stopped shaking.
He knew not to look a gift horse in the mouth.
'I know what you mean; I'll write the first name.'
He did this and passed the note pad to his becalmed friend. He scribbled on it and handed it to the officer, the officer looked at it.
'Are you sure?'
'Positive,' the youth said. The officer handed it to his partner. 'Are you having us on?'
'Look if they found out we gave you the name, we would be dead, that's the name, let us out now.'
'If we find out this is a load of shite, we'll get you, and remember we have your prints.'
'A deal is a deal; give me the pad and the lighter. 'The officer gave it to him.
He ripped out the page furiously and lit the page.
'I'm taking the pad; the name will be imprinted on the other page. '
The officer nodded, he was keen to empty the car of this cargo the youths were in a dangerous place, but they didn't try to disguise how dangerous.
'Take the pad and rip it up or use the lighter, do what you want, do you want out here?'
They didn't answer they opened the doors and left.
'Now that was interesting,' said the officer as he placed the heroin back into the glove compartment.
'Your pal in the Drug Squad is going to like this.'
'Let's think about this', said his partner as he started the car, 'let's think.'
'I don't know what there is to think about, we pass on the information to your friend, he passes on the money to us,' replied the officer.
'This is too big; I'm going to sit on this just now, things are flooding into my head here.'
'Fair enough…I'm hungry we'll head back to the cafe on Main Street, speak to the owner and tell him that he won't get any more bother from the yobs. This is not even our beat… I will speak to him and hopefully he'll offer us a couple of steak rolls on the house. Two steak rolls each, if I have to pay then its back to one each.'
'Greedy bastard,' replied his partner.
'No time like the present,' the car moves off. 'What did you think about that name that they gave us, did you have any idea?'
'I didn't have a clue and neither does my Drug Squad chum. What we have to do first is to corroborate the information that they gave us is genuine…and I have some doubt.'
'And how do we do that?
'By using our everyday skills, we can go any place and anywhere because we are policemen sorry police officers… and establish where she lives, find out who her friends are, who she comes into contact with. If we don't recognise them, we'll find out who they are and do they work? Are they businessmen with a dark side. Are they local people?'
'Do you mean, put her under surveillance?'
'Got it in one…we are the perfect people to carry out surveillance, we won't arouse any suspicion we have to drive near her house. It's a given, she'll have CCTV at her house. If we are driving past in the police car and her cameras pick us up; she'll be more pleased than suspicious.'
'How long do you think we'll have to keep an eye on her for?'
'As long as it takes, we don't know where this is going to end, this is just you and me, don't breathe this to anyone.'
'I know that… will you be able to fish for information from the DS friend without him noticing?'
'He always comes to me remember, he roughly comes to me about once every six weeks for information. Or say he's heard that, have you heard this, that's the type of conversation we have, then he'll leave a newspaper in the back of the car. I go to the racing page and see some horses circled in black ink, as soon as I see them I know where to go for the money. No one is there to hand it to me; I just go to the place and pick it up. He gets more and more ingenious.

'Last year I got a text message from him, telling me that there are nice plants at the outdoor bargain section at B&Q. The best time to go up is at 2pm. I looked there and an envelope was partly hidden I slipped it in my pocket. My wife thought I was just checking the quality of the plants. That's how he operates, I'm his only contact in the uniform section he knows about you being my partner, but we never discuss you. I give him a dealer's name on paper then immediately have a wee bonfire.'
 'Ah… so that's how the ashtray is there in the glove compartment, I knew you gave up smoking, I thought maybe your willpower sometimes lapsed every now and then.'
'It is good cover isn't it, we should be able to build a dossier on her and her friends, but trying to match her to drug dealing? That will be hard -work.'
'I find it hard to believe, but, she has the perfect cover, I'll give you that. On the other hand how do two low-lives like them know about her?'
'How many stories have you heard about senior officers that were up to no good? Then later on there is some substance to the stories. Then everyone said I knew he was guilty of this or that.'
'Yeah, you're right, what was that phrase you coined about them…hindsight detectives?'
He responded with a laugh. 'I'm like you, very sceptical, but did you see the fear in the laddies faces? That wasn't fear about us lifting them; that was fear about them being connected with a batch of heroin that had killed people. The dealers are having difficulty in selling their product because of the contaminated heroin; they want everything to return to normal as quickly as possible.'
'When I think about it, if they were charged with the contaminated heroin; they would be under a death sentence.'

***

    Mary stood there looking out over the Tay two hands clasping tightly the mug of coffee, the lights from Wormit shining brightly back to her. Her flat on the Perth Road had been her marital home when she had returned to Dundee, since then her marriage ended, somewhat embarrassingly after less than a year. The only thing that her husband left her was the twins; a boy and a girl she could have named them chalk and cheese. Brian the oldest of the twins by ten minutes, had rejected the educational system, Norma on the other hand had embraced and cultivated her education.
    She was at Warwick University, and had settled in well. She rejected Dundee University, even though it was on the opposite side of the street from the flat. Her mother was a lecturer there, she also wanted away from her indolent twin brother. She visited on rare occasions, never announcing her arrival. Each time she arrived one thing was guaranteed, Brian would be sprawled out on the sofa, watching television, or having a power nap as he liked to call it, not to get confused with a micro- sleep.
    Mary had met Alan when she worked as a linguist for the European Union, he was the archetypal accountant he was two years younger than her, that didn't please her mother. They decided to leave Strasbourg; both were successful in their search for positions in Dundee. Alan, who was born and bred in Paris, was obsessed by Scotland; he had many holidays in Scotland in his youth, and the thought of working and living in Scotland was a gift from fate. They had purchased the top floor flat for thirty -six thousand pounds, which needed completely renovated. The only external addition they made was having a balcony erected on the rear of their flat. Now they could open the French Doors and either sit or stand on their balcony taking in the vista of the road and rail bridges. Whatever the weather the view was persistently uplifting. Alan had received a phone call from Strasbourg, he had to leave in the morning it was his father who was ill.
'Would you like me to accompany you?'
'No, no, I'll be back in a week, ten days at the most, you have students depending on you.'
That was the last she saw of him. Seven days had passed and she had no contact from him, maybe he is caught up in his father's illness? He will phone soon, don't worry she told herself he will get in contact soon. Nine days later she received the fateful phone call.

His voice was different she knew something was wrong. She interrupted him.
'Is your father okay'?
'Yes, yes', now he was agitated, 'this is very difficult for me he continued, I...I... am not returning to Dundee, I am staying here in Strasbourg.'
She interrupted. 'Why, I can't understand...?
'I have met someone else, an old girlfriend, we still have feelings for each other, I'm sorry, but that's life.' The silence seemed to be infinite; his voice betrayed no emotion.
'You can keep the flat, which is not a problem; I will sign all the legal papers without question.'

Mary walked across the wooden floors in the lounge; she continued on through the kitchen, opened the French Doors and thought about it, why not? What is there to live for? Her husband had walked out; she couldn't afford to pay the mortgage on the flat, and they had borrowed additional money for the refurbishment of the flat. She felt light headed, but control gradually came back into her voice.
'Ah well, C'est la vie, send a letter saying that you have committed adultery and that you want your name taking off the title deeds, and that you have no claim now or in the future of the flat.'
'Is that all you have to say?' He was clearly taken aback at the matter of fact conversation.
'That's all I have to say, apart from wishing you well for the future, 'replied Mary trying unsuccessfully to suppress her laughter.

He ended the call. Five minutes previously she had thought about ending her life. An infusion of optimism had replaced the pernicious despair; time to look forward, not back. She walked towards the large brass mirror and looked critically at her reflection; she was petite, blonde hair, dyed of course, and at least a stone over weight and that was a conservative critique. No time like the present she thought, she went into the bedroom and flung open his wardrobe and manically emptied all his suits, shirts, and everything that he owned into black bags. She worked feverishly at this chore then stopped exhausted, and threw herself on to the bed. She pilloried herself was she that stupid she never saw any signs, that he was unhappy or had noticed any mood change? In all honesty, this was a bolt from the blue. She had been worrying about his father, but this had all been a ruse. She had been played like an old violin, how was she going to cope paying the bills, despair was taking a firm hold of her. Tears were flowing once again. Her life had been trundling along with little excitement, and then this. She would not go to the doctor and be prescribed anti- depressants; she could not contemplate this course of action. Why didn't she tell Alan she was pregnant?

***

Ian and his dad arrived back at the house, after removing their coats Margaret intimated to Thomas to go through to the kitchen. 'You boys settle down in here and watch the television, your father and I will bring the tea through.' She was impatient for information, how had the walk been, any trepidation vanished instantly when she caught Thomas's gaze. He gave her that wink of his that introduced him to her all those years ago. She followed him into the kitchen breathing a sigh of relief; she was more confident in the house now, it did not intimidate her as it had earlier. It felt like their house now.
'How did it go with Ian?'
'Couldn't have gone better, if I planned it myself... and how did it go with the boys here?'
'Tears from me, as you would expect, a few trips down memory lane... I was thinking about tomorrow when we go into town, I expect to see things have changed, how do you think we'll cope?'
'No problem whatsoever. I don't expect to see too many changes. I'm looking forward to going to see the old Caledon boat yard with Ian; I can't remember if he said we are going there tomorrow...I don't think its tomorrow. '
'Why, are you going to the old boatyard?'
'Ian wants my advice on something,' he said proudly.

'That's good', she switched on the kettle it started boiling immediately, 'and what were the topics of conversation then?'
'Oh the usual, just the things that father and son talk about. I got the impression that Ian was really trying to apologise for something, he would start something then move onto another subject.'
'What has Ian got to apologise for? His business is all right, is there a business opportunity at the boat yard?'
'He never went that far, but I suspect something is on the horizon.'
She poured the water into the tea pot, and placed it on the tray with the cups and saucers. 'Open the door please, and we'll enjoy the tea with our family.' She stopped as soon as she said it. They moved from the kitchen to the lounge.
'Where's Ian?' she asked.
'His mobile rang then he left,' replied Peter.

***

Linda Simpson is a successful high profile businesswoman, who loved publicity on an equal to herself. She is old money, the descendent of Walter Simpson who had owned three Jute mills in Dundee in the nineteen- century. If the Queen's Award to Industry had existed then he wouldn't have been a recipient of this prestigious award. He treated his family as he treated his two-thousand workers; harshly and with contempt.

The American Civil War a tragic event that had occurred in American History, but to Walter Simpson it was manna from heaven. His factories spewed out millions of sand bags for the Union side as well as the Confederates. The only regret he had; it was a war that ended too soon. However, as this was his first foray into the American market, he saw that America was indeed the land of a myriad of business opportunities.

Andrew Carnegie was a confidant of Abraham Lincoln, who had vanquished the Confederate Army. Abraham Lincoln had mentioned Walter Simpson to Carnegie that a fellow Scotchman had helped the Union side like he had. Andrew Carnegie was bursting with pride that a fellow Scotchman had seen this business opportunity. He telegraphed Walter Simpson praising him to the high- heavens He explained to him that he always came over to Scotland for the summer as the heat of the American summer was most disagreeable, would you and your wife like to join us for a week? Walter Simpson read the telegram over and over; Andrew Carnegie had invited him to be his guest! He sent a telegram immediately, it would be an honour.

When he returned from the holiday with the Carnegies, he ordered his accountant to meet him at his mansion in Broughty Ferry at six am. He intended to move the bulk of his capital into the fledgling tobacco industry. He had moved a proportion of his capital into the embryonic oil industry, Carnegie was aghast at this. Simpson and Carnegie had polarised views on his investment. Very few businessmen went against Carnegie's advice. In fact, Carnegie and a business partner had discovered oil on land that they had acquired for one of his steel mills.

Carnegie was not only shrewd; he was a gambler with businessmen's emotions. He said to Walter Simpson, the oil on my land in my view is worthless; if you think it is a commodity that is worth a lot of money. I will sell all the oil on my land; do you wish to buy this oil now? If so we will shake hands on the deal and I will have my Attorney draw up a business contract, it will be ready to be signed before you leave. Walter Simpson shook hands on the deal. Carnegie arranged to have a company to extract the oil for Simpson; obviously at no cost to Carnegie.

Then Kismet intervened on behalf of Walter Simpson; the combustion engine had not been invented yet, not only would the oil be used for lamps it would now be an integral part of the combustion engine. Simpson sold the oil field on to the Rockefellers' for millions. When Carnegie found out about this business deal he sent Simpson a telegram, with the brief message, 'a man after my own heart'. 'No animosity.'

They remained friends only death interrupted their friendship.

This was the fortune that Linda Simpson had thrown into her bank account when she was twenty-one. That was twenty- seven years ago and three husbands later. She was fortunate after each marriage had floundered her capital was left intact. The divorced husbands' had been wealthy in their own rights. They had to settle with her, parting with seven- figure sums. She lived in the seventeen- bedroom mansion in Broughty Ferry, the house that Walter Simpson had built. The mansion was originally meant to have fourteen –bedrooms; however, he had read in the newspaper, that a rival Jute Baron was commissioning a mansion that would have fifteen-bedrooms. The Jute Barons' had the mentality of the owners' of the great liners; they had to have their ships bigger and grander than their rivals. Walter Simpson ordered his builders, to increase the bedrooms from fourteen to seventeen; he would have the grandest, most elegant and of course the mansion with the most bedrooms in Broughty Ferry. His builder touched his forelock and agreed to the alteration. Walter Simpson was very pleased with himself; he sent a telegram to his dear friend Andrew Carnegie that he was having his mansion built, it would be an honour if him, Louise and Margaret could join him next summer? The cool breeze and fresh air from the River Tay would be conducive to his health.

Andrew Carnegie and his family did join them that summer. One evening as Simpson and Carnegie were strolling along the beach, Carnegie had succinctly steered the conversation to death; and how would he like to be remembered?

Simpson's reply no doubt assisted by the finest malt whisky, replied he couldn't care less.
The diminutive Carnegie came to a sudden halt; and took a puff on his cigar. Simpson saw the look of disgust emanating from Carnegie's face. Then his face returned to its natural exuberance.
He resumed to walk at a brisk pace; he mentioned to Simpson that a fellow Jute Baron whose mansion had been superseded by Simpson; was planning to develop the swathe of land that he owned to a public park. Had he heard this?

Simpson had heard nothing. Carnegie was surprised at this; he told him that he had heard from several businessmen at the party Simpson had given the previous evening. He had also heard other Jute Barons were to follow suit. Simpson was embarrassed and outraged; he was ready to burst a blood vessel.

Carnegie took a firm hold of his arm; 'Dundee needs a modern hospital more than three parks, his eyes were drawn to the leaden sky above Dundee; there were a multitude of industrial chimneys' from the Jute Mills, twenty-four hours a day belching out pollution. It reminded Carnegie of Slabtown in Pittsburgh, where the inside of buildings matched the outside; encased in soot.
'That's what I would do if I wanted to improve people's health; build a hospital and history would remember you fondly'. Carnegie had planted the seed firmly in his head, he was confident a new hospital would be announced and built as soon as possible. Simpson continued to walk with Carnegie barely communicating with him, the rage inside him building with every step.

The next day Simpson invited all the same people to an impromptu party in honour of Andrew Carnegie, on the invitation it said an announcement would be made by Walter Simpson.
Rumours were abounding in Broughty Ferry; from the ridiculous to the salacious. It was the hottest ticket in town. This would be the only occasion when all Jute Barons' would be in a room at the same time. They were all shepherded into the large ballroom the first thing the guests had noticed was the stage where the musicians would normally stand, had been set up bedecked by the Union Flag on a large table. There were five chairs occupied; in the centre Walter Simpson, to the left of him Professor Thomson a leader in his field of blood disorders, next to him sat their Member of Parliament, Roger Green. To the right of Simpson sat Andrew Carnegie and his wife Louise. Simpson rose from his chair. 'Ladies and Gentlemen, thank you for accepting my late invitation, I promise I will be brief, as you can see the table is occupied by prominent persons, I will not introduce any of them as you all recognise them.' He cleared his throat.

'Dundee will have a new hospital it will be one of the finest hospitals not only in Scotland but in the world. It will have the most advanced medical equipment; cost will not inhibit any part of the hospital. All the medical staff will be of the highest calibre; the hospital should be opened in less than two years.
   'This project has been on my mind for many a year', Carnegie's eyebrow raised then fell, no one noticed. Simpson continued. 'I have searched the globe for the finest architect who can design this wonder of the medical world. My friend Andrew Carnegie, as always was able to assist me in locating this genius. The architect is the most sought after in Europe. He is William Rice, from Dublin.' Audible gasps came from the enthralled audience.
   'William Rice is so enthusiastic about this that he has waived his fee'. What he failed to mention was that Andrew Carnegie had spoken to William Rice; he rejected the commission out of hand he was too busy, he had other commissions to give his attention. Andrew Carnegie said he didn't realise this, he went on to say he intended to ask him to design and oversee his mansion that is to be built in New York the following year; but as he was so busy, could he recommend another architect of the same calibre as him? William Rice had a very arrogant character within him; normally it was a beacon he proudly displayed. However, he was aware that Carnegie was close friends with the Vanderbilt's 'as well as the Rockefellers'. If he designed and oversaw Carnegie's mansion, which would make news all round the world. And it would do his spiritual side no harm if he was the architect for the hospital in Dundee. He could defer incoming projects to a later date.
   'Andrew, I will make my way over to Scotland as soon as possible, I apologise if I was a little abrupt, I have been working very late.'
'I understand,' replied Carnegie, 'are you sure that you will not be involved in a legal difficulty, as your clients may be disappointed?'
'I have excellent relationships with my clients, do not be troubled. I may lose some money, as I have been paid in advance, but...' said William Rice.
Carnegie, interjected, 'William, any loss that you suffer, I insist I will replenish.'
'That's very kind of you Andrew', replied William Rice.
'And my mansion in New York, would you be able to consider it..?'
'It would be an honour, Andrew an honour.'
Carnegie continued, 'as long as my mansion does not deflect you from the work at the hospital in Dundee...'
'Andrew, don't entertain that thought, I am looking forward already to seeing the land where it will be built.'
Carnegie replied, 'that is a heavy weight off my mind, it's not every day that the world famous William Rice offers his services free from any charge to design a hospital. I look forward to seeing you soon. I'll pass on this good news to Walter, is there anything else you want me to tell him?'
'No, I'll see you both when I arrive in Dundee, goodbye Andrew.'
   Walter Simpson saw the stir that this announcement had made he could imagine the newspaper headlines in his mind. His rivals may be endowing parks to the citizens of Dundee, which in itself was a wonderful gesture. He looked across at the faces of the Jute Barons; Baxter who was donating the land for the public park as well as the costs for the landscaping of the land seemed genuinely pleased at the thought of the hospital, he nodded his head slightly; he would take this head - movement as approval. For the first in many a year he was not happy but content.
The melancholic mood that seemed to be within him when he went to bed, and was there when he woke up; temporarily was gone.
   Andrew Carnegie was invited to address the array of Jute Barons and other wealthy individuals. Carnegie was a great orator and visionary, he contributed one million, five hundred thousand dollars for the construction of the Peace Palace in The Hague. If any countries were heading towards war, this was the place that they could talk instead of sending their youth to die in future futile wars.

He firmly believed that talking to each other would bring a common ground and an end to conflict, aided and abetted by the other countries.   He pulled himself up to his five feet three inches.

'What Walter has done is a magnificent antidote to death. Public health is a disgrace in Dundee; building the hospital will prevent premature deaths; that is also the case for the Public Parks. People will be able to go there, breathe clean air and have a place to relax. Eradicate poverty; this will eradicate hate; if mankind can manage to attain this, no wars need to be fought. In this room there are many wealthy individuals; all I say is use your wealth for the advantage of others less fortunate than yourselves. Projects like the hospital and the proposed parks, will benefit future generations, your names will never die; they will be spoken in fondly terms.

'What better thought is there, than in three hundred years' time, your future generations are enjoying the clean air of the parks and thinking that was my great, great, great grandfather who constructed this magnificent park, or hospital or music theatre? All of you have this town in your hands; you are in total charge of the destiny of its people. Walter told me over dinner last night that Broughty Ferry has more millionaires per square mile than Monaco; I was astonished at this information, but it is true. If the people in this room live in this gilded square mile, I would suggest you take yourself and others into Dundee. I have never seen so many street urchins, thin and pallor of skin that suggests that Death is near. The smell is over powering; sanitation if there are any, is very poor. Drunkards inhabit every street; the life has been squeezed out of these men. Why aren't these children in school being educated? Why aren't these men and women; I'm ashamed to say, in gainful employment? A tiny drop of the wealth in this room could go a long way to ease the appalling conditions of the workers' and the dispossessed.

'Hospitals and Parks are the icing on the cake. You all have the ingredients; pounds, shilling and pennies to make the cake more substantial. Do you want the future generations of Dundee to smile or spit when your names are mentioned?'

He sat down. Two thirds of the room were shaking by this outburst. They thought Carnegie was here to praise them not berate them. They left. The third that remained came from each corner of the ballroom to congregate in the centre under the French chandeliers. A quiet mumble could be heard at the table, coming from the group of men under the chandelier. Arms were moving from side- to- side. Walter Simpson turned to Carnegie and said, 'at least I know who I can trust now.' Carnegie lit his cigar and nodded.

***

She paced the lounge, every few minutes staring out of the large bay- windows, she lit a cigarette, her first in four- months; she only smoked when she was on edge. She returned to the window; still no sign of him. Again she glanced at her watch, was it only fifteen-minutes ago she had called him? It felt like an hour. This was her second cigarette; she only smoked them half- way down. Her video com buzzed. About time to she thought, as she made her way towards the video monitor. It was him. She didn't say anything. She pressed the button that activated the fifteen- foot ornamental gates. She watched them swing open and the expensive car enters the driveway. She then closed the gates, and watched the car come to a halt on the gravel driveway outside the door. He emerged from the car, and walked towards the imposing double doors; the door clicked open, he entered, the door automatically and silently closed after ten seconds. This person was familiar with this routine. He made his way up the magnificent spiral stair case. He never gave the Rembrandts' a second glance. His mind was occupied by events unfolding on a daily basis. He reached the top of the stairs and took a left into the lounge. She was sitting watching television; her demeanour suggested to him that she was perfectly relaxed. All trace of cigarette smoke had been removed.
'Is everything okay?'
'If it was I wouldn't have called you...take a seat.'
He sat across from her on the leather chair; she had a regal air about her as she sat opposite him on the sofa.

'We have had big problems with our supplier.'
'In what respect,' he asked.
'The supplier offered us more of the goods if we bought in bulk. We took up this suggestion, but when the goods were examined, the goods were not what they were supposed to be. They had replaced our goods with compost. We must have the most expensive compost in history.'
'Have you spoken to them?'
'Not me personally; but I've been told these things happen and I have been advised not to pursue them.'
'I would agree with that we can't go to the police can we? 'He continued. 'Maybe Ramage has worked out that we're using his suppliers and he has been stringing us along?'
'Surely not?' she replied.

***

The patrol car eased along the street known locally as millionaire's row.
'There we are number twenty-two, high walled and double gated. And for good measure, indiscreet cameras positioned.'
'Speed up a little and don't gawk.'
His partner whistled. 'I don't think many people here are on housing benefit, the gates are probably worth more than my house.'
'At least we know where she lives. Even the trees look good; the planners did well here. If this comes off, you will have enough money to buy one of these houses.'
'But I can't for obvious reasons, and if it doesn't come off?'
'Well you won't have to worry; because you'll be dead. No risk no reward.'
'That sent a shiver down my spine.' The car came to the junction.
'I'll do a U turn here and park discreetly away from the house so we can still see who comes and goes through the gates.' He completes the U turn and parks about a hundred- metres from the house. The driver takes a plastic bag from the rear floor of the car
His partner looks puzzled. 'What's all this?'
'Our camouflage', he hands him a small flask and sandwiches, he continued, 'if we are picked up on any of the resident's security cameras, they'll see it's the police having a break, nothing suspicious.'
'You have this all thought out, what's in this flask?'
'Coffee in yours amigo, tea in mine, just relax and enjoy… as well as keeping your eyes open.'
'How long do you think we should hang about here, without raising suspicion?'
'Forty -minutes, that will do us, oh I nearly forgot there's a digital camera in the bag as well, grab it just in case.' His partner took the camera and placed it between them. 'Is it easy to work?'
'It's just like a gun, aim and shoot, it's a top of the range camera my son bought it for my Christmas last year.'
'How is he getting on?'
'He's doing fine, he has started with the local radio station as a trainee reporter he likes it, so I'm happy. His mum wants him to go to London, but he has explained to her starting as a junior reporter reporting fires and occasional violent crime, that helps build up his CV; in a few years' time he will apply for jobs in London.'
'It's better than this job,' replied his partner.
'This job is not that bad, think of the perks, if you know what I mean,' the driver laughed. They had just poured their respective beverages, when the Mercedes elegantly exited from the mansion. It took a right turn, heading towards them.

'Take it easy; don't give the car a second look, just look straight ahead and keep talking and raise your cup to your mouth' said the driver.
The Mercedes gathered pace the driver was smoking a cigar; he looked at the police car fleetingly, typical lazy bastards he thought.
'Did you get the registration number?'
'Yes it was ABE 4, and I thought I recognised the driver… but it can't be him?'
'The registration number will be easy to trace. Who was the person driving it then?'
'I thought it was Ramage... Michael Ramage'
'It can't be him he's in the jail doing six years, what's he doing in Dundee? '
'That's what I thought, but I could have sworn it was him... how long do you think he's been inside?'
'At least two maybe three -years, Ramage the Damage, the facilitator for nefarious characters, that's what the judge said. Tomorrow I'll go to the Mercedes dealer and enquire about buying one I'll slip in the conversation that I saw the car in the town it had a vanity plate, I'll pretend to struggle remembering it, the salesman will help me; the salesman will say that's Mr X he's...'
'I am glad you are doing it that way, going down the data -base route or asking the traffic cops could be risky. In the old days you could have accessed the DVLA data base without anybody knowing, but today someone has to log on to the computer. The dealer is the best bet. I'll check on Ramage as well, I thought he was a high- risk prisoner and he was in Barlinnie?
'That will be easy enough to find out,' replied his partner, draining the last remnants of the tea from the cup. 'This woman,' he nods towards her house… 'It doesn't make any sense, her being involved in drugs. She has money and respectability.'
'The perfect cover; interjected the driver. 'We said at the start we had to find out who comes and goes to her house, tonight we have a registration, tomorrow we'll find out who owns the car. That's the first link to her.'

The following afternoon the police officer drove up to the Mercedes garage in a black five series BMW. The car is his sister's she is a nurse in the United Arab Emirates. He had the use of her car while she is in the United Arab Emirates, she worked four -months there then came home for a month. Usually she ached to get back after two weeks; Dundee was starting to lose its hold over her. She is happily married to an Arab doctor, he didn't like coming over to Dundee, the climate is too cold for him, but he enjoyed the rain.

She would come over to visit her mum and dad and her big older brother who is a police officer. On her last visit she mentioned to her brother that there would be a vacancy for Head of Security at the hospital where she worked. Her brother asked her, if this is an offer of a job. She replied that it is. He said that if it is still open in eighteen-month time he would accept it. But, he is not going to walk away from the police force without his pension. He explained to her that he could leave under ill -health, that's why he would approach the police doctor about back pains. He is confident that the doctor would concur with his description of acute pain.

That would make his exit easier from the police service. It also helped that they are in the same Masonic Lodge. To be truthful he thought the whole rituals absurd. However, it was an eye-opener and an irrefutable fact being a member of the Lodge, helped promotion aspects and achieving premature retirement on ill- health grounds with a generous pension and a more generous lump sum. Because of his infrequent attendance, younger colleagues were able to accelerate and by- pass the normal route to promotion .However; he is friendly with the avuncular police doctor and had helped the police doctor on numerous occasions, from ordering and installing a shower for him, to finding a flat in a good and safe area when his only daughter was studying for her degree at Dundee University. He had never asked covertly or overtly for a favour in return from the doctor; he would seek that favour when he prematurely developed sciatica.

 What would the doctor's reaction be if he knew that the electric shower, base and unit and Italian marble tiles had come from professional shoplifters, and that he had confiscated the goods in return for no charges be pressed against them?

Or that impressive two bed- roomed flat on the Blackness Road near the university that his daughter was renting for two -hundred pounds a month, is owned by a career criminal who is a member of the same Lodge? The doctor protested weakly, that his daughter only required one- bedroom.
'Your daughter will need a friend for company and to help her study. That's why a two-bedroom flat is more suitable. She will meet a new friend at the university, who will not be from Dundee. She would be able to rent the other room for two- hundred a month; thus costing your daughter zero.' The doctor's resistance capitulated; his wallet embraced this practical and economically sound idea. When he had inspected flat with his wife they was overwhelmed with the vastness of space, never mind the state of the art kitchen and contemporary bathroom with power shower. The next time he spoke to the doctor at the Lodge, the doctor said he seen similar flats in the same street and the landlord is charging six hundred and fifty pounds per month. He explained to the doctor that he knew the landlord, which was true; and he was returning a favour.

   The doctor explained to him rapidly in a hushed tone that if he needed help in easing out of the police service he would be able to facilitate this. That's what he wanted to hear. He never told his partner about the doctor, but he had no fears telling his beloved sister. If everything went to plan, this new position in the United Arab Emirates would be the perfect cover for his new found wealth. His health would improve in the arid heat. His wife had no inhibitions about leaving Dundee for months' at a time; she hated her job as a Legal Secretary, seeing all the low- life coming into the office everyday was affecting her mental well- being. All this monotony and drudgery for sixteen-thousand pounds a year; not forgetting the box of chocolates at Christmas. Thank God her husband had a good well -paid job in the police. He was the one who organised the holidays' to Tenerife in the winter. They always stayed in five star apartments; always on golf course complexes. The people who frequented the Clubhouse at night were a different class from the rabble who stayed in Los Cristianos. Her husband is so fortunate to have friends that owned apartments all over Southern Europe, her husband must be very popular for them to let them stay in their apartments for two weeks, sometimes at short notice. He intended to buy an apartment t before he retired; prices were moving upwards every winter, this did not concern her husband, he explained his pension lump sum would cover the cost of an apartment whether prices rose or not. He had been contributing the maximum from his salary to his pension pot. She believed every tainted word that fell from his lips.

***

   The salesman's eyes were alive when he saw the BMW arrive in the forecourt. He placed the bacon roll alongside the freshly brewed coffee on his desk. He wiped his mouth quickly, and straightened his tie, and then walked from the office onto the forecourt with a synthetic smile on his rotund face.
'Hi, my names Robert, are you looking for something in particular?' He thrust his hand out.
He met it immediately. 'I'm open- minded, I just fancy a change from the Beamers, do you have any special offers at the moment?'
'Any car is open to negotiation.'
That's what he liked to hear.
'Actually, the car I liked is a silver Mercedes, it was my wife that spotted it in the town it had a personalised number plate.'
'Could you recall the plate?'
'To be honest, I can't...' The salesman is dejected.
'Now what was it?' He was staring at the salesman. 'Could it have been ABE 3?'
The salesman was counting the commission for that top of the range car fly into his bank account.
'Could it have been ABE 4?' He knew it was.
'Yes that's it. You must have a good memory...'
'That car was sold by me to Albert Friedman, last year; it's a top of the range piece of kit.'
'Could I see it?' He asked expectantly. The salesman blanched; and his mood visibly deflated.

'Unfortunately, we have none in stock at the moment, that model has been flying out of here.'
'That's a great pity.' He feigned disappointment. 'Is there any other dealership in Scotland that can arrange a test drive?' When the salesman heard this, the holiday to New York from his commission dissipated. He coughed to regain some composure. 'How soon do you require it?'
'I could wait till the summer, as long as I can definitely have one?'
His mind filled with the vision of shops on Fifth Avenue once more.
'That is not a problem, we should, sorry, we will have another supply from February onwards.'
He explained painfully the car was not for him; it was a birthday present for his wife.
'Is it possible to order one in June; her birthday?
   He followed the salesman into his office. The salesman invited him to sit down. He punched the calculator on the desk; the worried expression is replaced with a smile.
'The car is offered for sale at ninety –six thousand. And how would you be financing the purchase?'
'It will depend on the level of discount on offer.'
'We have excellent financial options available… but cash is king.'
'Then cash it is then.'
'Excellent, I would be able to bring the price down to eighty-nine thousand and ninety-nine pounds, how did that sound?'
'Fine, you will throw in a three years free servicing as well?'
'I was going to suggest that.'
The salesman is cock- a- hoop at this, he could have brought it down another two maybe three thousand without a negative impact on his commission.
'Is Mercedes the preferred choice of Albert Friedman?'
The salesman didn't look up he is busily completing the sale agreement form. He placed the pen down.
'I have been at this dealer ship for over ten years, he always has had a Mercedes; he just upgrades. Albert is a very, very, very wealthy man. He has more pies than he can place fingers in, if you know what I mean.'
'To be honest I have never heard of him, I suppose he must live in Broughty Ferry amongst the other millionaires?
'You better believe it, seemingly, his house is worth four- million. He has businesses all over Europe. His main business is land and property and not just in Dundee, but international. He told me he has purchased a large piece of land in Romania or Bulgaria, he is going to build a five star hotel near a ski resort.' He liked this salesman, he didn't need to probe too deep, and he was forthcoming with information.
'That's worth knowing, my wife and daughter are keen skiers they are over in Aspen, Colorado, just now.'
'Skiing is too dangerous for me, I'm afraid.'
The salesman is keen to clinch the deal; he wanted to get the conversation back on track.
 'Would you want to leave a deposit or will you be paying in full in June?'
'I think it would be best to come back in June. Could I have your card, I don't want you to lose out on the commission.' He handed over his business card. He looked at it and placed into his well-stuffed wallet of fifty-pound notes. The salesman did not miss this lovely view.
'I will personally call you beforehand, maybe a week before I come back here, just too make sure the car is here. Then I will bring my wife and suggest she test drives the model that I want, and then say to her, it's a birthday present, then I'll pull out my well- worn cheque book and pay for it on the spot. My wife will think this has been a spontaneous purchase only you and I will know otherwise.'
The salesman was not surprised how these wealthy individuals operated.
'Don't hesitate if you require any further information.' He stood up.
'I'll see you in June then, he looked at the card… Robert.'

The salesman walked him to his car. When he drove away he saw the salesman continue to wave enthusiastically to him in his mirror and he kept on waving till he was off the forecourt.
Those salesmen don't miss a trick, he thought. He drove nearby to the disused industrial estate that is being demolished for a new industrial estate which would house a Digital and Media Park
He drove into a derelict unit and removed the false number plates; he placed them into the boot. His chin started to itch; he removed the goatee- beard and gave his chin a manic scratch.
The horned rimmed glasses with clear lenses joined the number plates and goatee beard in the holdall.

   He drove out of the unit slowly; he noticed the estate agents board, acquired by Friedman Estates. He then continued on to his sister's house a small bungalow in Birkhill, a small village four- miles west of Dundee. This quiet village is being slowly encroached by new housing developments springing up; mainly expensive executive houses. He had playfully suggested to his sister that she sell her house, but she dismissed this abruptly. He had no success when he gave her the alternative of letting her house, she could make a thousand a month. No deal.

   However, she had persuaded him to take the keys of the bungalow, where he could keep an eye on it, collect mail, and place the heating on in the winter months. He had considered using the house for card schools with his chums, but with the abundance of booze consumed his colleagues' tongues inevitably would become careless. He was glad that he had never exercised that option.

   The house would be the information centre of this web of intrigue. He would come here to think and plan his way to riches. The neighbours' would be not suspicious of him, he would be here looking after the house for his sister. The ten- minute drive to the bungalow was over he parked the BMW on the driveway a neighbour glanced at him from her window as he left; he smiled at the old woman she returned the smile. He went to his car an Astra, placed a Spanish Conversation CD into the player and moved off, after a minute he changed the CD to the radio, this Friedman character, is filling his head with questions, is he involved with Linda Simpson, illegal or otherwise? How are his businesses? Are they in trouble or are they successful? He would concentrate on Friedman; his partner on Linda Simpson.

***

   Ian is in his office enjoying a coffee with his dad, they're waiting on Peter arriving.
'So what do you need me for again…' asked Thomas
'Your local knowledge when you worked at the Caledon, that's all there's nothing to worry about,'
'But, but, didn't you get all the knowledge from the plans from the Council Offices?'
'Yes, but the plans don't go back far enough. Look dad if I wished to do a more thorough search that would raise suspicions, what I can tell you is that I am proposing to build five- hundred flats and ninety town houses. The plans are in at the planners' office now. As a matter of course, they'll reject this. They'll say there are too many it will have a detrimental effect on the area. It's all a game. The fact is I need one -hundred flats; forget about the town houses, to make this viable. When my company purchased the land years ago, it was commercial land. But now, the Government are encouraging companies like mine to turn derelict land, brown field sites into housing. The land that we bought is worth more, because we have been allowed to change it from commercial or industrial to residential. Other companies are annoyed that a local company like mine was successful in acquiring the land. They were more annoyed when we were granted change of use from commercial to residential.'
'How were you able to get the change?'
'That was so easy, there are too many commercial units lying empty. My company knew that if they built more units that would drive rents down. The last thing the council wanted was ninety -nine pence shops in an affluent area. So we had a meeting with the council officials and MSPs,' the company proposed that they had a solution.

'If we applied for change of commercial to residential and were successful in being granted permission to build houses; which would ease the housing shortage in Dundee and bring in much needed Council Tax revenues. At first they were taken aback by our candid plans. But the alternative was that we would build units causing companies to relocate to other towns.'

'And the council would lose money because the other companies moving out; and shops lying empty... you had them over a barrel son.'

'We have had another meeting with the council, but as I said it's all a game. My guess is our plans will be agreed on the third application. This would be the biggest thing that my company would be involved in. James would design the flats and town houses, much better than the legoland that is there presently. Peter as the Chartered Surveyor would order everything from the bricks to the low-energy bulbs, solar panels will be fitted on to the roof of the flats. We will receive government aid as its renewable energy.

'The flats will be more than the minimum insulated; the costs of heating and lighting for a year will be about two- hundred and eighty pounds. We have had it all evaluated. The first hundred flats would be built no higher than four storeys high. There will be unprecedented demand. We have the land to build more of these flats; but it is the council that are holding us up. The Scottish Executive will be impressed at these eco- friendly flats. But will not be impressed by the council, putting unnecessary obstacles in our way. After all the Scottish Executive are putting large sums of money into this pioneering development by a Scottish local company, and it will be a success. They will want their photographs' in the papers' and be on television.'

The phone rings on the desk; he picks it up. 'We'll be right down. C'mon dad Peter is running late he'll meet us at the docks.'

They leave the office and move down the stairs at a pace that Thomas was familiar with twenty-years ago; a car is waiting for them. Thomas is amazed at the change in the streets of the City Centre. The car makes its way onto Dock Street, past the old Custom House; it takes a right-turn to the Camperdown Rail Level Crossing that separates the old dock buildings from Dock Street. The barriers are up; and the car gingerly crosses the railway lines. The car moves towards the area where the old dog food producers had their factory. Thomas observes ahead a small gathering of people.

'What's all this then?'

Ian ignores the question. Margaret, Peter and James come into view. Six other people are there beside them he does not recognise them. As the car draws nearer to them he notices the glint of a camera. The car comes to a halt. Thomas's mind is in a whirl; his thoughts are interrupted by Ian gently pushing him towards the door opened by Linda Simpson. Thomas stepped out and is met by a round of applause; Margaret went to her perplexed husband.

'It's okay, everything is fine.' She moves with Thomas towards an area of derelict land, where the dog food factory stood, which is in a sorry state.

It seemed as if the numerous pigeons on the dilapidated slate roof are watching Thomas's every move. The cameras flash incessantly.

Linda Simpson on the first raising of the camera; stepped towards Thomas. Margaret halted Thomas in his tracks. Linda all teeth and hair, is smiling like she is greeting a long-lost relative. Margaret moved to the side to allow Linda to throw her arms around Thomas. The cameras clicked, whirred and flashed. She then stepped back, Ian took her place.

'You may have noticed that my dad is surprised at this stage. But I hope he will understand the secrecy. Let me tell you about my dad. He worked in the Caledon boat as an apprentice, and then worked his way up to be a journeyman. He and my mum gave me a wonderful upbringing.'

Margaret threw her eyes to the ground; she felt her cheeks become warm. The Press and dignitaries took this as modesty; she took this as shame.

Ian continued. 'He loved that boatyard. Now I will ask him to step forward with me and start the JCB.' he is helped on to the JCB via makeshift steps. The operator of the JCB takes his hand and coaxes him to press the button, the machine bursts into life.

Ian continued. 'This is the start of the project to bring life back into the area. This area will be called Caledon Quay; I think my dad agrees this is an apt name.'

Thomas is helped down from the JCB he makes his way to Margaret.

Linda Simpson initiates the applause, and steps forward. 'I would like to say a few words.'

All eyes are on Linda. 'Who would have thought that life would be brought back to an area that was bedevilled by lack of infrastructure and poor access routes. But these negatives were overcome by optimism and imagination, as well as substantial capital. Ian has been bold in this design for living, perhaps this is the way all new houses will be built or should be built. I know the Scottish Executive is blown away by the solar and light energy technology that will heat and light the buildings not just the houses. Street lamps will come on automatically and go off when daylight appears.

'From a personal point, it's good to see one of Dundee's entrepreneurs, pioneering new building techniques. Dundee has been too long looked upon which I'm sad to say from Glasgow and Edinburgh as an inward insular looking city. That is simply not the case. When we have individuals like Ian, who has vision and confidence to see an environment like this and turns it into a benign place to live we always ask why didn't someone see the potential previously? Perhaps it was you can't see the woods for the trees. Ian has given an assurance that this new building technique will speed up the building process, which is another plus point. I look forward to returning and seeing this new complex take shape, and to see the first flat completed and occupied. Thank you.'

At the rear of the crowd a young man is taking notes. When the Press and photographers had Linda in their view he was snapping away at Ian. The young man slipped the notebook and small camera back into his inside pocket. He gave a barely noticeable nod to the young blonde girl in the black trouser suit. She responded to him in a similar fashion. He walked away from the excited throng unnoticed, towards his nondescript car. She on seeing this pulled out her mobile and began and finished the call in fifteen seconds. They drove away.

Linda said her goodbyes to Ian and the dignitaries; she had more pressing needs to attend to. Her chauffeur opened the door for her; she gave a regal wave to all and sundry, the car smoothly moved off. Her mobile rang.

'No you listen to me! Don't you tell me what went wrong, I was there, and no I won't calm down! Stop talking! You have no idea how galling it was for some toe- rag to grab that land from me. And I have to say what a wonderful person he is blah, blah, blah. You my friend have a lot of explaining to do.'

The car made its way to the Hilton Hotel. Linda had a pre- arranged appointment with an investor. She told her driver that she would return to the car in twenty- minutes. That was her subtle way of saying don't move. She left the car with a face of fury, by the time she had completed the short walk to the foyer her pace was slower and she had the face of total contentment. She gave the receptionist a knowing smile, she never broke stride, and made her way to the table where a man in his late forties dressed in a dark suit complete with shirt and tie, sat reading The Courier. He saw her face change as she approached the table. She looked around about her before she sat beside him. He placed a well wrapped parcel displaying the Nike whoosh logo into her designer bag. He poured her coffee. 'Now calm down and listen.'

She ran her fingers through her hair.

'I realise something went wrong, I knew that you would not get the land. If you did, the police would be making arrests.' She looked relieved as well as puzzled.

He continued. 'Our friend in the planning department; requested more incentives than was on offer. Through our mutual friend that request was passed on to me. At first we agreed to his request, and as an act of goodwill we gave him five- thousand pounds to alleviate certain pressures that were affecting his judgement.

'However, we later discovered that he had a serious gambling problem; he was hooked on internet poker. A week after we gave him the five-thousand he requested more or he would not recommend approval...'

Linda interrupted him mid-sentence. 'You say he had a gambling problem, has he overcome it?' He leaned back into the leather sofa. 'Oh, he overcame it, but it was by accident rather than design. He threw himself over the Arbroath Cliffs; the post mortem will find he had been drinking heavily. Allied to the fact that he had massive amounts of debt and credit card bills from gambling web sites, I think it's safe to say that the Fatal Accident Inquiry if there is one will come to the conclusion that it was suicide.'

Linda had to place the coffee cup down as her hand was visibly shaking.

'When did this happen?' She whispered.

'Early this morning; at three a.m. to be exact.' It was a matter of fact reply.

'Was it absolutely necessary?' He just smiled. She lifted the coffee to her mouth and cast her enquiring eyes around the other tables, the hotel is quite busy, mostly men in suits and ties. Most of them would be reps of some kind meeting clients or putting off time till a conference started. Their tables had coffee cups and croissants.

He interrupted her gaze. 'Now you can understand, why one of your competitors was successful in his application for that land, and you were unsuccessful even though a third party was acting on your behalf.'

She regained her calm composure. 'You seem very calm in losing millions of pounds.'

'Don't tell me you didn't notice the other parcel of land, adjacent to the new housing development?'

'There are no vacant parcels of land next to Caledon Quay, that's occupied by a defunct ship repair company.'

'Who said that there is vacant land? 'He stood up and placed his jacket on.

'What do you mean?'

'All I'll say there will be an opportunity in the future to acquire that land.' He bent down and drank the dregs of the ground coffee, 'I'll be in contact later, I have to be in the Scottish Parliament for an important vote. He looked at his watch. The train is due in twenty-minutes I have ordered a taxi. I hope I have eased your mind... have I?'

She still couldn't smile. 'Now that I know the facts, things are not as dark as I thought.'

'There are millions to be made in Dundee and my office is privy to all subsequent sales and planning applications. It always makes good headlines for a local business person from a working-class background to triumph over established businessmen and women. If anyone has noticed us having coffee, you were just bringing me up to speed on the new Caledon Quay.'

He lifted the black attaché case from the floor. 'See you later.' He walked away.

She refilled her cup and pondered the lost opportunity was it a good thing? She wasn't convinced. But as he had said, future opportunities will be hammering at her door via a myriad of different companies in which there is no tangible connection; on paper at least.

She reminisced about the influence she had surreptitiously foisted upon malleable local councillors, regarding Government grants. She was aware she had influence when a piece of land in Broughty Ferry had become a dumping ground from unscrupulous traders; washing machines, mattresses and garden rubbish.

She was successful in lobbying the local councillor through the proactive Community Council. The council acceded to her demands; the site was cleaned up and fenced off. The owner of the land if he could be found was invoiced for fifteen-thousand pounds. This invoice was for clearing and disposing of all objects and dangers, decontaminating the land and making safe the said land, by robust fencing. The council took three days to complete this work. Linda knew that this could have been done in one day maximum. She set up three companies the next day through mutual friends, and she never looked back. In fact, some of her other companies were competing against one another.

She scanned the local papers for charity events; she frequently financially contributed to the underdog; single parents who were looking to start a mother and toddler group, but neither had the money or premises. Linda would gladly step in to fill this particular breach. Without exception the local newspapers' would be there to photograph her handing over the oversized cheque.

She is a member of the Tay Estuary Yacht Club, who was having great difficulty with the Port Authority. They refused to dredge part of the Tay the members' sailed; the yacht club insisted that shifting sands were causing a safety hazard to their well- heeled members. Linda approached the board of the Port Authority; they refused to move from their original position. Linda contacted her newly elected MSP; he was able to point out flaws in their argument. He met the soon retiring Chief Executive in an informal one-to-one meeting and casually mentioned the surplus land. The Chief Executive explained to him that the land was worthless.

The MSP told him that these rules and regulations regarding planning were made during world war two. It was his view that these planning restrictions belonged to another age and were an impediment to bring life and commerce into the peripheral Port Authority's land. He was supremely confident that he could muster the local MP's and MSPs to be a part of a pressure group to turn unwanted land into affluent housing developments. The Chief Executive was intrigued by this suggestion. But the MSP pointed out that he could only propose this if the whole of the community was behind him. That included the Tay Estuary Yacht Club. He didn't have to explain the minutiae. The Chief Executive took all this on board. The MSP repeated the conversation to Linda verbatim. She in turn informed her stockbroker that she would like to place an order to buy a tranche of nine hundred shares every six weeks until she cancelled the transaction. Her friends did the same but in fewer quantities. After the meeting with the MSP the Chief Executive met with the Tay Estuary Yacht Club, the meeting was very productive and amicable.

Two weeks later it was announced in the local newspapers that the Port Authority would be carrying out routine dredging that was in the area of the Tay Estuary Yacht Club. As a gesture of goodwill with their neighbours they would dredge the area that concerned the Tay Estuary Yacht Club. No fee would be charged. The Port Authority was just being neighbourly. Linda was there at the announcement and the Port Authority and the Tay Estuary Yacht Club publicly thanked Linda for overcoming their local difficulties and misunderstanding. This turn of events of course was given great reportage in the Press.

She looked forward to meeting the MSP Raymond Andrews, an ex- local planning officer who is well thought of by friends, seemingly he had no enemies. He listened more than he talked. He is good looking and he is able to request information that is usually off limits. The secretaries' didn't see this as unusual as he often gave his opinion on family and friends planning applications without seeking pecuniary gain. Even when the recipient of his advice was grateful, he refused whisky, chocolates and his passion; games of golf at private clubs.

His Modus Operandi would not deviate; he had to cultivate he is incorruptible; and did not seek favours. He stood as an Independent. The clue was in the name. Everyone from the main political parties was left in little doubt he was someone of independent thinking, and it would be a pointless exercise to try to curry favour with him. When Linda found out that his wife had left him for one of his friends, she knew that this was her opportunity to be a friend.

'Here alone are you?' She looked up, it was Mary.
'Sorry my mind was on other things'
'I noticed that,' replied Mary.
'So what are you doing here Mary… you're looking very smart.'
'I'm free lancing at the moment, I have a French delegation over on a fact finding tour, and I'm the interpreter.'
'Is it challenging enough for you?'
'It's okay, but hopefully I will be more successful tomorrow.'
'What's happening tomorrow?'

'Well I shouldn't really say... She sits down. 'I have an interview for selling property in Spain, the money is good and I can speak French and Spanish, that's what the employer's requires. I just hope I am not seen as too dowdy or old.'

'Don't be pessimistic, you have every chance, you have life skills as well as language skills. Maybe I can help, if it's possible for me to put a word in I will, what is the name of the company.'

'The name of the company is the Oak Investment Company.' Mary was dismayed to see it did not register on Linda's face.

'I can't recall that name Mary, is it a Dundee company?'

'Yes it's a new company, it is owned by Ian Williams he is a solicitor and has other investments mainly property and letting agencies in Dundee, this is his first venture into the Spanish property market.'

Linda was curious about this new company, and its plans. 'I really don't know him personally, but I will ask around, if I can help I certainly will.' Relief overcomes Mary.

'That would be a big favour if someone can vouch for me.'

'If I'm not being too nosey, and he requires someone with language skills, what are you doing exactly?'

'Of course you are not being nosey Linda! Nothing too complex; according to the telephone interview, he would need me to go out to Spain and assist clients. When I told him that I had lived in France, he was glad I mentioned that, as I could drive to the airport and pick French clients.'

'Well I hope the interview goes well tomorrow.'

    She stands up and said goodbye to Mary. She moves away from the table and is near to the door, when a voice shouts out to her. 'Miss! Miss!' She turns round and sees a police officer with her bag in his hand. 'Is this yours?' She feels everyone is staring at her, including Mary.

'Yes it is.' She walks towards the police officer. 'And is this yours?'

His colleague is in civilian clothes; he is holding and examining the Nike trainer box.

'Yes', smiling and walking towards him 'that's... my new trainers.'

'You should be more careful.' He hands it her.

'Thanks a lot... I'm just not with it today.' She took the Nike box and placed it in her bag. The police officers carry on talking to each other. 'Thanks again.' She turns around and makes her exit, the door seems miles away. She has to control her breathing, she feels like running but she knows that she can't. Her stomach is churning will they wait till I'm out of the door? Are there more police out there? Her mind is trying to calm her, but her imagination has gone into a pessimistic overdrive. Will they let her enter the car then ambush her?

    At last she reaches the exit and walks through the door, she welcomes the cold blustery wind, she takes a series of deep breaths. The concierge tries in vain to make small talk, he doffs his cap. Her driver sees her and starts the engine. She holds her hand up to indicate that she is coming over to the car. Nearly there; no sirens... no police officers wearing baseball caps shouting incoherently. She is just feet away from the car. She opens the car door expecting to feel hands on her shoulders dragging her to the terra firma. To her relief and surprise none of this scenario played out in her fevered mind manifests. Before the driver can say anything she tells him to drive her straight home, and don't break the speed limit. He just nodded and thought that was an unusual and odd instruction. Normally she instructed him to put the foot down. He moved off, she would glance periodically side to side and then behind her. He would never tactfully enquire if something was troubling her. She felt the tension build up in her stomach; she had to stop the car. He pulled over near the Tay Estuary Yacht Club. She ran to the grass area that overlooked the Tay. The contents of her stomach came forward like a torrent. He looked at her and thought how undignified she looked.

    She walked back to the car, trying to capture some of the dignity she had left in the car. He didn't pass any comment. He had left tissues and a bottle of water on the back seat as she worshipped the grass. She wiped her mouth and swigged the water and released it onto the ground.

'That's better I had sea food last night; I must have not prepared it properly. Thanks for the tissues and water.' He smiled and the car eased off to continue the journey to her house.
'Don't exceed the speed limit.' He was bemused by this repeated instruction. He had been stopped for speeding more times than he could remember. Her 'highness' would speak to the cops and a warning was issued again; never a ticket.

***

Mary sat in the reception area waiting to be called for the interview. She felt like a naughty schoolgirl outside the Headmasters office. Her confidence is waning; she now had serious concerns about her choice of attire. She felt she was too old to wear the black trouser suit
'You can go in now,' said the smiling secretary.
Mary returned the smile thanked her and then walked into his office with new found confidence. He had his back to her; he was staring into Reform Street. Should she cough to make her presence known? She dismissed that thought. If his aim was to make her feel uncomfortable he was very successful. She pulled the chair away from the desk the noise broke the silence. He turned around. Mary sat down uninvited. He went to his side of the desk and sat down.
'That's a good start, you showed initiative. Some of the people I have interviewed stand and say nothing or cough after a minute. No one pulled up a chair and sat down. I liked that.'
He stood up and held out his hand. 'I'm Ian, pleased to meet you Mary.'
She felt totally relaxed now. He examined her CV. 'Is this job going to be challenging enough for you? Compared to your previous employment in the European Union and your academic career?'
'It is a perfect fit for me; I rarely have the chance to use my language skills on a regular basis.'
'First of all your language skills are absolutely necessary. You will arrange the foreign clients' accommodation. Then pick them up at the airport and arrange golf, meals, and sightseeing. I don't want them getting bored. You can add these places of interest to the itinerary that I have drawn up. It's the repeat procedure with the clients from the UK.
'You will have an apartment in Spain, two bedrooms, two bathrooms with air condition and Sky television. You will meet and greet them at Reus airport. The apartments and villas are on a new golf course, which is just fifty-minutes away from the airport. Some clients' mostly from England fly into Barcelona airport which is two hours away from the complex. Over three days you will wine and dine them. At the end of the three days, I hope you have done enough to persuade them to buy. Unscrupulous companies try and persuade their clients sign on the first day. We don't. How does that sound to you?'
'Sounds fine...how long would I be based in Spain?'
'Four weeks at a time, then come home for a week, then back to Spain for four weeks. However, you have the option of staying on the complex on your week off, but you would undoubtedly be hit with a barrage of questions from clients. It is up to you, there are other places to visit near the complex, Vinaros for example is only a fifteen- minute car drive away; it is a small town with great beaches.'
Mary is trying to play down her excitement. She has to ask the salary and commission.
'It sounds challenging enough for me. What would be my salary?'
'It would be challenging, I can tell you are a gregarious person, the salary is twenty- five thousand plus living expenses, a commission of three per cent for the apartments and four per cent for the villas. Included in your salary package is a company car here in Dundee and private health insurance I may on the odd occasion and I stress the odd occasion ask you to pick up clients from Glasgow or Edinburgh airports; the arrival times at the airports could be out-with office hours, does that cause you any difficulties?'
'No... none, none whatsoever. The company car...?'
'It's a BMW. You have a choice of models.'
'Really!' When would I hear whether I have been successful or not in securing the job?'
'How much notice do you have to give?'

'A week... I am on a part-time contract at the moment.'
'I am offering you the job. If you want time to think it over, I have no difficulty with that.'
Mary's pallor has changed to a chalky white, her mouth is dry. She gulps down some air.
'When do want me to start?'
'As soon as you have worked your notice.'
'If you don't mind, I would like to ask some questions?'
'Be my guest. He placed his hands behind his head.
'Who will show me the ropes when I'm over in Spain?'
'I have a Spanish lady over there in situ, her name is Marta, she is very experienced and she is multi-lingual. She will show the office on the complex, the computer system is Windows. Marta will give you an IPhone. These will be useful when you are on the move or in your apartment. The clients' will contact you no doubt about numerous queries, which will not be in office hours. However, I will have you here in one of my offices giving you all the information you can think off. Your iPhone will be pre-loaded with useful contacts. When you arrive in Spain on the Saturday; you will be able to hit the ground running on Monday.'
'I don't know what to say,' she said laughing.
'Do you have any family?' Why is he asking this she thought, should I lie about my divorce?
'I'm divorced and have two grown up children childcare is not an issue...'
'Maybe it would be a good idea to take your children over to Spain for two weeks to show them where you are living, and to put their minds at rest. The company will pay for the flights and we will give you some spending money. You can get used to driving on the right- hand side again. 'How do you feel about that?'
She could feel her eyes filling up.
   'Everything sounds so perfect. Going over to Spain for two weeks before I start work officially...'
'You misunderstand me, you will have started work; you will be getting paid. The spending money does not come from your salary or expenses. It is just something that the company will do to erase any concerns from you or your children.'
'They'll jump at the chance for a free holiday; it will still be warm will it?'
'Last year some residents were having Christmas lunch on their balconies.'
'I can't wait to tell them. You mentioned driving on the right-side, I'll look forward to driving on the AP7, I have driven from Barcelona to Alicante, no speed cameras; it's a dream motorway. '
'The AP7 has speed cameras now; there have been too many accidents.'
'I suppose it was only a matter of time. Once I discuss the job offer with the children, I'll get back to you as soon as possible is that all right?'
'Take your time,' he replied. He stands up, she follows suit.
'I'll see you to the door... you were the best candidate by a mile. And I like your business suit.'

***

   The telephone rings incessantly in the cavernous and opulent hall. Albert Friedman is reading the Financial Times; he is drinking his obligatory second cup of tea. The telephone is still ringing, the shrill noise echoing down the hall to the kitchen. He turns to the share page. The ringing stops. He smiles, pleased with himself that he did not embark on the long journey from the kitchen to the hall. The ringing starts again; the smile melts. He rises from his chair and walks to the telephone; any anger that possessed him has dissipated when he reached the telephone.
'Hello?'
'Sorry to disturb you, Mr Friedman, its John at the service centre...'
'That's okay John, is there a problem with the car?'
'Not exactly, but there is a problem; could you manage to drop by this morning... I know its short notice, but I think you should come down.'

'Would ten 'o clock be okay?'
'Perfect I'll send a car up to pick you up.'
'See you at ten then, bye.'

Albert is intrigued, but not perturbed, one thing he could guarantee the garage would not be inventing faults on his car, they wouldn't be stupid enough to do that. He walked back to his chair, the morning light from the garden drew his attention, he bypassed the chair. He picked up the cup from the farmhouse table and walked slowly to the French doors and stared into his extensive garden. He brought the cup up slowly to his mouth, it's going to be a busy day, as it always would be; he had a flight booked from Dundee Airport to London City Airport at twelve -thirty. He intended to conclude the sale of some of his assets to Russian businessmen, which were surplus to his requirements. Notwithstanding that the land and property that he owned in London were in the process of being sold to the Russians for four times their real value. He had Ian Williams to thank for that. He persuaded the Russians that with the Olympic games being held in London; demand for Land and Property would exceed all their expectations. This coupled with their indecent haste to export money from Russia clouded their judgement.

Today would be the day when all documents would be signed, and assets as well as money would be exchanged. Ian had made sure that the money would be transferred from their bank in the Isle of Man to Albert's bank in the Cayman Islands; within one hour of signatories. Albert, on Ian's advice politely refused the Russians offer to be their guests at Stamford Bridge that same evening. The tempting offer to be their guests at the casino in Chelsea Village had to be turned down. Ian had told him, these businessmen were thugs and killers in expensive suits, they had to get out of Russia; Putin was in the process of filling up jails with these businessmen. They needed to convert their blood-soaked money into tangible assets in London. When Putin was eventually disposed of by the Russian people or other means, they would sell some of their assets at a profit and return to Russia, to once again conduct their brutal business. He had to be on the last flight up to Dundee, due to impending business. Albert now understood why they had to be on the last flight from London to Dundee that day. Albert was under no illusion he was dealing with ruthless gangsters.

However, Ian told him on more than one occasion their transactions were perfectly legitimate and legal. If there were a whiff of criminality Ian would have advised Albert to recoil from the bargain that would shortly be concluded. All he had to do is listen and follow Ian's premeditated instructions. They are not his ideal clients to do business with; all he had to do was smile and sign the papers. Albert had a latent admiration for Ian; a working class boy who had made good; not through inherited wealth or privilege but through his own endeavours. To a certain extent Ian's drive and determination mirrored his own early life.

Albert's Grandparents had fled the Communist Soviet Union to Dundee to escape persecution and poverty. Ian did not suffer as much as he had, but he had the same drive and single mindedness to escape from poverty and improve himself. When Ian told him it was more dangerous now dealing with Russians under Glasnost than Communism, he was silently offended. If only he knew.

The apple tree is now matured; fifteen years had passed since the gardener had told him it would not survive the first frost of its young life. Just because the roots looked spent and were withered. Albert did not concur with this professional opinion. With care and patience that young sapling became a tree and bloomed. The gardener refused to believe that it was the same sickly sapling. He was convinced that he had swapped the dead sapling for one with vitality. He loved proving professionals wrong; including doctors. If he had believed them he would have departed this world the same time as the sapling. They both proved the professionals wrong.

His tea had gone cold, but he felt good, time to be ready for this car coming to take him to the garage; or service centre as they liked to call it. After his brief visit there he would go direct to the airport. He deliberated whether he should have some toast; he didn't want the toast to take the edge of his appetite. He had booked lunch for him and Ian to be served in his suite at the Savoy.

His father had worked most of his adult life in London as a diamond broker; returning to Dundee on the Friday Night sleeper and returning to London on the Sunday night sleeper from Dundee to London. At Euston station he would have a taxi waiting to take him to the Savoy where he would begin his working day; clients would be waiting for him in the lobby, eager to do business with him.

This Land deal in London was a bittersweet transaction; his father had bought the land now he was selling the land, he felt uncomfortable, however Ian reminded him of his father's favourite maxim, 'a profit is only a profit when the money is in the bank.' In his heart he knew his father would approve of this deal. He would not give up the suite in the Savoy; his father had agreed a one off price for the suite back in the nineteen-thirties, the owners of the hotel thought they had extracted an excellent price. Albert had been able to lease the suite back to the hotel for the Millennium celebrations. The money the hotel paid him covered the cost of the price paid by his father in the wretched nineteen-thirties. His father would have approved that deal. The suite was a home from home for Albert. As a small child with his parents he went to West –End shows. He carried on this tradition; he took his grandchildren to the West-End shows

Now they stayed in the suite and slept in the same bed as he had slept in when he was a child. He decided to forego the toast. He felt he had grown into this big house; he enjoyed the solitude from Monday to Friday. It would be over flowing with the sound of his seven grandchildren from Friday afternoon till Sunday evening. The stillness came down suddenly when they left and it hit him hard. He overcame the temporarily melancholy when his grandchildren left and he closed the front door. When the door closed the memories of his wife came to the fore. He had railed against life and his family when his wife died in her sleep. He wanted to prove to his wife that he was like her, a fighter all the way. His four daughters wanted him to sell the house and move in with one of them. He declined they expected him to go to seed. They knew he was partial to malt whisky, they feared he would turn to the bottle. He kept the house and gave up on alcohol. At Christmas time all his daughters would sidle up to him and say he was right to retain the house, mum would have loved this. He would reply I know that, I see her every Christmas for a few minutes when I go to bed. His daughters didn't enquire that he had seen her, when or where, they just smiled. He was Jewish, however, he loved Christmas, and his daughters were members of different Christian denominations Catholic and Protestants He often thought at the table carving the turkey this is how the world should be all different creeds breaking bread.

The video com sparked into life. It was the car to take him to the service centre. He acknowledged the driver and told him that he was on his way. He looked around the kitchen for his jacket, he always went through the same thirty- second panic; that he had forgotten something, which he never had. The jacket is always where it is; he grabbed it and put it on, thumped his right hand pocket to hear the reassuring sound of his keys, then made his way to the front door. He closed the door with some force, and tried to open it again. When it resisted he was pleased, he would have been shocked had it opened. He turned and walked down the winding gravel drive. Forty- metres from the electronic gates he clicked the button in his pocket, they gracefully opened. The driver of the car had seen this routine with monotonous regularity he was no longer in awe of this angelic movement. He removed himself from the car and smiled. Albert returned the smile.

'Do you like the gates then?'
'Technology, where will it take us next?' replied the bored driver.
'Do you know why your boss phoned me?'
'Not a clue,' replied the driver.
'Ah well, all will be revealed.' He settled back to enjoy the ten- minute drive to the service centre. As the car drove along the esplanade he mentally checked- off the various flats and fishermen cottages that he owned and then sold off.

The nineteen -eighties were meant to bring prosperity to Dundee when the Conservatives and Margaret Thatcher came to power. It was all smoke and mirrors. The boatyard closed down followed by the Timex factory; thousands were confined to the dole queues.

They had been enticed to buy their council houses, at knockdown prices

It was a good time to be in the double glazing and fitted kitchen business. Smart talking salesmen talked them into taking on debt. Then the redundancies came in their thousands. Interest rates started to rise sharply. Cars that had been taken on the higher purchase agreements were repossessed with monotonous regularity. Marriages went as quickly as the cars. It wasn't just the naive working class who were caught up in this era of financial madness.

Albert had been mocked by the thirty-something's that entered the property game; because that is what it is a game. Albert had sold some of these properties on the esplanade to these young tycoons. They boasted to one another, that they had conned Albert out these fantastic properties for a song. Then the job losses came which was bad enough, however the second apocalypse came along the shore interest rates; with a voracious appetite. Their own houses in the salubrious addresses in Broughty Ferry were put up for sale as they had no money to service their own mortgages and personal debts. The final ignominy was that their children had to be removed from the High School of Dundee and educated at the local comprehensives. This must have been galling as they used to belittle anyone who sent their children to these schools. Their properties could not be sold or let.

Everyone and their dog were aware Albert walked along the shore. He used to be greeted by smiles and enquiries about his health. Then the conversation would be steered cunningly towards the precarious property market. Albert would not tease these budding millionaires about the derogatory remarks they made within earshot of him in upmarket hotels and restaurants. He was not a vindictive man; he was a businessman, with a social conscience to some degree. A price would be gladly accepted; Albert had his properties back, totally modernised courtesy of these young geniuses. Central heating, double glazing, new kitchens with appliances, and he had bought them back thirty- per cent under the valuation. He sold them recently for a healthy profit, prices were becoming unsustainable, there had to be a correction in the market sometime in the next few years. Interest rates were a friendly four and a half per cent for buy to let mortgages, personal debts were rising again. Instead of the double glazing, people were taking on BMW's; it was the eighties all over again. He had no doubt he would buy back at least some of the properties at a knockdown price in the future.   Debt catches up on the unaware and the financially illiterate.

The car came to a stop on the forecourt Robert the sales executive is waiting on him he had a worried look on his face. Albert opened the door then stepped out the car, the driver failed to emerge and open the door for Albert, this added to Robert's burden. Albert walked towards him.

'What's the problem Robert?'
'I think you should see this,' he beckoned Albert to the workshop. They stopped at the ramp where the car was in an elevated position; Robert guided Albert's vision to the internal area above the wheel arch. 'Do you see it?' Robert asked.
'Is that a mobile phone?'
'Yes.'
'But why is it strapped there?'
Robert is hoping for a plausible reason.
Albert shrugged his shoulders. 'I don't understand… could you remove it?'
'Sure, but I don't think that's wise, I think we should phone the police. It could be a detonator for an explosive device.'
'Are you serious?'
They all stepped back from the car, Albert was quite shaken. Robert turns to the mechanics.
'Everybody clear the workshop, no need to panic, I'll call the police.'
The workshop is cleared; Albert is in Robert's office drinking tea. The police had arrived earlier, and were examining the car. Two casually dressed officers come into the office without knocking.
'The area is safe you can get your men back to work...' Robert does not ask any questions he leaves the office.

The other officer smiles at Albert; he fails to return the smile
'You look so worried Mr Friedman, we have some good news, and it's not a bomb as Robert had thought or a detonator.'
'Thank God for that…why would someone tape an expensive mobile phone to the car?'
The officers looked at one another. 'It's a very efficient tracking device.'
The other officer explains. 'Someone buys a second hand mobile or pay as you go phone, attaches it to your car, accesses the Internet, it is now an efficient tracking device. Crude, but does the job.'
Albert places the cup down on the desk.
'Could I stop you there, I'm getting confused. Do you mean the signal from the mobile is the same as a tracking device?'
'Yes once they or the person involved attaches the mobile they insert the number of the mobile into a site and they can follow your car from their iPhone, any laptop or Internet cafe. This could be industrial espionage. Or something more menacing, have you had any threats or encountered any difficult individuals lately?'
'None whatsoever...'
'Have you received any hate-mail from Neo-Nazis groups or individuals?'
'You're kidding me…Neo- Nazis?'
'Have you had any anti- Semitic incidents, or graffiti?'
'Nothing... absolutely nothing; no incidents of any nature. What happens now?'
'That's up to you,' replied the younger of the two officers.
Albert shifts uncomfortably in his seat; he takes his glasses from his jacket, and polishes them.
'What do you suggest I do?'
'You can leave it on the car, or you can give us permission to detach and have it examined.'
Albert places his glasses on. 'I think I would prefer the mobile removed, but leave it with me.'
The older of the officers is dismayed by this. 'Leave it with us; our technical staff could get to the bottom of this.'
'No, I would prefer that the phone remains with me.'
'Okay, have it your way, do you wish to file a complaint, regarding the phone being secreted in your car?'
'No, we'll just leave it at that. I do not wish to take up valuable police time.'
'Then we will be going then.' They look at one another and leave the office.
Robert has observed the detectives in the office and watches them leave, he returns to the office Albert is nonplussed by their interview. 'What did they say,' he enquired.
'Nothing to worry about, it seems the mobile is some kind of tracking device, they think it's one of my business competitors; whoever they are; very amateurish if you ask me. They must have realised it would be found.'
'What happens now then Mr Friedman, are you going to be safe?'
'If it was a bomb, I'd been concerned, but the police explained everything to me. Could you have the phone removed, I'll take charge of it.'
'Have you had any other incidents at your home?'
'I told the police, no incidents, I can only assume it is industrial espionage.'
'Is this a coincidence? Or is the meeting in London with these unsavoury types connected to this? I would mention this to your lawyer. '
'I will.'

***

   In the cottage in Birkhill the police officer views the laptop screen with dismay. Then the melancholy quickly evaporates. I'm surprised the mobile was not found earlier, he thought. At least he had the movement of the car for the last two months. He had noticed that a pattern had emerged; the car on four occasions had been driven late at night from Dundee to Liverpool. It went to the same affluent part of Liverpool.

The car went into the underground garage, less than twenty-minutes there it made the return journey to Dundee. He had figured it out. The car had been called to the service centre for a service or a problem. The keys were held in the administration office, someone had passed them onto an unknown person. They used the car for moving drugs from Liverpool to Dundee. The car would have transported money from Dundee to Liverpool. Was Ramage the driver?

One thing was crystal clear; Albert Friedman was unaware that his car was being used for an extended test run. He had been out of the country while the shuttle service was being used. Or was that his alibi? The drug dealers would now know that the car was being tracked; there could be more activity at Linda Simpson's mansion. He was nightshift for seven nights now; he would have ample time to note any visitors to her house. He was due to see his chum from the Drug Squad that evening, maybe he would mention or hint that something was going on. He could usually tell by his demeanour. That would have to wait.

Today, he had one more visit to make; he looked at the carpet on the wooden floor. He closed down the laptop, removed the carpet and opened the floor safe; he took out latex gloves and fitted them on. He took out one small bag of heroin which had already been cut, and concealed it in his jeans pocket. He removed the USB stick from the laptop and placed it into his shirt pocket, and then secreted the laptop snugly into the safe. The workmanship is of the highest standard possible when the safe is closed you wouldn't know it is there. The knot on the floorboard is removed to reveal the lock to the safe. Then the knot is replaced to conceal the lock. He had built the safe himself and the rogue floorboard, only he knew that it existed. He is glad he had not turned the house into a drinking den and card school. Things would have escalated from booze and cards to women. He would have been cajoled into turning over the house for illicit romantic liaisons. He is far from innocent himself from extra-curricular nocturnal activities. The neighbours would have noticed the comings and goings of police officers from the bungalow at infrequent hours; notwithstanding the late-night card schools. Taxi drivers' would have had a field day taking police officers home in a tired and emotional condition and if women were involved, the jungle drums would have been incessant.

***

Raymond Andrews is fond of Linda, but he loves her house with a passion. He is very interested in local history. This house had had many fine guests throughout its illustrious history Linda on the other hand, couldn't have cared less about the house, she knew she would sell it one day, but that is far into the future. She had lost hundreds of thousands buying cocaine and heroin, but millions in real monetary terms when the cocaine and heroin were cut and sold on the street. Raymond is also her business partner; he didn't seem perturbed about losing hundreds of thousands, three hundred thousand to be exact, Linda had lost the same amount.

Raymond had some explaining to do. She stood against the black granite worktop smoking he sat leaning on the island in the kitchen. The silence needed to be broken, she drew on the cigarette her eyes fixed on him; she tossed the cigarette into the sink he anticipated raised voices.

'So what went wrong?'

He took a deep breath. 'We have been conned, there is no doubt about that.'

'Raymond that's history, I know we have been conned, but why now...? We have been using the same suppliers for two years... we have never had any problem with the gear; and they have been happy with our payments I just can't understand it.'

He moved towards the American style fridge, he took out a bottle of water, and turned around and faced her. He took a swig of the water.

'We were too complacent for starters, and too trusting. Let's examine how it all came about, and let me complete what I'm going to say without interruption...' She nods her head.

'Good. We have been using the scousers for years, without a hint of dissatisfaction from them.'

'They said that they had come into more supplies than normal; they said rather than take the normal consignment, why don't we take three times the weight, but just pay for double instead of treble. It will also save you coming down to Liverpool once instead of three times. Everyone profits from their generous offer. Why should we be suspicious? We have had numerous transactions with them. So what they did was give us three holdalls of compost; with bags of talcum powder on the top of each holdall, the mule looks at this, everything is in order or so it seems. He hands over the money, drives back to Dundee thinking he had earned three times his normal fee. They have not made contact with us; however, we are back in business. She looks incredulous.

'Let me explain. We have always used another supplier from Liverpool for smack, for the Dundee and Aberdeen market. The dealer that supplies the smack has had a few violent run in's with the person who ripped us off. It was mentioned in a roundabout way that we may have to end our agreement with him, due to us being ripped off. He was far from happy; he promised he will deal with the rip-off merchant. The rogue supplier would be no more; courtesy of our new supplier of cocaine this would be an act of good faith. He also said that the rogue supplier had done this to other people, from Scotland and Ulster. He is finished, a dead man walking. He told one of our associates to click on the Liverpool Echo website over the next few weeks something of interest will be there. In the Liverpool Echo this evening this story appeared; 'Yesterday a man was shot in Benidorm; he died in hospital of gunshot wounds to the head, police sources have revealed he had served time in prison for drug offences. 'He hands her the print-out of the story, she studies it. 'That's what I meant by saying we are back in business.' Linda didn't know whether to laugh or scream with joy. Instead of cracking open a bottle of Bollinger, that was so passé; she went to the drawer of instant happiness and pulled out a small silver case. She made two lines on the granite worktop.

'Will you join me?' He walked over and snorted the first line; he handed over the small trumpet shaped nasal appliance to her. She in turn expertly ingested the powder. She rubbed her nose in a familiar fashion; she placed the equipment back into the drawer.
'Will the coke be of the same quality as the defunct supplier?'
'It will be the same; it's coming from the same source.'
The coke is raising his sense of well-being.
'It's just a pity that we couldn't retrieve our money...'
He interrupted her. 'In the circumstances we have done all right, don't get hung up on losing the money. We are back in business that's the main thing.' She wasn't convinced by this, she still had lost three hundred grand.
'What else could we have done? She couldn't answer. He was getting agitated.
'We could have gone down with all guns blazing, which would have been crazy, or we just smile and accept our losses. We have personally made five million each from this enterprise, more than we can ever spend. Our money is clean. You have the perfect cover your great, great grandfather left you millions in a trust fund.
'I suppose when you look at the situation through an accountant's eyes it is very difficult to argue against what you have just said.'
'Another lesson learned. Trust no one.'
'I trust no one, apart from you.
This vote of confidence washed over him.
'Linda you have to admire the cheek of our old supplier, who would have thought of pulling a stunt like that?
'But, this stupid situation cost him his life.'
'He must have had protection from someone to even think of a scheme like that.'
'Ripping off people from Ireland is another matter entirely; you don't contemplate something as dangerous and stupid as that if you don't have protection, maybe he was being double-crossed by his protectors?'

'Well, I have no sympathy for him; he did not live long enough to enjoy his money.'
'These guys that pull these stunts, I suppose they treat it as an occupational hazard.'
'How is our mule? Is he stilling willing to do the run to Liverpool?'
'He's fine; he's well experienced it's just been a blip. He's earning again.'
'Good, business returns to normality.'
'I will keep you up to date if there are any major developments. It's been an expensive lesson for us, but we have been fortunate, that this has been the only problem we have encountered. However we are in an unusual business with unusual ethics, doing business with ruthless people sometimes throws up problems.'
'No, you're wrong Raymond; there are no ethics just consequences, sometimes fatal.'

***

'So did you recognise the male visitor then?'
'No, did you?'
'Yes I did, he's her boyfriend, he's an MSP for Dundee, I don't know which party he represents, but I'm sure he won't be discussing social deprivation in Broughty Ferry.'
He laughed. 'You sounded surprised when I told you that Ramage is still serving time in prison.'
'Wouldn't you be surprised if you saw him in a car driving about; never mind driving someone else's car, and a well- known millionaire at that?'
'But there's an explanation, Ramage is in Castle Huntly; he is allowed out to work in Dundee under the Training for Freedom programme. He sometimes works in a charity shop in Broughty Ferry...'
'But how was he allowed to be on the outside at night, and is there an explanation why he was driving somebody else's car and being at Linda Simpson's house?'
His colleague looked at him. 'I can't explain the car or why he is allowed out at night.'
'Well, you must do better, will you.' His colleague took this as personal criticism.
 'I will.... and what have you been doing then?'
'First of all, as I told you many times the car is not Ramages' it's Albert Friedman's car, and it's being used to ferry money from Dundee to Liverpool...'
'And drugs are coming from Liverpool to Dundee,' his colleague finished the sentence for him.
'That's more like it, now you're thinking like a policeman...well done!'
He was lifted by this praise.
'Now we have the difficult task to link Ramage to Linda Simpson, and both of them to drugs.'
'That will be the hardest part and dangerous as well. But... if we can figure, who is who and who is the courier, we can intercept the money going down to Liverpool for short term gain, but if we are patient we can get the drugs and the money.'
'Have you worked out how to get the money and the drugs?'
His younger colleague had an element of surprise in his question. His partner returned a look of disdain, along with arched eyebrows.
'Sorry, I just got carried away.'
'That's all right you're young and slightly stupid. This Albert Friedman; is he involved in this, and if not, why is Ramage using his car? That's another question to be answered, but my gut instinct is he put his car in the garage for a service and somebody is using it for the Liverpool trips.'
'Would it be Ramage doing the trip to Liverpool?'
'That thought occurred to me, has he the balls to do that, or is he just too stupid to see the risk?'
'He will know all the dealers in Liverpool, that's where he got busted.'
'Naw, he wouldn't risk that, I think he is organising the money from Dundee. He's got the perfect cover, he's in jail! We have to be patient, the link has to be Linda Simpson and Ramage, and it could be innocent... but it can't be, why is he here at night? Tomorrow, I'll dig up more about Ramage, you concentrate on Linda Simpson.'

'How did you find out about the car, and are you sure it's going to Liverpool'?
'I tracked it; I was watching it on my computer Dundee to Liverpool and back, don't ask how.'
'Are you sure it was definitely Albert Friedman's car? The arched eyebrows returned. 'I'm not saying you are stupid...'
'Well thank you,' his partner laughed.
'Listen hear me out, just supposing it is his car, wouldn't he notice the mileage had gone up considerably?'
'That's a very good point, if someone is doing drugs runs; somebody from the garage is there when the car is returned, do you agree? His partner nods his head sagely. 'When the car is returned a laptop and some software is used to return the electronic odometer back to the correct mileage.'
'I see,' he said slowly.
'This mob has thought through every eventuality they think like police officers and prosecutors.'
'If they are that smart why is Ramage driving that car about without a care in the world?'
'But what if he knew he would never be stopped; is he being protected by us, the police I mean?'
'You have said what I was scared to think, you could be right, but who is protecting him and why are they in on the deal or are they being paid to ignore his late night soirees?'
'My brain is racing do you want a coffee?'
'You my friend have grew a detective's brain tonight, that's how we have to think, maybe, my contact in the DS is mired in this, I'll have to be so careful with him and see if he is questioning me when I think I'm pumping him for information...'
'Do you want coffee I said?'
'Sorry, yes, hopefully Ramage can lead me to someone, and if it's a cop, we could be in more danger than I had previously thought. He looked at his colleague and continued. 'You realise what I'm saying?'
'I am not that daft, I know what I'm into.'
'I don't think you do realise how the landscape has changed. Two multi- millionaires' from Broughty Ferry, Albert Friedman and Linda Simpson, and If that was not complicated enough, we now have thrown into the mix Raymond Andrews an MSP. What is his link to any of them? The one thing that is eating away at me, why is Ramage driving Albert Friedman's car? I just can't figure that out. And who is Ramages' guy in the garage? Does that guy use anyone's car that is being serviced or repaired to nip down to Liverpool?'
'To add to your woes I have thought of something else.'
He places the coffee cup on the dashboard.
'I'm scared to ask...but go on.'
'Your contact in the Drug Squad, if he is involved with Ramage, if something happens, I don't know what, but has he got anything on you that he can use as a bargaining chip, if he is caught doing anything unprofessional?
'Don't concern yourself; to be honest I don't think he has the balls or brains to be involved in something as big as this.'

***

   Albert Friedman is sitting in the lounge at Dundee Airport; the bugging of his car could not be removed from his mind. The pecuniary benefits of his disposal of his assets in London are secondary. There are fifteen other people in the lounge mostly business people, young and old. The younger ones are tapping away at their iPhones. The older more portly of the men are reading The Financial Times and The Telegraph. This airport is becoming more and busier with flights to London and Manchester. If he had his way and the City Council had listened to him there would have been flights to Spain and more European countries. Five years earlier the population of Dundee were up in arms about the year on year Council Tax rises.

They became more incandescent when information came into the public domain, when a citizen wrote into to the Evening Telegraph asking if the City Council still owned and operated the airport, and how much did it cost to run, and did it make a profit? The reply from the Council was that they did own it as well as operate it; this was a well -known fact. The operating costs outstripped the income; they didn't have the figures at hand.

This brought more irate letters into the papers; did the Council have anything to hide? Eventually, the Council released a short statement the airport was losing a million pounds per annum. Council Tax payers were up in arms, what benefit were they receiving from this cash draining airport. Albert saw an opportunity in Dundee's difficulty; he would take over the airport, extend the runway, and operate it. Flights would extend to Spain from April to October. Council Tax payers' would not be invoiced for one thin dime. He had plans drawn up; various low-cost airlines were fighting to operate the flights. Nevertheless, when the plans and timetables were displayed for public consultation the myopic Community Council vetoed them; they said there would be too much noise and pollution. Bus and Taxi firms also put in objections; they would lose the lucrative routes to transport passengers to and from Glasgow and Edinburgh airports. This was an opportunity lost not delayed; the public vented their feelings on the Transport Companies. Some set up small firms to compete with them and the local taxi firms. Council contracts were put out to tender.

The cartel was smashed into a thousand pieces and scattered to the wind. Firemen and the general public applied for taxi licences that became available. The owner- drivers in addition to the taxi companies had made the biggest mistake of their business lives. They had not studied the plans with an open mind. Albert had made only forty -spaces for car parking available at the airport, there would be no long term parking. The forty- spaces were for setting down and picking up only. The taxi companies would have made more money from picking up people from their houses in Dundee and surrounding areas, rather than the laborious trips to the main airports. The Scottish Executive was dismayed by the short- term thinking.

There were plans for a train station to be built at the airport; this was a condition of the new rail franchise that was coming up for renewal. Albert still winced at the thought of that great opportunity lost. The city would have benefited greatly from his plans. He recalled that the Council had ignored the well- founded fears of the residents of Douglas and Whitfield when the waste to energy plant was first cited. The Council waved through the application and ignored the well-organised petition with legitimate concerns about air pollution. The reason that they ignored the residents of Douglas and Whitfield was that they were council estates, and the Community Council in the West End had their objections upheld were well –heeled. Someone's pump had been well -primed. Looking around the lounge made him embarrassed; two vending machines one for cold drinks and one for hot drinks. Someone's imagination had run wild.

Five years on the Community Council for the West End were complaining about noise pollution from students at the weekends. Letters had been printed in the paper regarding the noise and vandalism from the students. At the same time some students were asking why the airport could not be extended, to allow flights from Ireland to accommodate the massive influx of Irish students who were studying at the Universities. They suggested that the city would lose out by millions of pounds if the students went to other Cities to study; it was a veiled threat of a boycott. The West Enders' knew that if the students studied elsewhere, their valuable rental income would disappear, and property values would plummet.

'Sorry I am a wee bit late Albert,' it was Ian.
'That's okay; I had a small problem at the garage this morning.'
'What was that then?'
'Someone had bugged my car,' he was laughing. Ian was not.
'Someone had placed a mobile phone in the underside of the wheel arch, the police were called, but I told them that I was not making a complaint.'
'It must be industrial espionage,' responded Ian.

'I know; that's what I think... do you think it's something to do with the Russians in London?'
'I wouldn't think so; I think they have more sophisticated resources at their disposal. Using a mobile as a crude tracking device sounds to me pretty amateurish; they would have used a tiny tracking device and removed it before the car went into the garage. Have you had any unusual business dealings lately?'
Albert visibly blanched at this. 'No, no...everything in the garden is rosy.'
'Not even a little touch of greenfly anywhere?'
'No, everything is ok.'
'Okay. Do you want to talk about this or do you want to concentrate on the business in London?'
'The business in London is more pressing, Ian.'
'Good, everything is relatively straightforward, if they deviate from the agreed price, stand up and say to me Ian let's go, then walk to the door, I'll follow.'
'Do you think the Russians will try to pull something out of the hat?'
Ian looked up to the ceiling. 'Without a doubt, but it will not come to brinkmanship, and if they have legal papers that they say supersede ours...'
'I say this is not acceptable,' Albert replied. 'I stand up then walk towards the door.'
'That sounds as if you have done your homework Albert,' replied Ian.
'That's what you have told me time and again, fail to prepare; prepare to fail.'
Ian smiled at his mature diligent pupil. 'If everything is agreed, I anticipate that the money from their account should be in your account in the Cayman Islands in less than an hour.'
'Good that's what I want to hear, no hitches in the transfer of the money. I was under the impression it would have been less problematic for them to transfer the money into my Isle of Man account.'
Ian shakes his head. 'Yes, that would have been the case a year maybe two years ago, but not now. The European Union is clamping down big time on this.'
'I don't understand,' replied Albert.
'In a nutshell, the banks' in the Isle of Man have been under scrutiny for some time, it will only be a matter of time before the Isle of Man has mutual agreements concerning banks' throughout Europe. The Cayman Islands will not be co-operating with any countries, including the United States or the European Union. The Russians don't want anyone to know how much money they have and where it came from for obvious reasons. They will close down their accounts in the Isle of Man. The Cayman Islands shields their money from prying eyes so to speak.' The Tannoy bellows out their flight is now ready for boarding. 'It's time to go Albert.' They move towards the exit that leads to the runway.
'I hope you are hungry Ian, the lunch at the Savoy is fantastic.'
'So you say; I'll be the judge of that.' His mind drifted fleetingly to the time when he was fourteen. He came home from school for his lunch, because there was no money for school dinners, and had seen his mum was placing a whole chicken in a chip pan; she was drunk. Ian took the chicken which was too big for the chip pan and placed it on the table; he guided her back into the living room, where his dad was sleeping in his chair with cigarette ash spread down his stained waistcoat. He removed the burning cigarette from his fingers and crushed it out into the full ashtray. His mum went through a charade as though Ian had interrupted her from pressing housework. He turned off the two bar electric fire; the dry heat had a pungent smell, the room needed aired. He opened the window. He told his mum to have a lie down on the sofa which was strewn with old magazines. He picked them up and placed them neatly in the magazine rack. He told her that he would make himself lunch.

   He closed the door and went into the kitchen; the only thing in the otherwise empty larder was hard bread. He toasted the bread and ate it hurriedly. He looked around the kitchen, it was filthy; the sink had plates that had been there from previous nights. The floor had linoleum that was ripped and was encrusted with dirt.

He looked at the decaying crusts on the floor; they looked more edible than the ones he was gorging.
'Did you hear me Ian?'
'Sorry Albert, I was miles away.'

CHAPTER THREE

The two police officers were back on nightshift; their car is parked in St. Vincent Street in Broughty Ferry. 'Have you any news for me?'
The young officer had anticipated the question.
'Plenty, who do you want to start with?'
The older officer turned down the volume of the control radio. 'You choose.'
  'First of all Ramage has been allowed out of Castle Huntly, including night time visits to a prominent businesswoman; our friend Linda Simpson. She has set up a charity, to help convicted drug dealers see the error of their ways. Ramage signed up for this course. Linda likes a one to one interview; she asks the offender how he got into the drug trade; what his family background was like etc. She charts his history from birth, where he lived; what the parents did for a living; how many sisters he has; how many brothers; what is his relationship with them. She is able to predict where his life will lead to and the inevitable where it will end. She leads him back to school, his education, when the first trouble erupts in school. That leads on to secondary schooling, how well or poor did he do, what was the average pass marks in academic studies. Once she has completed the study from birth to sixteen when he leaves school, this is when he opts out of society. He neither seeks employment nor wants it. She tells him, this is him on the escalator to crime and prison. If he accepts this prognosis, she pulls out another case history of a male born into a more stable family. Both working -class parents work, they have four children, they live in a more prosperous area, but they have a hefty mortgage.
  'The son sees his parents go out every day to work, the parents point out the benefits of education. They instil their work ethic into their children. They encourage them to take part time work. Their children take this all on board. When they leave school either they take up apprenticeships or go on to University. This is laid out to the offender; they have to figure out, it was when they were six or seven; they were on the road to crime. They were unaware of this. Linda asks them if they can see where they went wrong in their lives; and what do they think were the key differences with the other family. The dealer, if he is not that dumb, points out that stable family background, working parents and children, who pay attention in school, are less likely to step on the crime escalator. Once they accept Linda's theory, Linda takes them back to the first offence that he committed. She then skilfully guides them to his involvement in drugs, who were the person or persons that first introduced them to drugs, was their father a user? Was he a dealer? Was any blood relatives involved in dealing?'
'Don't tell me Ramage goes all Jeremy Kyle and confesses he's been a bad boy and names dealers?'
'It gets better,' he laughs. 'Ramage at first is reluctant to say too much. Linda has built a rapport with him, including wearing short skirts that barely covers her arse; he thinks he is in with a chance. Linda takes him to Art Galleries in Edinburgh, all the middle- class babble with bells on it. She takes him to meet her MSP friend and explains how he is the pioneering force to refrain dealers when they are released from prison from becoming recidivists. I had to look that word up. It means...'
'I know what that means, carry on.'
'Okay. It's taken her months to gain his confidence. Ramage asked, what options did he have when he is released, these people are his friends. She tells him not to avoid them completely but don't frequent with them on a regular basis. If he doesn't he will be lured back to drugs. She suggests that he starts a business. 'Doing what? Where would I get the money,' he replies. She laughs; she tells him that the Courts may have confiscated five million of his ill-gotten gains.
  'But, she would be astonished if he did not have a tidy sum tucked away in an account sheltered from Government agencies. He goes all defensive at this. Now this is where things get very interesting. He replied to her. 'If I did have money, and I used it in a legal way as you suggest, the Government will confiscate the business and his money.' She shakes her head, 'Not if I loan you the money, or I use your money to set up a profitable business.' He is taken aback at this. 'How much money would you require to set up a business?

' She tells him she will see him the following week at her house; she will discuss it then. She is a Director of this Charity; she is paid over sixty- thousand a year from the Scottish Executive.'
'Where did you get this information?'
'From inside Castle Huntly, that's all I can say just now, the information is copper bottomed.' He puts the typed A4 documents into his inside pocket in his jacket. He is looking pleased with himself. His colleague arched his eyebrows again.
'Are you that confident in this information?'
'It is better you don't know my source. It's safer; for all of us.'

   The smug smile that appeared on the young officer's face is illuminated; he is very confident that his source is solid. The control radio cackled into life, he held up his hand, to stop the young officer from continuing to talk. He turned up the volume. A fly tipper had dumped effects from a house clearance, at a lay-by on the Kellas road. He had dumped an old fridge in the adjoining field. He became aware of a body of a male lying face down in the field. Detectives and Forensic Officers were in attendance. The Kellas road is only a five -minute drive away.
'I think we should go up there.'
His colleague replied, 'it's on our beat, might as well.'
They drove to the Kellas road. Approaching from Drumgeith Road they saw in the distance a road block had been set up; all traffic is being diverted via the Drumsturdy Road. They approached the lone police officer directing the sparse traffic from the Kellas Road to Drumsturdy Road. These two roads are country roads, four hundred metres from the beginning of the Kellas Road is the lay-by. A new housing development had been started between Ballumbie Golf Course and the Kellas Road six years previously. The second phase of house building had started just a few months ago. The development was in the middle of nowhere according to the many sceptics; it was just two- minutes away from Dundee. They parked their car in the small turning adjacent to the Drumsturdy Road. The older officer told his colleague to stay in the car. He walked towards the young police officer directing traffic away from the lay-by. He did not recognise him. He looked in his early twenties.
   'So what's the story up bye, at the lay-by?'
'I have not been up there myself, but according to the forensics, it is a young boy about eighteen, he had been shot in the head and dumped. The body has been removed from the field and is due to be taken for a post mortem. This road will be closed till seven am. The floodlights are in the field, the place is crawling with white boiler suits.'
'Has he been identified yet, or is it too early?'
'I've heard nothing, but more than likely he'll be from Whitfield, another scumbag I suppose.'
'Okay, thanks for the info.' He walks back to the car. His colleague has been monitoring the messages coming from the control radio.
He opens the door, his colleague face is ashen. 'What's up with you? You look terrible.'
'No, no, he replied with terror in his voice... it's just came over on the radio... another body has been found... another male... a young male.'
He closes the door behind him slowly. 'Where about was the body found?'
'Not far from here... in Monikie Country Park. A dog walker found it.' His colleague started the car.
'We have to get out of here; we will head down to the esplanade, get thinking and listen to the radio.' The car moves off. They drive onto the Kellas Road, heading back to Broughty Ferry, three police cars pass them in the opposite direction with blue lights blazing.
'I wonder where they're going.'
He looks at his partner, his partner is staring ahead, no response. 'I said I wonder where...'
'I heard you...' He is still rigidly staring ahead. 'Do you think they are the two young lads that we lifted on the Hilltown?'
'I hope not, for our sakes, they might have given our names to their killers.'
'That's what I'm worried about, we could be next. I hope to God it's not them, you don't seem too concerned?'

'Nobody is daft enough to kill us that's stupid; but I am concerned; I'm just hiding it well, but believe me a lot of other things are going through my mind, and they're not pleasant thoughts. We will head back to Broughty Ferry and get two fish suppers, I'll pay. We can go over things at the Esplanade. Things might not be as bad as we think.'
'How can you think about eating, my stomach is in knots?'
'I would advise you to eat.'
'Why?' The car glides to a halt not far from the chip shop.
'Because you look terrible, you look like you have seen a ghost.'
'I can't get over the young boys being murdered, if they can be murdered, what about…'
'Relax …do you want a fish supper?'
'No, I want to find out who they were... you go ahead, I'll listen for news.'
He enters the chip shop and orders a fish supper and a can of Coke, diet of course; he doesn't want to add to his burgeoning waist line.

   The proprietor is not there tonight. Serving is a young long haired student; it looks as though he'll have to pay for his supper tonight. He tries to make small talk with the student, but he is having none of it, he paid for everything and checked his change very carefully, and congratulated the student on his accounting skills, the student turned up the television volume and turned his back on him. Time to leave with dignity, he thought. He couldn't wait to tell his colleague about the surly student. He returned to the car, his colleague is slumped over the steering wheel, an unusual smell was present. He recognised it, and instinctively threw the fish and chips on to the pavement. The smell was still in his nostrils; it was cordite.

   The inside of the windscreen had a whoosh of blood on it, similar to the Nike logo. Part of his skull is on his seat. He slowly withdrew his upper body from the car, his legs are going limp. He looks up both sides of the street, no one is present. He stoops to re -enter the car, keeping his fragile legs on the pavement. His colleague's hand is gripping his radio. He had better leave all in the car as he found it. He would use his mobile phone. He contacts the police control, identifies himself, and told them that his colleague has been shot, he is dead. He is told to stay where he is and instructed not to enter the car; it is now a crime scene. He acknowledged these instructions; he would wait at the crime scene. He took the Coke from his pocket, and opened it and takes a long drink. He finds to his astonishment he is calm and thinking coolly. He has no doubt now the two males are the young neds who gave up Linda Simpson's name.

   Who is the contact that gave all the information about Ramage? All he knew is that it came from Castle Huntly; is it an inmate or a member of prison staff? He suddenly felt nauseous and overcome by fear. His dead colleague has the information on the A4 paper in his jacket. He steps forward and pulls the door open, he leans forward trying not to look at his dead colleague's fractured face. He rummages through his inside pocket, calm is restored, his hand triumphantly extracts the damming information. He backs out of the car calmness personified. The street is eerily quiet. He walks into the entrance of the tenement close and continued on to the rear courtyard where the bins are stored.

   He looks quickly about the courtyard, thoughts coming into his head and departing at a more lightening pace. He walks toward the bin recess and pulled the heavy bin forward, he looks at the flagstones underneath the bin, his eyes take on an added sheen, there is a gap at the rear of the recess, he folds the A4 page into a small square and pushes it into the crevice, it could not be seen now, he would return sometime later and retrieve it.

   The forensics team would be looking for the gun not a piece of paper. He pulls the bin back onto the flagstones. Darkness would have made it difficult for anyone to identify him from the tenement building. The silence of the night is broke by wailing sirens.

   He ran to the entrance of the tenement close and sat on the windowsill of the To Let ground floor apartment. He is breathing deeply; nerves that were taut are now relaxed. He knew what would be coming his way.

His lifestyle would be under intense scrutiny. His bank accounts would reflect a police officer's earnings. He is so relieved that he had not been slovenly with the money from his friend in the Drug Squad. Ordinary life. Ordinary house. Embarrassing car. That would be the net conclusion of the internal investigation. His eyes veered towards his colleague; only he knew the killer, however that could or would change, he would be digging around surreptitiously when he is placed on gardening leave, he would unearth the killer or die trying. The police cars come from both directions; they are followed by large forensic vans.

The tenements that are on both sides of the street come alive with lights, curtains and blinds opening as if they are synchronised. An abundance of lights are now showering the normally dimly lit street. Two police cars are positioned at both ends of the street preventing any vehicles from entering or leaving the manic street. An unmarked car pulled up parallel to the police car where his colleague lay slumped like a drunk. Two males emerge from the car; they stood observing him as they place on latex gloves. One opens the passenger seat and places his fingers on his dead colleague's neck. His pulse went the same time as his skull expanded. The detective searching for a pulse shook his head, the other one signalled to the van and a large white screen is thrown around the car. The two detectives come together in the street, heads are nodding and shaking, then they stop and they both stare at him intently. He felt their accusatory eyes on him, he felt very alone but very much in control. He anticipated what is coming next. They move towards him, he felt an icy tinge run up his spine.

'My name is Joe Feeney and this is Valentine Eddings we are with the Serious Crime Squad.'
He nodded at them. 'How are you coping with this? He didn't have time to answer. 'We need you to answer some questions, we would prefer you to answer them now, rather in the back of a car, are you happy with that?' This is not a request.
'I am okay answering questions here.'
Eddings gestured for him to hand over the can of Coke. When he hands it over, Eddings places it in a forensic bag as evidence, he shouts for Pete, a forensic officer, he then hands him the sealed bag. His attention returns to the officer.
'Tell us what you were doing fifteen- minutes before you came into the street?'
'We heard on the control radio that a body had been found near the Kellas Road, we drove up there. I spoke to the young officer diverting the traffic away from the crime scene, I asked him what had happened, he told me a youth had been shot. I told Jim what the officer had told me, then we came down here for a fish supper.'
Feeney has a scowl on his face. 'Why didn't Jim Swithers come into the chip shop with you?'
'He didn't want anything to eat...'
'That was convenient, was it not?' Feeney interrupted.
'Not really, he wasn't a big eater...' They were trying to provoke him, but he remained cool.
'When you came out of the car to go to the chip shop did you notice anybody or anyone walking in the street?'
'No I didn't notice anything unusual.'
'What about when you went into the chip shop was there anybody else there?'
'No, I was the only customer in the shop.'
'When you went in to the chip shop was anybody coming out?' He thought for a minute.
'No, nobody came out as I went in.'
'How long were you in the shop then,' continued Eddings.
'Five minutes... maximum'
'Did you hear any noise, never mind gunshots, I mean anything, car door been slammed, anything?'
'No, the television was on.'
'How convenient,' interrupted Feeney
He stared at him hard and moved from the windowsill. 'Convenient? Convenient for whom?'

Eddings is annoyed at Feeney being confrontational. 'Have you ever owned a gun?
He turns away from Feeney to answer Eddings question.
'No, never.'
'How well did you get on with Jim Swithers, and did you know him socially?'
'Jim was my partner for the last four years, we had a lot in common, he was younger than me, but...we got on well.'
Feeney had enough of the soft questions. 'Did you have any major disagreements with him?'
'None... pity that's inconvenient, eh?'
'Look, don't try to be a smart arse, just answer the questions. Did he have any problem with other officers male or female?
'I wasn't aware of problems, any problems. If he did have any he kept them to himself. But I doubt it if he did, he got on well with everyone'
Feeney smirked. 'Are you sure about that?'
'As far as I am aware, they were no problems with me or anyone else.'
'Had he or you had any threats from criminals?'
He felt his head starting to swim. He shook his head, his throat had run dry.
'Was he friendly with known criminals?' Eddings enquired.
'Not that I am aware. Is it okay if I move from here? I don't like looking at the car.'
'No, just stay where you are we won't be much longer, then we will take you down to Headquarters,' replied Eddings. He turned around and signalled to Pete, he came over with a white boiler suit.
'Robert, I want you to place this on.' He took the suit and climbed into it. Now come with us.'
Eddings led him to the car that they had arrived in; they invite him into the back seat where they manoeuvre him so that he is between them. Eddings instructs the driver to take them to Bell Street, Police Headquarters. As the car swings out of King Street, he feels pangs of guilt overcome him.
   What if he didn't suggest going for a fish supper, Jim would still be alive. Then cold calculated reasoning replaced this speculation, if they had went to their usual place on the Esplanade to enjoy their supper and the views of Fife, he would be dead as well.
   The assassin or assassins would have shot them dead. Plural. He would soon be down in Bell Street and interviewed again. Had the Serious Crime Squad had any inkling about their suspicions about Linda Simpson? Was Jim set up by his copper bottomed informant from Castle Huntly? Was the information on the A4 misinformation?
Could these detectives link Jim to Ramage, Linda Simpson and the two bodies that had been dumped on the Kellas Road and Monikie Park?
   He still didn't know if the bodies were officially the two neds that had implicated Linda Simpson with heroin. He is hoping against hope it isn't them. As the car makes it way out of King Street, the street is lined with rubberneckers.
He has to suppress an urge and tell the driver to put the foot down. The car is painfully slow leaving King Street, far too slow.
   This is a tactical manoeuvre, when the car reached the end of the street; it unexpectedly did a U-turn and drove back. When it approached the chip shop the driver changed down a gear, why?
The youth who had served him is on the pavement talking into his mobile. He caught the youth's eye for a second; the youth refrained from talking into the mobile and stared at him. Is that a smirk on his face?
   The driver stepped up a gear, and turned onto the Broughty Ferry Road. The car is doing seventy now, why the big hurry?
He only has a short window of opportunity to anticipate the questions that will be thrown at him when he arrives at Police Headquarters. The car is doing sixty now.
   'So how are you coping now Robert? A contemptuous smirk is on the questioners face.
This the first time he has called him Robert. 'C'mon now, Robert's just been through a traumatic experience, no need to treat him like a criminal.

He understands we have to do this, being rude to him doesn't make our job any easier.'
'That's okay detective Eddings; maybe detective constable Feeney, has always been a bully, but he won't bully me because bullies stop being bully's when …'

Feeney reacts badly. 'You shouldn't make any plans for the night; it's going to be a long, long night for you. I on the other hand, am looking forward to tonight when you are kept overnight in the cells if you don't co-operate fully. And for your information sonny, I am the senior officer in this team.'
'I won't be in the cells overnight, you know and I know it. And you are the senior officer?'
He laughs. 'Why am I surprised at that? I heard a couple of months ago that someone was disciplined for their, let's call it their interview technique and was banged down to a detective constable, any idea who that was?'
Feeney was not taking the bait. 'No idea who you are talking about constable, but maybe, just maybe the officer concerned appealed and it was upheld. Ever think of that?'

The car has arrived at Police Headquarters. Robert is clearly unnerved by this. He has been in and out of Bell Street many, many times. However, this time he has a feeling of dread and hopelessness. Should he ask for the Police Federation representative to be called before the interview commences? If he did the response would be, 'if you are innocent, why would you need the Police Federation rep?' Think quickly, and breathe slowly. Feeney is taking great pleasure in Robert's discomfort. Feeney grabs hold of him to march him through the doors to a wide-eyed audience. Eddings moves quickly and removes Feeney's hand from Robert's arm.
'He's here for questioning, that's all. You holding him like that will give a wrong impression, people will jump to conclusions.'
'No problem, we will do it your way then.'
'No, we won't do it my way; we will do it the correct way.'
'C'mon lads I don't want you two falling out over me. I will only be here a short time. Now behave yourselves, people are watching, especially you detective constable.'
Feeney winces. 'You could be here overnight, so less of the bravado, you're fooling no one, and no semantics at the desk.'

CHAPTER FOUR

Mary looked out of the plane window as it began its descent into Dundee. The sky was overcast, but at least it wasn't raining. She flicked her hair from her eyes, her hand was tanned. The twins had loved Spain, she was apprehensive when she drove up to the security lodge and asked for the keys to her apartment. Her Spanish was faultless. Brian always seemed to be embarrassed when his mum switched seamlessly from English to Spanish or French. The security guard handed over the large brown envelope, she in turn handed it to Brian who was in the passenger seat. Brian ripped open the envelope without tact. He pulled out the keys, and read the directions out loud. The apartment was less than five minutes away. The ground floor apartment exceeded their expectations. The rooms were expansive and furnished tastefully. When Brian opened the French doors they were met with the lush green of the golf course. Between the apartment and the golf course was the pool, Norma who had been unusually quiet from Reus Airport to the complex, now had an infusion of enthusiasm.

Mary had met Marta the Spanish manager of the sales, the both of them seemed to gel instantly. Marta knew that Mary spoke Spanish, but not as well as this. Marta explained that the apartments practically sold themselves, if finance needed to be arranged; they had a reputable Spanish Bank with the mortgages in place at a reduced rate compared to the UK banks'. Mary's job was to build a rapport with the clients. Marta saw that Ian had chosen well in Mary, she was pleasant and not too tactile. Some of the clients were from the Dundee and surrounding area, and they were reassured that Mary was from the city herself. Marta had shown Mary all the local bars and restaurants as well as the beautiful small villages that were dotted around the area. She introduced Mary to the owners of the restaurants where the clients would dine. After three days if the clients wished to purchase an apartment they had the advantage of a Spanish mortgage, and they would sign for their apartments at the Bank with the English solicitor. Ian had intended the purchase to be problem free. The two weeks at Panoramica flew by too quickly, much to the annoyance of the twins. Marta insisted the she took a few days off because she absorbed information so quickly. The last few days in Spain were spent at the Country Club, enjoying meals and meeting the ex-pat community who lived on the complex. Nuggets of information regarding car hire and airport runs were thrown at her. Her small note book was bulging; business cards were left behind the bar for her. Marta laughed at her with her pen and paper. Mary explained this painstaking archaic method was her iPhone's back-up.

They were just minutes away from landing at Dundee Airport. If Ian was true to his word there would be a black BMW 5 series awaiting her. She had no reason to doubt him, but the doubt was still there. She knew he had other businesses outside Dundee to tend too; perhaps her car would slip his mind? She would find out soon. The two weeks in Spain had a positive effect on Brian, the lethargy that affected him had gone; he now had a zest for life. Norma on the other hand had placed Spain out of her head. She was thinking of her studies, and the long train journey down to Warwick University. The plane swayed on the approach to the runway, she gripped her seat, landing was not her favourite flight manoeuvre. The plane landed safely despite the bumps; they collected their luggage, she instructed the twins to stay with the luggage. She went to the desk and enquired with a smile and some doubt in her voice if car keys had been left for her?

The girl behind the desk smiled and handed them over. Mary felt guilty about doubting Ian. She had not mentioned to Brian and Norma that she would have a company car. They made their way out of the airport foyer, Brian walked to the Taxi rank. Mary told him to follow her. She clicked the key, the lights started flashing, Brian and Norma looked at each other in amazement. Mary strode towards the car with a sense of anticipation and opened the boot and placed her luggage in, she invited them to do likewise. They didn't notice the cold damp weather now, and then the questions came, 'you never told us about this,' 'how much did it cost,' and 'would you be able to drive me down to Warwick?' Mary's look said no. They drove the short distance from the airport to the flat on the Perth Road.

For the first time in years she felt happy, really, happy; long may it continue she thought. Mary felt her life was turning for the better when she was able to secure a parking space outside her tenement. The builders', who had been renovating a flat below hers, were gone, or so she hoped. She came to this conclusion when the large skip that had been resident for the last three months and taken up two rare parking spaces was gone. When they retrieved their luggage, Mary took great pride in using the clicker to lock the car. She casually looked about her; she was disappointed that none of her neighbours were there to admire and enquire about her car. The Perth Road was busy with the omnipresent student population.   Brian and Norma had left her to ascend the stairwell to their flat. Even with her luggage Mary didn't curse the long journey up the stairwell to her flat. She entered the close, turned around and glanced affectionately at the BMW, and made her way up to the flat. Norma enquired when Mary reached her front door, what had taken her so long?
Mary replied, 'Joy.' It had been an infrequent visitor in her life; she hoped it would stay for a while. She turned the key, and pushed on the door, mail was strewn about the hall. The flat was cold.

'I'll put the heating on,' volunteered Brian. Mary stooped to pick up the letters and junk mail. She walked into the kitchen, placed the letters on the table and deposited the rest in the bin. Norma was close by and filled the kettle ready for a much sought after pot of tea. Mary stared out of the kitchen window over the Tay to Wormit; a train was on the Tay Bridge coming into Dundee.

She felt the temperature in the kitchen rise. An icy cold shiver ran up her spine, what if this dream job turns into a nightmare? To rid herself of this melancholy, she busied herself by producing mugs for the long awaited tea. Norma noticed the sudden change in her demeanour, and asked what was on her mind. To her surprise Mary told her. Norma told her that was a natural reaction, after all the heartache and trauma, as well as the financial problems that had embedded her for years. Confidence had deserted her years ago. It would need time to return and establish itself. Mary was dismayed at this shockingly accurate diagnosis. Norma knew that she was being too candid. She changed tact.

'You were oozing confidence in Spain, you heard Marta say that on numerous occasions.'
Mary agreed, and a faint smile returned to her face. Brian came meandering into the kitchen.
'Do you think we will ever move to Spain?' Mary burst out laughing.
Norma stared at her intently. 'Well will we Mum?' Mary stopped laughing.

***

The train snaked its way off the Tay Bridge and into Dundee Station. Ian was disappointed that the negotiations with the Russians were delayed due to some improbable; or potential contamination that was in the land near the old railway goods yard. Ian pointed out and produced reports from the most thorough and respected environmental company in Europe, that the land was toxin free. The Russians knew that they were booked on the last plane from London City Airport to Dundee. This was a stalling tactic, as far as Ian was concerned. He was prepared for delaying tactics that would eventually mean the price paid would be less than previously agreed. He would not move on the price

Albert watched the arguments ebb and flow. He was enjoying this; this was how business used to be done in the old days. Ian had called their bluff, he stood up gathered his papers placed them neatly in his briefcase, Albert stood up, Ian said goodbye to his hosts, and walked out with Albert in tow.   The two Russians were left to ponder their next move. Ian and Albert were in the elevator, when one of the Russians scampered along the corridor towards the elevator. He was waving his hands in an animated fashion.

'Please come back into the suite, there has been a misunderstanding.'
Ian held his finger on the open button inside the elevator.   He told the Russian that all the papers had to be signed in two minutes, as far as he was concerned the negotiations were over.

The Russian nodded his head in agreement; he was still encouraging them to leave the elevator. Ian told Albert to move from the elevator, back into the corridor, Ian followed suit. Ian walked quickly along the corridor into the suite. The Russian was still sitting in his leather chair but the smug face was gone. Ian opened the briefcase and indicated where the Russian should sign.
The five papers were signed promptly and without comment. His signature was worse than his manners. Ian examined them and nodded to Albert.

The Russians spoke to each other in their Mother tongue. Ian caught the Russian in mid-sentence, he reminded them that they had to authorise their Bank to release the funds and transfer them into Mr Friedman's account in the Cayman Islands. The Russian smiled, spoke on his mobile for ten seconds and continued to speak to his colleague. His mobile rang; he answered it then turned to Ian and told him the money was released. Ian pulled out his phone and placed it on the table. Albert, who had said little during this new cold war, watched the two Russians continue with their conversation. Ian's phone rang; Ian still kept the poker face.

'Thank you,' he said, ending the conversation.
'Are you happy now?'
'Totally,' replied Ian. 'Would you like to join us later on for lunch?' The Russians were taken aback at this unexpected invitation. 'I thought you had to be back in Scotland by tonight?'
'Our schedule is flexible, if you have business to attend to ...I understand.'
Now the Russians were apprehensive, why the change of heart? They were very suspicious, they had seen many set ups in Russia after Yeltsin came to power.
'No, thank you for the gracious invitation, but we have other urgent business to attend to.'
Ian stood up, thanked them, and then left. Albert followed.

In the elevator Albert asked Ian why the change of plans. Ian explained that he had booked them into the Hilton at Marble Arch. They would be catching the train tomorrow morning.
He was just taking a precaution that's all. The bugging of Albert's car weighed heavily on his mind. Russia was still in turmoil even with Putin in power and his steady hand on the tiller. Putin was systematically scrutinising the chequered histories of all these new multi-millionaires. Most of them had accrued their massive wealth by corruption and intimidation. That's why many of these new money millionaires and billionaires were ensconced in London. They were in self- imposed exiled along with their wealth.
'The Russian who purchased your land was an ex- welder from a shipyard; he worked there until eight years ago. He then bought the shipyard himself, then other land in the centre of Moscow.'
Ian continued. 'On which now stands one million dollar apartments. Dangerous individuals Albert, if you had refused to sell them the land, well...'

The train slowed then came to a halt in Dundee Station, Ian and Albert were already at the door ready to avoid the mass of people who were also leaving the train. They made their way to the taxi rank, they shared the taxi, Ian would alight first, and then the taxi would continue onto Albert's residence. The taxi driver recognised Albert; he knew he was in for a good tip. He recognised Ian vaguely, he knew he is a solicitor, Albert is the prize.
'Were you down in London?'
Ian replied that they had been down there on business and had stayed the night.
The taxi driver asked them if they had heard about the double murder.
Albert and Ian looked at each other; the taxi driver glancing in the rear view mirror knew they hadn't before they mentioned that they hadn't.
'Two young lads, one was dumped on the Kellas Road, the other was found in Monikie Country Park... both had been shot in the head... and a policeman was shot dead eating fish and chips in his car, in King Street in Broughty Ferry.'
There was no stopping the taxi driver. 'I heard drugs were involved.'
'Did you say that it was a double murder... do you mean a triple murder? Ian asked.

'No, I said it was a double murder, what my mate told me was a policeman told him the young boys had threatened to tell the police that the policeman was using both of them for sex, as well as other rent-boys, he was giving them heroin in exchange for sex. Seemingly, he had sex with both of them, shot them, dumped the bodies, then when his partner went for a can of Coke, he shot himself.'

Albert was open mouthed at this information.

Ian was sceptical of the taxi driver's theory. 'Has this been the official statement from the police?'

'No, this is inside info. Obviously I can't say too much.'

'Seems a lot has gone on when we were away, Ian. Three people dead, all been shot, including a policeman.'

'I'll find out more from a contact I have in Bell Street,' Ian replied.

The taxi came to a halt outside an imposing house in Douglas Terrace, it had magnificent views over the Tay, Ian had lived here for eight years. His young wife and baby daughter were on the steps of the house waiting for him.

'Remember what I told you about your parents Ian.'

'I will, Albert. I will.'

The taxi moved off towards Albert's house, the driver had done this trip many times. 'Is he your lawyer, Mr Friedman?'

'He sure is, he is young but he is bright.'

'That's some house he has there,' said the driver.

'It's a lovely house, I used to live there over forty- years ago, Ian doesn't know that, or if he does he's keeping it quiet. When he was at University studying, he used to wash the windows of that house. He confessed to me that when he was washing the windows, he couldn't help peering in to the house, he was totally enchanted by it...I wonder if he knew that one day he would own it.'

'Is he of good stock' asked the driver?

'The finest, he had a tough upbringing, but he applied himself to his studies, and he has reaped the benefits. He has looked after his parents well.'

'It's all right you saying that Mr Friedman, but to make money you have to have money...'

'But, you have to work to make money, and then make money work for you. Everyone has the opportunity; the difference is so few see the opportunity. Faith and confidence in you own vision, doubters and never do wells will be in abundance to taint and laugh at your plans. However, years later the council boy's plans start to bear fruit, he moves out of his council house, he buys a small flat, in a less desirable area, he stays there for a few years, and his money is working for him, don't you see?'

'I see Mr Friedman.'

Albert continued. 'While his friends or so called friends see him move up the ladder of life, they start to question their own mortality, what have they achieved in life?

Meanwhile, their friend has sold his flat he is now in a nice house in a more affluent area.

They, his friends that is, are still stuck in their same routine, living in the same house, going to the same pub. They might buy their council house then sell it to move into a more desirable area.

But our friend is now moves ahead of them; he is now living in a house in Douglas Terrace need I go on?'

'And that's how your lawyer got to Douglas Terrace?'

'Correct, and remember he is just in his early forties.'

The taxi stops nears the gates of his mansion.

***

'George' was studying his laptop with interest; the money from the Bulgarian land scam project had been in and out of many accounts in Europe and the United States, all going to individuals or companies.

But in the end the money was going from bank account to bank account which he controlled. The early morning sun was reflecting off the Tay, he completed the last of the transactions on the laptop. He closed the lap top triumphantly. He went into the bedroom and changed into his running gear. His early morning run took him from the City Quay to Broughty Ferry Esplanade then back to the City Quay. This was an excellent way of cross-referencing the area where he would be ascertaining the side streets that would enable him to complete his business in Dundee. He was able to establish when the police officers started and ended their shifts.

From seven- am till eight- am no police were patrolling Broughty Ferry; this was because the nightshift and the early shift conferred over the previous night's incidents, which were trivial if anything. After he had completed his run and had showered he altered his appearance again in case any potential Bulgarian investor in Broughty Ferry recognised him. The office manager was running the City Centre office diligently, there would be no need for him to go there, until the day his work in Dundee was complete, and even then it would be during the Christmas holidays. Gone was the sober suited businessman with nice short blonde hair, he was now sporting dark hair with moustache and clear lens glasses. His attire was jeans and a shirt with trainers. He was now a software consultant. That was the only thing that rang true.

He had studied computer science in America and worked with two computer geeks. The students in the campus where he had studied had made fun of him and his two friends, because they were obsessed with technology that was changing at a whirlwind speed. They were known as the geek triangle they did everything together. The triangle was broken when his parents divorced and he returned with his mother to the UK. They settled in London where his mother took up a teaching post, he went to the London School of Economics. He was dismayed at the lack of enthusiasm from his fellow -students and more so from his tutors, they were still battling left- wing causes from the seventies, he dropped out.

He started his own software technology company in London. He was successful when he tendered for the contract to update computer systems in Lambeth City Council. That contract made him a millionaire. Hackney Council followed suit, then came the City of Westminister. Unofficially a condition of the securing these multi-million pound contracts was that he was 'encouraged' to employ as a consultant, a young lady at fifty- thousand per year. He was mystified at the interview at her lack of basic education never mind her blank look about her degree which gave her a 2.1 in computer science. He was later told that she was a blood relative of one of the panel, who would select his company to update the computer systems for Lambeth Council. If she was not selected the contract would go elsewhere. That was the way of the land

He, with a shrug of the shoulders concurred with this. He never signed anything regarding the employment of the young lady in question. After four years in London he sold his share of the company to the two other directors, one of them was the cerebral challenged young lady. This netted him ten million pounds plus five percent of the gross profits for five years. Secured financially for life, he needed excitement; he was bored with life at twenty- eight. He relocated to Spain. He met a Liverpool girl who sold timeshares in Benidorm. He never mentioned the fact that he was a multi-millionaire, he thought that would spoil the think on your feet type mentality that she possessed. He was amazed at the sheer stupidity of the Brits abroad. Scratch cards produced winners at an alarming rate, but still at the presentation and hard sell, they still didn't walk away. They were financial lemmings, running to hand over their credit card details to the sales reps. After two years in Benidorm he moved to the south of Spain, near Murcia.

This time he wouldn't be a timeshare sales rep, he would be the sole proprietor of the two hundred apartments that he had built on the land he previously bought. These apartments were all two bedroom. The most expensive cost twenty five thousand for July to ten thousand for a week in February. These came with an annual maintenance charge of fifteen- hundred pounds. Still they came and signed up, and this was all legal.

Bulgaria was the next big thing, according to the media. He flew into Sofia; he was booked into the five star hotel for two weeks, it was winter, snow flurries were frequent. Land was cheap; several German speculators were carrying out extensive surveys. They were staying in the same hotel. They enquired what his business was in Bulgaria. He told them that he was interested in acquiring land for apartments. They told him that they were acquiring land, then they would sell the land to a Hotel Chain, they couldn't tell him which chain it was. But they knew that they had struck gold. Pan-European hotel chains knew that Sofia had excellent piste for wealthy skiers. The infrastructure was however archaic; millions of Euros would have to be spent to bring the sewers, electricity and roads, up to an acceptable standard. Once that was done it was Euros from Heaven. George asked how they knew that Hotel chains wanted to build Bulgaria. They both laughed.

When they join the EU trillions; not millions of Euros will flood in. George, intrigued by this information, ordered more beer for his new friends. They asked him how he knew where to buy land for his apartments; George laughed and raised his glass that they clinked with him, 'couldn't comment commercial confidentiality.' They laughed, and toasted secrecy. They were all more relaxed now; information was flowing from the Germans lips. They reckoned, that the land they had bought for two hundred thousand Euros, would net them over two million Euros each. The land was sold as seen. They didn't have to do anything else.

George had worked out how they had managed to make a fantastic return on their investment. He did not broach his theory with them to perceive if he was correct. He knew how they worked. One bought the land and registered the name of the company. The other was looking to buy land for a hotel chain, in which he would be paid a fee for acquiring the land, at a certain price, he would be also be paid a premium if he acquired the land at under a certain price. The one employed by the hotel chain knew that the hotel had a very impressive budget. Another hotel chain was tipped off about the prime location site.

Documents were produced to prove the rival hotel chain was willing to offer a more substantial sum to acquire the land. The German advised the original hotel chain to act quickly. They did. The land was sold and the former owners were sitting across from him toasting his health and their wealth. This was the new Klondike gold rush. Get in, get out and count your money. George had breakfast late the following morning; the waiter was impressed with George's manners. George complemented him on his manner and efficiency.

He had a rapport with the waiter, he said his English was excellent, he then enquired if the two Germans were still in their beds with a hangover from the night before. The waiter said they had left early that morning and had ordered a taxi to take them to the ski resort about an hour's drive away. George thanked him, and continued with his breakfast, as the waiter was passing, George asked would it be possible if the taxi could take him to that area, as he had to see the Germans about documents. The waiter said that was not a problem, when would wish the taxi ordered? Immediately was the reply. He smiled, went to the desk, and ordered it personally. He told George it would be there in fifteen minutes. George thanked him went up to his room had a quick shower, and then returned to the lobby. The waiter was there, he told him that the Taxi driver didn't speak any English, but he knew exactly where to go. He gave the waiter fifty Euros and twenty U.S. Dollars; joy radiated from his face, he escorted George to the taxi. Thirty- Euros would cover the complete journey, and that included the tip. He was amazed at the area near the ski slopes.

He had been previously informed that there were only two estate agents for the area. He told them what he wanted, they told him the price. Over the next six days he was shown the land where he would build ski lodges. The estate agent was showing him the area, he noticed the two Germans with three other men in suits, it was obvious that they had recently landed. The two Germans were pointing and moving their arms in an arc, this was them explaining what area that the hotel owned; it was expansive. George quickly came to an agreement with the estate agents. If he were to buy the land at the price that he mentioned they would receive a hefty bonus in U.S. dollars.

The two agents colluded and spoke to the elderly farmer who owned the land, they told him of the interest from George, but they had to move quickly as he was leaving the next day.

The farmer had no children to guide him through the maze of selling to a Westerner, he went ahead and signed. He received more money than he would spend in the remainder of his life time, but he should have received more.

When the legal work was initiated George sought out the two Germans at the hotel portraying a sense of naivety, the Germans were impressed with his plans for ski lodge apartments. George, asked if they would be interested in overseeing the construction of the lodges, including connecting to the services; sewers, electricity and telephone lines.

One of them replied. 'That is where a large portion of the budget would go, the planning permission, even with the greasing of palms, would take six months.'
George thought for a moment as if he was ruminating and replied. 'But once the services for the power, sewers, were in place for the hotel, surely connecting the lodges to the hotel's services; would be relatively simple?'
'How far are the ski lodges from the hotel?'
'Eight hundred metres... but the services would be less than fifty metres, adjacent to the road.'
The Germans were puzzled 'Where is exactly is the land, and where will the lodges be built?'
'Just twenty metres from the mountain track, beside the fir trees.'
They knew exactly where he meant.
'Is that the old man's land you are talking about?'
George sipped his beer, and then nodded his head. 'The estate agent wanted four -hundred thousand Euros just to allow the new road to be built on his land. Things changed rapidly, I now own the land, I will allow the road to be built; on the condition that the hotel will maintain the road, and they allow me to connect the services for the lodges to the hotel at no cost to me.'
'I think they would agree to that, because the new road that they're proposing would take many months to build, with the difficult terrain.'
'But if you allow them to go through the old man's, sorry, your land, that will save them time and much money.'
'That's what I hoped to hear, could you arrange for the hotel's lawyer to be here tomorrow?'
'That is not a problem ... how much of a kickback do you require from us?'
'Nothing, all I ask is the conditions that I mentioned are adhered to, and you and your silent partner, build the ski lodges at a fair price with good finishes internal and external.'
'Leave it with us, I will contact my local lawyer, he will ensure that the plans go through quickly, and construction starts in the spring. That is not a promise but a fact. We will take care of him financially, do not worry about that. The German skiing market is booming; we can sell them no problem, at a price that will make you weep with joy.'
The lodges were built, to a very high standard, the Germans kept their side of the bargain. The money was rolling in once again.

George had met a con artist while he was looking at other properties to develop, his name was Bruce, he tried pitifully to entice him into a Holiday Ownership deal, George explained to him that that side of the business didn't appeal to him. He told Bruce that he did that scam in Spain years earlier. He advised him that his approach was too suspicious, and that he needed to dress to impress and be more receptive and smile more. Bruce found it difficult to smile.

George had seen the depression envelope him. He invited him to lunch at the hotel. Over lunch Bruce started to relax and confessed to him that he had split up with his wife earlier in the year, and came out to work in construction, he was an electrician by trade. When he arrived he was met by a Dutch agent, he worked for four -weeks without pay, while his papers were being processed, he was to meet the agent at the Bank where he would be paid. When he arrived at the Bank, there were four other Brits waiting on the Dutchman; he failed to show.

With no money he was threw out of the basic hotel, because the Dutchman failed to pay his wages. He met another Londoner, who told him about the Holiday Ownership scam. George was instantly dismayed at his lack of fight. He told him he would make them both rich.

Bruce looked at him; not only had he seen and heard that movie, he was the principal actor in it. George plan was simple. He would rent two of the finest newly-built Villas for a year, money up front. Bruce would stay in one; the prospective new owners he would send over to Sofia. Bruce would meet them at the airport. Take them to the best hotel and wine and dine them for two days. The villa that they were viewing was the finished product. They would be taken to one of the building sites that ubiquitously dotted the country side of Sofia, and shown foundations that would be their dream villa.

The secret of this scam was a whistle stop tour of the site where building was actually taken place. Their eyes would be their judge. After less than ten minutes on site, it would be lunch time, they would be whisked off to a mountain restaurant to drink in the views as well as consume the copious amounts of the finest wines available. Then back to the hotel with brochures copied from legitimate companies. With the market being fluid and prices increasing by the month, this was all in their heads as they flew back into Glasgow Airport. George had him hooked.

He would need an impressive office; that would cost big money, but he would take care of that side of the business. He told Bruce about sales techniques, a consummate actor he was not, but he would shave the rough edges off him.

George needed an answer, if he felt he couldn't do it, now was the time to tell him. George knew he would say yes. When George struck out his hand Bruce automatically shook his hand George laughed, that was the first lesson, hand out, and it would always be met. Bruce asked how long the scam would operate. George put his knife and fork down, and pulled his hands together; six months; no longer. They would meet in Spain, where George would give him his money. Bruce aged when he heard this. He put him at ease he wouldn't rip him off.

The only problem was where to set up the office, it had to be in Scotland; the scam had not been tried there. After lunch, they set out for new villas to rent. There were a plethora of villas available. Bruce would be the prospective renter; he was honing his thespian skills on the fledgling property management companies that had ensconced in this area of Bulgaria. This he achieved with remarkable success. Two villas were secured, the rent paid in advance with cash. Bruce even managed a discount of two months' rent. George was pleased with the aplomb Bruce now possessed. He told him that the money he had discounted from the rent he could keep. But for now he should keep a low profile. George gave him money to open a Bank account; this money would be his living expenses which would tide him over till the first owner arrived, probably in the next two months

It was imperative to have the professional web site up and running. This area of Bulgaria was going to be the in place for skiers, and property developers, villas and apartments were springing up every week. Property experts and first time developers were swarming about the area. This would be the area for the fictitious villas. The area was teeming with bulldozers and building materials. Ten tonne lorries criss-crossed the lunar landscaped building site in a reckless manner. This made the laconic visit to the site more plausible; the builders hated these tourists on their site. George, first of all thought about setting up an office in Edinburgh, but the location that he wanted had to be in the City Centre. The Agents wanted a lengthy and expensive lease and the offices were in a very poor condition. They told him he was compelled to refurbish the offices that they had shown him. Another added expense.

One night in the Caledonian Hotel, he was surfing the net, Dundee was a city that was once on its knees, but it was on the up and up. He browsed commercial properties in Dundee; he was amazed at the low rents and flexible leases compared to Edinburgh. The following morning he took the train to Dundee, he wandered about the City Centre.

There were very few shops vacant and even those were under offer, the streets were bustling with shoppers, there were an array of Audis, BMW's and four- by- fours on view. In the Overgate Shopping Centre he meandered into one of the many coffee shops, he sipped his coffee slowly, his eyes watching the busy shoppers with their designer logos on the bags. This would be the place to open an office.

That morning he registered with a Letting Agency, he was aware that a credit check would be compiled on him from the Letting Agency that would cost sixty pounds, could they do that as soon as possible? He briefly explained he didn't want to stay in a Hotel for longer than absolute necessary. The credit agency contacted his software company, everything was in order. Bruce had been able to vouch for him. He would be in Dundee for a year. Four days later he was in his flat by the River Tay in the City Quay development, everything that he needed was in the flat that was the beauty of a luxurious furnished flat. He would keep a low profile avoiding contact with the neighbours.

That first night in his flat, he opened up his laptop, and checked his emails, one was from his two former college friends in America, would he like to invest in their new company it would be a unique search engine. He gave quick reply, he laughed as he responded, he wouldn't invest, but if they needed working capital he would give it to them as they were his friends; interest free. They had developed a social-media website two years ago and sold it to Google. He would be astonished if they needed a fresh injection of cash. Perhaps this was a thank you to him for bridging the funding gap between the Venture Capitalist's money and securing world-wide patents. The last thing he needed was to be identified as an investor. He closed the laptop and then called Bruce and told him that he had a flat; tomorrow he would be viewing shops and small offices in the City- Centre.

The next time he would contact him would be when the first client would be flying over to Sofia. The bank account for the Bulgarian villas had been opened in London. The ideal vacant office was in the next street to the Letting Agency in Crichton Street, but it was too risky. Too many solicitors' offices were in that street, but to counter -balance this fear; it added respectability to the premises. He would sleep on the decision. He met the Agent at the office, it could be converted quickly and cheaply, no planning permission or change of use was required. He signed that day; the Agent was able to recommend a reputable shop fitting company. The shop would be ready in fifteen days including telephones and computers. He was compelled to employ twenty- something's with an engaging smile and a pleasant telephone manner.

Their salary would be well- above average for this type of work. He wanted them to believe in the product. Two nights a week he would need them to cold call potential customers, not to sell them the villas but just to arrange an appointment. If they didn't agree to an appointment, they were invited to the office for a coffee and a chat when they were in town. The potential clients had nothing to lose, apparently. This softly-softly strategy worked remarkably well. George had hacked into and plagiarised various Specialist Ski and winter sports Travel agents, he had harvested the data base of customers who were regular skiers, all in a radius of sixty -miles of Dundee.

The young ladies would be surprised at their knowledge of the skiing area of Bulgaria. It had helped that George had supplied a wonderful script that would answer any question about the area; the young ladies even had photographs of the villas, with mountains in the background. The clincher would be the exclusive financial plans available. George had taken out double page advertisements in the local morning and evening papers. The photograph with smiling staff, except George who had to fly to Bulgaria unexpectedly, shone out to the readers. Tomorrow the office would open.

***

He sat in the interview room for an hour. He knew that he was being videotaped and watched by a body language expert. Any movement could be interpreted, towards innocence or guilt. Sweat was building up in the suit, he wanted to wipe his brow and scratch, but he daren't, would that expert condemn him as a guilty man if he did scratch or move in his seat?

He wasn't going to take that chance. Voices were coming along the corridor, towards him. It was Feeney and Eddings. The door opened, they walked in with a young woman in her late twenties.

'Before we start the interview, we would like to take a DNA swab, if you don't mind?' said Eddings.
'Go ahead,' he opened his mouth; the young woman took a swab around his mouth.
'Do you have any objection if this went on the National Data Base or would you just like it to be held in relation to the murder of your colleague?' asked Feeney.
'Place it on the National Data Base, I have no objection.' Feeney looked dismayed.
The young woman placed the swab in the pouch wrote on it his name, date, time and asked for his signature then left the room.
The two of them took their jackets off, and sat directly across the desk from him.
'Jim Swithers was a bit of a lad then?'
'What do you mean by that?'
'C'mon Robert, it was an open secret...'
Robert looked at Eddings then Feeney. 'If you have something to tell me, come out and say it... what was an open secret?'
Feeney got up and walked round to the back of Robert, he bent down his mouth nearly touching his ear. 'You must think I am a fucking idiot...'
'Well, that did cross my mind,' replied Robert. Suddenly, the heat inside the boiler suit seemed to recede. Robert continued. 'Look if Jim had a secret, and it's an open secret, could you let me into it?'
'So you don't really know then? He was a user of heroin, we just found out when he was stripped for the post mortem and the result indicates this.'
Robert stared then laughed. 'That's rubbish, two weeks ago; we went to the swimming together, I would have seen needle marks on his arms.'
'You're wrong Robert, but you're right as well... he injected into his toe.'
Robert's eyes went from Eddings to Feeney who nodded.
Feeney stared at him. 'You expect us to believe that you didn't know?'
The heat in the boiler suit increased. 'Are you telling the truth?'
'He is Robert; do you want to tell us anything?'
'Likes of what?' Robert said mystified
'Like you fucking set him up!'
Robert rose from the table, and went head to head with Feeney, Eddings just sat impassively. Feeney backed away from Robert.
'It would be better if you sat down Robert, or do you prefer Rab?' said Eddings.
'Joe, go and bring a pot of tea... for three.' Feeney glared at Robert, then left.
'What do you prefer to be called Robert or Rab?
'Anything but a liar,' replied Robert. 'You would think it was his partner that had been killed.'
'That's the problem Robert; he thinks you are not showing any emotion.'
'And what do you think?' asked Robert. Eddings didn't reply immediately.
'I've got an open mind, that's why I am a detective. You have to look at this from our point of view, you go to the chip shop, he gets shot, and he takes heroin, and you don't know...' he shrugs his shoulders.
'Are you telling me that you just looked at Jim and noticed he's a junkie right away, I'll bet you and Sherlock were surprised as me, go on admit it.'
'We were shocked, I'll give you that,' replied Eddings,' he continued,' you go in for chips, your partner gets shot. Look I will lay my cards on the table; we are looking to see if you were involved in this...'
'Naw, you are kidding, I thought I was coming to a snowman competition,' screamed Robert.
'Don't shout Robert, it doesn't help you.'

'As I was saying, we are trying to ascertain if you had something to do with this murder, you might be worried now, but if you are in the clear, we will make sure that you are one hundred per cent innocent.'
'And am I meant to be thankful for this, being the number one suspect?'
Feeney came through the door with a tray of tea and biscuits he places them on the table.
'Has he wanted to make a statement yet?'
Eddings looked at him, 'No, statement, no need, I don't think he was involved, not at this time, anyway.'
'You have your opinion, but I think he's up to his ears in it,' replied Feeney.
Robert poured his tea, added milk and a sweetener.
'By the way, Sherlock, have you given a DNA sample?'
'No, why would I want to do that?'
Robert smirked. 'Have you something to hide then?'
Feeney slams down the tea pot, and grabs Robert.
'You fucking set him up! You're a lying murdering bastard.'
Robert was tempted to defend himself in a robust manner; he thought that would play into their hands. 'If you want to go ahead with me Sherlock, allow me to take the snowman outfit off, then we will sort this out.'
Feeney looked at Eddings seeking approval.
'What are you looking at him for; does it need two of you? What do you want to do then, Sherlock?'
'Anytime, anytime...' Feeney replied.
Eddings pulled his partner away. 'Take the tea back to the canteen.... now!'
Feeney left with the tray. 'Sorry about that Rab, he can be emotional at times.'
'He has a problem that's for sure...' Robert replied.
Eddings mood swung to visible anger. 'Problem... what problem, he doesn't have a problem?'
'Anger, he doesn't know how to control it.'
'Oh, and you are an expert..?'
'He has violent anger; he is going to hurt someone, if he can't channel his rage somewhere else.'
'That's your uneducated opinion, but he is not here helping with enquiries.'
'And I won't be here much longer,' replied Robert.
'You'll be here as long as I say you'll be here,' pointed out Eddings.
'I will be here as long as I am assisting, not helping with enquiries. I want the assistance from the Police Federation Legal Dept.'
'So you must have something to hide then, maybe Joe is reading you correctly?'
'I am requesting the services of the Police Federation, please!'
'They could be hard to contact, you know Liam Macintosh, likes to have long lunches, liquid lunches, he could be sleeping it off,' taunted Eddings.
'Well, you'll just have to try then will you, from now, this moment; I am saying nothing till the Federation representative is in my presence.'
'If you take that attitude, suspicions will arise, and you know how stories can get into the Press.'
Robert grabs Eddings and pulls him towards him. 'You fucking get the Federation now,' he throws him and he collides with the door, the noise reverberates along the corridor Feeney comes in just in time to see Eddings rise from the floor.
Feeney moves towards Robert. 'Do you fancy your chances with me?'
Robert calmly pulls the upturned chair and places it neatly flush to the table. 'I fancy putting money on me and I think your partner would as well.'
He moves towards Feeney.
'Forget it Joe,' said Eddings.

***

Linda made the train with a minute to spare she had officially been in Edinburgh as a member of a quango on environmental issues. Green issues were being sought, she was a great supporter of renewable energy; energy costs were having a negative impact on small and large business users, electricity and gas prices were also hitting domestic consumers. She had used the time in Edinburgh to her advantage, her inherited row of town houses in the New Town were being refurbished she took a stroll to see if the work on these beautiful houses were progressing. Always inclined to go in to inspect the work personally, she changed her mind and observed from the pavement and was pleased to see a whirl of activity on the final house being refurbished. She had received very generous offers from property companies for the town houses and rejected them out of hand. Prestigious tenants were straining at the leash for the lease of these properties.

One of her investor friends had submitted an offer in writing to her solicitor for the town houses. The Scottish Executive was acutely interested in acquiring the town houses for top level Civil Servants. She was able to produce the figures from the private companies to the Scottish Executive; however, as she was a supporter and campaigner for the establishment of a Scottish Parliament, she would be willing to lease the town houses to the Scottish Executive for less money. This she did, for five pounds less. This way she could not be accused of cashing in on her influence in the Scottish Executive.

Furthermore, when any VIP's were in the Dundee area, she would invite them to her mansion free of charge to the Scottish Executive. This generous offer had been taken up many times. She was sitting in First Class; her costs would be refunded by the Scottish Executive, the steward enquired if she would like a drink from the well-stocked trolley.

She chose a gin and tonic and she asked for the receipt by rote. She slipped her shoes from her feet and felt better instantly.

On the front page of the Edinburgh Evening News was the spiralling cost of energy. Companies were asking the Scottish Executive to subsidise them. She released a wry smile; little did she know that a problem awaiting her would be related to energy. She arrived in Dundee to be greeted by the bill board of the Evening Telegraph; Romans set to pull out of Dundee' this was not the last legions of the Roman Empire; this was a factory near her home in Broughty Ferry, she had a friend who previously sat on the board as a non-executive member for Romans.

Romans had been in the city for over twenty five years, they had made assorted rubber products for industry and consumers. They were the best paying employer's in Dundee for factory workers who earned over twenty- thousand a year. The factory employed over two thousand people.

She hurriedly made her way the news kiosk at the station to buy the Evening Telegraph. She took a taxi from the station, and devoured the front page news. The gist of the story was that the factory was a voracious user of electricity. However, their products were becoming un-competitive due to the spiralling cost of energy. In fact, Romans had a working- party over in China at the moment with a view to relocating the factory from Dundee. She was mortified.

The Chinese Government had identified several sites where the factory could be set up. The Chinese Government had offered incentives; from building a bespoke factory at little cost to Romans; and exemption from all taxes for five years. Reading between the lines as a business woman, she knew what she would do. She explored the disturbing thought of all the new occupants of the new houses in Broughty Ferry. If the factory closed, this could be the start of a housing price crash, which in turn, affected pubs, restaurants, not forgetting Council Tax returns. She would contact the former non-executive board member to establish if this was a fact or sabre rattling. When she had established the facts, she would contact her MSP lover, to find out if Romans had been in contact with the Scottish Executive. Why hadn't the local MSPs or MPs not had an inkling this was in the air?

She was still devouring the story when the taxi came to a halt outside her house. She paid the fare, and took the receipt and walked up the driveway to her house.

If Romans did withdraw from Dundee the city would take years to recover, if it did recover. Surely, there was something that she could think of? She had a pre-arranged meeting with the Chamber of Commerce; there would be only one subject raised and discussed at the meeting; she would make sure of that.

***

Ian was on the steps of Dundee Sheriff Court, enjoying a cigar. The rest of the solicitors' were enjoying a tête-à-tête amongst themselves. They overtly shunned Ian; he blew circles of smoke into the air. He glanced at the circle of five, four ex- High School of Dundee pupils and one ex- failed entrepreneur and pub owner, who was looking at him in a contemptuous manner, Ian could hazard a guess that he didn't suffer from anorexia. If only he knew that they despised him; the one and only reason that they were talking to him, were they knew Ian spoke to him on occasions. They were always fishing for information about Ian. The cigar smoke had a pungent smell to the group of solicitors, but to Ian this smell was sweet success. The VAT man had cometh, and walked away empty handed. Ian had picked numerous flaws that were minute, but they were still legal flaws.

The VAT men who walked into his client's pub and aggressively demanded that the gaming receipts should be displayed there and then were dismayed to find three months later in court; that the pub had been sold two hours earlier than planned and his client was just helping while the new owner was at his solicitor's office. Ian had been advised about the visit by one of his contacts. He had brought forward the sale in anticipation of the VAT officials arriving he would not be the de-facto owner. Even if his client was the legal owner the charges were spurious to say the least. A new inspector had come to Dundee and wanted to make a name for himself; when he was the inspector in Glasgow numerous court cases he had instigated were thrown out through lack of evidence.

He was advised to move to Dundee as his *talent* would be more conducive there rather than Glasgow; he was assured this was a promotion. When the hapless inspector took the witness stand Ian was able to build up a case that he was a vindictive man and was ostracised to Dundee because of the many 'no case to answer to' acquittals. He was out of control and he was sent to terrorise upstanding publicans in Dundee.

When the alleged evading of taxes were the fulcrum of the case, discrepancies in the procedures that the inspector had taken were openly ridiculed. However, the nub of the matter was that his client was not the legal owner of the licensed premises when the raid took place; the word raid was peppered throughout his legal argument. The inspector feebly explained that the ownership had been brought forward to impede or weaken his case. He could not explain when this impromptu business arrangement was arranged and by whom. He was respectfully informed by Ian his narrow opinion differentiated from established facts. The Crown deserted the case. The Sheriff opined that was a wise move

Another solicitor came down the steps from the Sheriff Court and made his way towards Ian, who was shocked at his dishevelled appearance. The group had their envious eyes fixed on him.
'How are things going then Grant?' Grant eyes said it all, they were losing their shine.
He gave a quick glance to the group watching him, and muttered 'fucking awful.'
Ian threw the cigar in the direction of the solicitors.
'C'mon let's take a walk.' They walked down the steps of the Sheriff Court, in the direction of the Abertay University; Ian took off his gown, wrapped it up neatly and placed it under his arm.
'How bad are things?'
Grant stopped in his tracks. 'Do you really want to know, I mean really?'
'Give me the unvarnished truth, Grant, you look like shit and you smell like shit.'
'Thanks Ian...are you trying to build up my confidence by any chance?'
'I am trying to help you, but if you don't tell me your problem how can I help, spit it out.'
'Okay, you ask for it but its problems not a problem. I am paying the mortgage on my credit card; clients are cancelling appointments at the last minute on a regular basis.

I know my clients' are the scum of the earth, but I went into Law to help these people. The Lease on the office runs out in six- months' time I have an option to lease for another four years, you can imagine the increase I'll be paying. If business doesn't pick up soon, I'll have to go back into the pub game.'

'Who do you think is behind the cancellations then?'

'Does it fucking matter,' replied Grant exasperated?

'Of course it does, who is behind it?'

'Adam Bingham, are you not surprised at that? His voice sounding resigned to defeat.

Ian grabs him by the arm. 'So that's it then, you are giving up on your Law career, because of him?'

'Grant, I'm really, really, disappointed in you, where has the fight in you gone?'

Grant throws Ian's hand off his arm, his face full of hate and anger.

'That's easy for you to say! You have money and success, and businesses coming out your ears, I have fifteen clients, paying the minimum Legal Aid Fee, I'm finished...'

'Are you going to allow Adam Bingham and his pals back there to finish you?'

Ian's thumb is jabbing back at the four solicitors observing them from the steps of the Sheriff Court.

'They have probably cancelled your clients.'

Grant is incredulous.

'C'mon, Grant, you know how Bingham works? He cajoles the junkies and shoplifters to cancel with you, then he calls them up, your pals back there, tells them he has clients piling up, looking for a solicitor, they pay him a commission. Don't tell me you didn't work that out?'

'Of course I knew, Bingham was behind the cancellations, but I think you are way off the mark with them,' his head nodding towards the Sheriff Court.

'Let's walk back.' Ian is amazed at Grant's naivety, he was tempted to say that his mother probably taught them, but he didn't want Grant to segue onto another matter.

   They turn on their heels, and walk for a minute in silence. Grant's head is leaden and he is gazing at the pavement. Ian knew he is in despair; he has to break the silence.

 'Times that tough; that you are looking for pennies on the pavement?' Grant lets out a laugh, his head levels out.

'I'll get through this, I always have.'

'That's better, when we get into view of the vultures; smile as though you have just had twenty clients pushed into your lap'

' I wish, I wish, that was the case...'

'I'll send the files round about three; they are straight forward, breach of the peace, shoplifters, low-level crime. That will tide you over, and if Bingham gets in touch with you, just tell him Mr Williams sends his love.'

Grant grabs his arm. 'Are you serious?'

'You're hurting my arm, of course I am serious, friends help friends don't they?'

He releases his iron grip. 'I can't tell you how thankful I am, I really can't, you have saved me from a death sentence.'

'No worries.

***

   Liam McIntosh bursts in the room. 'How are things Robert, have they been treating you with respect?' He brings his briefcase down with a loud thump on the desk; he takes out a note pad and places it beside the briefcase.

'Believe it, or not Liam, according to him;' pointing at Feeney, 'I am up to my neck in this murder'

'Is that right Mr Feeney?'

'I think Robert, is a wee bit emotional...'

'Did you say Robert was up to his neck in this murder, if it was murder?' McIntosh asked aggressively.

'I never said that, Eddings will back me up on that,' replied Feeney.
Eddings nodded. McIntosh puts his hand to his ear. 'I'm sorry, I missed that, was that a yes or a no?
'Yes, I agree with my colleague...'
'And which colleague is that... Robert?' He stands against the wall.
'No, no,' a flustered Eddings continued, 'Feeney never said Robert was up to his ears in this enquiry'
'So it's not a murder, as yet, is that correct,' badgered McIntosh?
'It's not a murder... yet,' interrupted Feeney.
'Sorry, I was addressing Mr Eddings; Robert is assisting you as his colleague was found dead in suspicious circumstances, am I calling this correct?'
'You are,' said Eddings.
'Has Robert assisted you fully; in your enquiries; and I mean by that has he voluntarily gave you a sample of his DNA, and answered all your questions?' Eddings and Feeney look at each other. Well? Has he assisted and answered all your questions, yes or no?'
'Yes he has,' said Eddings.
'Then get him out of that white suit, into the shower and get his clothes... now, he's going home, I'll need the forensic report on his uniform when it's completed. I'll see you out the front in ten minutes, do you fancy a pint?'
Robert stood up and placed the chair against the table. 'I could do with a pint now Liam.'
'I thought you could do with a shower and a pint you must be sweating like a pig in that suit. Mr. Eddings will escort you through to the showers, then to your locker, where you can get your clothes. Tell me when you are out of the shower then all four of us will inspect your locker, photograph and note the contents of it, you will then get dressed then we'll go for that pint, does that sound reasonable?' He looks at Eddings and Feeney. They look at each other again. 'It's not a hard question.'
'That's okay with us,' replied Eddings.
'I thought so.' McIntosh winked at Robert, he moved away from the wall and returned the notepad back into his briefcase.
Feeney is irritated. 'You do realise that Robert could be called in to clarify matters sometime in the future?'
'Oh, what clarification is that then?'
'The forensics will be coming in with their report soon, and let's hope there is nothing unusual when the forensic team examine his uniform.' Feeney smiled.
McIntosh stifled a yawn. 'I'm sure that you will keep Robert informed... and myself. C'mon Robert, it's starting to smell in here.' Robert follows McIntosh out the door.
'He really thinks he is some kind of top lawyer, when he is just a piss head,' stated Feeney.
'McIntosh knows his stuff... I know he has completed an Open University degree in Law,'
'Law by numbers, a total joke and he is backing a loser in this one. The forensics should be through about the two young lads as well... it would make our life easier if the bullets came from the same gun, we would know that we have three murders from the same gun,' replied Feeney.
'If that was the case, we would have to establish a link. Up till now we know Swithers was a user of heroin, if the two young lads are junkies, then that point's to drug involvement. We start from that premise,' said Eddings.
'For a police officer to use heroin, raises more than an eyebrow, but to have him killed... he was involved in something big, how big is anyone's guess.' Eddings nodded in agreement.
Feeney is becoming more manic in his theory. 'His partner conveniently nips into the chip shop; you're not buying that shit are you?'
Eddings is annoyed at Feeney's impatience. 'You are fixated on Robert Lotus, a law abiding police officer of the old school, have you thought maybe someone is trying to set him up?'
'Yes that entered my head for a second, he is involved up to here,' his hands are parallel to his neck.

'I'm not so sure… we have to delve into Swithers private life, his wife, was she aware he was taking heroin? Was she herself taking it, after all she is a nurse, where is their house? How much of a mortgage do they have, insurance policies, investments, bank statements, credit cards, there must be clues in there,' replied Eddings.
'I know all that, background stuff, you put a couple of men on to Swithers bank accounts, and I'll go through our friend Lotus, I'll link him with the execution of Swithers,' said Feeney.
'No… you stick to Swithers, and I'll go through in a clear concise manner, and examine every facet of Lotus' habits and social life.'

***

McIntosh and Robert are sitting in the Trades Bar in Union Street.
'That Feeney fucking loves himself; doesn't he?'
McIntosh pulls the pint reluctantly from his lips. 'He gets results, legal or otherwise, you've got to admire him for that.'
'What do you mean?'
'Well… put it this way, when he was in the Drug Squad, there were rumours that some officers were understating the amount of drugs, the dealer wouldn't argue with that, he would still be going to the High Court, but it would be better for him to be charged with half- a -kilo of heroin rather than four kilos of heroin. The same with the money; half a kilo of heroin and five grand, rather than four kilos and fifty grand.'
'And Feeney put an end to this scheme?
'Robert, it's hard to believe isn't?'
'I can't believe that…Feeney having a moral compass?' Robert wasn't convinced.
'He wanted the officers involved in this charged with corruption as well as dealing in drugs, but it was covered up.
'They resigned, and Feeney was promoted, big office, big car and of course a big salary. That was his pay off. You are not the only one, who doesn't take to his sunny disposition.'
'He is not squeaky -clean then, he's just less corrupt as the corrupt drug officers,' retorted Robert.
'I know that, you now know that, but he is still a good police officer, even though he is an arse hole…another lager then?'
'Yes… I need another and another.'
McIntosh went to the bar, a man in his late fifties engages him in conversation Robert is spooked by this; the man keeps turning his head towards Robert but avoids eye contact. McIntosh is pulling the man towards him, whispering in his ear, the man is glancing at Robert again. The barman has left the lagers on the bar; Robert is unnerved when the man pays for them. McIntosh makes eye contact with Robert, then turns his head quickly away, the man nods towards the lagers on the bar and walks away. McIntosh grabs the lagers and returns.
'Was that a friend then?'
McIntosh looks irked as he stares around the bar.
'That was one of drug squad that resigned; he's heard already that you had Swithers taken care of because of some involvement in drugs.'
'Who told him that then?' Robert was visibly shaken by this revelation.
'Feeney.'
'I just can't believe this, why is he doing this to me?'
'Because he's a vindictive bastard, that's why.'
Robert takes a long drink and places the lager on the table; he clearly expects another lager from McIntosh. 'Why would Feeney tell a corrupt ex-drug squad colleague about me, I can't understand that?'
'He's fishing for information. Another lager?'
Robert is startled. 'What information?'

'Information what happened to your colleague, and where the investigation is going. Do you want another lager?'

'Yes, another lager please, don't give him any information, he'll probably sell the info to the newspapers.'

'You have to learn to relax, no one can blame you for being agitated your colleague has just been murdered. People are just curious, that's all. I'll go up and get the lager.'

'Fair enough, but don't give a chapter and verse of the events of the last couple of hours.'

'I won't, I'll try and find out what he has heard; if he has heard anything. I won't be long.'

The pub is filling up, he looks at the clientele some are laughing and joking. How he envied them.

***

Grant McEwan is on the telephone in his cramped untidy office, files are everywhere; floor and desk. He allowed the cleaner to seek other employment, as he couldn't pay her anymore.

'As I told you earlier Adam, I don't need the loan, I received a better offer from Mr Ian Williams; he said he knows you very well... hello Adam... I thought you had gone; the line went silent as I was explaining, Mr Williams is lending me money at a very competitive rate. I will be renewing the lease on the office, thanks for asking, yes business is picking up as well, I will be exercising the option on the lease and I will be taking up the option to secure the empty office next door, with the lease for the next ten years. Thanks for the call, talk to you soon, bye'

He is leaning on the chair with his feet on top of the files on his desk. He removes his feet from the desk and walks over to the neat stack of files to the right of the door he picks them up; he is delighted at the hefty weight of them. He places them down on the chair, removes other files from the desk, and then takes the files from the chair onto the newly acquired space on the desk. He sits down on the chair, and counts them with his finger touching each one in turn, forty- five, forty -six, forty seven.

'Ian you are an angel.' He cries out loud. Grant smiles for the first time in months; he was totally aware that Ian would call in the favour sometime in the future, whether next week or the next decade, the favour would be called in. But this was now; and he saw a future not entirely rosy, but definitely a tinge with a reassuring red hue. He looked around the office with a sense of shame and embarrassment; the office was a mess, a burglar would have left it tidier. The windows had a thick layer of dust upon them, and he noticed for the first time the air was not fragrant.

He moved towards the window, he could see where he had written telephone numbers in the dust. He was so embarrassed, had he lost that much self- respect? He opened the window and air rushed in accompanied by the din from the streets. This was music to his ears; he welcomed the sound of humanity. He stared at the throng of people going about their daily business; soon he hoped a proportion of them will be making their way to his office where they can unburden their troubles to him, albeit at a price. He moved away from the window and called the cleaning company to arrange a cleaner for Monday. Pride was once more in his voice.

CHAPTER FIVE

Linda Simpson was having a meeting with the Chambers of Commerce in the Lord Provost's Office. The oak panelled office with the large walnut table had chairs for twenty people. Seventeen chairs were all filled. The empty three chairs attracted ominous stares from the overspill that stood all around the walls of the room. Trade Union officials were present as well as local councillors, MP's and MSPs. It had been agreed no Press were allowed to remain in the office when the meeting commenced, senior management had been covertly brought in earlier; they did not want to be button- holed by the Press when entering the City Square offices.

When the Press had departed, the management from Romans took the three empty places at the table. It was quite obvious that they didn't appreciate being held in another office until the Press departed. The meeting started with startling bald facts. The senior manager from Romans insisted, that what he was preparing to say would bring hurt, anguish and anger to the people of Dundee. There was a sharp intake of breath around the table, colour drained from many faces, colour replaced white pale faces, as relentless anger built up. The manager went on to insist, that he be allowed to read the prepared statement in full without Interruption. All eyes were directed to the Trade Union representatives. They all nodded like compliant martinets, what else can they do? The manager read aloud the last will and testament of Romans, patronisingly he wished to place on record his thanks to the workforce. In over twenty –years there had never been a single dispute that had halted production. His monotone voice droned on and on, thanking everyone

The Trade Union official, felt as if he was at the Oscars; he tried to follow what was being said, but his whirring mind was constantly reminiscing. The workforce and management had grown old together but now it was the end and nothing it seemed could change the wind that would bring heartache to the work force. He brought his mind to the task in hand. The manager was on the last paragraph of the prepared statement. Romans have been up front with the Trade Unions, energy costs were the principal reason that the factory would close, and the Chinese government were offering financial assistance to Romans, the British government and other agencies could not or were not prepared to offer any financial packages. While the Trade Unions looked after their members, Romans had shareholders to protect, and paradoxically, the Trade Union Pension fund was a shareholder. They agreed to close the factory and relocate to China, because it was in the Pension Funds interest. The manager concluded that if the closure went unopposed from the Trade Unions, redundancy terms that were already generous, would be increased by fifty per cent. This placed the Trade Unions in an invidious situation. If they opposed the closure, the members' would say that the Union cost them money. If they went along with the closure, they would be accused of selling out the work force, then the malicious canards would circulate; that they had taken back – handers; and money had been placed into secret bank accounts.

Certain facts would arise and add credence to these malicious rumours; the Trade Union official had placed a deposit on a four bed roomed detached house in Castle Green a new development in Ballumbie; a short distance from the factory. He was not showing any concern how he was going to pay the hundred thousand pound mortgage, on the purchase price of two hundred and fifty thousand pound. It would all be perception; the rumour mongers would point out the quarter of a million pound house and say, 'someone has done well, out of the closure.' The perception would be that he had accepted a bribe from Romans, and then bought the house. He had inherited his mother's ex- council house and had sold it for a hundred and two thousand, plus the money from the sale of his own house, would still leave him with a sizeable mortgage. The facts always came a poor second to a salacious rumour.

The manager placed the last page on the desk, his two colleagues looked approvingly at him he invited questions. The Trade Union official looked at the manager, he had no notes this was from the heart.

'I was extremely disappointed in the manner in which management had leaked the news to the Evening Telegraph first then broke the news to the Trade Unions.

The Trade Unions would explore every avenue to keep the profitable factory open. My national officials are meeting with Government Ministers next week. I would like to point out to the politicians that they are all in marginal seats, and if they are seen to be doing very little; they would be out of a job as well. In the past the Dundee Electorate had thrown out Winston Churchill on his ear. Whether the politicians liked it or not, they were involved, and they knew it. Troubled times had entered this room, all the people who were present would be praised or vilified by future generations.'

   The managers' looked uncomfortable at this stark statement, closure looked far from certain. Silence came and went after a long twenty seconds. Linda Simpson was perceived by everyone in the room, including her MSP lover, as a light-weight, born into money, and failing to grasp real life, asked the first question.

'Taking an extreme pessimistic view if the factory does indeed close, are there any plans for the site?'

The manager briefly consulted with his colleagues then replied no plans were in place.

Linda came back at him. 'I was told by someone, that I can't name, that Romans have had a quotation for the demolition of the factory, is this correct.'

All eyes were fixed on the manager. 'I am aware for insurance purposes, and that some costs must be prepared for the shareholders report, there is nothing sinister in this, and I am disappointed that you are trying to project Romans in an unflattering light.'

'I want to see the factory remain open, after all it is profitable, I just can't see the indecent haste in which you want to close the factory'.

The manager started to shift uneasily in his chair.

'I think political capital is your aim... at this meeting, nothing else, you are not interested in the work force.'

Linda smiled at him. 'I will ignore that misplaced comment; is it true that you have had the land that the factory stands on valued as well?'

'Again, that is for the shareholders report,' the manager said exasperated.

'If another buyer came in and wanted to buy the factory, would Romans be difficult to deal with?'

'Do you have someone in mind?' asked one of the manager colleagues.

'Oh, you startled me; I didn't know you are allowed to talk.'

Linda's stock rose in the eyes of the Union officials. She was onto something unsavoury; what did she know? She was like a dog with a bone; she would not give it up. The managers' air of control and confidence had evaporated.

'I am of course talking hypothetically... if a third party showed a genuine interest in buying the factory, would Romans be difficult to deal with?   The manager took a deep breath, and abandoned the monotone management speak.

   'Look, don't try to play games here; you know as well as I there is no interested party, third or otherwise. Don't play politics with people's lives, and build up hopes, when there is no foundation.'

'All I am trying to do is establish facts, if a buyer comes in and wants to acquire the workforce as well as the factory, will you sell it to them, and if not, why not?' Linda asked in a pleasant but icy manner.

   'If a bid comes in it will be considered, by the Board, but till then, you should deal with the here and now not mystery buyers, make no mistake I am addressing everyone in this room, Romans are relocating to China, full stop.' The Lord Provost had seen jobs come and go. Many well -known and high- profile political figures had been in this office, but this woman, had something about her. She was more impressive than the historical mentioned political giants. Now was the time to pour oil on troubled waters.

   'Would anyone like tea or coffee?' Before anyone could reply, Linda interjected.

'No, it would be inappropriate to drink tea, when we are discussing the fate of thousands of families... but thanks for the offer Lord Provost.

'We are still trying to establish if Romans would be willing to sell their profitable factory, or had Romans an alternative plan for the site?'
The manager's patience was diminishing. 'You have heard my reply to your questions, is there anything else?'
The Union Official piped up. 'Have you plans for the site if, Romans leave Dundee?'
'No plans, we are taking this day by day, we want an orderly closure, with your members receiving the most generous redundancy terms ever offered. Do not build false hopes from someone who has never done a day's work in her privileged, cosseted life. She was an accomplished actress when she was at a Swiss finishing school....As we have seen today.'
Linda refused to take the bait.

   The manager's colleagues passed around the table the terms of an orderly closure. Employees who had over twenty years' service they would receive sixty- thousand pounds, which was two thirds of the workforce. The other third would receive forty- thousand, whether they had five years' service or fifteen. The bribe was gilded. No one in the room apart from the management team was aware that the redundancy terms would be splashed across the Evening Telegraph that evening.

***

   Eddings and Feeney are in their car in the small car park on the Law; one of the few places that you can view Dundee in a three- hundred and sixty degree vista. They had the forensic reports on the two youths who had been shot. The bullets that killed them came from the same gun that killed the police officer outside the chip shop. The youths had been shot less than an hour apart. The police officer was shot thirty- six hours later. Feeney is comforted that they had all been shot from the same gun. All he had to do now was connect Robert Lotus to the youths. Eddings interrupted his thoughts.
   'Well, what's the theory?'
'Nothing just now, but give me time...time is what I have plenty of.'
'Do you not think it is just too easy to link the three bodies, all killed from the same gun, it could have been different killers?'
Feeney had another theory for Eddings. 'Or it could have been someone contracted to kill all four of them including Lotus... you seemed to be surprised at this.'
'God, you haven't half changed your mind! What brought this on?'
'I know that McIntosh is well in with all the men, and he can't keep his mouth shut, sober or otherwise. If everyone thinks we are after Lotus, we can run a parallel investigation, one on Lotus and the other on the killer or killers. Lotus is involved in something, I don't know what, but he is involved,' said Feeney.
'McIntosh has plenty of clout with the men, I told you he is well respected, even though he is fond of the odd shandy, but he is smart as well as devious,' replied Eddings.
'As long as he thinks we have Lotus marked down for setting up his partner that will keep him occupied. Swithers' funeral is tomorrow; I'll visit his widow next week, and ask questions. If she is trying to hide anything, let's hope grief will bring something to the surface, you concentrate on Lotus he's more likely to bond with you rather than me.'
'That's what I had in mind, the bank statements, from the last five years should be through in the next couple of days, then you'll have a clearer picture of their spending habits, same goes for Lotus, I'll ask him to furnish us with his bank statements, and if he has any investments for the last five years. He'll cooperate.'
Feeney is not convinced. 'I wouldn't bet on that, he is one devious, lying individual.'
'Softly, softly is our approach, this bawling and shouting has not been productive.'
'We have to make inroads into the case, but I can't be bothered with this political correctness, it just slows things down, but I will go along with your strategy, for as long as it produces results.'

Eddings is pleased and surprised to hear this.

***

The Trade Union official pressed the button of the video com on the wall of the entrance, it was answered immediately, he didn't have time to say who he was.

'Come on up,' said Linda. The gates silently opened and he meandered up the gravel winding drive. He looked all around him; this is a different world, beautiful trees and flowers in abundance. If there is a Heaven let's hope it's like this. This was the Baronial Mansion that the Jute Baron Walter Simpson built, or more accurately the workers' who worked twelve- hour shifts built. The Mansion came into full view now, his mood changed from disgust to envy, this is absolutely beautiful he thought, he came to a temporarily halt to observe the many gargoyles that seemed to be peeping at him.

'Are you going to stand there all day?' She was smiling. He was embarrassed, that she had caught him gazing adoringly at her house.
'You can't just walk by without absorbing the beauty of this house,' he replied.
He quickened his step, she elegantly came down the stone steps to greet him, she held out her hand and he shook it.
'Tea has just been poured, we will take it in the sun lounge, much more comfortable, follow me.'

If he was wearing a cap he would have doffed it, he pulled himself together, and followed her through the long corridor then into the drawing room, then he continued on through to the large sun lounge. Tea and toast were on the small table. He moved the Financial Times and the Courier from the old leather settee. She indicated with her hand inviting him to sit across from her on the chair. He nervously sat down.

'Thanks for coming, at such short notice; I'll come straight to the point, the management at Romans are not telling you the whole truth they will close the factory, no matter what the Trade Unions or for the matter what politicians say. He made that very clear to me. The meeting was intended to be informal and all discussions were meant to be kept within the four walls of the Lord Provost's office. But lo and behold we come out and the headline in the evening paper is 'Workers to accept sixty -thousand pay off.' Brian, he is mounting a dirty tricks campaign against you and the other Trade Union officials. Next week they want you to organise a ballot, so the result is out in the open. If you mount any credible opposition to the ballot they will smear you.'

Brian suddenly lost his appetite; he returned the toast to the plate. 'I am in an impossible position, the workforce *will* vote to close the factory, I'll point out that what they are doing is stealing their children's future away from them.'
She was disappointed in his weak response.

'Brian, that is all well and good and I admire your sentiments, but we must go down the legal route. At the moment, I have information that will greatly assist us in retaining Romans in Dundee. I am unable to tell you where this information has emanated from. However, I am sure you can understand my reticence. All I can tell you at the moment, there is a way to stop the closure for at least two years, but only if the Unions pursue the route that I am suggesting.' Depression reluctantly made way for the incoming rush of endorphins. Brian's posture became rigid, he was curious to hear more. He had spent hours consulting the STUC and the TUC, he wished he hadn't bothered. Their unanimous opinion was cast in stone. 'Romans will close, grab the redundancy money for your members.' Both of these august organisations made it transparent they would not contribute a penny to a futile posturing campaign to retain Romans. His heart sank as he tried to argue his case. When he met the Labour list MSP he was shocked at her lack of grasp on basic economics, and the knock-on effect of the economy of Dundee. He walked her through the figures; he estimated that in addition to the workforce losing their jobs, the sub-contractors who varied from catering companies to window cleaners would lose millions of pounds, when their contracts were cancelled, as well as a minimum of three hundred jobs.

Her solution; 'I can lobby for a zoo to be built in Camperdown Park. That will create jobs to replace Romans. And when Romans close the air quality in Dundee will improve.'

He was astonished at this banal response. But, he kept his anger in check. He thanked her for her valuable time; he stupidly thought that as she pointed out to him over many times in the conversation, that she had vast experience in European Law. She could offer something that could make Romans consider their decision. She offers a pie in the sky prospect of a zoo?

He had a meeting with his MP and informed him of their banal conversation. The MP and former fire-band shop steward at Timex; interrupted him. 'She has never worked in her life, her CV reads Dundee University, Labour Party researcher, then she had to leave London due to a personal problem which aided her relocation to Brussels as a Liaison Communication Director, fuck knows what that is. And then List MSP for Dundee. Don't waste your time with her, and if there are any positive developments tell her fuck all, she will have a Press conference, giving the impression she has been the forefront of the hard-working team. Oh, and as for her Law Degree her only use she has made of that is to scratch her back. She has never practiced Law.'

However, he was not on his own, he had an unlikely ally. The absurdity of the situation sat uneasily with Brian. The TUC, STUC, Labour MSP shrugged their shoulders and told him to accept the closure. At least the MP pointed out the obvious to him; he was on his own. However, in an opulent mansion before his very eyes sat a woman of inherited wealth and a descendent of a vile Jute Baron offering hope.

'Brian, are you listening?'

He nodded. 'Sorry, carry on.'

'Romans will not be keen to move to China. Next year the European Union will have Laws, which prohibit profitable Companies moving to non -EU Countries. If the workforce; vote to close Romans, then they can move to China, legally.'

Brian was puzzled and then exhilarated at this news. He sat back in the leather chair an air of bewilderment overcame him. 'Could we go through this slowly... correct me if I am wrong, the EU will not allow Romans to move out of Dundee to China, in more than a year's time, but Romans can move between now and then.'

'That's correct. The EU anticipated many years ago, that China with its cheap workforce would suck all the factories in Europe towards it; this could cause a slump in employment. The EU accountants; went back to the very beginning when these factories were first set up. The most up to date figures I have is, that ninety per cent of them were giving EU money to help them build the factories and finance the plant and machinery. Romans benefited most handsomely, to say the least.

'The EU will serve a Court Order on these companies prohibiting them from moving Capital and Assets from within the EU. The EU will argue in court that they were entitled to the money that set them up to be a profitable concern, and they are entitled to a share of the profits, from the first year till they leave. The EU intends to put as many legal obstacles in their way as possible to make other conglomerates ruminate, is relocation worth it? Then they will endure a massive consumer backlash that could result in an organised boycott.

'The narrative from the EU will explain that the companies had benefited from assistance from the EU and now they were throwing the loyal workforce onto the scrap heap. And to make matters worse they were relocating to a country with an appalling human rights record. All these factors will be brought into play.'

'Linda you have convinced me, but the workforce will see the large cheques, being waved under their noses; and they will like the smell. They will take their chances in the jobs market; most of them will be able to clear the mortgages on their homes. What also will enter their minds, is Romans pay well, but a large percentage of them hate what they are doing for a living, so they will see the cheques as a passport out of hell.'

Linda was visibly shocked at this. 'I didn't realise that Brian,' she slumped back into the Chesterfield sofa. She thought for a moment then regained her posture.

'On a more personal level Brian, you will be aware that certain information about yourself will make its way into the public's domain, innuendo, that sort of thing.'

'Now what innuendo is this Linda?'

'Your intention to move into a large house, that cost's nearly a quarter of a million, you don't need me to explain to you the whispering campaign that will ensue. Photographs of you playing golf with the management, things that were innocent at the time, but will now take on a new insidious meaning,' explained Linda. She poured the tea. She was studying him carefully; there were no signs of embarrassment or defensive traits. He sat back deep and brought his hands behind his head.

'Just milk please... I have been in the Trade Union movement and seen every trick in the book, nothing will surprise me...'

'Including sending you daughter to a fee paying school; that will not go down well with the comrades,' interjected Linda.

'Hold on! ' He practically jumped to his feet in indignation. 'I am not someone who says one thing and does another. My daughter was being bullied at her school, I spoke to the headmaster, and he did nothing. The bullying continued, in fact it got worse. Again I spoke to the headmaster; again he said he would deal with it. Then words were exchanged. Insulting words from him I may add'.

Linda poured the tea. Brian continued. 'He has a hatred for Trade Unions, he spoke in glowing terms about Thatcher and the wonderful world she had created. Whether he did this as a diversion to steer the conversation away from the bullying that my daughter was suffering; is a matter of opinion. I mentioned to him I agreed with one policy that the Conservatives, championed; his curiosity got the better of him, and he asked me what policy was that. I told him the school's league tables, knowing that he was bitterly opposed to them. I asked him where his school came in the tables, Champions League or relegation?

'He knew that the school was way down in the league tables, and the school had been heavily criticised by Government Inspectors. He ignored the league tables, but he was fuming, what didn't help was that I brought out the newspaper cutting which screamed 'Dundee School Failing Pupils' the article went on, and reported that members' of staff had lost faith in his Leadership. One member of staff was quoted stating the Headmaster was nicknamed 'Conference Charlie' because he spent more time at conferences than in the school. Oh, and he was the Manager of the group that opposed School League Tables. Obviously, because his school was near the bottom, and obviously that didn't colour his views. The meeting ended abruptly, I had effectively demolished all his arguments. The following week my daughter was badly injured in the school, she had been assaulted by two girls, miraculously, my daughter had summoned up enough courage to fight back.

'She had wiped the floor with the two bullies, even though she was badly injured. I was summoned by the Headmaster and was told that my daughter was being excluded for fighting. I told the Headmaster that my daughter was only defending herself. He said because she had raised her hands she was being excluded.

'I told him that the two bullies were well- known troublemakers, and were known to the police, and I was not accepting my daughter being punished. She had been the victim of an unprovoked and vicious assault. He went on and told me their social workers had given them a glowing report. He also told me that the social workers had tried to persuade him that the police should be called in and charges should be pressed against my daughter! But he told me, smiling, that he wouldn't be doing this. I pointed out to him; that the bullies being under care of social workers, might have gave him a clue that they weren't Prefect material. And that they were from a family who dealt drugs. He dismissed this as irrelevant. He said my daughter was excluded for a week, I told him I would be taking him to an Educational Tribunal. He was aghast at this. I told him in the meantime that my daughter would require a Tutor until the Tribunal set a date.

'That's when he lost it he started to scream and shout about, the cost of a Tutor and he had to be at conferences and I was a Communist. No Tutor was ever provided, not even a scrap of homework, so me and my wife stared to educate our daughter ourselves.

'One day; I came home and the house was empty, I shouted on my daughter, there was no response. I went up to her room, and she was hanging from her wardrobe, her face was blue, I ran down stairs grabbed a knife and cut her down. Thankfully, she survived. She was driven to take her own life because of the bullying, and being excluded. Anyway, I won the Educational Tribunal, but I told the panel that the school was badly run, and the Headmaster was a despot. I also told them that I would be seeking an apology from the Education Department for failing to remove a Headmaster who was clearly unfit to manage a school that had weakness and glaring obvious problems. I quoted these damming words from the School Inspectorate's report. My wife and I have cashed in endowment policies; the proceeds will pay for my daughters last three years of her education. That is the reason she is going to Dundee High School.

'Before you say couldn't she be transferred to another State School, the answer was yes. But I couldn't trust other Headmasters' not to be influenced by the despot Headmaster. Even though it is against my principles, my daughter's education comes first. I have spoken to the Rector at Dundee High; I told him exactly what I have just told you, he was horrified. He told me he would be delighted to accept my daughter, he is from a humble background, his father was a Tentor in a Jute Mill.'

'I didn't realise Brian, does anyone else know the background of this case?'

'Apart from my wife and daughter, you are the only person to know. Everyone is aware that my daughter was being bullied, but they didn't know to what extent. They don't know that she was less than a minute from being brain damaged, and less than two minutes from death. I would appreciate this information staying confidential.'

'Of course, 'I hope everything works out for your daughter at her new school... and I'm sure it will.'

'So do I, I am more confident now that I have spoken to the Headmaster; he seems to have a good handle on everything, my daughter seems a lot happier,' said Brian.

'Romans attempting to pull out of Dundee, has added to your woes hasn't it?'

'Everyone is worried or should be worried, some more than others. From the Union's perspective we were pleasantly surprised at your genuine concern at the meeting in the Lord Provost's office, compared to the independent MSP, you can tell he was bored stiff, even when I said that the electorate will throw them out on their ear. The rest of the politicians were worried but he wasn't; maybe he has plans to leave the Scottish Parliament?'

'He's a bully as well,' Linda blurted out. Brian was surprised at this outburst. Linda was embarrassed.

'Sorry, my feelings got the better of me, ignore what I said.'

Brian shrugged his shoulders, and lifted the cup that Linda filled, he was curious and concerned.

'Is everything all right?'

'Everything is okay... sorry, what were we discussing?'

'The MSP, I pointed out that he was not too concerned...'

'That's right, and your observation of him was correct, he looked bored, but he is very, very, interested in Romans. Avoid any contact with him, if you happen to meet him, don't mention that you were here, is that understood?' She was quite forceful. She wanted him to get the point.

'That's fine,' replied Brian who was understandably uncomfortable. Linda rose from the table, she was uncomfortable.

'Thanks for coming Brian.' He stood up.

'Thanks for inviting me. I really appreciated what you had to say. I am more optimistic now than when I entered your house. '

'We have a long way to go, but at least we can pursue the legal route, if that's what the employees want and I am sure when they have all the facts laid out in front of them minds will be changed.'

Brian was not convinced, but he would not succumb to the nagging pessimism that engulfed the factory. 'If I come across any information positive or otherwise I'll keep you informed.'

She led him to the door. They said their brief goodbyes. She closed the door and stood with her back clinging for support on the inside of the door. She looked at the sweeping staircase and the classic paintings that adorned the staircase walls. Nothing could ease her turmoil. Things were difficult at the moment, but much more difficult times lay ahead. Confidence in the future was in short supply. In a perverse way the threatened closure of Romans was a welcome distraction from her own personal problems. If she had one wish it would be to turn back the clock.

She knew that this wish would never be granted, but she continued to battle against the inner feeling of impending doom. The door had worked its magic again. Problems still swirled in her mind, but problems could be eradicated by analysis. She hadn't realised the anguish Brian had been experiencing, but she was sure that the money spent on educating his daughter would be money well-spent. The High School had an excellent reputation, and had alma mater that had contributed to the enhancement of science, education and sport.

***

Robert was enjoying being on gardening leave, but when he left the house, he was acutely aware of cars or individuals that passed his house. He knew that he would be under covert surveillance; McIntosh even gave him the registration of the car that would be following him. Early in the morning he drove up to Birkhill, with the intention of going to his sister's house. But right on cue the black Astra emerged from the slip road and stayed behind him at a discreet distance on the Kingsway dual carriageway. The registration matched McIntosh's information. He abandoned the drive up to Birkhill; instead he detoured to Camperdown Golf Course for a game of golf which he enjoyed. The round of golf gave him time to think, he beat himself up mentally, why didn't he twig Swithers was using heroin? His reasoning countered the pernicious self -criticism, he was *just* a recreational user. This brought him no comfort. McIntosh assured him that he was not an addict.

He had been using heroin occasionally for the last two months. The post mortem, suggested that he used heroin only once before, but this was not conclusive. But he was his partner, he should have known, shouldn't he?

When he completed the round of golf, he went for breakfast at the golf club, and then returned to his car, the Astra was there. Three rows behind his car, no one was in the car, he wondered where the occupants were? As he was placing his clubs in the boot he glanced round the car park and surrounding area. He couldn't see anyone who looked like detectives. He closed the boot, looked around once more then went into the driving seat. He viewed the mirrors no sign of them, he gunned the engine, waited, and then drove off; the black Astra was still stationary in the car park. He made up his mind; he would require another vehicle which had to be cheap and nondescript.

A favour would be called in; he knew the man that would arrange this. He drove into the City Centre and parked in the East Port car park. Again, as he was buying the ticket he didn't notice anything untoward, he returned to his car, and stuck the ticket on the side window. He walked towards the Wellgate Centre, he looked in shop windows, walking slowly; he made his way to the phone box. He dialled and spoke to his contact in code. He was talking to the owner of the auto breakers about an alternator. He was pleased at the response. Robert came away from the phone box fulfilled. He had never been let down by the auto-breaker.

Tomorrow he would have a different car; it would be in the usual place, the keys would be in the glove compartment, the driver's door would be unlocked. He would be able to go home tonight, close the curtains and switch the lights on. He would then exit by the rear door, jump across the fence into the next street and the car would be there in the same spot as before. His wife assumed he was being thoughtful when he suggested she went abroad for a few weeks with her friend, so that she would not be harassed by the Press.

She gave her statement to the police and they were satisfied with her answers, or so it seemed. However, she welcomed the vision of two weeks in a five star hotel in Benidorm, with her fun loving friend.

Tonight he would drive up to Birkhill and think for a few hours, then return to his house. The surveillance team would observe his car outside; and his lounge light on and settle down for the night. To be doubly sure that the surveillance car would not move, he set up a small camera from one of the upstairs bedrooms. It would be fixed on the police car, and he would be able to watch the car via his laptop when he was in Birkhill. He would leave about ten and return at four in the morning, which would give ample time to analyse everything. From the two young junkies murders to his partner's unexpected and horrific demise; he was convinced that Ramage was involved somehow.

Linda Simpson kept popping into his head as well. Then his mind went back to Swithers taking smack; this made his blood run cold. He still found it extremely difficult to accept. Even though the autopsy confirmed he had used heroin. Perhaps this was the red herring? Or was he thinking this because Jim was his friend. Would he come to the same conclusion if it was just another addict found dead in Whitfield? The answer was negative. If his partner was involved in the drug trade, he must have been very careful. Otherwise his friend in the Drug Squad would have known, or had he deliberately omitted to tell him? Every rumour had some substance to it, but there was no rumour concerning Jim, or else he would have heard it. When he was in the house at Birkhill he would retrieve a section of surplus lining paper from the cupboard and use it as a spreadsheet. The Mercedes trip to Liverpool would be his starting point.

***

Mary sat on her balcony, even though it was now late September the temperature was still warm, the sky would start to darken about eight. She placed her book down, and wandered to the other side of the ornamental balcony. She looked all around the surrounding tenements; she was the only one to have a balcony. There had been many objections to the planning committee how it would be out of character, but she was able to convince the planning committee in person, that it was for her family's enjoyment. After all satellite dishes were in abundance, they didn't enhance the tenement. Not long after the balcony was erected, the planning committee came round to see the balcony. All were suitably impressed. They congratulated themselves in so many words.

Even the most belligerent and vociferous objectors were invited, and they too couldn't find fault. The ornamental Victorian balcony was pleasing on the eye. Two years later Health and Safety legislation was halting pleasing additions to similar tenement buildings. Some owners from adjoining tenements applied to have balconies. Their applications were rejected on safety grounds, and that they would have a detrimental and corrosive impact on the buildings. It was rumoured but not substantiated, that the Council were concerned that buy- to- let speculators had purchased far too many flats in the tenements in the Perth Road area.

The flats would be let to students, the planners were concerned that when the students had parties, horseplay would no doubt emerge sometime in the evening. If there were balconies present, there were legitimate concerns that a student or students would have an accident and deaths would occur. Mary was fortunate to have been the pioneer for a balcony; the others were just too late. As a result of the rejected applications enmity was directed at Mary. The owners' who had had their applications rejected knew that the balcony cost her fifteen –hundred pounds, but once it was in situ her property went up in value eight thousand pounds, and that was in a becalmed property market.

Dundee was now in the grip of an avaricious property boom, her flat, courtesy of the balcony was much coveted. She had unsolicited letters from numerous solicitors, advising her that they had clients willing to pay a premium for the flat. Her solicitor strongly advised her to sell; she smiled at this then declined to heed his advice.

Her eyes gazed towards the east of the River Tay; the skyline of Dundee was altering on a weekly basis. Some buildings were less pleasing than others. The first apartments in the dockland area; were a disaster as far as she was concerned. They looked like buildings from the austere Soviet times. Little imagination had gone into them, bland, was the term she used for them.
Non offensive was the builder's description. Her curiosity had defeated her outright hostility towards them. She went to view them, she felt pleased that her perception matched the reality. They were absolutely awful, she apologised in her mind to the Soviet builders. The lounge was spacious if you lived alone and owned a chair. If you owned a cat, one of them would have to go.

After the viewing she felt smug, her spacious flat, or was it an apartment, on the Perth Road was absolutely stunning. She had many arguments with Alan and if she was honest, some physical fights if she lived in those dockland apartments, she wouldn't have room to raise her voice, never mind raise her fists. The building was continuing at the docklands she could see the skeleton steel work taking shape. They were meant to be finished early two thousand and seven. For a one bedroom apartment, the price would be one hundred and twenty-five thousand, she shook her head.

She sipped her tea. They were all sold now. In fact, they were all sold before they were completed. Investors had purchased the one bedroom flats; they would rent them out to students. The Council's vision was the polar opposite; the apartments would be occupied by young professionals; and more importantly the dock land apartments would be a lucrative revenue stream for the Council. The Council Tax base had been diminishing caused by people moving out with the Dundee area. The Council's projected Council Tax revenue was in tatters; the builders had built the apartments but the buyers' failed to materialise. They were bought by investors not nesters. They at first tried to let them to the professionals, but there was not a surfeit of that much coveted class. They were forced to let them to students, to retrieve some of their expenditure.

The Council were also dismayed; students were exempt from Council Tax. The docklands were now populated by students, and seagulls; not a benign marriage. Who made the loudest noise, seagulls in the morning or the students at night? The few foolhardy professionals; who moved into the apartments at the inception, moved out when the students moved in. However, the building continued. Mary placed the empty cup on the table. Her eyes continued away from the dock lands; more high-rise apartments are proliferating the sky line. These buildings were designed for students renting, again no Council Tax income to the hard-pressed Council. It was not just developers who were targeting the lucrative student market it was the Mr & Mrs Smiths; who were borrowing money to finance their dreams to a financial el dorado.

Mary's analytical process concluded that this property boom would crash, not any time soon, but soon enough to catch everyone unaware. If she felt that strongly, why didn't she capitalise on her flat and move to Spain? She was probably living in a flat that could easily attain one hundred and eighty thousand pounds, maybe more. This thought was now a regular visitor, usually after watching those ubiquitous property programmes and accompanied by the bottle of wine that she had as her viewing companion.
If the truth were to be told, she loved Dundee too much, for its many faults and perceived failures she could never leave the city.

Ian had shown her four apartments that he owned and were used by the frequent businessmen that came into the office. The apartments were in the old Dundee Royal Infirmary, spacious and luxurious, with every modern convenience apart from the glaring omission of Sky. There seemed to be a misunderstanding with the other wealthy owners.

The property management company assured Ian that a communal Sky Dish for all the apartments in the block would be erected. The cost would evenly split but this wasn't to be, frustrated Ian arranged to pay for the dish himself, fortunately his four apartments were on the left hand side of the block. He went personally knocking on every apartment door. Every apartment owner on the left hand side agreed with Ian that having a Sky Communal dish would be better than having individual dishes on the block. They were prepared to contribute to the cost.

However, the right hand side of the block they took the contrary view. Some of the varied opinions were that Sky was the opium of the masses, they preferred reading, the others were buy to let, and they saw Sky as an unnecessary cost. Ian politely pointed out that people would rather rent an apartment with Sky rather than without. When this suggestion was dismissed, Ian was quite mischievous. He told them that he would pay for the Sky Dish himself, would you like the engineer to wire up their apartments just in case they changed their minds. Their demeanour changed, feeble excuses came spouting out their mouths, 'maybe, I will sign up to Sky in the future,' and from the buy to let investors 'It will be handy if the tenants want to subscribe to Sky.... and of course I can adjust the rent accordingly.'

Ian ordered the Sky Dish and the engineer wired up the left hand side of the block, he had no instructions to wire up the owners flats that weren't prepared to pay on the right– hand side of the building. The owners were glad to see the engineer erect the grey dish; a white dish would not have been as discreet. The owners on the right- hand side were mystified when the engineer failed to wire up their apartments. Every one of them had the audacity to contact Ian and complain that he had misled them. Ian did apologise to them for the misunderstanding, 'but why should people benefit when they have not contributed?

Mary admired Ian's style, either in interior design or dealing with shysters. Those apartments were always on call twenty- four hours a day. Ian never let them out on the open market; they were strictly for his clients. Ian had mentioned to Mary about his clients, who turned up unannounced, would she mind being on call? He explained that if she agreed, she would pick them up at Dundee Airport then take them to one of the apartments at the DRI Mary, not long being in this job, agreed with alacrity. Ian continued that sometimes she would have to pick them up at Glasgow or Edinburgh. That would not be a problem; that would give her a chance to give the BMW a run out.

Ian anticipated this response, her salary would be adjusted. Mary was embarrassed at this, but she was expecting Ian to offer her some type of monetary award. Within a week, she was asked to go through to Glasgow Airport and pick up a client. The client was in his late thirties, smartly dressed in a black suit, he came off the last London shuttle. He had no luggage only a laptop. He was pleasant, but made it very clear; he didn't welcome questions or small talk.

The journey went quickly, at that time of night the roads were sparsely populated. Mary was glad that the client was not talkative. She enjoyed driving the BMW at one hundred miles an hour; it had been fitted with a radar detector; that warned of speed cameras and hand held speed detectors nearly a mile in advance. She was being asked to collect clients from Glasgow and Edinburgh on a regular basis. She would rather do this than work in the office. Ian was happy enough for her to work from home, sometimes Mary was certain he preferred her to be away from the hustle and bustle of his office. After a number of these trips, Ian asked her if she could suggest any improvement to the flats that the clients were staying in, there was nothing that could be improved on. Fridges were groaning with replenished fine food and various bottles of beer that juxtaposed as equal partners with Krug champagne.

Wardrobes were stuffed with suits to fit midgets to giants; shirts, ties and shoes were in plentiful supply. On the entertainment side the forty- inch plasma television and the latest DVD releases, would satisfy any film critic. No, there was nothing that could be improved on. One thing that unnerved her, there was no computer, and obviously the clients that she picked up all had laptops, maybe for security reasons they preferred their own laptops.

Now that winter was peeking over the hill Ian's Spanish properties would be interesting people with one eye on retirement, or just seeking a winter antidote to the cold damp Dundee climate. She hoped that she would be sent over to Spain, now that warmed her blood. When she was there she had spoken to Marta about golf lessons Marta had told her that she would arrange this, the next time she came over. Ian thought that Mary showed initiative, he thought that playing golf with potential purchasers or clients that had bought apartments, was putting a personal touch to her sales technique.

It was a given that some of the semi-retirees would love to go on the course, but their spouse had no interest in golf. Mary could always make herself available. When playing golf with the semi-retiree, she would enquire how they were adapting and how was the apartment? She would ask if they were missing their families. If they replied that they had grandchildren, and they were missing them, Mary would skilfully bring into the conversation that Ian was going to be building four bedroomed villas around the perimeter of the course, had they thought about trading up? If they any showed interest Mary could drop by that night with the plans, prices were not released yet, but she was sure because they were clients of Ian, he would give them a generous discount. Mary would suggest that their grandchildren would be frequent visitors because the villa had ample room for their daughters or sons and their children. Mary would take the stress out of selling their apartment, because Ian would buy their apartment from them. This would have the desired effect, Ian was cock sure of this, the golfing holidays were burgeoning; he had to turn away disappointed golfers as all his apartments were booked. By buying the apartments from the clients who were upgrading to a villa, he was increasing his property portfolio, thus satisfying the increasing demand for his golf holidays.

Buying existing apartments was more cost effective than buying the new apartments that would be completed in a year's time; they cost an additional thirty thousand euros. The client would receive a loyalty discount on their new villa, thus creating a more personal relationship rather than the numerous estate agents that fleeced naive buyers in Spain. Mary would encourage the client to enquire if their friends would be interested in buying a new villa. They couldn't receive a better recommendation, could they?

Mary was always available if something went askew with the air condition or the shower head needed renewed. Thankfully the apartments and villas were built to a very high standard that she was rarely called upon. Marta was guiding potential business opportunities to Mary from unlikely sources. Marta told her that she had a phone call from a wealthy hotel owner, who was due to arrive at Panoramica with potential investors for his new hotel in Benidorm. He owned two four star hotels near Levante beach. He was planning to build a new five star hotel in that area as well. Could Mary welcome him and his two guests at the entrance and show them to the villa that they were renting for the weekend? Mary acceded to this, and it was a profitable experience. The three Spaniards were impressed by her flawless Spanish as well as her knowledge of the surrounding area. They also liked her can do attitude. The hotel owner had commented that the British people enjoyed coming to Benidorm throughout the year. Mary reminded him it was because of the sunshine and the value for money. He told her that the British taste was becoming more and more sophisticated, three star hotels were being shunned; four and five star hotels, with the accent on being family friendly were becoming more attractive.

He saw a niche market for the ex-pats now ensconced in Spain. When the family came for their week or two weeks in Benidorm, mum or dad or grandparents would sometimes drive down to see their family from various locations in Spain, and then drive home in the evening. He had noticed when he was on the golf course, that there were many English accents.

If Mary could subtlety point out the benefits to the residents in Panoramica, that if they wished to meet their families in Benidorm, he would offer generous discounts, and of course Mary would be well rewarded with a commission; a room would always be available to her and her children at no cost to herself. However, that depended on how much business she generated.

Mary took his business card and the link to the hotel web site. This would be another incentive for the ex-pats to meet their family and friends. Mary would emphasise Benidorm was only two and half hours down the AP7 toll road, and because they were special guests they would have their car valeted before they returned to Panoramica. This was another positive selling point when she was escorting clients around the villas, new apartments or resale apartments. Mary was overwhelmed by the amount of ex-pats on Panoramica who texted if any weekend breaks in Benidorm were available.

Mary received a phone call from the hotelier thanking her for the business that was coming his way. He had placed champagne in the guests rooms as she had suggested. Mary knew that extras like that though unexpected, were undoubtedly welcome.

Soon four and five couples would travel down to Benidorm together, although they all lived in the same complex, most of the couples had only seen each other on the golf course and exchanged brief pleasantries, they had never met socially. Mary was the glue that brought them together. Now they were frequently congregating in her office enquiring about weekend breaks in Benidorm. Mary had found out that some were also interested in acquiring a villa either for themselves or friends, she invited all of them over to the show house, where the potential clients could look over the villa, and the rest could watch the DVDs showing the hotel in Benidorm. While Mary was showing the client the beautifully appointed villa some of the residents could not take their eyes off the forty- inch plasma, and cast their envious eyes over the expansive lounge. When Mary and the client returned to the lounge Mary would make coffee and discuss the benefits of acquiring a villa on Panoramica.

Mary had turned into the go-to person if anyone needed travel information or financial information regarding mortgages. The Bank manager had emailed Ian praising Mary for the amount of clients coming into his branch in Vinaros, the small but bustling town. He in turn had contacted his Head Office in Madrid regarding the sales of property on Panoramica; they allocated additional funds to accommodate the anticipation surge of new mortgage applications. Mary had exceeded Ian's ambitious sales figures, there were no doubt this was down to Mary.

He would not share this information with her; however, she would be well –rewarded in the spring when the sales figures would be collated along with the profits. He had chosen well. The nagging thought in his mind was to persuade his parents to move out to Panoramica for the winter months. This would be difficult but not entirely impossible. He had seen with his own eyes couples older than his parents rediscover a renewed zest for living again. The warm climate in the winter months allowed them to go for walks and have lunch at the Country club. Their pensions stretched further and their diet improved. Exercise was the mantra. They had all the comforts of home, plus the benefit of lower energy bills and satellite television where they could watch the local Dundee news, with their balcony doors open. There were very few people never mind pensioners who could leave their balcony doors open in Dundee in the winter months. Pensioners in particular were under self-imposed house arrest because of the cold and damp weather. If snow engulfed Dundee this caused more restrictions of their mobility. Spain was the place for his parents in the winter.

***

Raymond Andrews knew everything about Ian Ramage. Linda Simpson had confided in him. Ramage didn't know it at the time, but he was the architect of the drugs plan that Raymond and Linda had implemented. He told her every contact he had made over twenty-years as well as the highs and lows of the drug trade; he was able to tell her where the corrupt officers were, not naming them individually, but which city and department they were in.

Raymond brought Linda's money and his stepbrother in contact with Ramage. Ramage was not directly involved because he was laughingly *incarcerated* in Castle Huntly.
This was where he would serve the last year of his prison sentence. Castle Huntly was a relaxed place, drugs were in plentiful supply. Ramage had assiduously befriended a young prison officer over six months. The young officer asked plenty of questions about his wealth. Ramage was understandably coy about his wealth, but his innate inner instinct was that this young officer was in a career that was unrewarding financially and was lacking in intellectual stimulus. He built a rapport with him and flattered him. He tested the young officer to the hilt with various illegal requests; the officer showed no inclination to resist and acceded to his numerous requests, now was the time to spring the ultimate request on him. He told him that in his car was five thousand pounds; the money was secreted in the spare wheel. 'Tomorrow, you will bring in a small package, that's all I ask, it will be in your bin when you get home.

When you are taking rubbish out tonight, it is in an M&S bag. When you arrive at work don't lock the car leave the M&S bag in the boot. When you finish your shift it will be gone simple as that.'

The officer did this without any introspection, he hated this job it was dull and the salary was not consistent with his lifestyle. This lucrative arrangement was repeated until Ramage was released. Ramage advised the young officer where to invest the money, he strongly advised him not to invest in any criminality. The officer assured him he was not interested in anything criminal. Ramage was considered a financial guru in Castle Huntly. He spent most of his time reading financial newspapers and other publications. Other officers came to him seeking advice regarding investments, pensions and mortgages. The sage advice was free.

However Ramage guided them all to an esoteric cadre of Financial Advisory Companies. Unbeknown to the officers these companies were owned and controlled by Ramages minions. The officers' money would be acting as a detergent for the soiled money that had lain dormant in bank accounts offering poor returns; now that money could be used to purchase legitimate investments; notably high-risk bonds. The young misshapen prison officer was advised not to invest in these bonds. He never queried why? This was all perfect cover for him. He was just another officer seeking financial advice.

The Governor also sought out Ramage, but only in his private office. This Canadian had seen every penal system in most of America and Canada. Castle Huntly was a shining example of how redemption should be encouraged. To the outside world, Castle Huntly was seen as a soft option. Most of the public would rather have seen the prisoners breaking rocks and returned to Spartan conditions. However, the academic world had a polarised position that would not change, education was the way forward to the depressing cycle of recidivism and it would save billions over the years and lead to less crime and a more cohesive society. Time would be the final arbiter. The Canadian Governor in unguarded moments used Ramage, not by name, as an example of why education was the key, when he was called before various Scottish Executive committees and think- tanks. Saving money and less repeated offenders was music to their ears. Castle Huntly was to be the model for future 'unsecured rehabilitation behaviour centres.' Prison would be systematically removed over a period of time from the Scottish Executive's lexicon. A new word to describe individuals in URBCs would be 'habitees' not prisoners. There had to be a re-education of public thinking. Sending drug addicts to prison did not achieve anything that could be construed as positive. The cost implications had to be raised in any debate in the Scottish Parliament. The small rump of Conservative MSPs during the emotional Social Justice debate would not countenance that crime committed by drug addicts were linked to poverty. The cost-benefit study that proved that prison had no benefit to the tax-payer; was rejected by the Conservatives. Send them to jail was their mantra.

***

The cacophony of threats could be heard outside in the car park. Differing opinions were evolving into physical threats; the meeting could turn into an orgy of violence. There was no room for anyone else in the canteen despondency was all around. The workforce was divided; the long serving employees were desperate for the factory to shut.

The young employees were vociferous in their opposition; the nights of broken sleep were impairing their judgement.   In the various pubs in Broughty Ferry that the employees from Romans had frequented for years were turning into citadels of animosity and personal hatreds. Certain pubs had become pro –closure; and the other pubs became meeting places for retaining Romans. Animosity would rear its head if any of the opposing factions came face to face in neutral pubs. Alcohol loosened tongues and increased hostility. Inevitably, fists would be exchanged instead of insults. Certain pubs were now no- go areas. Older workers stayed in their own comfortable fiefdoms, The Fort and The Fisherman's, the younger set made Jolly's their meeting place, and then they would move on to The Anchor Bar. Families were being split. In many cases the sons and daughters refused to speak to their parents.

The Father had been instrumental in securing the daughter's boyfriend a job in Romans. Both sides saw the merit in their case but refused to consider the other side's argument. Solomon would have been scratching his head to bring about a mutual solution.

Some had placed their homes on the market; they wanted cash to reduce their personal debts, the shiny new car on the drive which was a badge of affluence; became a symbol of reckless borrowing. Uncharitable neighbours who were in unattractive jobs that paid less than Romans were enjoying the negative stories that had been leaked to the Press regarding the redundancy settlements. There was no escape from the constant rumours either at the factory or in the confines of their homes.

Brian banged the table, the hum of voices receded to a murmur. At the table to his left was Linda Simpson; to his right was the Trade Union Pension Advisor who had flown up from London. 'Thanks for the large attendance; before I begin could I please ask anyone who has a mobile phone to switch it off.' Ringtones are heard all over the canteen; Linda reaches into her hand bag to switch her phone off. Brian glanced out of the cathedral windows; the sky is turning from slate grey to biblical black. Rain starts to assault the large windows. He feels unsettled.
'Okay is everybody settled?' Shouts of yes are hurled back at him.

'Right, to bring you up to date regarding the fate of the factory, Management are still insisting the factory will still close...' voices of disapproval echo from the floor. 'However, we have verified significant information, which may help us keep the factory open. As you know the Union's Pension Fund is a significant shareholder in Romans; the Pension Fund value would increase significantly if the factory closes, in the short term; however, taking a long term view, the fund would benefit more if the factory remained open. Martin Arthur is here, he is the best person to explain,' Brian sits down.

Martin stands up; he is clearly ill at ease. 'I do not wish to raise false hopes, but I am confident that when the full facts are made aware to the Pension Fund Trustees, they will look to the medium to long term view, which is at least five years hence. Thus far, the Management of Romans have indicated to the Trustees, that it is to the benefit of the shareholders that Romans relocate to China. Ergo close this factory. In the short term, that is certainly the case. However, we have ran figures through an independent company, and they have come back to us saying it would be economic madness and detrimental to the Pension Fund to close this profitable factory.

'There is not a single cogent economic reason to close this factory. They stated that opening a factory in China was an excellent business decision, that factory would supply the growing Chinese middle classes, and this would have not any detrimental or material effect on the Dundee factory. They cannot fathom any financial reason why Romans should even consider closing Dundee. They stated that expansion of the Dundee factory rather than contraction would be their advice. There would be a short- term boost to the share price if the factory closes; that would undoubtedly happen, but in the medium to long term the share price could suffer. The economic impact on Dundee will be catastrophic. Let me explain, there are two thousand employees at Romans.

'If the factory was to close, people would down size houses, imagine if this downsizing happens at the same time? In simple terms, prices would be at least depressed, but in my view, there would be a down turn in prices, possibly a crash. Everyone is fully aware that there are new builds coming on stream, add to that, the Romans employees' houses going on the market at the same time... well you don't need me to elaborate. Prices will flat line for years; you will have people offering you less, because you are maybe desperate to sell. That should be in your thoughts when you have the vote on the closure. I will recommend to the Trustees of the Pension Fund that we do not support the closure of Romans.' He sits down. Cheers ring out from the workforce, some older employees walk out of the canteen. They are booed by the majority.

Brian bangs the table to bring some order to the meeting some older employees are exchanging insults with the younger colleagues. Brian continues to bang the table, eventually order is restored.
'Now, we have Linda Simpson, who has something positive to say... I hope.'
Linda sips her water then stands up.

'Martin; is a very experienced actuary, he studies figures in a cold calculating way, that is his job. But I am glad that he has alluded to other unknown reasons why Romans seem to be hell bent on closing this factory, if it was not economically viable; you may not agree with closing the factory, but you can understand their thinking.

'As a shareholder myself, I receive the annual report, usually I go to the Chairman's page. I then read his report, he gives a synopsis how the Company is doing and what the future holds. Profits are up; share price is up twenty- five per cent in the last eighteen months. He went on to praise the work force for their efforts over the last year. This is a puzzle. Romans have four other factories in Europe; Spain, France, Germany and Lithuania. All these factories are profitable; it states this in the Chairman's report. However, the Dundee factory is the most profitable; in fact the Chairman calls Dundee 'the jewel in the crown.' Romans have had a change in Management over the last year. This was due to the incumbent Chairman being incapacitated; he suffered a brain haemorrhage, it was not fatal, but the recovery will be slow. When the Chairman was taken to hospital, an emergency Board meeting was called by Eric Cameron.

'As Vice Chairman he assumed that he would be given a free reign, but the other Board members disagreed; they wanted to plot the same course. Mr Cameron is a very strong willed individual; he used the Chairman's plight to settle old scores. He vetoed steady, profitable course, he unilaterally changed course, hence the proposed closure of Dundee. He made life unbearable for two Board members, coincidentally women that they resigned for 'personal reasons.' He opted onto the Board two of his acolytes. The Board is in a state of flux at the moment; my information is that they are not unanimous in agreeing to close the Dundee factory. Eric Cameron has for the last six months being going round investment companies in the City of London, with an alternative business strategy to the incumbent Chairman. These investment companies commonly known as hedge funds; are not interested in sensible long – term plans, if they can force a company to close a factory that would then see a spike in the share price, they would agree to the closure, then sell the shares take their profits and invest in another company and repeat the same procedure. They will be the key to Romans demise in Dundee or they will be the saviour. Romans principle reason for wanting to cease operations in Dundee is the high cost of energy.

'This undoubtedly will have an impact on the profitability of the Dundee factory. But that will only be in the short term. Romans are not the only business in Britain suffering from high energy costs. If anyone reads The Guardian, they will have read that a pipe line from Norway to Yorkshire is due to be completed in the next few months; gas will be flowing from Norway to Yorkshire in less than a year. In addition the Russian company Gazprom has been buying up energy companies in Europe, they want to sell gas and electricity to Europe.

'The rise in energy prices is because energy companies in Britain have created a shortage to boost their profits and share price to make their companies attractive to Gazprom. In three years' time maximum, energy prices will be cheaper than five years ago, if and only if, Gazprom are successful in purchasing European energy companies.

'Russia has an incalculable amount of gas; they view Europe as a customer waiting and willing to buy their gas. There must be another reason not an economic reason, why Eric Cameron desires to close operations in Dundee. And why the indecent haste to close the factory? I would implore the more senior employees to think and gather all the facts before casting their vote. I am sorry I cannot answer any questions from the floor on this occasion, but if I have any other information positive or negative I will let Brian know, and I assume Martin will do the same.'
Martin nods his head. Linda sits down to thunderous applause.   Brian stands up.
'Thanks for letting the workforce know that information, I was not aware of the Chairman's health problems, I hope good health returns to him soon. It was encouraging to hear your view on energy prices, I wasn't aware of the pipeline, or Gazprom buying up other energy companies in Europe. If energy prices come down, there would be no other reason to close the factory. The candle of hope is burning a wee bit brighter.

He turns to the workforce. 'I hope everyone who wants to take the redundancy package will now have second thoughts, but that is down to the individuals concerned. All I ask is give thought to your colleagues and your families. Your decision will impact on the future generation. They have no vote, but you do. If you vote to reject the closure you will be leaving a living vibrant legacy. I understand how tempting it must be to get away from this factory with money in your pocket. But on behalf of the workforce who wish the factory to remain operational; I ask you to think of them. How many of them have helped you in the past when you had difficulties, either personal or financial? Many of you have been helped by the Social Fund; it was your colleagues' money that alleviated your financial difficulties. This is not emotional blackmail; this is an example of when everyone sticks together we can overcome our difficulties. If we do not have a united workforce, then that is the beginning of the end, the rot will set in. At least have a good think over what you have heard today from not just me but from the previous speakers. I am sure you are all aware redundancy money is tax free up till thirty-thousand, after that the rest of the money is taxed. All that glistens is not gold. Vote in haste repent at leisure' He sits down to rapturous applause and some jeering. The assembled workforce has heard enough; they file out in a sombre mood. Linda and Philip look at each other they can't figure out if Brian has helped or hindered them.

***

Feeney and Eddings arrive at the house of the police officer's widow. She invites them in with a broad smile. The widow does not seem to be in mourning. 'Come in and sit down,' she says. She leads them into the lounge.
'I'm sorry that we have to disturb you not long after the funeral but we have to go through procedures,' said Eddings.
'That's okay, I understand.'
'How was Jim's mood before he went on duty, did he seem anxious, irritated?'
'He seemed perfectly normal, everything seemed okay.'
Feeney interjected much to the annoyance of Eddings. 'How did he get on with his partner Robert Lotus?'
'If he was a woman, I would be worried! All he talked about was Robert, how Robert was a *real* policeman; if there were trouble with youths he would talk to them, and gain respect from them, he thought the world of Robert. How is Robert anyway?'
'He's fine… was your marriage okay?
Her posture became rigid, she wasn't expecting this question.
'Very strong, couldn't be better, has someone said anything different?'
'No, no, we just have to ask these things don't worry.' Eddings butted in apologetically. He turned to Feeney with gritted teeth. Feeney smirked at him.
Her face was creased with anxiety.
'Financially, were the two of you okay?' Eddings was reaching boiling point. Feeney ignored him.
'We have a mortgage of eighty -thousand on this; we have, or had 15 years to go on this.'
Feeney was getting impatient, he continued. 'It's a lovely house; a mortgage of eighty grand on a house worth about two –hundred and fifty grand is not much nowadays... were you aware Jim was taking heroin?'
Eddings looked at Feeney mortified. Silent tears were streaming down her cheeks.
'I heard that, but I don't believe it, I would have seen the needle marks.'
She was pleading with her eyes for help to Eddings. He was shell shocked. Feeney is not finished.
'He was injecting into his toe, are you sure you weren't aware?'
'Absolutely, and before you ask, no I don't take drugs, the detectives who came the day after he was shot, and took his computer away would have mentioned there were no drugs in the house, they must have been in the house less than two minutes.'
Feeney shot Eddings a perturbed look. Eddings shook his head; this was disturbing news to him.

'Did you catch the names of the detectives who took away the computer?'

'I can't remember, as I said they were in and out, then gone.' She seemed calm now.

'When you answered the door, they must have introduced themselves and showed you ID?' Eddings hoped his quiet questioning would release vital if seemingly innocuous information. Feeney disapproved of this inoffensive form of questioning.

'The bell was ringing continuously, I answered… let me think what they said.' She thought for a few seconds. 'Yes, when I answered the door, they brushed past me, one of them said police, showed his ID and asked where Jim's computer was, I told them it was in the bedroom, I led them to the bedroom and one of them took the computer away.   As I said it was all over quite quickly.'

'Did they say when they would return the computer?'

She thought for a moment, and then shook her head.

'No, the bell rang, I answered the door, and one of them said police, showed his ID they brushed past me, asked for Jim's computer and took it away, that's an accurate description.'

'When they left did you happen to notice what type of car they had?'

'No, I just closed the door behind them when they left.'

'Okay, the detectives came and went in a short space of time, we've got that… Jim taking drugs; are you being truthful when you say you weren't aware of this?'

She stood up and walked towards the bay window.

'I can't remember what type of car that they arrived in. This is a very difficult time for me…' Eddings walked over to her.

'I know this is very difficult, could you describe the two detectives, how old were they, what colour of hair, did one of them have facial hair.' She only responded with tears. Eddings took some tissues from the wall unit and gave them to her. Eddings indicated to Feeney it was time to go. Feeney was having none of it. He had something else to ask her. And he didn't need Eddings approval.

***

Robert was in Waterstones sipping a coffee, he felt comfortable amongst books. He was thumbing through the book The Law Killers; it was a book that detailed a brief description of murders that had occurred in Dundee. Jim's murder when it was solved, or if it was solved would no doubt be talked about for years' maybe a book would be born out of this tragedy.

He had visited Jim's widow the previous morning; his visit was monitored by the same two police officers who had been following him since he was suspended from duty. He wanted to find out how the police were treating her, and he hoped that their questions were not too intrusive. She was genuinely so glad to see him. He told her that he hadn't visited earlier, as he was suspended and a shadow of suspicion hung over him, but he could reassure her he had no part in Jim's murder. She reassured him she had no doubt that he was totally innocent. She made him coffee and they reminisced about Jim's life, his strengths and weaknesses. He was feeling good. She thanked him for convincing Jim to buy this house on Arbroath Road; she had doubts about the affordability of this house. They had only been in this house for five years, but they both acknowledged this was their forever home

She was almost in tears as the episodes of Jim's life came to her. But she caught herself in time; she forced herself to laugh at Robert's present to them for the house, a seven foot snooker table that was delivered and assembled the previous day of the house warming party. She reminded Robert about the time when the party was in full swing all the men went into the games room to play snooker; she had to go in and plead with them to come in to the lounge and enjoy the party. She tapped the floor with her foot; Robert twigged straight away what she was alluding to. The survey said the floor was infested with woodworm.   Robert had oak flooring delivered and installed by 'friends.' She was well aware that the wood was ill-gotten gains, but she had learnt not to ask any questions.

Robert was and still is a great friend. She knew he worked in an unorthodox way, Robert's wife had told her that, the secret to their relationship was she asked questions, but not the probing or unsettling ones. That was the template of her marriage to Jim. No questions, no lies. Robert's plan was to stay an hour, he told her not to worry about her large garden that was now showing signs of neglect. He knew a gardener who was due him a favour; he would be in touch to arrange a fortnightly cut and tidy-up. He would not mention this just yet to her, she had other more pressing difficulties swirling around her head. She pleaded with him to stay for one more coffee which multiplied into several. How could he turn this request down? Her pain was so deep and wounding, dark circles had made an unflattering imprint around her almond eyes. The strain on her could not be hidden. He would just let her ramble; she was veering from sadness to joyful recalling of past incidents. She never brought up Jim's use of heroin; he could not bring himself to ask the obvious questions. When did Jim use heroin and what was the trigger that drove him to heroin? The question would be raised, but today was the day when he would be compliant to her many memories. When she moved from tears to laughter, he felt hopeless and helpless.

His state of mind was trapped in melancholy, which was a natural high to him; he was engulfed in a semi- permanent haze of depression. He found great difficulty draining this swamp of depression from his mind. Why hadn't he picked up any warning signs from his deceased partner, had he sublimely been pleading for help? He didn't know. However, he did care about the myriad of theories going viral amongst the rank and file uniformed officers implicating him in Jim's murder. Theories which in circulation were through unadulterated malice, apparently he had 'brought upon himself.' How could he feel sorry for himself when Jim's wife was breaking her heart in front of him? He was genuinely worried about her mental health. She had suffered from depression in the not too distant past. Her mistaken gateway from this depression was consuming wine after dinner. Then having a couple of glasses during the afternoon, she never got smashed. Jim asked him for some advice, he told him he would ask his wife's friend to look in on her and take her to lunch. They became firm friends; they filled their day with trips to the Olympia participating in swimming, then having a sauna. She was slowly retracting herself from the scourge of becoming alcohol dependent.

***

Eddings put down the pint in front of him. 'Well, where does that leave your theory now?' The bar was very quiet. 'Exactly where I thought it would lead, maybe not to the killer, but to someone involved... step forward Mr Lotus,' replied Feeney.
'Could you explain a wee bit more for me?' The quizzical look settled on Eddings face.
'The forensic report said it was the same gun that was used to kill all three of them. I have spoken to Strathclyde Police and their forensics; they are going to check if the gun was used in any unsolved murders there.'
'Do you think the gun had been hired out?'
'It could be, or the gun and gunman could come as a package, we will have to be patient.'
'I am starting to get an uneasy feeling about this case I feel as though someone is dragging us away from logical and rational thinking,' stated Eddings.
'I'm glad you have decided to go up a gear a police officer shot dead in his car, no one sees or hears anything. Most of the residents in the street were watching Big Brother, how sad is that?'
'Are you more annoyed that they were watching Big Brother or a police officer was shot dead?'
'Are you serious?'
'That's the way it came across.' He looked at Feeney.
'I can see I was wrong.' Feeney was embarrassed.
'That's all right, I was wrong as well I jumped down your throat. He paused then continued.
'Another thing that is niggling at me is this heroin, the autopsy revealed he wasn't a heroin user till recently. How recent is recent? Robert Lotus could be telling the truth, that he wasn't aware Swithers was taking heroin. Where does that leave Lotus, in your thinking?'

'He is still the prime suspect. His wife has gone on holiday to Benidorm now why is that? Shouldn't she be comforting him?'
'Maybe she has gone on holiday to get away from the newspapers?'
Feeney was dismissive of Eddings assertion. 'Or maybe she has gone to Benidorm to launder money, or buy a property over there?'
Eddings was smiling at him. 'What has money laundering got to do with Swithers murder?'
'Why was Swithers murdered, why was he taking heroin, it has got something to do with drugs and or money, it has to. If it is property in Spain, then that's not a good idea, Spain is overpriced. And it is full of crooks. Bulgaria is the place to buy property, when they join the EU prices will rocket.'
'I admire how you can discuss a brutal murder, than segue into investment property. Leaving the trivial murder aside for a moment, if you are that confident in Bulgaria, why don't you buy property over there then?'
'I have, it's in a place where five star hotels are being built for the skiing market. I went over there, there are loads of conmen going about, but this is kosher, the company I have bought through, have an office in the town centre. They have even done me a deal to save on my legal fees'
Eddings is shocked at this revelation. 'Why didn't you mention this before, to me?'
Feeney burst out laughing. 'You're kidding me, right? When I bought that flat in Lochee Road five years ago for fourteen grand, you said that was fourteen grand's worth of trouble, well now if I decided to sell it I would get sixty to seventy grand on it. Don't you recall telling me you don't want to hear of any investment opportunity?'
Eddings remembered that statement, he felt embarrassed.
'Okay, I remember that... but now I am interested in Bulgaria, tell me more.'
Feeney signals to the barman for another two pints.
'The villa won't be ready for two years, but when it is built, it will be worth double, and then I will sell it, simple as that.'
'It can't be simple as that, surely?'
'It is. Ask me any questions.' The barman comes over with the drinks. Feeney pays him.
'How much of a deposit did you put down?'
'Fifty grand; and I saved money on the legal fees, I paid them up front and saved on VAT and tax'
'Fifty grand! Where did you get the money?'
'I released equity from the flat in Lochee Road, next question.'
'How much did you say the villa was worth?'
'A hundred thousand, but when it's ready, it will be worth two hundred grand at least, oh and it is in the area where diplomats and ambassadors have bought.'
'Wow! 'Any other person from the force bought there?'
'The Assistant Chief Constable, he has done the same deal as me, paid the deposit and paid the legal fees up front.'
'I feel as though I have missed the boat on this one, again.'
'Nip down into the town tomorrow and pick up a brochure, before it's too late.'
'Money is a wee bit tight at the moment I'll have a look at that, area, on the internet tonight.'
'Money is tight! I find that hard to believe… everybody is aware that you're a shrewd cookie.'
'This is not up for discussion and I am not explaining… I'll have a look at the area.'
'Are you really struggling, I'm not probing... maybe I can help.'
'Look, I'm sorry for snapping at you, but, I don't want to take any risks, my marriage is not as solid as everyone thinks; we are just drifting apart. I am looking at my life just now, the two kids have graduated from University, they both have jobs in Australia; they leave next month. That means me and Jean will be rattling in a five bedroom house. We hardly go out socially together, she likes ingratiating with the neighbours.'
'What's the matter with that? Surely it's better to get on than fall out?'
'No, I really mean ingratiate; sucking up I think she finds me embarrassing …'

'Sounds to me that you are going through a mid- life crisis pal, it'll pass, believe me, I thought that the house in Fairfield Grove was the dream house?'
'It was, and still is, Jean has never believed in a multi-cultured society; for God's sake that's how we moved from Clepington Road. Too many of *them* were moving into the street, well she got the shock of her life when we moved into Fairfield Grove. Eighty per cent, of the houses are occupied by *them*.'
'Whoa…what do you mean by *them*?'
'Asians.'
'Jean… a racist! This is a bit of a shock to me.'
'She's a closet racist, or rather she was, when my son brought home an Asian friend from the University, Jean was so hostile, and she didn't try to hide it. There were major ructions in the house. My son wouldn't bring back any Asians female or male.'
'You would think that at Fairfield Jean would be less happy, then?'
'That would be the logical path to follow but she has gone the complete circle because the Asian neighbours are mainly doctors, she sees them differently from Asian shopkeepers… it's pathetic really.'
'But surely, that would just be an argument, or a disagreement that shouldn't affect your marriage, ach, you know how women are.'
'I haven't told you the classic line she came out with, we were watching Newsnight one evening, it was about racism in the Met. She was saying that was terrible, I couldn't listen to this anymore, I told her three months ago she was calling them, them people. She denied this, she even looked shocked. I told her she should be put forwarded for a BAFTA. She burst out crying, and then she said I was a racist! And I was bad as them! I told her I was confused, was I as bad as her new found friends, the Asians? No, I was bad as them, the Met she said.'
'Don't worry, you will work things out, at least Fairfield has changed her perceptions of Asians for the better.'
'You are right there; she has traded one prejudice for another; race for class.'
'Everything will work out in the end, just don't take things personally,' advised Feeney.
'Thank you Rocky for that advice don't take things personally. You didn't think like that last Christmas, remember?' Feeney looks at him mystified. Then his thoughts crystallised.
'Remember you broke that ex- Drug Squad detective's jaw on the Perth Road, at the Christmas night out, near Thompson Street?'
Feeney straightened his tie, even though it was sitting perfectly. 'He deserved it.'
'On what grounds?'
'Because he was a hundred per cent arse hole,' replied Feeney.
'In your opinion.'
'I can't recall you disagreeing at the time, can you?'
'I hauled you off him when the two of you were rolling about the pavement; and that woman shouted, 'stop it or I will call the police...''…and you replied 'it's a fitness train trainer you need, not the police.'
'And I stopped 'defending' myself because I was pissing myself laughing. The woman came over and said 'are you insinuating that I'm overweight' and I said 'no you misunderstand me, I'm not insinuating that at all…' and she walked away triumphantly, and I continued 'you're a fat bastard.'
They both burst out laughing uncontrollably.
'Point taken,' said Feeney still laughing.
'Same here,' Eddings replied wiping his eyes.
'Things are not that bad, are they?'
'You were right... I take things too seriously I'll just let Jean get on with it.'
'Mention Bulgaria to her, see what she thinks, it will impress the neighbours.'
'We will see how she reacts, and if she agrees, we would want to visit the place first.'

'Of course, if that's how you feel, but I think you would be wasting time, what are you hoping to see...a forest that will be in situ or a forest that has been razed; or at best a building site?
'My son is bound to know some Bulgarian students from his University days; they will know a lot more about the area. Once I research it a wee bit I'll get back to you.'
'That's entirely up to you, but I'm worried that you will miss out on the opportunity by not getting in early. Prices will have risen by the time you do pointless research.'
'I am listening to you, but I want to feel comfortable, that's all.'
'Look, I am that confident that there is serious money to be made there, as a friend, I don't want you to miss out,' said an exasperated Feeney.
Eddings drained his Guinness then looked at his colleague a smile flickered momentarily.
Feeney returned his smile. 'So, are you in then? '
'You have talked me into it... but I still want to speak to Jean, okay?'
'That's more like it, show initiative and bravery... another Guinness my friend?'
'That'll do nicely.'

***

Raymond Andrews was parked across from Linda Simpson's mansion. He was seething with volcanic anger. His hands were tight on the steering wheel with anger. The pressure was on him, he had to change her point of view. Where the fuck is she? She was meant to be here at two it was now five past two. He was becoming more and more irritable. He had convinced himself that the cause of his erratic behaviour was Linda; he knew it was not being an MSP; he was surprised how little there was to do.

Linda had mentioned that he had lost weight, and he was prone to violent outbursts, this of course had nothing to do with his voracious appetite for his best friend 'Charlie,' aka cocaine. He viewed the rear view mirror again, no sign of her. His heart was beating faster, he was grinding his teeth, he glimpsed into the rear- view mirror through habit. At last, he saw her driving up towards him, she flashed her lights at him and smiled, then turned slowly towards the gates, they opened slowly, she motioned for him to follow her. What did she expect him to do walk up?

He slowly drove the car up the drive, why does she drive so slowly? His hands were tightening on the steering wheel. She stopped short of the house, and emerged from the car, talking animatedly on her mobile. Then the regal wave to him, who the fuck does she think she is! Out of the car he leapt and slammed the door violently, and then walked angrily towards her. Seeing this Linda hurriedly ended the call. Fear was on her face oh no, not again she thought. He was now five metres from her, his pace quickened, then it started, he launched a barrage of blows at her. She screamed, but no one would hear her. She fell to the ground, her hand bag and mobile lay beside her. And then she heard the crunching sound of gravel, she saw his black shoe coming towards her. She closed her eyes tightly. Kicking her in the stomach and face he did not utter a single word, grunts instead of insulting words.

She just lay there compliant, she was numb she stopped feeling pain after the third kick. A surreal moment had taken over her mind; she saw her tights were ripped, and her knees were bleeding; one shoe was lying upturned on the flower beds. Must phone the gardener about the roses needing pruned. Her head felt as though it was floating, but the fear had dissipated, then she heard him drive away. Calmly rising to her feet, he picked up her hand bag took the clicker out and opened the gates, and then hurled the clicker at her.

Raymond Andrews felt triumphant when the gates opened he felt as though they were bowing to him. He looked in the mirror he was sweating and smiling inanely. He was heading towards the Esplanade. Opening his window, the cold winter air rushed in, he was taking deep breaths now. His heart rate was accelerating; he threw admiring glances at the mirror again. He was in control of this relationship, he would be ending it soon, not that bitch, not a flicker of regret. He had other women on the go as well as Linda. He had used her and now he had abused her...again.

She had tried to end their relationship amicably. She had pointed out to him, that he was becoming paranoid, and his mood swings were becoming increasingly aggressive but he was not violent. No, he could never accept being dumped again, this time he had insurance. He was invited to her mansion where the fragrant Linda would be telling him lovingly that their tempestuous relationship had run its natural course the same with their import and export business. Smiling lamely at this he suggested she would be changing her mind immediately. When she told him that she was never so sure in her life about ending the relationship, he suggested that she make him coffee, and then he would leave. She came in with the coffee, he drunk it and left. Fifteen minutes later he phoned her and told her to press play on the DVD player; he then abruptly ended the call. She pressed the play button on the DVD player reluctantly and with trepidation. She was now filled with unknown dread. What filled the forty- two inch plasma chilled her. There in glorious colour was her having sex with him, then her snorting cocaine. She recalled that event instantly

This was their first million pound profit from their business with the Liverpool dealers. He must have slipped the disc into the DVD player when she was making coffee. She had to call him, and she would know the tone of the conversation. She called him, no hysterics, and no rants. The relationship would not be severed. He was pleased to know that, she didn't even ask if there were copies, she assumed that in all probability there were. Time would be her ally, not her enemy. She would have to extricate herself from this disastrous relationship. That was certain. It was more easily said than done. How was she going to end this disastrous and criminal partnership; without implicating herself? She was not religious, but she believed in Karma. Her options were limited; she couldn't go to the police because of the stark facts. Raymond Andrews had far too much information about her and her legal and illegal business transactions. And then the incriminating DVD, how could that be explained?

***

Dundee was heading towards Christmas with a sense of foreboding, even though the Wellgate and Overgate shopping centres were bursting with shoppers, and credit cards were being flashed and processed rapidly, Romans was occupying everyone's thoughts. The majority of people were inextricably linked to Romans; either through blood relatives working there; or Tradesman carrying out maintenance down to the window cleaners, and numerous suppliers who supplied components to cakes for the canteen. Newspapers replicated the Management line that it was the high energy costs that were forcing their hand, albeit reluctantly to close the factory.

Radio Tay, the local radio broadcaster which had a phone- in show on Sunday morning was dominated by the workforce saying they had been betrayed. Real not imagined fears about losing their homes, because they had increased their mortgages on the solid belief that Romans was deemed a long –term profitable employer. Linda was listening to the phone- in this had come as a relief to her sanity.

She had been ensconced in her mansion for over a week, due to the facial injuries inflicted by Raymond Andrews. Her friends were concerned of her conspicuous absence from the social scene; she explained she had a serious bout of flu, a plausible reason why she was in voluntarily quarantine. That was eight days ago. Her injuries had cleared up, due to ice cold water and expensive moisturiser. She had reflected on her life since coming into this World, why had she come under the spell of Raymond Andrews? Her conscience kicked in, 'you got involved with him because he was an influential politician, and you hoped to profit from the relationship.' She couldn't quibble with her conscience. However, financing drug deals?

She was in a period of introspection, no excuses; she had exercised her own free will. She asked herself again what possessed her. She was a millionaire many times over. In fact, she was a millionaire before she was born, thanks to Walter Simpson. The money she had spent was instantaneously replaced by her investments appreciating in value, so why did she get involved with drugs? It was easily answered; boredom, the curse of the idle rich.

She needed excitement to course through her veins, now because of her, the youth of Dundee and the small enclave of villages surrounding Dundee, were coursing heroin through their veins. Romans' was her path to redemption, as well as insulating her business interests.

Some of the callers to the phone- in had praised her intervention and genuine concern. If only they knew. She chased these black weighty thoughts from her train of thought and went to the kitchen, poured herself a cup of coffee, and walked towards the large bay window. The Tay was looking magnificent; the wind was whipping up the waves, the plethora of small boats seemed to be attempting to leap over the waves. The trees in the grounds were swaying in a melodic hypnotic manner. In a strange way they seemed to inspire her, how, she didn't know, but her well -being was being uplifted. She was listening to the continued barrage of calls regarding Romans, the common theme was high energy costs, she was starting to tire of that phrase. Watching the oak and willow trees sway, her melancholy was receding, another caller came on again using that tiresome phrase; high energy costs.

She was minded to look in the direction of the radio in a moment of contempt, when it hit her. The trees swaying; the boats bobbing on the Tay; the wind would be the saviour of Romans! Wind Turbines! She moved quickly towards the phone, and then changed her mind. In a state of delirious panic she was trying to locate her laptop. Why was she panicking she asked herself, she wasn't panicking, this was pure magical adrenaline.

She went to the bathroom and turned on the shower, she always thought more clearly and concisely in the shower. The radio was brought into the bathroom; she turned the volume up unnecessarily loud. There was still half an hour to go before the phone in ended. Shit, the jingles were on. She stripped off, instead of neatly placing her clothes on the chair; she cast them on the Italian marble floor. Her ribcage was still sporting the purple bruising; she quickly looked away from the Venetian mirror. The infuriating and inane advertising jingles had stopped now. The calls flowed quicker than the water from the shower. 'High energy costs...blah, blah, blah.'

She caressed her bruised side, it was still tender, and that was the sixth call that mentioned the high energy costs. This would be the stick that she would beat Romans over the head with. After the shower she would go on the Internet and research the potential of wind power, she had a rudimentary knowledge of the benefits, but the set-up cost could be prohibitive. However, she looked to counter act any negativity from Romans. It was early days, but confidence was now emanating from her. She would do research on the Internet, Europe was embracing wind power; this would be the chance for the Scottish Executive to back up their proposals with cold hard cash. The German environment department would furnish her with all the relevant costs of wind turbines.

***

Camperdown golf course was becoming a regular haunt for Robert. He was more at ease on the course, and it helped him think more clearly. His wife would be coming back from Benidorm next week. He would be back in uniform the week after that. Playing golf on his own kept his mind sharp. Ramage was the most frequent visitor to his mind. There was something going on between him and Linda Simpson, drugs was the obvious connection. But was it the correct assumption? She would be the financer and Ramage would be the distributer. The great difficulty with this assumption was she was supplying money to Ramage maybe for a legitimate start up business and he could be using that money for buying drugs; his first love. It did not make any sense a multi-millionaire being the banker behind Ramage.

She had more money and no doubt thriving businesses. Why would she do that? Then his dead partner came to mind. What did he know? Someone needed to kill him to prevent him talking. And this heroin lark... him injecting into his toe? Instead of things becoming clearer, they were becoming more opaque. He started to feel irritated.

Eddings and Feeney had arranged to come out in the afternoon to see him, he declined to meet them.

They would be annoyed, but that was the legal advice he had been given. He did not intend to deviate from this advice.

McIntosh had told him that rumours were swirling in Bell Street, he would not disclose what they consisted of or who was the principal spreading them. McIntosh would neither confirm nor deny that bastard Feeney was the malicious disseminator.

The darkness was descending; he looked at his watch, ten to four, he was on the fifteenth green, his ball was about ten feet from the hole; he tried to regain his composure his breath was showing up in the cold air, it was a distraction. If this would go in it would be his second par of the day. He concentrated and let the putter swing back slowly then forward it came, and the noise from the ball inferred it was good, it was and the ball went into the cup. His breathing became more controlled and it eerily illuminated in the half- light. He walked with a sense of pride and purpose to retrieve the ball from the cup; he bent down and placed his hand in the hole.

The figure came out of the darkness at speed; he was too slow to react; the punch knocked him over, he was winded; he tried to rise up and turn round to see his assailant, the last thing he saw was the outline of his putter; lifting his hand in vain to protect his head. His eyes closed he heard the sickening sound of his skull collapsing.

***

Eddings stood on the fifteenth green; it was now floodlit. The body had been given a cursory examination, photographed and then removed and taken to the mortuary for a comprehensive autopsy. His face was beaten beyond recognition; the skull had been hit with such ferocity that it was in eight pieces. Blood still lay in pools, the golf bag and clubs were still beside the green, except for the putter which was missing. It was obvious that the putter was the murder weapon. The early frost had exposed the sets of footprints of Lotus and the murderer.

The proverbial dog walker had found the body at six thirty p.m. He phoned in a state of panic the police and ambulance services they were on the scene within ten minutes. When the body was identified as a police officer, they knew in the pit of their stomachs it was Robert Lotus. They were not surprised when their stomachs were correct. Where were the surveillance team? The surveillance team had been stood down from ten pm the previous evening. It was deemed 'expensive and counter –productive and no intelligence had been gained.' The bean-counters had won again.

Feeney would now realise that Lotus was not the killer, up till now they were up a dead end street trying to solve these murders; two police officers and two junkies. They were all connected in life and now they were connected in death; violent deaths. Lotus's death was the most savage and horrific. Gratuitous sadistic violence was used to extinguish the last drop of life out of his body; he had never seen a body with so much damage inflicted upon it. This was not a warning that had overstepped the mark and resulted in an unplanned death, this was a premeditated murder. It was a warning to others.

This would make headlines around Britain, four murders in less than a month. MPs would be raising concerns about the Mafia style murders. Pressure from the top brass would be cascading down in torrents; they would demand arrests first evidence can come later. Lotus's wife was in Spain, the police officers who had her under surveillance would inform her of her husband's untimely death. Then the routine would start again, checking relationships and bank accounts. While this was going on the murderer or murderers would be reading the Press regarding the progress of the investigation. Stalemate was staring him in the face.

He wished Feeney was here with him he needed guidance and help. Feeney was convinced Lotus was at least involved in his partner's death, later when he had viewed the forensic teams gruesome photographs he would be acutely aware he had been wrong. He would not lecture him, he would not berate him with his blinkered views on the case, he would not utter, 'I told you so.'
He would hope that Feeney would self-medicate with humility. That was his hope.

They had to dovetail together from tonight.

***

Mary was told at eight pm the previous evening that Ian wanted to see her at ten am in his office. Her scheduled run to Manchester Airport to pick up a client then take him to Dalgleish House (the former Dundee Royal Infirmary) was cancelled. Though she would have to rise at three thirty am for the journey south, she was disappointed that the pick up from the airport was cancelled. She enjoyed the journey, the roads were quiet and she relished the solitude and darkness. She was not too concerned about the unexpected meeting with Ian.

Everything had been running smoothly Christmas would be shortly upon her again, but this year she was welcoming it instead of dreading the festivities that came with it. Last year she failed to dig out the Christmas tree or decorate the flat with decorations of any kind. When Norma or Brian chided her about her lack of festive sprit, she would respond, 'what was the point?' This year Christmas *had* a point, and if she was truthful she had had a Christian reawakening. When she was strolling down the Perth Road to the small newsagents next to the Queens Hotel for her newspaper and milk, she had an uncontrolled urge to enter the Church near bye. She felt as though she was being guided into the Church, before entering she looked around to make sure no one she knew saw her enter the Church. She walked to the area where the Holy Water was located. She dipped her right hand into the vessel and blessed herself. As she was walking towards the pews she felt a strange warm feeling tingle up her spine she convinced herself that this was the shame and embarrassment for abandoning her Faith.

Instead of taking the nearest pew to her, she walked up to the front of the altar kneeled down and bowed her head then blessed herself. Her embarrassment was gone; in its place were vigour and vitality. She sat in the pew one from the front and placed her milk and paper on the pew, then knelt down and prayed. After she completed prayers she sat on the pew and turned around slowly, she was the only person in the Church, she stared at the magnificent altar, the colours seemed to be more vivid, and then she gazed at the ceiling above her. She was in awe of the architecture and plethora of intricate carvings.

'Are you interested in architecture?' Startled she turned around and saw the priest smiling. He had an East European accent.

'I have not been to Church in a long, long time.'

'That's quite all right; we welcome visitors then hope they become friends. Christmas is the time of year of reflection. People come here for solace of the soul, or for giving thanks.'

'My name is Mary I live on the Perth Road a short distance from here...'

'Will you become a frequent visitor to the Church in the future? Or is it because we are near Christmas?'

Mary looked aghast. 'I have fallen away from worship to be honest, but I hope to return in the New Year.' The priest was smiling; he must be in his late twenties thought Mary.

'I was only teasing.'

He sat in the pew behind her. 'My name is Vlad; I have only been here for three weeks, I came over here from Krakow in Poland. The Church in Scotland has a shortage of priests, so I have been sent here.'

'How do you find Dundee?'

'I find it most interesting, I didn't know William Wallace attended school in Dundee, the city seems to have much history about it, but the citizens don't shout about it why is that?'

She was more relaxed now. 'That's what I like about Dundonians; they understate everything, good and bad.' The priest looked puzzled. Mary helped him understand.

'Dundonians, that's what you call people who were born in Dundee... William Wallace, did part of his education in Dundee, and then he moved to Italy and France and to complete his education.'

'I will have to do more research on William Wallace, any more history that I should know?'
Mary moved from the pew. 'Come with me.'

The priest moved from the pew and stood in the aisle, Mary grabbed her milk and paper; he followed her down the aisle to the entrance of the Church. Mary was pointing to a tree on the opposite side of the Perth Road. 'Do you see that tree over there?'
He nodded. 'That is the Liberty tree, when the French Revolution was at its height, the citizens up rooted the tree from the old Townhouse, that was where the politicians met and did business, and replanted it there. Dundee was caught up in fervent political fever at the time.'
'I will have to go to the library and look up the local history. That is a very interesting story.
The Perth Road was teeming with people even this early.
'May I point out something to you Mary?'
'Of course', she replied.
'They do not know it yet, but some of these young people will be my flock. Most of the congregation are quite old; new blood is needed if the Church is to survive. But last week the church was full, I was astonished the congregation were nearly all young people. Then, when I was serving Holy Communion the replies were in Polish. Dundee for some reason has become popular with Polish students and workers. It made me very happy, because the older congregation welcomed the Polish people. Some have come to me and said that they have rooms that are available, if the students need them; they don't want Landlords exploiting them, which I found was very good for my heart.'
'How are they integrating, with the other students and workers?'
'Very well... but some of the workers have said it would be nice if there was a Polish bar, just like the Irish Bars, it would be a good meeting place to make friends and also where they can source work, place a card on a notice board for work and accommodation, things like that.'
'Father, that's an excellent idea, I'm sure there are enterprising Polish people out there who can turn it into reality.' Mary started to shiver, the priest noticed this, 'Mary, I don't want you to catch cold go home maybe I will see you on Sunday?'
'It is getting cold; I'll see you on Sunday then, bye.'
She made her way up the Perth Road, it was bitterly cold. Some of the students were only wearing T- shirts, they must be mad, and then the first snowflake fell, the first of the year

The snow started to fall more heavily, the wind was blowing more strongly, people were shielding their eyes now; cars were slowing down to a crawl. She was moving more quickly but gingerly over the pavement. The magnificent Christmas tree was swaying, as long as she lived on the Perth Road, she couldn't recall the Christmas tree ever being vandalised, no traffic cones placed on the top as a jape and no discarded beer bottles at the base of the tree. It was treated like a religious icon, it brought people together. The first year it was erected, fresher students unfamiliar with the layout of Dundee used the tree as a meeting place, they may have forgotten the names of the myriad of pubs that ran the length of the Perth Road, but there was only one Christmas tree.

Later Carol singers came on the scene, they sung their carols, people stopped in their tracks observed then began joining in; humanity had found a focal point to express hope. Every year they came, the Polish students now in the city the Christmas tree helped forge friendships and alleviate personal problems and homesickness that bedevilled some Polish students. Mobile phones were in evidence recording the carol singers at the tree, the recordings of joy and hope would be sent too many countries in the World.

At last she reached the entrance to her building; she kicked the snow of her shoes, and then made her way up to her flat. When she entered the flat, she went into the kitchen and made herself a welcoming cup of coffee. She went to the French doors to view the River Tay, but she may as well stare at a A4 piece of paper from her printer. Outside it was a whiteout, the large snowflakes were settling on her balcony. The wind was swirling the snow, which was changing direction every few seconds. She appreciated the coffee and decided to have another one; she switched the radio on, and then quickly switched it off airports are being closed and roads were becoming treacherous.

She looked at the clock, just past nine; she had plenty of time before she met Ian at ten. A fifteen minute walk to the office would be sufficient time to reach the office with time to spare. She wouldn't be taking the BMW today, too risky, and someone might leave their car overnight in her place because of the deteriorating weather. She went to the lounge with the steaming cup of coffee in her hand and looked out onto the Perth Road, the mass of people had thinned out, her eyes were drawn to the other tenements on the other side of the road. People were doing the same, people watching; others had opened their windows and were calling to friends in the street. Mary guessed that they were inviting them up, and they accepted the invitation without hesitation.

The coffee had lost its soothing powers. She felt a wave of melancholy slowly descend upon her. She didn't have many true friends, very few if truth had been told. True, she had a wide circle of acquaintances but few friends. How she wished she could call down to a passing fiend and invite her up for a coffee. She looked at the coffee with disdain, and placed it on the small table under the window sill. Then decided to chase away the debilitating sadness and count her blessings. She had lovely children, and had raised them on her own. She had a lovely home and had a well-paid and stimulating job and of course a BMW. However, the overpowering sadness still stubbornly remained. At that juncture the sadness started to dissipate; her mind took her back inside the Church, now a triumphant smile returned, she lifted up the discarded coffee, it was so hot and comforting. She took another careful sip. No doubt about it, it was so good.

The snow was showing no sign of relenting; she was so thankful that Ian had cancelled the trip to Manchester airport; driving conditions would have been horrendous. She felt guilty about the permanent sadness that lay dormant in her. She was puzzled that when some event triggered happiness within her, sadness would suffocate the joy immediately. But today the joy was withstanding the relentless negative thoughts that attempted to contaminate her happiness. This was going to be her year; she had faith in herself once more. Her smile diluted when her eye observed an old man sitting on a bench staring aimlessly at the snow laden Christmas tree.

***

The Lord Provost welcomed her into the office the large table was practically bare, Brian the Trade Union official was sitting at the table; he had his head down and was stirring the spoon in the cup continuously, he perked up when Linda walked into the room. Linda was momentarily deflated when she saw Brian who was physically showing the strain.

Before the Lord Provost had pulled the chair out for her, she had made up her mind to cut short her 'glimmer of hope' speech, and get to the point. Linda had declined the offer of tea or coffee, she invited the Lord Provost to sit closer to her, she was sitting directly across from Brian. He was looking terrible this close up, the dark rings encircling his eyes made him look years older. He had lost a considerable amount of weight.

'Brian, I've got good news, no I will rephrase that I have great news...'
Brian stopped stirring his coffee, and looked up. 'And what's that? ' he replied without a trace of enthusiasm. Linda noisily pushed her chair back over the oak floor and stood up.
'C'mon Brian are you really not interested?'
'You haven't a clue haven't you?' replied Brian'
'Do you want me to leave?' asked the Lord Provost
'No' both of them replied in unison.
'What's troubling you Brian?' asked Linda
'Last night I answered the door about ten thirty, I was just settling down to watch Newsnight; two men smartly dressed, and this was the exact words; 'You have done your best, Brian, just let the men vote to close the factory,' then one of the men thrust this Asda bag into my stomach, I instinctively grabbed it then they walked away.'
'What was in the bag?' enquired Linda. Brian reached under the table, came up with the bag, and he pushed it towards Linda, who opened it up, and then she stared at Brian.

'How much is in here?'
'I haven't touched it, be my guest, and count it.'
'Will you do me the honour and double check with me Provost?' He nodded in agreement.
   The money was counted three times, individually by Linda, Brian and the Provost. They all agreed the sum was forty- thousand. Silence had descended on the room, and it was only broken when Linda swept the money back into the bag.
'You realise the police will have to be called in now?' Brian looked at her and smiled nervously. She placed the bag into the centre of the table.
The Lord Provost thought this was apposite to mention beverages.
'I'll phone them now; do you want tea or coffee brought in?'
'Yes please, and what about you Brian?'
'I could do with something I feel a lot better now, I've hardly slept... and what's the good news?'
'Let's wait till the Provost returns with the tea or was it coffee I asked for?' They both laughed, the Provost returned with the tray crammed with tea, coffee and cups.
   'It's good to hear laughter through the door, I've brought in more cups for the police, I assume they will be here for some time and taken statements.' He placed the tray on the table.
'Sit down Provost Linda is going to tell us some good news.' The Provost smiled and sat down.
'As everyone is aware, Romans want to close the factory, not because it is not profitable, but because of... over to you Brian and John, its less formal than Lord Provost... because of?'
'High energy costs,' replied Brian.
'And you John, why are they closing the factory?'
'High energy costs.' He pours the tea.
'Well, gentlemen, I have spoken to Cabinet members of the Scottish Executive, and they have in turn spoke to other professional bodies, everything has been evaluated and if the high cost of energy is the reason then we have shot their fox so to speak.'
Brian and the Lord Provost, are perplexed at this, Linda notices this.
   'In plain English, wind turbines could be erected on the site within nine months and could be producing electricity not just for the factory but for the surrounding small businesses and houses, any questions?' Brian is sipping his tea he then places the cup down on the saucer.
   'Linda, are you saying that wind turbines could be built and the electricity that they produce could power all the factory; and the surplus could be sold to the houses that are near the factory?'
'That's the way I see it, and the small businesses will also benefit,' replied Linda.
'What are the costs of the wind turbines and who will finance it?' asked the Lord Provost.
Linda had expected this question.
'This will be borne by the Scottish Executive the surplus electricity will be sold to the businesses and houses in the vicinity of the factory, in a one mile square radius, at half the price that consumers are paying now.'
'Will Romans own the wind turbines?'
'That was just the question that I was going to ask Brian,' said the Lord Provost.
'No, not an earthly chance, the money will be coming from the Scottish Executive, a new non-profit company will be formed, it will be owned by the Council, and the profits will be able to pay back the ten million pound costs to the Scottish Executive, that way the Executive is not contravening or breaking any laws, especially from Europe, in fact seventy -per cent of the cost will come from Europe. So to sum up; Romans will not have to pay, the Council taxpayers will not have to pay, and the surplus electricity will be sold to consumers in the one mile radius at fifty per cent of the rate they are buying it at the moment.'
   'I don't wish to be negative, but no wind turbines have ever been erected in an urban area and however the emotional aspect of the factory, the wind turbines will have to go through the same planning application, you do realise that, don't you?'

'Of course everything will be subject to planning permission John, but I can't see any difficulties or insurmountable problems can you?'

'Well Linda, I can see plenty of problems. The owners of neighbouring houses having issues with noise etc… I think there will be many objections.'

Brian was infused with optimism, now it was slowly dissipating; the Provost was injecting reality into the discussion. He picked up the teaspoon and started to stir his tea slowly again.

'Yes I realise that John, but I can't see the residents, many who work in the factory and they will have the opportunity to halve their electricity bills manning the barricades. We have to initiate positive information, from Romans reducing their power bills to the residents' reducing their power bills. Wind turbines will be a landmark of clean, inexpensive, renewable energy, for businesses large and small, domestic consumers will also benefit from clean, inexpensive, renewable energy, that's the phrase that must be repeated time and time again, at every opportunity. We want to hear the members of the public use this phrase; clean, inexpensive renewable energy. Everything has been looked at John; from costs to visual impact... moreover the Scottish Executive want this to succeed.'

'Linda do I detect this planning application has been given the green light?' asked John

'Even today the sky is green.'

Brian stopped stirring his tea. 'Could I say something?'

'Please do,' responded Linda.

'Say for arguments sake, all the planning permission is given, the finance is in place, the vote rejects the company's offer but Romans decide to close anyway have you looked at that? I'm sorry to be pessimistic, but it's been gnawing at me.' The Provost looks at Linda slightly dejected.

'Brian that's a very good point, and I'm pleased to tell you that the worst that can happen is the factory will be put up for sale. The pension fund trustees have considerable power and influence. The shareholders' will be made aware of everything, and by that I mean the Romans family. They were aware of environmental issues, decades ago, before it was in vogue, every year they donate millions of euros to Greenpeace, they are a family that do things, but they shun publicity. I wasn't aware that they contributed many millions of Dollars to cleaning up Chernobyl, the nuclear power station, and in addition have taken the children affected out of the area, and moved them and their families to other parts of the then Soviet Union. This was the brainchild of one of the daughters. Mr Romans, whose health is incapacitated at the moment, is showing slight signs of improvement. I can assure you, that the Romans do not want to sell the factory never mind close it down.

'It is because the son has power of attorney that we are in this situation. The son is a maverick; the reason he has a power of attorney, is he is the only son. Mr Romans has four well- adjusted daughters with the same characteristics as himself; unfortunately, the son did not inherit his genes. He has no business acumen, and from the age of twenty has pursued a hedonistic lifestyle, and the consequences of this lifestyle have caused the family some concern.

'While his father is ill, he still can't speak or use his hand; but his daughter has told me his eyes are getting brighter, she is positive that some of his hearing has returned, but the doctors don't agree with her assessment. It is my personal assessment that the manager of Romans must have been promised some financial inducement from the wayward son, why else would he be trying to close the factory? The daughter insisted that none of her family wishes to close the Dundee factory, Dundee has a special place in their hearts.'

At this Brian spluttered. 'Linda, all that maybe well and true, but do you not think, the Romans family are using the son as a patsy?'

'Not at all Brian, if someone has power of attorney, they can do what they want, when they want. On face value, the son however wayward is not diminishing shareholder value. In fact he is increasing it, even though it is in the short term.'

'Okay, that maybe the case, but I have my doubts, but I don't believe that Romans have Dundee carved in their hearts, maybe they are using you and the son to ease themselves out of Dundee, good daughter, bad son.'

'I understand your scepticism, let me explain. Mr Romans married a Spanish girl during the Spanish Civil War, she and her family were lined up in their barn ready to be executed suddenly a band of Spanish Republicans burst into the barn, they killed the three would be executioners, and saved the Spanish family. After they had untied the family and reassured them that they were now safe, they buried executioners a good distance away from the family farm. When they returned the family had prepared a meal and wine for them. The leader of the Republicans told the family to move away from the area, which they did. The future Mrs Roman never forgot her brave rescuers, nor did the rest of her family, the leader was from Dundee. When she attended the University in Barcelona that is where romance blossomed with Mr Romans. She was the catalyst in setting up the factory in Dundee. Mrs Romans never found out the name of her rescuer, all she knew was what he told her, that a hundred and fifty volunteers from Dundee joined the International Brigade. In all probability her hero from Dundee was killed in another conflict in Spain, but he and his family didn't know that the Romans factory was his legacy.'

Brian looked thoroughly ashamed of himself. 'My grandfather fought in the Spanish Civil War... he was one of the International Brigade from Dundee, he never came back, he died in an ambush, that's all my dad said. I take it back what I said, about Romans.'

'It's understandable why resentment comes in Brian, but I hope I have explained that the Romans are the most philanthropic family in Europe. The European Union do not object to Romans opening a factory in China. When Mr Romans was in rude health, he was planning to open a factory in Hungary.'

'As well as China...?' the Provost asked

'No, no, when Mr Romans took his stroke, his lawyers had to contact the son who was living in Monaco, Mrs Romans had passed away two years previously. However, when the son was told of the impending plans for a factory to be opened in Hungary, he was contacted by dubious advisors, that China would be more beneficial financially rather than Hungary. The European Union had agreed to pay substantial sums of money to Romans to open the factory in Hungary; no factory would close because of high energy costs or any other reason.'

If the father regains his health, mental as well as physical, will the power of attorney be returned to the father?' asked Brian.

'I'm sure that will be the case, however, we have to come to the conclusion that the father will not recover sufficiently in time, sad but that's what we have to do,' Linda replied.

'What is the strategy you intend to take now Linda?' asked the Provost

'What we have spoken about; will be made available to the public through sympathetic newspapers, drip by drip, that way not only will Romans management be questioned by the Union officials, trustees from the Pension Fund; and with no disrespect to these bodies the European Union.

'The European Union has had a great working relationship with Romans, they are or rather they were at a loss, why the sudden change in a sound business strategy?'

A loud series of knocks is heard on the door, the Provost went to the door, and he closed the door he was having an animated conversation of some kind.

'So how do you feel now Brian, now that the facts are slowly emerging,' asked Linda?

'A lot better, but, I'm still uneasy, what will Romans management do, when they are given the solution to their energy costs?'

***

CHAPTER SIX

Feeney is hunched over his computer; he is staring at the screen in disbelief, Eddings is talking to another detective at the other end of the office. The detective lost interest in Eddings conversation, he nodded towards Feeney's desk. Eddings instinctively knew that Feeney was building up to a foul mouthed rant. The detective smiled and moved away from Eddings and left the office, returning briefly to retrieve his coffee. Eddings moved towards Feeney, who looked up from the screen.
'What were you talking about Eastenders?'
Eddings had seen and heard this movie before; he refused to take the bait.
'What's the bad news?' Feeney turned the monitor towards Eddings.
'Be my guest.'
'Go and grab a cup of coffee, and I'll take a look at this.'

Feeney took his advice and left the office. Displayed on the monitor was the report from the forensic accountants, nothing untoward was in any of the police officers bank accounts, credit card bills were up to date. No massive debts outstanding, no jaw dropping investments. Eddings was acutely aware that Feeney would have placed a hefty wager that the forensic accountants would have uncovered secret bank accounts, property portfolios as well as unsustainable lifestyles. To date Feeney's theories were insipid and fanciful at the start, now they were shown to be non-existent. No wonder he was volatile, perhaps his legendary gut instinct is waning. He should be examining his conscience, as well as his method of detection. He would be either lying low with his opinions or he would be biting off everyone's head off, if they were brave or foolish enough to offer another more credible theory. Feeney would tell them where to stick their theories.

Eddings was keen on theories, now was the time when he would give his theory on the murders to Feeney, it should be interesting. He would be going back to his training methods when he was a young detective. His lecturer always reminded him and others even though forensic science was improving detection, there will come a time when you will hit a wall. That was when you must return to back to basics. Back to basics it will be on this case. He would be going back to interview the widow of Jim Swithers, something troubled him about Swithers injecting heroin. He would tell Feeney his theory.

Feeney was in the canteen, he would never be seen dead there, that's what he opined to all and sundry because that's where the plastic detectives had their coffee. He would ask Feeney later what attracted him to the land of plastic. He gestured to Feeney, who was laughing and gesticulating wildly, the young constables were in a state of uproarious laughter. Feeney held up two fingers to him, he would be with him in two minutes. Eddings knew if he walked over, Feeney's party piece would come to a shuddering halt.

He had known Feeney for years; when he joined the police he was a constable, unlike Feeney who came in as a detective constable and he treated constables with visual contempt which he did not attempt to disguise as humour. Female officers were ignored, even if they were attractive. They wouldn't be using him as a reference to expedite admission to the coveted detective division. The party piece ended with laughter, the young constables were still in a state of mirth, the older experienced sergeants sat unimpressed and poker faced, they had not forgotten how they were treated by Feeney years ago; they would not be joining in with any back slapping.

Feeney joined Eddings at the canteen door. 'You should come down here now and again, instead of being aloof in the office; it helps keep your feet on the ground.' Eddings refused to comment. They both left and made their way up to their office. At Feeney's desk the computer was shut down and the paperwork pertaining to the case was in his desk.
'Getting paranoid are we not?' Feeney asked.
'No, far from it, I don't want you going back to the original case notes, we are going to do this my way, if you are going to be undermining me, fine stay here, and expound on your theories. I'm starting from scratch. I am going to visit Swithers widow, do you want to come and observe or do I take one of the team?'

'Swithers widow?' His raised voice drew embarrassed looks from other detectives at their desks. 'There is nothing there; didn't you read the forensic accountants report?'
'Of course I did, I just want to eliminate her altogether, and I'm going to ask her some questions that's all, and if you are coming leave the questions to me. Do you understand?'
'Are you questioning my competence in interviewing witnesses?'
Silence replaces the hubbub of the office; all eyes are on Eddings and his reply.
'Yep, are you coming, or do you want to stay in here and entertain your new found pals?'
Some brief laughter is heard, Feeney is far from amused. He gives the suspect of the laughter an icy stare.
'Hey, fat boy, you find this funny?'
The young overweight detective tries to ignore Feeney, unfortunately his face cannot ignore Feeney, it reddens, his eyes return to his computer monitor.
'You're not laughing now are you? Anybody else think this is funny?'
He looks at each detective individually. They cannot meet his malevolent stare.
'Funs over ladies, back to your computers to fuck up more cases... chop, chop.'
   Eddings is distinctly unimpressed by this boorish and bullying behaviour. He shakes his head at the overweight detective. Feeney grabs his jacket from the back of his chair. He lowers his voice and said to Eddings. 'I'll tell you about the canteen later, lead on I can't wait to see this master class.'
Eddings stands toe to toe with Feeney. 'Remember, total silence, I'm asking the questions, ok?'

***

   Jim Swithers widow has made tea for Eddings and Feeney.
'Look, I am going to be upfront about this, and I need total honesty from you.' Eddings stares at her with intensity.' Feeney looks bored.
Sitting on the sofa she is very relaxed. 'Go ahead feel free.'
Eddings stands up. 'What is niggling me is the heroin in his body, you are a nurse, it was obvious that he was not a regular user, was he just starting to use heroin?'
She bursts into tears; her head is in her hands. Feeney is interested now; he stares at Eddings bewildered at the speed and turn of events. Eddings puts his finger to his lips. Feeney nods. Eddings does not offer her any of the tissues from the box on the table.
   She blurts out, between fits of raw anguish. 'It doesn't matter anymore; I handed in my resignation, I leave next month, and to be honest I'm not bothered if you charge me... since Jim has gone my life is empty...'
   'Did you have something to do with his murder?' Feeney blurted out. Eddings glared at him.
She continued laughing and crying in bursts. 'No I injected him with diamorphine, when he was out jogging months ago he stubbed his toe, the pain killers from the doctors weren't alleviating the pain, so I took some diamorphine from Ninewells Hospital, just as a pain killer, he could hardly walk, I know it was wrong, but I couldn't bear to see him in pain.'
'That's all I needed to hear, thanks for all your help. C'mon let's go,' he said to his partner.
'Will I be charged or will something happen to me?'
'I can't promise anything, when we get the murderer or murderers, it will come out in court, as for charges, I would be very surprised if anything came out of this, you have suffered enough.'
Feeney stared at him in total disbelief now he's a fucking social worker! If it was up to him she would be charged with stealing and supplying an illegal drug and perverting the course of justice by withholding crucial evidence.
'Thanks for coming here, I had to get that off my chest, I don't want Jim's name to be tarnished, did you see the headline in The Sun: 'No leads in junkie cop murders?'
'We can't control the Press I'm afraid,' replied Eddings.
'Are we going?' asked Feeney. Eddings ignored him and continued to talk to her.

'Here is my card, if you remember anything, just give me a call. Thanks for clearing the heroin business up.' Feeney feels angry at this perpetrator is the victim mentality, is Eddings going round the bend? He walks out. 'I'll see you in the car.' Eddings continues to ignore him.
'Thanks for your help,' she calls at Feeney. Feeney ignores her.

Feeney has been sitting in the driving seat for ten minutes. Feeney watches her wave from the front door as Eddings makes his way to the car.
'I'm glad that's cleared up, now we can start solving this murder,' Eddings said triumphantly.
'Where now Boss?' Feeney said sarcastically.
'Back to the office, I have another hunch. Ramage is becoming less secretive and he is spending less time in Glasgow and more time in Dundee, where he is living I don't know, but that will be easy enough to find out.'
'And why have you been keeping this from me?' Feeney is angry
'Because you were becoming obsessed by Swithers mate, now he's dead as well, that's your number one suspect eliminated, now we have to start with a clean sheet. We know that if two junkies are murdered then two police officers are murdered, what connects all of them... drugs.'
Feeney has become more interested and his anger has subsided.
'Do you think Ramage was involved in the murders of the police officers?'
'Well... if he was involved in the murders of Swithers and his mate, killing two junkies would not bother him, would it?'
'Good at last you are thinking like me, Ramage is involved, I know it,' said Feeney convincingly.
'Thinking like you...really? Ramage has walked away from two murder trials in Glasgow; he thinks he's untouchable here in Dundee.'
'Untouchable?' Feeney raised a sceptical eyebrow.
'So I have been told and I have been told certain officers in the Drug squad have built a rapport with him through intermediaries.'
'You mean he's passing on names of low level dealers,' interjected Feeney.
'If you'll let me finish... Feeney is mockingly nodding his head... your right he is passing names to the Drug Squad, dealers and others as well, that way he is helping the Drug Squad make good headlines in the media, but on the other hand he is creating a bigger market for himself, and the Drug Squad know this of course.'
'Look, don't preach to the converted, the Drug Squad that I had broken up because of corruption, this lot is more corrupt than the previous lot, and that's from one of the young plods.'
'So that's how you were laughing and joking with your new pals,' replied Eddings.
'One of the young plods is from Edinburgh; you would never know that from his accent. He is from the Serious Crime and Drug Agency; he is in uniform to gather information.'
'How the fuck didn't you tell me?' Eddings replied
'Boohoo! Who is hypersensitive now, you never told me about Swithers wife supplying him with heroin, did you buddy!'
'Point taken, from now on everything on the table, do you agree to that?' Eddings feels chastised.
'I don't have a problem with that,' replied Feeney feebly.
'Has the young plod found out anything yet?'
'I'm not holding back, but he told me he thinks Ramage is running the Drug Squad, never mind supplying information.'
'I find that hard to believe, influencing it, but running it, surely that is an exaggeration, is it?'
'Not only that, he has four plods in his pocket as well, that is definite, no, let me rephrase that he has two plods in his pocket, the other two were murdered, any idea of their identities?'
'You are kidding me, Swithers and Lotus! Are you sure?' Eddings is clearly taken aback by this revelation.

'One hundred per cent, believe it or not, Ramage is a small cog in this massive wheel; it's international, see that new block of flats getting built at the City Quay; its dirty money that has financed it. The Bank that supplied the finance for the construction of it was a subsidiary of a disgraced Bank in New York; it was the Colombian Cartels that set that up.

'That is where the money originally came from, but it has been laundered many, many times. If you think that's bad, legal financial advisors who are totally unaware of the back ground of the Bank, are advising potential owners to take a mortgage out from the bank at a ten year fixed rate, the high street banks' can't compete. The Bank said to the advisors that they had only a finite amount of these special rate mortgages, everybody that applies for one has got one.'

Eddings is white faced at this news. 'So the Bank gets good honest hard earned money back in, then they lend clean and dirty money out again.'
'Welcome to the murky world of dirty money, how does it feel?'
'I need a drink to help me think straight, this is getting more complicated, where can we go?'
'No drink, you have to be sharp twenty- four hours a day, I thought you would be angry with me?'
'I am... what am I involved in here? Pull over I need air.'
Eddings was trying in vain to keep the contents of his stomach from going sightseeing.
'Hold on for a minute, I'll drive into Baxter Park, the air will do you better than any drink.'

Feeney was concerned that he wouldn't make it, he opened Eddings window he wasn't taken a chance. 'That's better,' he gulped in the freezing air, then closed the window.
'Do you still want to go to the park?'
'It's bitterly cold out there, but I can do with a walk to settle my stomach and try to make sense of what you have just told me,' replied Eddings.
Feeney parked the car in Baxter Park Terrace. 'Will the car be safe here?'
'Park Avenue is around the corner; once inhabited by old money, but alas the poison of drugs stalks every close, twenty -five years ago Park Avenue was where the moneyed classes would start on the property ladder. Now it's a dumping ground for junkies.'
'Thanks for the history lesson; the car should be safe surely at this time of day?'
He glances at his watch; the pubs are not even open yet.
'The junkies will not be wakened yet, two in the afternoon is when they waken from their slumber, to start another day of crime...how are you feeling now?'
They made their way to the top of the park past the play area.

'I've not been sleeping well, this case is driving me mad with frustration, and you'll appreciate the news that Swithers and Lotus had been bought and sold has knocked the wind out of me.'
'I can agree with that, the same gut wrenching feeling happened to me when I was told. You're taken aback, it's a natural reaction.' Eddings stops walking and grabs Feeney by the forearm and also comes to a halt. Eddings face is betraying his inner feelings of anguish.
'International finance, corrupt banks'... all in a provincial city like Dundee, I am getting worried, really worried.'
'Can you let go of my arm please, it's hurting.'
'Sorry...where will this case take us?'
Feeney rubs his arm and starts to slowly walk up the gradient to a park bench.

'So you should be worried, I have the same concerns as you, everything is done from computers in New York, London and other major cities, money is transferred electronically, millions of transactions are done every nano- second of each day, cyberspace has no borders, the days when suitcases full of money being brought in by couriers are long gone.'
Eddings is still overwhelmed by this international financial intrigue
'Just carry on as normal with the murder inquiry then?'
'Of course, we keep this financial business to ourselves, you understand?'
'Yeah, I understand.'

They reach the park bench and sit down. 'Exactly carry on as normal. Plods and civilian workers will ask for information, just tell them what you normally say, 'we're working on leads.'
Eddings loosens his tie. 'Swithers and Lotus, how had Ramage managed to corrupt them?'
Feeney laughs. 'They didn't know they were working for Ramage they had him under surveillance.'
Eddings heart rate has slowed down to normal. Eddings thought process was less excitable now.
'Then why were Swithers and Lotus watching Ramage?'

'That's the question still to be answered, but there must be a relevant reason, and that throws up another unanswered question, who told them to watch Ramage? Were they doing it for someone else or were they doing it for themselves? The forensic accountants found nothing, two police officers are murdered and two junkies are murdered we are no further forward in solving this case even though we have more information,' replied Feeney.
'Ramage, is he still under surveillance?'

'Officially no, but he is being watched, everything he is doing is normal, he is even talking to Linda Simpson about setting up a charity for ex- prisoners, it looks as though he is trying to screw money out of her to set up the charity. More than likely he will be successful; apparently she is quite dense, more money than sense.' Eddings is perplexed at this revelation.
'Surely she is not that thick to give him money? The money would be on the streets in less than an hour after the money is deposited in the charity's bank account; doesn't she know he is a loan shark?'

'That's where we are in a dilemma, if we warn her that, in all probability the funding of the charity will make its way to organised crime either purchasing drugs or illegal lending, he will know that we are on to him, and secondly her pride will be damaged, she has contacts in the Press, and we don't want police harassment stories do we?'
'Softly, softly is the approach then?'
'That would be the wise move at the moment, it's getting cold let's have a walk down to the Arbroath Road I'll treat you to a pint in Rossies.'
Eddings was still having great difficulty in taken all this information in. He had underestimated Feeney. He was not deceptively stupid as he had originally thought.

***

On the train from Edinburgh to Dundee, Linda was relaxing in First Class, the meeting concerning the wind turbines had been met with unbridled enthusiasm; funding was nodded through. If planning permission was denied by the Dundee City Council, the decision would be overturned; if there were a myriad of public objections they also would be overruled. All bases had been covered she had done her homework. Her lobbying of the Appeals Committee individually had borne succulent fruit.

When she arrived home she would have a bath then phone Brian with the good news. Her mobile rang, it was the Lord Provost he was enquiring if she had heard from the police regarding the money handed to Brian, he was obviously fishing. She replied that had heard nothing officially or unofficially. The Provost told her that he heard from a source he wasn't prepared to identify, that the money had being examined and large traces of cocaine contaminated the majority of the notes. Drug money was permeating society now, ended the Provost. She thanked him for the information and promised that she would keep it to herself.

The feel good factor and sense of achievement was slowly disappearing like the daylight as the train trundled over the Forth Bridge. Her edge of happiness was blunted. Let no good deed go unpunished came to her mind, she absolutely hated that saying. Pessimism was in the air. She refused to inhale this toxic strength sapping odour. Her analytical mind kicked in, follow the logic; a bribe offered to a union official laced with traces of cocaine, why would drug dealers do this? If they were setting him up by handing in the money, then they could have contacted the police with an anonymous call to Crimestoppers or the Drug Squad.

'And say a deal was going down now, money and drugs were there now. That didn't happen, why? They had an opportunity to discredit Brian, which would have brought the closure of the factory much closer. Again that didn't happen, why not? The trolley steward came through and she ordered a gin and tonic. Her mind went over everything again and again, and then a horrific cataclysmic thought entered her mind; the police had found traces of drugs on the money. Last year Raymond Andrews came to her house drunk with a case full of money. He opened it and started throwing the money around; he hadn't been wearing gloves.

***

The Press and photographers were out in force at the gates of Castle Huntly. Ramage was personally assured by the governor that his debt to society had been paid in full, the previous evening he went round the inmates and staff and bade his farewell. He was doing that now because he would be released at seven a.m. Thus avoiding any Press; that was the theory the reality was slightly different. His car was waiting outside and his associates had been involved in a series of insults with the Press; that in turn resulted in a barrage of savage blows to the reporter and photographer of one newspaper. This could have been a coincidence, then again maybe not.

The reporter concerned had run a series of stories highlighting Ramages' time inside Castle Huntly, a penal colony it certainly wasn't. The reporter ran a front page story insinuating that he was still running his crime empire from inside the relaxed regime at Castle Huntly. It was obvious that the reporter was gleaning information from an inmate or a member of staff. Ramage had managed to persuade the Parole Board that he had seen the error of his ways. When his solicitor spoke to the Parole Board he told them that his client would be hounded from the moment he was released from incarceration, would they accede to his request that his client would benefit from four weeks in Tenerife where he had a villa, ergo taking his client out of the public eye?

The Parole Board unanimously agreed to the request. Police had been called to Castle Huntly to quell the disturbance between Ramages' employees and the Press. The reporter and photographer had sustained serious facial injuries; the police were unable to elicit details from any witnesses. The injured reporters' were unimpressed at the senior police officers attitude towards them. Professional jealousy had trumped natural justice. They did not see anything that could be described as an assault. Various reporters were convinced that the alleged victims of the assault were agent provocateurs. Some explained in great detail that in their opinion they were baiting Ramage.

No charges were brought against the Ramage employees. After the brief but bloody skirmish, Ramage effortlessly entered the back seat of the Bentley. The Press glimpsed champagne on ice awaiting him. Once Ramage was safely ensconced in the Bentley he lowered the blacked out window and smiled at the bloodied Pressmen, the window then mockingly returned to the closed position.

Ramage had been booked on the noon flight to Tenerife; the warm sunshine would bring back the fading tan that had been mistakenly identified as jaundice. Even though he owned hundreds of Tanning Salons throughout his fiefdom in the west of Scotland he never used them. During his stay in Castle Huntly when he was allowed to have visits to Linda Simpson in Dundee his business brain was always ticking over. He contacted his associates and they bought over existing salons in Dundee, the owners some bona-fide, others ran by local crooks signed over the legal papers without too much truculence. Some, however, were querulous individuals they received more than the compliant salon owners.

Ramage converted one salon where 'extras' were offered, the police knew this, as well as the Council, however, sex workers who worked the streets were high-risk and intravenous drug users, sexually transmitted diseases were rampant amongst them. Those who worked in the salon were not drug users and were checked on a weekly basis. Condoms would be the *de rigueur* at all times even though exorbitant sums were offered to discard the condoms.

Health Officials and police unofficially welcomed this well run establishment, in fact it had reduced the sexually transmitted diseases by forty per cent in the first year alone. Officially no praise was forthcoming from these professional bodies. But it was common knowledge in police circles that Ramage was being praised. Praise meant no harassment from the police. A torrent of money flowed into the salons bank accounts fleetingly, and then into his various companies. He paid tax on these earnings amoral or not.

His entourage had been booked into one of the VIP lounges at Glasgow Airport, they had exclusive use of the lounge to themselves, they paid handsomely for this exclusivity. Any members of the public that had booked months before were transferred to another lounge. This had come about because sometime before another figure high in the echelons of the crime world had booked the same lounge as well as the same flight to the playground for organised crime figures; Tenerife. The lounge was wrecked, families were screaming with fear as the mobsters henchmen went head to head, knife to knife. From then on an uneasy peace had broken out. Each other's itinerary was exchanged with a nod and a wink, often helped by police officers wishing to avoid the repetition of the bloody fracas that occurred in front of the eyes of holidaymakers.

Ramage had optimistically invited Linda Simpson over to his villa in Tenerife set high up in the hills near the Golf de Sur. He could see everything and everyone from the villa it was called Vantage for a reason. There was only one road to and from the villa, he felt more secure there than in Glasgow. If he chose to go to any of the resorts he could with the minimum of fuss, shorts, T-shirt and sunglasses. Sometimes if he went to Los Cristianos in the evening he would wear a light-weight bullet proof vest. This did not cause him much discomfort as he wore one twenty-four hours a day in Glasgow.

He was not supremely confident that Linda Simpson would accept his invitation but he was a gambler by nature. He had come a long way from the depths of poverty, he had killed other human beings but he had not a trace of guilt, even though he was in juxtaposition he classed himself as a Christian. When he was serving his sentence he agreed to go for a psychiatric evaluation, the report said he was not psychotic, and he had a higher than average IQ and in the psychiatrist's view he was a well-rounded individual. He smiled at that one. Maybe the evaluation would have been more balanced if it was not a friend of a friend, his solicitor's second cousin. The minder next to Ramage gave him his omnipresent bullet proof vest. Ramage was keen to place this on as soon as possible; this was quite evident; he was given his passport and a wallet full of Euros by his other minder, one room in his villa was exclusively stocked with clothes. Everything was on hand and in place, topping up his tan would be his first priority. The thought radiated across his face.

When he arrived in Tenerife he would arrange for the hair stylist to colour his hair, grey was spreading wildly over his bouffant hair. He accepted the bottle of beer from his minder; the champagne was for the benefit of the Press, he hated the stuff he couldn't understand why the wealthy placed it to their lips. He was seriously wealthy and he craved the good things in life, but champagne mystified him.

Five hours later he was sitting on the largest of the sun terraces, beer in hand as the sun slowly descended. Six new pay-as-you-go mobiles lay in a row on the table. He picked up the third one then instantaneously returned it to the table, then picked up the one to the right of it. It was time to throw his friend in the Drug Squad a bone. He told him that the sleeper train from London would arrive at Dundee at six am. A youth dressed in a dark green jacket with New York emblazoned across the front would be in the seating section he would be carrying a holdall, inside would be four kilos of cannabis. The Drug Squad officer did not doubt this information, he didn't ask any questions there was no time; the call lasted twelve seconds.

Ramage omitted to impart other information regarding this youth; he was a means to a lucrative end. While the youth was being spread-eagled on Platform Four by the highly-efficient Drug Squad, one of Ramages' more mature couriers would exit the sleeping berth section of the train at the rear.

They would walk straight across to Platform One and exit the station that way; other unsuspecting passengers did this as well. A member of the station staff remembered them from a previous trip and the generous tip he received from them.

He offered a trolley to accommodate the suitcase and the other bags with the Harrods name adorning them. Then politely asked if they had enjoyed London, general chit chat went back to and fro as they walked down Platform One unaware of confusion that was reigning on Platform Four. By the time they reached the elevator at the station concourse normality was returning to the station. The porter placed the luggage in the Taxi's boot with utmost care the man gave him ten pounds. That was the best tenner he had ever tipped in his life.

He was in his fifties dressed smartly carrying a suitcase containing twenty kilos of uncut heroin. His wife accompanied him also in her fifties. They had stayed at the Hilton in Marble Arch; they had been on a theatre break. They went to see Les Miserables and dined at various restaurants at Covent Garden. When they were enjoying their meal, a member of the hotel staff went to their room and secreted the heroin in a panel of the bespoke suitcase. The husband was aware of this his wife wasn't. This was the fourth time he had done this, at one hundred thousand a trip it was worth the risk.

He had had a successful business but unknown to him his accountant had been filching his business for years this only came to light when the VAT men came to his office and explained about the unpaid Tax and VAT. The accountant had being issuing phoney invoices, everything apparently was in order. His accountant was on leave, he never returned from his holiday. He sold the business as a going concern, but there was still a significant shortfall, he would have to sell their magnificent villa in Broughty Ferry there was no other option. But there was. One of Ramages' myriad of associates explained a way out of his financial morass. What had he to lose? He was in his fifties he had lost his business now he was going to lose his home. Prison seemed a worthwhile risk. Everything was explained in great detail to him, there was practically no risk he would not handle any of the heroin and when they were back in Dundee he would leave the suitcase in the garage as they had always done, the garage shutter would be pulled down but not locked. After they returned from the Tay Estuary Club the heroin would be gone. He had built up his business again slowly, not arousing suspicion. Many friends had offered him substantial sums from ten thousand to thirty thousand to start again.

He accepted their bountiful largesse with a grateful smile. Next year he would start paying back the money, he could pay it back now but he tempered his antipathy towards debt, slowly, gradually he would pay it back. He would also forego his annual joint to the Sandy lane Resort in Barbados; he would rather build up the business. His friends were impressed with this penance and how he was placing his family in penury all to rebuild his business; the theatre breaks in London were his only overt expenditure.

The Drug Squad officer who led his team at the train station was cock- a- hoop at this 'intelligence led operation.' His team looked up to him because he had informants throughout Dundee, what they didn't know was that the cannabis they had intercepted was low- grade. If the truth was to be told it had been rejected by other dealers in Glasgow because of its poor quality, therefore the drug was brought down to London where the young cerebrally challenged youth was given the holdall.
He was promised heroin for his own use when he brought it back to Dundee, where he would be met. The meeting would never take place.

Ramage would allow this cannabis to be intercepted. His contact in the Drug Squad was elated at this solid–gold information it made the television news as well as the evening paper. A costly diversion it was to Ramage, but in a cost to benefit analysis it was a no brainer. After he ended the call he took out the sim card out of the phone and walked into the villa and threw the sim card into the open fire. He returned to the terrace and watched the twinkling of the resort below him. When he had finished his beer; he would be driven into Los Cristianos and relax; to a certain extent. He would dump the mobile that he used into a bin in the resort.

Tomorrow he would ease himself back into work. Some of his associates from Morocco would be sailing in tomorrow. Others unbeknown to the police in the UK would be staying in apartments in Golf de Sur. He would be telling them not advising that he would be easing himself out of the front-line, his time in prison even though it was far from austere had a cathartic effect on him. He would be examining the commercial property market on Tenerife then he would be investing in a hotel preferably a five star one. He would leave the financial side to his trusted solicitor, and then he would start the financial maze all over again.

Nothing would ever be traced back to him. He had owned this villa for more than fifteen years, and it was in his name, no need for any aliases. This was the opportune time to live most of the year here, that way he could observe the construction of his new hotel. He had purchased land in an area which was pointed out to him by an accommodating official. The official was confident that permission would be granted as long as the hotel was five stars.

She fascinated him and she gave the overt impression that he in return intrigued her. He had researched her great, great grandfather's life. Moreover, he researched her life; she had much in common with the deceased Jute Mill owner, both had an appetite for money and a distaste of failure and the working class. His two uniformed police officers had kept him informed of her liaison with Raymond Andrews, when he had collated all the information on Raymond Andrews the police officers would immediately become expendable.

***

The secretary had buzzed the manager at Romans; 'there are two men to see you, I explained that they were not scheduled to see you, but they insist you will see them...'

'Send them in,' the manager replied. The queasy feeling returned to his stomach, he reached into his desk drawer, yes it was still there. His facial features went into smiling mode. He had been manager here for nearly two decades, and he would take everything in his stride. They entered the office and one sat down without being invited, and the other more robust character stood at the door. 'Progress report Mr Anderson,' asked the one sitting across from him.

'No progress… this is getting out of hand, look here is an email from Brussels for God's sake,' he stands up. 'This closure was all meant to go quickly according to your boss, but it is becoming more and more complicated.'

'That is your fault, when you accepted the money; you told us that it would be a straight- forward closure, there would be no opposition, the residents' near the factory would be glad, less noise. The workers' would be delighted with the redundancy money. Why hasn't that happened?'

'Here, don't turn this around, you and your chums are to blame not me.'

'You said the union man would roll over, didn't you, he had just bought a house.'

The manager was uneasy he could not deny this; maybe he had shown too much confidence.

'That was my opinion at the time; I had all the employees' names and length of service on a spreadsheet brought to my office. I calculated how every one of them would vote; which amounted to seventy per cent to close. I even built in a ten per cent margin. This Linda Simpson has been the problem; she has turned around the work force with her meetings here.

'She has been glad handing senior politicians the vote is taking place in two weeks' time maybe it will go our way, but I'm not so sure now.'

'Has she been in contact lately?'

'I have a meeting at the City Chambers on Friday, the Lord Provost, Unions, Pension Trustees and Linda Simpson will be there, before you ask I don't know what the meeting will be about, it will not be an agreement to close the factory that's for sure.'

'You just have to fight your corner that's all, and if things are desperate you can increase the redundancy terms by ten thousand, but the vote must take place on the agreed date.'

He was pleased and relieved to hear this but he didn't wish to display unbridled joy.

'That might swing it, if that's the reason for the meeting.'
'What else will it be about? Of course it will be them trying to screw more money out of Romans disguised as increased redundancy terms, can't you see that?'
'No I didn't see that, and I wouldn't place any money on that happening.'
The suit betrayed the thug wearing it, he leaned across the desk. 'You'll have to explain...'
'If Linda Simpson is there, I sense trouble that's all; I feel that she has something in her possession that we are unaware of.' He leaned back in his chair again and tried to look calm.
The thug stood up. 'Just be composed, attend the meeting, you know the script, and here are the new redundancy terms.' He opened his old style teacher's case. 'You won't see us again, if the meeting goes to plan.'
'And if it doesn't go to plan?'
'You will see us again.' They leave the office.

Anderson reproaches himself the second the door closes. Why was he so stupid? He was earning over one hundred thousand pounds a year, not forgetting his five figure bonus because profits had exceeded expectations. He knew what he was getting himself involved in. He had forsaken his workforce many of whom were his friends. They had shared laughter at golf outings and at Christmas parties. He was well respected. He had saved many of the men's jobs when they had personal difficulties. How many factory managers had golf clubs given to him from the workforce at Christmas that cost over a thousand pounds? He was full of self-loathing that he had took a bribe to carry out the closure; he had bought the villa in Florida with some of the money. Even if he could give it back he couldn't; he would end up in jail. The meeting is two days away, the dread and nausea combination had sapped all the energy from him. Avarice had taken over all his senses, his conscience had been muted by the thought of money and a lifestyle that was a reality instead of a fantasy. He feared for his life now. If only he could turn back time.

***

Linda Simpson stared at the telephone. She had smoked four cigarettes and had two drinks, yet she still couldn't bring herself to call him. The thought turned her stomach. Yet she knew the call had to be made. She picked up the hairbrush and manoeuvred herself to the mirror. Even when she was brushing her hair, she saw the telephone in the background. She gave up fighting her conflict. She sat down trying to rehearse what she is going to say. The more she thought about it the more reluctant she became. She grabbed the telephone and punched in the digits.
'Hello, could you put through to Ian please.'
'Who shall I say is calling?'
'Linda Simpson.'
'He is on a call, will I take a message or I can give you his voice mail.'
'I'm prepared to wait, the call is very important.'
'Hold on I'll see if he will be long.'
'Thank you.'
There was a pause, and then he came through.
'Hello Linda, how can I help you?' She had to take deep breaths.
'Hello Ian, thanks for taking my call, I need to see you as a matter of urgency.'
'How urgent... is everything all right?'
'It's very hard for me to speak, especially on the telephone, could you see me tomorrow?'
'I'm very sorry tomorrow is a very busy day...'
'Could you come to my house tonight, it's very important.'
'Is everything okay?'
'Could you come to my house tonight, I'll explain things better I'm not thinking clearly.'
'What time would suit you?'
'Seven, is that okay?'

'Okay, see you at seven.'

She placed the phone down. She took a sharp intake series of breath. How am I going to explain this?

Ian didn't dwell on the call she was worried that came through in her voice.

She must be really desperate if she was calling him. She is a snob, and a patronising snob at that. She is a class warrior; she hated the working class oiks residing in her beloved Broughty Ferry. The many tradesmen that populated the once cherished exclusive streets were out- bidding the old moneyed cabal for houses. Ian had never sought approval from Linda and her ilk. He was a home bird; many of his former school friends resented him using his brains. He gave up justifying his lofty position in life now. Erstwhile friends were acutely aware that his childhood had been besmirched by his parents' alcohol problems. He resented his parents until a short time ago he used to laugh at whining middle classes that sought therapy. Now he had changed his mind, therapy saved him and had slayed his demons real or imagined. His wife helped him through the really dark times; she was the one who told him to stop feeling guilty because he had a horrendous childhood. She told him too ignore the friends who spoke in unflattering terms about him now. Who did they turn to when their out of control off spring had run into trouble? Ian had listened to them feigning concern then passed them on to the hapless Grant McEwan. He chose his friends like he chose his holidays; very carefully. Many people thought they were friends of Ian. They weren't, Ian had a simple weather vane, if they had been in his house at Douglas Terrace they were his friends. In all the years he had lived in Douglas Terrace four people had been invited to his house.

His phone rang; it's his secretary who told him that the builder had been on the phone, they would be starting a week before Christmas. They would be working right up to five o clock on Christmas Eve. He was pleased with this news but not entirely surprised, he had incentivised the builder if the contract was completed he would add two thousand pounds to the agreed cost, however, if the job overran three thousand would be deducted from the bill.

He was a high profile individual and wealthy to boot, anyone who a tenuous link had declared they were friends of Ian's. They wanted to stand at the bar or say over a restaurant table that they were working for or being represented in court by Ian. He was selective in choosing builders or clients, and his fees reflected that. Being resented or hated by former school friends' and his peers in the Legal Establishment caused him no anguish; the thought brought a satisfying smile to his contented face. He had decided at the last minute to walk to Linda Simpson's house rather than take the car. He retrieved the black full length overcoat from the rear seat of the car. It was cold but there was no wind he looked at the bay window of his house.

Not a fissure of light escaped from the lounge, the old heavy curtains had been in place since the Second World War they were only removed for periodic cleaning, they were imperious to any defects. Turning round he faced the Tay and heard the soothing noise of the lapping waves. The stars were out in force tonight, he made sure the car was secure and left the driveway and made his way on to Douglas Terrace. Twenty minutes would be more than adequate for the walk to her house. This would give him ample time to analyse the potential problems that were concerning Linda. Money problems were ruled out immediately. A proposed pre-nuptial agreement prior to marriage running into difficulties?

He smiled at that, Linda was more versed in matrimonial law than most solicitors. Perhaps it was Romans; she had been in the media spotlight over the last few weeks haranguing the management over the plans to close the factory. When he had read in the Evening Telegraph the plans to close the factory he knew the impact that this would have on the Dundee economy. When it became fact rather than rumour the factory was going to close, he swithered whether to offer his legal expertise to the Union. But he thought better of this, the many critics he had would say he was an opportunist; somehow he would be making a pile of money out of the workforce's misery. Nevertheless, he was keen to become involved and offer his services on a pro bono basis.

However, Linda took up the mantle for the work force and she was doing an excellent job, better let her get on with it, rather than the media spotlight shining on him. He walked past The Estuary, the pub was busy, disposable income was passing over the bar from outstretched hands. You wouldn't think the owner had financial problems, but they were winging their way to him. His wife was smiling beside him, unknown to him she had been to see one of Ian's colleagues, she wanted a divorce and she wanted the pub. She had been tipped off that he had been having an affair with the young nubile barmaid. She had employed a private detective to monitor their movements. The camera was an unimpeachable witness. Ian had wondered how many of the customers in The Estuary would be affected financially by Romans closure.

He glanced at his watch another five minutes and he would be at her house. Another thought from left-field came to him. He knew she used cocaine; maybe she had been arrested and charged with possession of a Class A drug? No, that would have been in the papers. She used cocaine there was no doubt about that, he was at one of her charity functions, and he pointed out to her after she returned from the bathroom at the hotel that something was on her nose. Traces of the drug, though minute, were still visible. She returned to the table where she was flanked on either side by the Chief Constable and an expert on drug abuse, she thanked Ian for the advice. The high walls that surrounded her house came into view. He terminated his theories; all will be revealed soon. He pressed the button on the intercom she viewed him on the monitor and he was ushered in.

Her voice seemed high pitched. The stars were less visible because of the topography of the ancient trees that lined the winding drive. His walk was accompanied by the loud crunching from the gravel. Lights were shining from every window; she was standing on the bottom step she started to shiver Ian quickened his stride. The worried look on her face receded as Ian came up to her.

'Cold tonight isn't?'

'Yes it is...coffee is waiting on us upstairs in the lounge.' The staircase was beautiful; this was the universal reaction from everyone who entered her house for the first time. She took his overcoat and beckoned him upstairs to the lounge. Once again wonderment came to his eyes. The lounge was spacious and expensively furnished with antique furniture. The coffee was poured and polite chat commenced.

'So how can I help you Linda?'

She placed her coffee cup down stood up and walked to the bay windows she couldn't tell him face to face. 'It's a delicate matter... I don't know where to start.'

Ian remained seated he just looked at her. She knew he wasn't going to ask again and turned around quickly.

'Do you mind if I smoke?

'It's your health and your house.'

She lit the cigarette and returned to the table. 'This is very hard for me... you know Andrews, Raymond Andrews?'

'The MSP, I know of him, but I don't know him personally, I have seen him at functions.'

'I had a relationship with him, but I ended it or so I thought I did, but he is blackmailing me.'

'Why is he blackmailing you and what does he want?'

'There is a DVD of us having sex... and me snorting cocaine.' She felt like her old confident self again, her burden had been released.

'That's unfortunate, and is he proposing to release it to the newspapers' if you...?'

'I don't drop my interest in Romans.'

'That is bizarre, if the DVD gets released into the public domain his political career is finished, he has the same humiliation.'

Any nerves or tension that had afflicted her had evaporated.

'There is a pattern emerging, last week the Union Convenor had a knock at his door late at night two men were there, one thrust a plastic bag into his arms and told him to forget about saving the factory.'

'What was in the bag?'

'Money, a lot of money, forty- thousand pounds in used notes in different denominations.'

'A blatant bribe, then this DVD... well Romans is the common factor and Raymond Andrews wants Romans to close.'

'It gets worse...' she lights up another cigarette; 'the money was contaminated with cocaine, Brian the Union Convenor called the police, we were at a meeting with the Lord Provost he counted the money so did I.'

'Organised crime and an MSP wanting Romans to close, you being blackmailed by the MSP, he must have a connection to them and has been paid enough to risk his political career'

'I can't go to the police for obvious reasons; this is why I need your advice.'

He looked at her she wasn't going to appreciate his uncomfortable advice.

'Raymond Andrews, have you spoken to him recently?'

'I spoke to him earlier today; he warned me if I go to the police he will say I am stalking him, because he broke it off, our engagement which is pure fantasy on his behalf, we were lovers once and I was a cocaine user. If I continue to offer support to the employees, the DVD will sent; anonymously to a tabloid newspaper and posted on the Internet, he will indicate I sent it in and uploaded to the Internet to ruin his political career.'

'Is he capable of doing that?'

She laughed. 'Capable? He is capable of many things including disseminating lies, anything to damage my reputation. He uses cocaine more heavily now than when we were together.'

'He could be bluffing, however, you would only find out if you carried on as normal and assisted the employees at Romans.'

'That's where my difficulty lies. He will send the DVD into some media organisation and he has the chutzpa to spill the beans for money, he is shameless.'

'There are two separate problems as I see it. First of all he is playing the woman scorned card and secondly why is he keen for Romans to close? There must be a monetary inducement for him. Perhaps he is being blackmailed by some other person or persons, bearing in mind forty -thousand pounds laced with cocaine, was that deliberate, was offered as a bribe to the Union Convenor, is he behind that as well?'

Linda is alarmed how Ian is getting to the root of the problem. 'He is capable of saying anything as I have said, I wouldn't be surprised if he said anything so outrageous, that I took heroin or was even supplying drugs to him.'

'Tabloids thrive on lies and facts being embellished. Did he have money problems? Did he ask you for money?' Ian took out his notebook and while he was waiting on an answer he scribbled furiously.

Linda was just about to answer a resounding no then she thought if Andrews said she was financing drug deals, she could indicate she gave him substantial sums to invest for her. She felt more relaxed now, more confident.

'He seemed to do very well out of his investments; he asked me if I would like to invest in emerging markets, China to be precise. He suggested five hundred thousand, we talked it over and I gave him the money. Unfortunately I gave him the money over a period of a year. Every three months if I remember correctly.

'However, to avoid tax issues Andrews said it would be best not to inform my accountants. He would take responsibility for the tax liability as everything was in his name.'

Ian stopped scribbling when he heard this, a multi-millionaire following the well-worn path of dodging taxes

'I don't think you have to worry about where the money went you would be unaware of what he actually did with the money. Maybe he was using your money to profit from the drug trade. You would be surprised of the number of legitimate businessmen who are fully -aware that their money is financing drug deals.

'However, it does not make any sense why you would knowingly contribute legitimate funds to drug deals. Everyone is aware you were left millions of pounds from your family's trust fund going back to the Jute Baron times.'
She was so glad he had written this all down.
'How and when did the relationship end?'
'To be blunt he was using coke more and more and he wanted me to use it when he was using it. I refused and he started to beat me up he was getting more and more paranoid. That's when he told me he had filmed me using coke; that was his insurance; he would decide when the relationship would end not me.'
Ian closed his notebook and returned it to his pocket.

'Just leave it with me just now; I'll try to find out more about Raymond Andrews, if he gets back in touch call me immediately. He is obviously addicted to cocaine, he is violent and he is a blackmailer. You said he is capable of anything, do you think he could harm you?'
'Without a second thought, but if I go to the police then everything comes out.'
'Is it possible for you to have a friend or friends to stay with you while this is going on?'
'I really don't have real friends I'm sad to say, I just have acquaintances, sorry if I sound like a poor little rich girl.' Her vulnerability she couldn't hide. He felt pity for her rather than sorrow.
'Surely you know one person who would stay without asking too many questions?'
'I'm afraid not,' she replied embarrassingly.
'Would he try and break in and harm you?'
'No he wouldn't do that, or I don't think he would.'
'You have good security here, I mean I used the video com, alarms will all be in good working order?'
'Yes that is one thing I'm confident about the alarms and monitors. The police patrol here on a regular basis. He used to see them outside having their coffee break.'
'Does he know the security number for the alarm system?' Dread came into her voice.
'Yes he does he used to stay here sometimes on his own if I was away on business.'
'Do you know how to change the sequence?'
She laughed. 'Ian blondes are not all stupid; of course I do I'll change it when you leave.'
'Sorry, I hope I didn't come across sexist... as long as you change it tonight. I'll be going now I am advising you, you may have to be candid with the police if we can't resolve this any another way.'
She folded her arms her she was staring at the floor shaking her head.
'That's out of the question I can't go to the police, surely you will come up with a better solution?'
He placed his overcoat back on. 'If there is no other way, the police will be your only option.'
She didn't want to hear that.
'Bu t we aren't at that juncture yet.' He didn't sound confident.
She lifted her head and smiled. 'I'll see you to the door.' They both walk out of the lounge and down the staircase. 'If he does get in touch try and be nice with him, tell him you understand that he has a problem. Tell him that you reported an attempted break in and you have changed the numbers on the pad. Again mention that the police are patrolling more frequently. That'll give him something to think about.'
'He will be angry when I mention that I will be stepping up the Press campaign against the closure, I will call his bluff and see his reaction.'
'No, don't mention that, let him read about it in the newspapers, let him worry. Remember and change the numbers on the pad.'
'I'll do that now, thanks for coming round.' He smiles; she closes the door and groans that the phone begins to ring. She is in two minds whether to call Ian back and ask him to answer the phone she continued to walk into the kitchen. Too late the answer machine activated. No one spoke.
 She picked up the phone with a feeling of overpowering dread and dialled one four seven one. It couldn't possibly have been an anonymous number as her phone didn't accept numbers when the caller withheld their number.

The phone started to ring again. Tentatively she picked up the phone on the second ring. Raymond Andrews's manic voice spoke with menacing tones, speaking slowly then rushing to finish his sentence. It was difficult for her to hear clearly what he was saying, but she heard the last part. 'Time is running out for you financially and physically.'

She placed the phone down without seeking an explanation. Her doorbell rang. That was Ian; maybe he had forgotten something, perhaps his pen? She walked to the front door and opened it expectantly. She was greeted with a flurry of fists; she fell on to the floor and let out a scream, the door was closed behind her now, she was rolled up into a ball she closed her eyes, the kicks that she was expecting never came. The lights were switched off, she heard a sharp sound hitting the tiled floor, and she dare not look up. The door is left ajar, the cold air rushes in, she starts to shiver the assailant has left.

Blood is streaming from her nose the pain is more numb than excruciating she could taste the blood that is filling her mouth. She lay motionless, paralysed with fear. Slowly opening her eyes nothing stirred, the cold air continued flowing in from the open door. Lifting her head slightly off the floor she heard nothing stir, her eyes had adjusted to the darkness all around her. Easing herself onto to her knees after she has convinced herself that the assailant had gone she stood up, the blood had slowed to a trickle from her nose, she accepted it was broken.

Her first thoughts were to close the door, and then she would call Ian. Walking on her toes to the door she is scared that maybe he is still in the grounds of the house. Her foot struck an object on the floor that echoed in the hall and she let out a blood curdling scream. She instinctively ran towards the light switch fumbling till light flooded the hall. Staring at the object puzzled, it is a golf club. Confused and overcome with fear she hurriedly closed and locked the door. Realising how sensible she was by not fighting back or he would have used the club on her. Her throbbing head had derived from her head striking the floor.

A small pool of blood lay where she had been felled. Her clothes had small splashes of blood that resembled red paint as though she had been decorating. She moved back from the door and gazed up the winding staircase and looked up; the Rembrandts were still in place. This was not a bungled burglary, if it was the Rembrandts would have been ripped from their mountings. She had been a victim of violence, naked brutal violence, not once but twice. In her mind Raymond Andrews was the unseen hand behind this attack. Was he brazen enough to be the assailant? This was a painful and violent warning. Her eyes were fixed on the golf club. Had it been left behind because he had been in a state of panic? She dismissed this, it had been left behind as a warning, she was fortunate she could have been struck with the club.

Her thoughts were all over the place she had to call Ian. She dialled his mobile number and told him briefly of the assault she was all right no ambulance was needed. He replied that he would be there as soon as possible. He cursed to himself that he should have taken his car. He couldn't run not that he wasn't fit it was because of the heavy overcoat. She called on his mobile he couldn't recall giving her the number. The walk back to her house would let him think things through again.

The thug must have been in the vicinity of her grounds, the thug must have had a clear view of the house and watched him leave, and then when he was walking down past the curve of the drive, the thug rang her bell. She thought it was him that was at the door and then the thug attacked her when the door was opened.

This had been a premeditated, a military executed operation. Raymond Andrews may have been the perpetrator, if he was, he was clearly deranged. The police would have to be informed now whether she liked it or not. He pressed the intercom she opened the gates, he was mentally preparing himself not to show any signs of shock at her injuries.

Striding his way up the drive which seemed to have lost its benign design; the trees that were swaying looked more hostile and malevolent than before. He quickened his pace. This time she was not standing welcoming him from the step. The allure of her house was diluted from his first visit. Still the trees kept on swaying in a demonic and unsettling fashion.

How could she live in this house on her own? He felt a shiver run up his spine. At last he came to the steps that led to the door; he took the steps two at a time and pressed the bell. She answered after he had pressed the bell for the third time. He was shocked at her appearance, he couldn't disguise it. Less than an hour ago he was struck by her beauty, not a trace of make up or lipstick. She was like an actress made up to look like a victim of domestic abuse. His face must have shown his true feelings.

'Is it that bad?'
The prearranged reassuring words were locked in his head, he couldn't utter a word. She led him in and locked the door she was holding her jaw.
'I'm just shocked at your face; it must have been a terrifying experience.'
She pointed to the golf club. 'Did he leave it behind? Did you disturb him?'
They both sat on the stairs.
'No, I think it was a warning.'
'Did he strike you with it?'
'No. I didn't know it was there till I kicked it, after I opened the door I was punched by him he was wearing a baseball hat, he never threatened me or said anything. I just lay there; he switched the lights off and just left.'
'How long do you think he was here?'
'Roughly thirty seconds if that.' His eyes were scanning the hall, nothing seemed to be missing.
'Oh, before the doorbell rang the phone rang; I was too late reaching it, the answer machine started no message was left, I did the number recall I didn't recognise the number, it was a mobile. I had just replaced the handset when it rang again. It was Raymond Andrews he sounded if he was hyperventilating, he was babbling, but I understood his last words, you're finished financially and physically.'
'You are sure it was him?'
'Definite, absolutely without question it was him alright.'
'You do realise that the police will have to be notified?'
'I thought you would say that, maybe you can come up with some kind of solution...'
'You are kidding yourself Linda, this is the second time you have been assaulted; the next time you may not have a choice whether to call the police.'
'Will I have to mention... the DVD?'
'There is no other way, you have to tell them everything, including your recreational use of cocaine, I don't see any problem.'
He could see the humiliation in her eyes.
'Of course, you were coerced into using it weren't you?'
She was feeling less apprehensive now. 'He'll deny that of course.'
'Well he would wouldn't he?'
She was so glad she called Ian, she still had to explain about the DVD, but it would be better her explaining to the police rather than the police asking her to explain about the DVD.
'Do you think we should call them now?'
'That can wait, how are you feeling now?'
'I'm a lot calmer now.' He stands up, she follows suit.
'Could you show me where the security monitors are so we can see if they have picked the perpetrator up?'
'Follow me, there are six monitors all together,' she leads him into a small room, which is in complete darkness apart from the white light emitting from the security monitors.
'Could you go back, say an half an hour ago then we'll take it from there?'
This she does the CCTV camera that is positioned on the front door showed Ian walking up the drive. The other CCTV cameras positioned at the rear of the property showed nothing untoward, the one sited at the right side elevation of the house draws a blank.

However, when Ian left the house and made his way down the drive and exited by the front gates, a male crept in from Ian's blind side before the gates had closed. He then sprinted up the drive and rang the bell, the door was opened and the vicious assault took place. The assault lasted nine seconds. Ian was shocked at the ferocity and the speed at which the assailant carried out the deed. He watched him run from the house; he did not leave via the drive he ran across her garden and climbed up a ladder, then he pulled the orange rope ladder up after him. Ian didn't see him carry the golf club, he didn't mention this to Linda he just asked her to play the same segment of video again; much to her chagrin.

'Start it again but at a slower pace when the assailant was close to the door'. When it was slowed down, he saw him proficiently remove the club from his jacket almost magician like. When he played it again at natural speed he couldn't see the club being removed from the jacket. The assailant would be impossible to identify, his attire was made up of dark clothing, a dark baseball hat pulled down to his eyes, and dark gloves. Ascertaining his age would be problematic, he ran very fast with a natural, even purring motion. Raymond Andrews had completed the New York Marathon the previous year.

'I have seen enough, I'll phone the police now.'
She felt nauseas. 'I feel more afraid of the police coming here than the thug who assaulted me, I know that is a crazy thing to say.'
'It's called victim guilt... it'll soon pass. Do you have a digital camera?'
'Yes... why?
'So I can take photographs of his handiwork. It's best to do this. Sometimes the police records of incidents go missing for one reason or another.'
'I will take your advice on that I have a camera in the kitchen drawer, would you like a drink?'
'I'm fine thank you; I'll take the photographs then call the police... oh did you touch that golf club?'
She thought for a second. 'No, yes... I mean I kicked it when the hall was in darkness, but I never touched it with my hands.'
'He seemed professional enough but maybe some of his DNA is on the club.'
They went into the kitchen where she rummaged through the large drawer without success. She closed the drawer and went to the next one; she was relieved when she located the camera. When she held it up and smiled triumphantly, she winced with pain her jaw was fractured, but he wasn't going to mention this. 'Sore?'
'Just a bit, here's the camera, where will I stand?'
'Just where you are, is this easy to work?'
'Very simple,' she gave a demonstration. He snapped the photographs, two straight on and two side profile shots.
'I will call the police, I'll make the call from the hall you stay here, don't wash any blood from your face or hands, they'll want to swab you.'

He left the kitchen closing the double-glass paned doors behind him. This was one occasion when she didn't want to hear the conversation. She caught her reflection in the pane of the old sash window the darkness outside made the glass give an almost digital reflection, nursing her hand up to her jaw she felt it move slackly. She heard his footsteps come along the hall.

'They are on their way detectives are coming along as well. I gave them a brief rundown on what happened; I didn't want to say too much on the phone.
'However, when I mentioned the golf club, a detective came on the line and asked what number of club was it, I told him to wait a few seconds, I told him it was a putter, he shouted at me not to touch it, and then cut me off.'
'They won't be too long, will they?' He looked at her the side of her face it was turning purple.
'They'll be here very soon. I told them there was no need for sirens or flashing lights.' Her intercom from upstairs burst into life. They both looked at each another.

'I have another intercom here in the kitchen as well; she made her way to the opposite side he followed her, it's the police.'

Eddings and Feeney were looking at the outside of the building. Feeney is pointing to the CCTV. 'We might get lucky...' Ian opened the door. They both exhibit their identity cards. Ian recognises them both. He has had a frank exchange of words with them previously when he was cross examining during court cases. Eddings accepted that was his job, but Feeney still bears a burgeoning grudge. He has never been slow to let him know when their paths had crossed professionally or socially. They couldn't hide their surprise when Ian answered the door and beckoned them in.

'Most unusual for a victim to call a solicitor before the police, don't you think,' opined Feeney. Ian stopped in his tracks. 'Still making assumptions, or have you forgotten what the Sheriff told you about assuming things?'

Eddings decided to be the oil on troubled waters. 'How is she?'
Ian turned his back on Feeney; a deliberate snub.
'Her face is in a mess...' Feeney interjected. 'Where's the golf club?' Ian pointed to the club and walked with Eddings to the kitchen. Eddings was shocked at her face which had swollen; her eye was starting to close. He asked her if she had recognised the assailant, or his accent. There was not much of a statement to give. The paramedics were in attendance and they sat her down and examined her injuries. Meantime Ian had led Eddings into the room where the monitors were. He played the tape for him, and Eddings pointed out that he didn't see any sign of the golf club. Ian played the tape again at the slower speed and the golf club became visible. They both watched the assailant run from the house across the garden then scales the wall.

'He certainly didn't hang about.' By the time he entered from the front gate, ran up the drive, committed the assault and had disappeared over the wall it was ninety seconds.'
'We may as well be a watching ghost no one would be able to identify him.'
Feeney comes into the room. 'I was right, that's the club we wanted.'
'Are you short of one for your set?' asked Ian
Feeney turned to him. 'Have you given a statement, explaining why you were here?'
'Yes he has, he was here to give legal advice on a delicate matter,' Eddings explained apologetically.
Ian stares at Feeney. 'And if this confidential information makes its way into the newspapers I'll know where it came from, will I?'
Feeney looked so smug. 'First of all you will have to explain to me the delicate matter.'
Feeney was bursting with anticipation when Ian explained Linda's relationship with Raymond Andrews and then the lurid content on the DVD and then finally the assault on her; he went on to explain Andrews had 'encouraged' Linda to take cocaine. She took it because if she refused Andrews may well have assaulted her. Ian then asked the two officers that the information remained under wraps and confined to the three of them; or four if they were counting Raymond Andrews.

Ian then left them to watch the tape again. He met Linda in the corridor she was in a wheelchair being taken to the ambulance. She explained that her jaw was fractured at the very least. She handed him the keys to lock up along with the alarm code. When he was watching her being pushed to the door, he noticed the golf club was gone. He turned and went back to join Eddings and Feeney who were gesticulating at the monitor.

'Sorry to interrupt, but I noticed the golf club has gone, has that any significance to this case?'
'Could do,' replied Feeney without turning round.
'In what respect?'
'Significant.'
Eddings once again stepped in. 'We can't say just now, but the club could be linked to another crime.'
'I see; the police officer who was murdered at the golf course?'
'I'm sorry we can't say till the forensics examines the club amongst other things.'
'What other things?' Ian pressed.

'The footprints on the grass for one,' replied Feeney.
'I'll get the forensics in here to have a look at the tape they might notice something that we've missed,' said Eddings keen to end the conversation that was turning into a cross examination.
'You do that, I want to have a look through this tape again... alone,' replied Feeney.
Ian followed Eddings out the door. 'Good to see he doesn't bear a grudge,' said Ian.
'He never forgets a favour or a slight.'
'Has he still not got over that case yet?' Ian asked expectantly.
'Do I really need to answer that... you know he doesn't like you?'
'You surprise me, you know you have your job and I have my job, one tries to send people to jail and the other tries to stop them going to jail.'
'Even bent cops?''
'Some went to jail, others didn't... you know how the justice system works.'
'Your partner was impetuous if he waited just one more month he would have seen five sent to jail instead of two.'
'He couldn't afford to wait any longer; they were going to kill him...'
'Allegedly going to kill him, inadmissible evidence,' Ian countered.
'That's why he hates you with a vengeance. He was or is convinced that you are part of an organised conspiracy that operates in Dundee. He believes that your rapid expansion came from dirty money.'
'You are not telling me anything new. I have heard this regurgitated time and again. If you're looking for corruption you'll see it every day in Bell Street, so don't delude yourself.'
Eddings looks flushed. 'That's just rumours; you know how it works...'
Ian stops him angrily. 'Whoa! One of the biggest thugs in Dundee is involved in everything from drugs to supplying children from disturbed families to known paedophiles; he was even caught passing heroin into Perth prison when he was visiting one of his friends. When he was up at court and he pled not guilty the Crown accepted this and deserted the case. That is corruption.'
'He has contacts in the drug squad and in organised crime...'
'You don't say, he has been grassing up his fellow dealers for years, and yet he has never been convicted. We are not talking a master criminal here; he would have difficulty in spelling mum backwards or forwards.'
'I know, I know.'
'That's the problem you do know, but he still walks the streets, don't you realise that I know it's Ramage that controls him and the drug squad '
'Keep that to yourself, or if that gets out you could be in danger yourself.'
'Is that a threat?'
'No of course not, I'm just offering you friendly advice that's all.'
'It's just a pity you didn't offer the same advice to the two police officers that were murdered.'
    Feeney comes out of the room. 'Ladies, ladies, what are you two arguing about?'
'Nothing much... just discussing how the police in Dundee are in the pockets of hoodlums; that's all.'
Feeney has taken the bait. 'Are you saying I am corrupt?'
'Officer what gave you that idea, oh I remember, some of your colleagues were jailed and some weren't, I recall you in the corridor after the verdict you said they were all corrupt, have you changed your mind?' Ian waited on his response.
   Feeney felt the temperature rise in his head. A measured response was called for. He took deep breaths. 'Information or hard evidence hand it over, if not I advise you to keep quiet.'
Ian was impressed and a little surprised that he didn't go into a rant, perhaps he had upped his frequent use of Jamaican cigarette additives were having a more calming effect on him.
   'No doubt someone will come out with the evidence; he will probably be roughly six foot tall, wears a dark blue uniform, has a corpulent physique and has a healthy diet of fish suppers, not forgetting the intrinsic health value of diet coke.'
Feeney erupted. 'You are corrupt I know it I just don't have the evidence at hand at the moment...'

He was walking towards Ian. 'That could be the flaw in your case.'
'I'll get you one day,' continued Feeney.
   Ian was feeling supercilious he was in total control of the situation. 'I hope you mean that in the Legal sense and you are not implying violence against my person?'
Eddings came between them. 'Concentrate on the matter at hand, don't try to relive past battles.'
Feeney stopped short of Eddings outstretched arm.
'I am just warning you if you are involved in this...' Feeney instantly regretted what he had just said.
'You seem to have personal enmity towards me, would it help if I wrote to the Chief Constable and pointed out or made him aware of these disturbing outbursts?' Ian waited on his response.
   'You are still a prick from Fintry as far as I am concerned,' retorted Feeney.
   Eddings interrupted any intended response from Ian. 'There is nothing more we need to do here, the forensics has been and taken away the club, but I'm not holding out anything of forensic value emerging. We will be going now, we will be in touch.'
   Sometimes Feeney wished he had the common touch like Eddings, the way he could leave skilfully without losing face or losing his temper. Eddings nodded to Feeney, the nod that said 'don't say anything just leave.' They left but Feeney couldn't resist one more barbed comment. He stopped and turned around and faced Ian, Eddings just nonchalantly walked on. 'We'll be in touch, stay safe okay?'
   Ian could have let that comment whistle over his head, but he enjoyed goading him. 'Thanks for your advice officer, your advice is priceless, you actually don't know how valuable that advice is to me.' Ian was in court room mode now, and he was drawing his prey in skilfully.
   'Oh, and what do you mean by that,' a crackle was in his voice his throat craving for moisture of some kind. Eddings cringed when he heard his colleagues reply, he reached the door stopped briefly shook his head then closed the door behind him. He knew his colleague was going to be barbecued.
'When you said we will be in touch... did you mean you and Ramage, I believe you two are quite close.'
'Close? Define close?' Feeney is irritated.
'Like man and wife close.' Ian yawned, another tactic to rile his opponent.
   Feeney walked towards him now, looking back over his shoulder, he was expecting Eddings to be observing this verbal joust. Ian took off the heavy overcoat and hung it over the balustrade. This unnerved Feeney, he wasn't expecting that.
'Are you saying I'm bent?'
'Bent in meaning corrupt? Most certainly!'
'Are you saying I'm gay?'
'I think in your case the correct term is bisexual, we live in a more tolerant world now.' Ian just let a trace of a smirk appear on his face momentarily.
'For your sake I would advise you to keep that comment to yourself, I know who spread this rumour it was one of the corrupt drug squad sent to jail, who happened to be bisexual he tried to smear me, but it didn't work he still went to jail.'
'I'm just quoting him from the public record, he went on to say you were lovers, and you set him up after he said the romance was over.'
'Just because I wore a pink tie, my colleagues started calling me names, just banter that's all, it was just banter.'
'You were lucky you didn't go to jail as well, lucky for you some statements went missing. If I or any of my staff are stopped on a frequent basis in our cars, I'll put you on the front page of the News of The World, that's certain. There are many of your colleagues and ex- colleagues would love to see you in jail, you know it and I know it. Ramage is a despicable human being but he is a very clever human being. He can descend to a low life thug or he can elevate to talk with Judges, MPs and journalists and won't be embarrassed with his vocabulary, one side of him is erudite and urbane, that's the side he reveals to the professional class. We all know his other side.'

Feeney wasn't interested in this aspect of Ramages' education. He wanted to know how he and Ramage were perceived as close. He had to change tact and become more receptive to Ian's concerns however misguided.

'All I can tell you at the moment is we are very close to breaking up a drugs ring. I know for a fact that the two police officers', who were murdered, were being paid by someone known to you and me, I can't tell you, you must realise this. However, because we are progressing with the case, misinformation about me will come to light, that's a warning for me to back off. I was told that you have been laundering money for years. It has just occurred to me that someone is briefing against me and you. We are filling up our heads with rumours dressed up as facts.' Feeney's body language changed from aggressor to facilitator.

Ian's thought process was churning and dismissing some facets of information, but he was starting to see that Feeney had a point. Ian picked up his overcoat and placed it on, turning up the collar for the long walk home, the rain was battering against the staircase window. Feeney was relieved to see Ian place his overcoat on; he was not going to be intimidated by a loud aggressive detective even though countless others were. He knew that Ian was a match for him if the argument escalated into a brawl. Ian had not replied to the theory of Feeney, his face remained stony, no expression appeared. The silence was having a debilitating effect on Feeney; at last Ian was going to say something. 'That may be the case, I expect my staff and I to go about our lawful day to day business, if we are harassed in any shape or form, I do not see any incentive for others not to continue to propagate unsavoury and salacious facts about your personal life, you can take what I have just said as a quid pro quo. In layman's terms you don't spread stories about me I return the favour.'

'Agreed,' Feeney said with relief. Ian didn't reply but nodded his head; Feeney took this as a resounding agreement. 'If you'll excuse me I want to lock up,' said Ian.

The rain had evolved in to hailstones which were pummelling against the window. They stared at the window; the security lights were illuminating the bouncing hailstones.

'I can drop you off if you want,' Feeney offered but hoped he would decline.

'No I'll just walk, thanks for the offer, close the door on your way out,' he turned and went to the room where the monitors were and the security alarm pad was. Feeney felt more at ease now; he decided not mention to Eddings the ludicrous suggestion that he and Ramage were lovers, the thought made him queasy. Ian had reset the code for the alarm, he felt quite pleased with himself; no one had told him about Ramage and Feeney he had made that up on the spot, it certainly changed Feeney's attitude.

He knew for a fact that Feeney had taken a lot of ribbing from his macho colleagues when one of the corrupt drug squad officers had made that outburst in court that they were lovers, the courtroom was stunned at this allegation. Feeney started to wear the pink tie *after* the High Court case had concluded as a joke, his accuser also said he was having an affair with a prominent Sheriff. The allegations could not be qualified. Feeney was the star witness; he loved the intense cross examination he was a born thespian, he was not fazed about this high profile case. Ian felt no shame or guilt by bringing up the allegation again, even though it was more outrageous than before. Feeney didn't want to revisit that episode of his life again. The public mentality would think there was no smoke without fire. Ian had managed to glean some information regarding the two murdered police officers.

Feeney had gone on at some length about breaking up a drug gang, but never mentioned the police officer's murder and how that was progressing. The golf club that was left in the house, was undoubtedly the murder weapon, would there be any fingerprints on it? He looked at the monitors and watched the two detectives move off slowly down the drive, he opened the gates and watched them take a right turn, he then closed the gates. He had reset the alarm to allow him five minutes to close the door and exit the gates on to the street. He made his way along the hall; he decided to leave the lights on. He locked the door; the hail had turned back into rain.

'You walked into that one didn't you?' asked Eddings.
'How do you know? You didn't hang about did you?'
'If you were going to give him a square go, I wasn't going to be a witness. What did I say to you? Don't try any threats with him; he is well connected with the higher echelons of the Chief Constable as well as the heavies.'
'I didn't threaten anyone, you jump to conclusions...'
Eddings smiled at this. 'He wouldn't be intimidated is what you really mean...'
'We had a chat, no threats were issued from either side, and can we concentrate on the matter in hand?'

Eddings was thinking Ian must have beaten him into submission with threats dressed up as questions.

'I think we will have to visit the much respected MSP Raymond Andrews to account for his whereabouts tonight, then we can ask him about his relationship with Miss Snooty aka Linda Simpson, and point out that if there was a hint of blackmail that would not be an appropriate way to end the relationship.'

Eddings was pleased that his partner was focusing on the inquiry into the assault on Linda Simpson, he had no time for the haughty prima donna but he was hoping that Raymond Andrews was connected even in a tenuous manner to the murder inquiry, because they had no progress in even scratching the surface of the case. He was far from certain that Raymond Andrews was involved in this assault never mind the murders of the two police officers unlike his partner.

'Mr Andrews lives up on the old Dundee Royal Infirmary complex. There are two main buildings one is called the Caird Building it is built in red bricks the other is Dalgleish House which is built from stone, Andrews lives in the Caird Building. Tonight is a perfect time to visit him; I can't see him being out on a night like this.' Feeney was surprised that Raymond Andrews lived in this expensive location.

'He must have a substantial income the flats up there are pretty expensive, I looked at them a few years ago, they were too expensive for me then, I would guess they have appreciated in value by at least twenty-five percent... If he is in he could be making a DVD, perhaps we can be extras?' Feeney waited on the reaction.
'Highly unlikely don't you think?

They drove gingerly into the DRI complex the car park was full; cars were parked on the pavement at ridiculous angles. He parked the car on the pavement. Feeney whistled as they walked past the glittering array of expensive cars. BMW was the favoured choice of the residents.

'Like a car showroom isn't it?'
'Cars do nothing for me, probably most of them are leasing contracts, fur coat, no knickers.'
They continued on through the heavy rain to the entrance of the Caird Building. Eddings pressed the flat number which was on the third floor. He pressed it again then waited. No reply.
'At least the rain's going off,' said Feeney.
'It looks like he is not in; I'll try his mobile number.'

Two young women came out of the building, Eddings and Feeney took the opportunity and they went in and took the elevator to the third floor, they walked along the carpeted corridor to Andrews flat. Feeney pressed the bell, Eddings hammered on the door, they waited. He pressed his ear against the door. They both continued to knock on the door.
A neighbour next door came to see what was the noise booming in the high vaulted corridor. He was young in his twenties.

'Can I help?'
'We are looking for Mr Andrews, have you seen him today?'
'He moved out last week, he had a flood, workmen were in there last week they said it would be two weeks before he returned; the chemicals would need to dry.'
'Have you seen him since, maybe when he came to collect his mail?' asked Feeney.

'No, I haven't seen him since the flood. I've only seen the workmen that took out the damaged carpets and other stuff.'
'Do you know where he is living now?'
'Sorry, I have no idea, has he done something wrong... you are detectives, right?'
'No we are insurance assessors; we come out to inspect the damage that speeds up the claim we just wanted to see for ourselves.
'That the work has been carried out to Mr Andrews's satisfaction,' said Feeney.
'Oh, I was convinced you were detectives.'
'Don't worry about that, a lot of people come to the same conclusion, it's just because the way we dress, I suppose.'
'None of the neighbours have complained about water damage below, so they were lucky.'
'We will just check with them, in case water is trapped somewhere, thanks for your help.'

They rang the bell at the flat directly below Andrews flat. The neighbour was very obliging or gullible, she didn't ask for any ID. They did their 'routine inspection' the young woman was so pleased that there was no damage to any of her ceilings. They thanked her and she closed her door.
'Try his mobile again,' requested Feeney. Eddings shook his head. 'It's going straight to his voice mail.'
Feeney was looking out of the corridor window looking perplexed, snow was falling heavily.
'What are you thinking?'
'I'm thinking if I bought here four years ago I would have doubled my money... and if I rented it out I would have made seven hundred a month in rent, why was I so cautious!'
'And there was I thinking you were thinking hard about this murder inquiry, but no, you are thinking about property investing.'
'C'mon over here and see this, see the old part of the DRI they will be converting that into flats probably in the spring, I won't miss this opportunity again... I'm going to buy two flats, sell one when it's finished making about twenty grand, and renting out the other, the rent will cover the mortgage, I won't be cautious this time amigo.'
'Your brain never stops does it?'
'Perpetual intelligence... don't worry about Andrews, we'll go and see him in Edinburgh at the Scottish Parliament, we'll take the train through, parking is a nightmare in Edinburgh.'
Eddings was clearly troubled. 'He has not been at home since the flood... the neighbour below has no sign of any water damage, strange, mighty strange.'

'It is not really strange; this place was a hospital, walls floors and ceilings were built more robust back then, there is probably at least eighteen inches between Andrews floor and the downstairs woman's ceiling. Andrews will be able to show us around his flat soon enough; there could be a plausible explanation...'
'I don't think Andrews will be at the Scottish Parliament either.'
'You don't believe there was a flood, do you?'
Eddings raised his eyebrows then shook his head. 'This is getting more complex by the day; we will have to start making inroads into this case, I mean the murders,' Eddings said.
'Relax, the golf club could be our first big break, once the golf club has been through forensics, we might be able to link Andrews... that's one theory, if it doesn't, we start again. The thing that bothers me is why leave the club?
'Which I would bet my house in Bulgaria on is the weapon that was used to beat Lotus to death with.'

Now was the time for Eddings to curb his partner's enthusiasm. 'You were convinced that Lotus was implicated somehow in his colleagues murder; were you... what makes you sure Andrews is involved?'
'I just know it, I can't explain... but I know that I'm right this time.'

One of the residents opened her door. 'Do you mind..? Your voices are echoing throughout the hallway,' the elderly woman then closed the door without waiting for a reply.
'It's time for us to go... Imagine living next door to her, 'Feeney joked. The old woman opened her door again. 'Still here?'
'We are just leaving...'
'Good, and please leave without making too much noise.'
They felt scolded by an old style schoolmistress. They made a hasty but quiet retreat. The snow started to settle on the ground; the car roofs were covered. The snow was falling more heavily than before. They carefully made their way to their car.

'Where do you want to go now?' asked Feeney.
'I've done my shift; I'm going home, where are you going?' replied Eddings
'Home for me as well,' he sighed.
'Home it is then, you can take me home then you can take the car back to Bell Street...'
'What if I want to go for a pint?'
'But you don't want to go for a pint; you said you are going home didn't you?'
'Oh all right then, next time you drop the car off, okay. Why is it always me that gets lumbered with the car?'
'Stop moaning and drive.'
Feeney moves off slowly the car is finding it difficult to grip the road, the wheels are spinning.
'What time do we get the train tomorrow?'
Eddings was enjoying seeing Feeney struggling to keep the car under control and conduct a conversation simultaneously. 'Eight am; does the council not grit the roads?' replied an exasperated Feeney.

***

At Ninewells hospital the x-ray identified Linda had a slight fracture in her jaw; she could still talk albeit in a slow and painful manner. Soup was the sustenance that she could only manage through a straw; she thought this enforced diet was the one positive outcome of the assault.

She called Brian with good news; the manager of Romans had got wind of some of the story, he had been told at the Press Conference she would be announcing something positive, the manager didn't know how positive. Brian replied ecstatically, he couldn't wait to hear the manager's response to the good news. Her information was correct up to a certain degree. The manager had been briefed by a reporter from the Evening Telegraph.

The hopeless and opportunist MSP was trying to elicit some credit for the wind turbines, she had leaked this to the reporter; a golfing partner of the manager. The MSP had the reporter's word that she would be written about in 'a positive manner.' This would not happen; the reporter would blame the editor for omitting her completely from the story when it was published. The reporter would be spinning this impending announcement to the manager's advantage.

He had prompted the manager to brief the Romans Board &family. He did this with modest aplomb. He had told them the factory could now stay open; there would be no need for closure due to his discreet behind the scenes lobbying of the Scottish Executive. The son was bitterly disappointed his plans were now in ruins. The manager succinctly pointed out in a brief and heated telephone call to him in Monaco that things had got out of hand; he would not be implicated in 'other' matters. The manager was in a reflective and sanguine frame of mind.

The Romans family would be saving millions of pounds in energy and labour costs, he had calculated the factory could still lose at least one hundred workers without a negative impact on production, he recommended that the company seeks voluntarily redundancies on less generous terms, but still enticing enough for the offer to be oversubscribed. Some workers' would be bitterly disappointed. He acknowledged that his benign relationship with the Trade Unions would never be the same; he would be resigning after the Press Conference due to ill health.

A bonus payment from the Board would be included in his severance package due to the savings from energy and employee costs.

On Friday Linda Simpson had called a Press Conference where she would be revealing for the first time about the wind turbines; or so she thought. The narrative in the Evening Telegraph would give the impression that the local manager (him) had been working flat out to retain the factory; he had been lobbying members of the Scottish Parliament about 'renewable energy 'he had mentioned this to Linda Simpson and suggested the wind turbines. To the readers' it would seem Linda Simpson had hijacked the manager's unselfish and selfless political lobbying even though it had had a corrosive impact on his health. The Romans family had been dismissive and sceptical of his renewable energy plan due to the enormous start-up costs for the wind turbines. However, after listening to him and being informed that the Scottish Executive would be contributing a large tranche of funds along with Dundee City Council they agreed that his arguments to retain the Dundee factory merited further examination.

His time on this earth would come to a premature end when the news of the factory remaining open broke in the Press, he would not be hanging about for the inundations of praise that would be coming his way. Dundee had been a great place to live, work and bring up a family. He had to leave Dundee quickly and by his own volition in a removal van, if not he would leave in a hearse.

***

Linda was recuperating in her house; she was thankful that she had not heard from Raymond Andrews. She checked her emails on her laptop, no emails from him, great. Her jaw was less painful now and it had more movement, she would be able to give her original speech at the Press Conference tomorrow. She would set up her mobile phone to record it, play it back and hear how she sounded, if she came across sounding like she had an alcohol problem she would pass over the speech to Brian. If on the other hand she sounded reasonably coherent she would go ahead and deliver it. She glanced at the clock it was ten past three. As she was on her laptop she would download the Evening Telegraph website and have a look at the Readers Letters page, Romans had dominated the page for some weeks now. Some correspondents had opined that they were lucky to be offered such generous redundancy terms. This had provoked an angry response from the workers' at Romans, laying bare their financial commitments mentioning their mortgages, credit card bills etc.

Linda was feeling excited about the Press Conference, where she would deliver the great news about the factory remaining in production; and the news about the wind turbines. The headline of the Evening Telegraph exhibited: "Wind of Change for Romans." She read the story not once but twice, she was mortified. The story said a "source close to the senior management at Romans" had indicated that they had come up with a solution to the energy costs at the factory. It went on some length and explained that the manager had been lobbying Ministers in the Scottish Parliament about wind turbines, not only would they solve the factory's predicament the surplus electricity would be sold at a very competitive cost to households and businesses in a one mile radius of the factory. The one mile radius was outlined on a map. The response from the Scottish Parliament and the European Union were positive; they could see no difficulties from planning permission to construction costs. All this was due to the selfless manager at Romans in his quest to keep the factory open. The manager at time of publication refused to comment.

Linda was apoplectic. Anger and disbelief overcame her. She felt giddy. She read the story again. She knew or thought she knew who had leaked the story; Ian. She had never truly trusted him, the bile that had lain dormant over the land that he had purchased returned with a vengeance. She would tell him immediately what she really thought of him. She grabbed her mobile and dialled his number, he was not available would she like to leave a message.

'Tell him to call me ASAP,' she shouted at the hapless receptionist. She needed a cigarette. She made her way to the bay windows where she stared out onto the Tay.

This was the well-worn path she took to gazing out the window in times of anxiety. How could he have done this? She was sucking voraciously on the cigarette. He knew she was the engine behind the campaign to keep the factory open. In between puffs of the cigarette her thoughts switched to Brian and the Lord Provost who was anything but publicity shy. He was a voracious gossip, and there were local elections next year. Romans remaining open and the electorate in the one mile radius from the factory receiving cheap electricity would benefit his Party.

Brian was ruled out; he wouldn't give the management the time of day. Had *she* even mentioned the wind turbines to Ian? She explored the recesses of her mind, now she was not so sure. Embarrassment had replaced the pent up anger for Ian. She was now certain she hadn't mentioned it to him. She felt ashamed and embarrassed.

She began an exercise in introspection on herself. So what if the manager was trying to claim the accolades for the factory remaining open? She as well as the work force, Trade Unions and the Lord Provost knew he wanted to close the factory with indecent haste. He was a mendacious individual who couldn't care less about the heartache and turmoil that would have affected hundreds of families. Her ego was the cause of the resentment; she wanted to be remembered like her great, great grandfather Walter Simpson the Jute Baron who gave the citizens of Dundee the best hospital in Europe at the time. Would she go down in history as the power that kept the factory opened or would she be remembered as one of the peripheral figures who gave lip service?

The vista over the Tay had done its job again; the anger was almost gone now. The phone rang; she picked it up praying it wasn't Ian. It was Brian who was ecstatic at the news that was in the Evening Telegraph. He hadn't read it, but had taken a telephone call from a reporter who explained that the factory would not close, he refused to give too much detail away, everything would be laid bare in the special supplement; who were the characters that had played their part in the campaign? It was clear the reporter wanted Brian to disseminate to the employees what was going to be in the Evening Telegraph's special supplement. A spike in the circulation of the Evening Telegraph was anticipated.

***

Eddings and Feeney had spent most of the day at the Scottish Parliament. Raymond Andrews was nowhere to be seen. He had not attended the Parliament for over a week, ten days in fact. He had 'personal problems' and had advised that he would not be attending the Parliament or his constituency surgery until further notice. This advice had been relayed in a brief telephone call to the Scottish Parliament's administrative officers. They asked to see his Parliamentary office, everything seemed in order. They told the official that they would be arranging for the uplift of his computer as a matter of routine. The official knew not to ask why, but he knew something was up.

Eddings and Feeney were on the ten past two train back to Dundee. 'I don't think he will be coming back to serve the Nation,' said Feeney.
A frown appeared on Eddings face, Feeney was gearing up for a theory fanciful or not. Eddings listened intently.

'This is becoming a more complex case; Linda Simpson may be able to give a more detailed statement, where he may be, or does he have another place to go to that she is unaware of?' Eddings didn't reply to Feeney, but he agreed with every single word. Feeney continued.
'When his computer has been examined we may have a clue that comes in his emails, sent or received...'

Feeney's mobile rings he listens to the call without interrupting; he gives the thumbs up to Eddings and ends the call. 'Forensics... Andrews's fingerprints and DNA are on the club which explains why he has done a runner, things are starting to make sense, the sooner we locate him the sooner we solve the murders of Swithers and Lotus,' said Feeney triumphantly.

'You have forgotten to mention the two young lads as well. They have families grieving as well.'

'Yeah… grieving till the scumbag families get the compensation cheques.'

Eddings trademark frown appeared again. 'That's a wee bit harsh?' Feeney's face reflected the frown. He replied, 'no its not, their families sell drugs, use the sword, die by the sword, forget about them, concentrate on the police officers.'

'Fair enough, to quote your favourite word. Don't you think it's too *convenient*?'

Feeney's face is changing colour. 'It's a breakthrough; things are starting to make a semblance of sense, why the dismissive look when I told you that Raymond Andrews's fingerprints and DNA are on the club? Which is the murder weapon in case you have forgotten?'

'Don't you think it's just too *convenient*?' Eddings remained impassive.

Feeney is becoming more agitated. 'Convenient? It's a fucking breakthrough, we have the murder weapon.'

Eddings interjected. 'I'm not buying it just yet, the picture will be clearer when Andrews emerges.' Feeney is incandescent. 'We have positive prints on the weapon, we have DNA on the weapon, and when we get Andrews we will have his confession what more could you wish for?'

'All I am saying is don't get fixated on Andrews, make a more clear and measured judgement once we take him in for questioning; it's the adrenalin that's impairing your judgement, maybe his emails will give us a clearer picture.'

Feeney stands up. 'Unbelievable. Fucking, unbelievable!'

'Keep you voice down, passengers in second class are looking in our direction. Okay, where is the motive?'

'Motive? He's went AWOL. He's a cocaine addict. He's deranged. In his state of mind he's capable of anything. We won't know till we interview him, why he did it. Put it this way, he's not acting like an innocent person is he?'

***

Ramage sat contentedly on his veranda sipping non- alcoholic Becks. He had made a sacrosanct rule which he adhered too; no alcohol before seven p.m. He had seen too many retired businessmen' become bloated and their judgements become impaired when they moved to Spain. He learnt this lesson years ago.' He used to jet out to Marbella for 'business summits' the lean men he had met before now had expanded girths and struggled to move from their chairs in restaurants when their bladders were full. He had assiduously studied that they drank copious amounts of alcohol sitting at the same tables day after day. This was filed away in his business plan for future reference when he would finally relocate from Glasgow to Tenerife; not Spain.

His contact in the Serious Crime Squad advised him of the proposed co-operation between the United Kingdom Government and the Spanish Government about the brazen untouchable swagger the British organised crime figures were displaying on the Costa del Sol. They had been under surveillance for years; both Governments were keen to formulate a more harmonious relationship.

Notwithstanding the Spanish Government were overtly keen for these undesirables are repatriated home. Within the next two years warrants would be issued against them from the United Kingdom Government primarily about unresolved tax matters, the Spanish Government would simultaneously serve warrants regarding undeclared income from hidden assets. The advice from their lawyers would be return to the United Kingdom, there would be more room for negotiation; some charges could be settled on a voluntarily basis. On the other hand the Spanish Government were pursuing a more stringent policy; imprisonment for ten years minimum. After digesting this information, Ramage did not have a dilemma in choosing Tenerife over Spain. He had always had a conciliatory relationship within the Tenerife Government who insisted he led a low profile existence. He had 'business assets' in Spain that he wished to divest of in an expedite and orderly manner, the meeting would take place tomorrow at his villa and would conclude in a fire sale of his Spanish assets to other businessmen.

The same ones' who would fall foul of the more punitive legislation that would be coming their way soon. They would come with lawyers to place a value for his businesses; below commercial value. But that was tomorrow, he had other matters that had been taxing his mind. A year ago he had been approached by a political figure that had information that would benefit him. Through a convoluted system of contacts he was advised land in the prosperous area near Broughty Ferry would become available.

It was suffice to tempt developers, however this land would not be placed on the open market; it would be sold to a preferred developer. Unfortunately it was occupied by a factory: Romans. When the factory was closed and razed to the ground the sale would go through rapidly, the Council would be under pressure to do something and do it quick.

The developer would lodge plans for a gated community complete with twenty -four hour security for the houses that would cost a minimum of three hundred and fifty thousand pounds to a maximum of eight hundred thousand pounds. There would be one hundred homes of the three hundred and fifty thousand pound types.

There would be also two hundred of the more expensive abodes. That was the reason Ramage had set up and financed a new building company; now the millions that he would have earned had evaporated, notwithstanding the money he would have earned from the factoring charge of one hundred pounds a month from each home. He owned the garden maintenance and security companies. He blamed one man for this and one man only: Raymond Andrews. He always felt comfortable with Andrews; he was his biggest earner in Dundee. But that relationship had irretrievably broken down.

Ramage was the *de facto* supplier of heroin and cocaine (via Liverpool) in Dundee; Andrews had no notion that Ramage knew from the very first deal when he was in Castle Huntly, that Andrews financed the drug deals.

On route to a meeting with Linda Simpson, Ramage passed the Romans factory and was amazed at the acreage which the factory appropriated. He researched the Romans family history and knew the wayward son would inherit the business if the father became incapacitated in any way. He did this research when he was in Castle Huntly, one Sunday morning he read in The Observer business section that the father had a stroke and the outcome was expected to be less than positive.

He had contacted one of his associates in Glasgow with his business plan; befriend the son promise him two million pounds to close the factory, he would be found a site in China to build a factory and the overall costs would be met by a third party; Ramage. When the site had been cleared his building company would buy the land from Romans at a very good price. As an act of goodwill a hundred thousand pounds had been lodged at the son's favourite casino where he had considerable debts. The son was befriended over several months' by the associate of Ramage. The son would not have lived to see or spend the two million pound, apparently he would have died of a drugs overdose; he had been in rehab but had succumbed to heroin once again.

Ramage had gone over every legal eventuality with the much respected Law firm that he had founded at a cost of five million pounds. His associate induced the most honest and upstanding mature and young solicitors by the same method. They would be wined and dined at the world's most prestigious sports events, which included the US Masters, Football Cup Finals, Henley Regatta and the Kentucky Derby. They were seduced at the glamour of these events, the salaries paid well above the norm. The fringe benefits included the top of the range silver Mercedes to the interest -free mortgages. All the potential homeowners at the Romans site would be amazed at the incentives on offer from the Legal Firm. Mortgages that were two percent below the high street banks' rates to the conveyancing fees that were cut to the bone. But this was not to be.

Raymond Andrews had ruined this ingenious and profitable business plan. He would pay in monetary terms at a minimum. Andrews had the perfect profile; he was brought up in Broughty Ferry the affluent suburb of Dundee and was educated at the prestigious High School of Dundee.

He was scandal free in his political career and he had a relationship with Linda Simpson; the wealthy ice maiden. One outstanding feature that Ramage admired was his discretion. He was careful in his finance of drug dealings no one would be able to trace a bad penny back to him, only Ramage knew he was the money man. He had obviously given Linda Simpson a plausible story about an investment, he then used her money to finance the drug deals, and he would give her a sum of money every month explaining this was her dividend or share of the profits.

But that was all in the past Raymond had started to become erratic and less careful, the mundane image had now became prominent, he was taking cocaine on a more frenetic and conspicuous basis. At one of these parties taking cocaine was seen as innocent as asking for an olive. Most of the well-heeled would disappear into one of the bathrooms and take it; Raymond Andrews seemed to revel in taking it openly and invited others to join him. He was embarrassingly rebuffed. Linda Simpson was livid at this brazen and foolhardy attitude, especially when one of her guests was a senior ranking police officer who indulged in it, but in a less conspicuous manner.

A solicitor witnessed this confrontation; he was employed by Ramage's Law firm. He was in the minority and politely refused any of cocaine on offer; overtly or covertly. This news was relayed to Ramage, who was alarmed at this exhibition, then came the news that Romans were likely to stay open; that was Raymond Andrews get out of jail card used. Ramage was appalled at this information; he went over in his mind to question if he was losing his judgement.

All the information coming back to him was negative; his judgement had not diminished, he decided Raymond Andrews was no longer an asset to him. His political career was coming to a halt, he was less sure of himself; while he used to smile at his political foes and use flattering language he was now openly being abusive. His private life was also in turmoil, on three occasions he had been stopped for speeding along the Broughty Ferry road, Linda Simpson had managed to persuade her friend from the party that Andrews was going through 'unpleasant emotional issues' that needed to be addressed. He was frequenting the area along the Broughty Ferry road where prostitutes plied their trade openly. His personal number plate had been noted at this area. Everyone was concerned at his behaviour. A decision had to be made and made quickly.

In Tenerife, Ramage explained to his visitors how he orchestrated the solution to the problem. This he achieved by walking through the extensive grounds of Castle Huntly, two hours he walked, then stopped. He had come to an unlikely oxymoron scenario; Raymond Andrews who was a liability had metamorphosed into an asset, unlikely though that seemed a couple of hours ago. He returned to his room, no one called them cells anymore and initiated the solution to the problem.

CHAPTER SEVEN

Eddings was studying the forensic report, a fingerprint and DNA was conclusive; Andrews had held the golf club. An intelligent defence QC would be able to accentuate this point; he had only *held* the club; that would also account for the DNA. He looked across at the ebullient Feeney; there was no convincing him this was the only evidence against Andrews, they had not even spoken to him yet. But he knew if he injected caution into his unbridled optimism he would be called 'too cautious, the evidence suggests... we have done our job it's up to the Crown now.'

Eddings demurred and decided to leave him taking the plaudits from the lickspittles that were shaking his hand enthusiastically. He closed the forensic file and slipped away from the office to attend the Press conference regarding Romans at the City Chambers; then request a few private words with Linda Simpson when the Press Conference had concluded. Feeney never saw him leave the office

When he arrived at the Press conference the Lord Provost was in fulsome praise of the dedication and diligence that Linda Simpson had shown throughout the long and arduous campaign. Eddings immediately noticed that the manager of Romans who was sitting at the opposite end of the table between the Lord Provost and the Union official was in a benevolent mood. He explained that he had to display a draconian and aggressive stance when news of the closure was announced but this was at the behest of one the more influential member of the Romans family. However, he was surreptitiously working furiously behind the scenes taking the opposite view and speaking to MSPs with an alternative vision. Linda Simpson raised her glass of water, her thespian skills that she had learnt at the Swiss finishing school came to the fore when she heard this.

The Union official looked at the manager with undisguised contempt; but he had been advised by Linda that they had to display a united front for the television crews and newspaper journalists, even though he would hear unpalatable inconsistencies. When the manager halted the platitudes on himself, he praised Linda; but not too highly. His eyes caught Eddings and the glowing smile was replaced by a solemn stare, he decided to take a question from one of the throng of journalists that were screaming a barrage of questions at him, anything to avoid looking at Eddings.

Eddings was unnerved at this eye contact from the manager. It made him lose track of the reason why he was there. Linda Simpson noticed him as soon as he came into the Press Conference; she had nodded politely to acknowledge him. The PA of the manager came and whispered into his ear like a bodyguard that whispers in the President's ear with uncomfortable news. He looked at his watch, stood up and apologised to the assembled Press Corps, he had overstayed his time he had to get back to the factory to address his employees. He was displaying the trait of a modest individual concerned about his employees.

The Press Conference continued for a further thirty minutes, questions were being repeated and were becoming banal. Linda beckoned Eddings into the corridor when the Press and Television Crews had collected all their equipment and departed, she was anxious to hear any news; good or bad regarding Raymond Andrews. After the informal chit chat, she asked him if there were any developments. He told her that they had travelled to Edinburgh to see him at the Scottish Parliament but he was nowhere to be seen, they had tried his mobile and visited his flat but he was not there and had not been there since the flood.

Linda was clearly disappointed in receiving this news. She was concerned when Eddings told her that his computer was being examined in case there was relevant information that could lead them to him. She was hoping he had not become less vigilant when he was concerned with the drugs from Liverpool, and God forbid she would not be implicated. He suggested that she may join him for a coffee. She relaxed at this offer and suggested that they go to the Hilton.

He smiled when he agreed to this, the expensive coffee will be made to last and hopefully he would glean more information about their time together; she might let her guard down. She said her farewells to the Lord Provost, and the cypher MSP that had crawled out of the woodwork to bathe in the glory that in her vacuous mind she had created.

The MSP was explaining loudly to anyone who would listen that she was proud and happy to play an active role in retaining the factory. Success has many parents; failure is an orphan, Linda thought. Eddings could practically taste the contempt for the MSP that Linda exuded listening to her telling bare faced lies. The MSP saw Linda observing her, she decided to go over and speak to Linda.

She wanted to find out who the gentleman that Linda was with. Linda turns her back on her and speaks to Eddings. The MSP taps Linda on the shoulder; Linda does not appreciate this, and turns to face her with a glowing smile. 'Hi I am...'

'I know who you are...vaguely; you said 'when the factory closes there will be less pollution, I hope the employees remember you at the next election... time for that coffee Mr Eddings.'

Ian asked Mary if she would do him a favour, his secretary had fallen and broken her ankle, she had slipped in the snow strewn street. Would she fill in for her?

Mary said yes but felt she had to explain that apart from typing, answering telephones and operating the computer her office skills were limited. Ian was able to reassure her that her skill base was more than adequate. He then asked her how her business plan for Panoramica was progressing. Mary had told him that she had finished the final draft, but did not wish to exhibit the business plan to him as he was occupied by events concerning Romans. He thanked her for been so professional and showing foresight, he was pleased that Romans would now stay open. He noticed that she looked as if she wanted to ask a question but seemed to be reluctant.

'Is there something on your mind Mary?'

She looked embarrassed. 'I was going to ask you something... it's a legal matter, but it effect's me too.' He beckons her into his office and asks the office junior to bring in some coffee into his office. He takes his seat behind his desk and invites her to sit in the chair opposite him. He saw she was ill at ease. 'Before you start Mary this advice is free, a perk if you like, so get it off your chest.'

She is just about to start her well- rehearsed opening gambit, when the office junior knocks at the door and brings in the coffee. Mary decides to abandon the speech; she will say what she really feels.

'Ian as you know; there are a lot of Polish workers in Dundee as well as in Angus, I have become friendly with a Polish priest who is the priest for the Chapel on the Perth Road. He has a lot of Polish and Lithuanian students that form the majority of his congregation. I read a lot of history particularly about the Irish immigrants that had immigrated to New York, it was very tough for them; they were accused of stealing the indigenous people's jobs or undercutting their wages. They were not prepared to put up with this behaviour which would now be called racism. So they formulated a political strategy. They met in the pubs and organised a strategy to garner the Irish vote.'

Ian pours the coffee without interrupting her; she was in full flow and had obviously a point but he couldn't second guess her.

'The problem today in Dundee is the Polish students, workers and professionals do not have any meaningful place to meet. I know there is a Polish club in the Perth Road area, but I have been there, and to be frank I can't see what the attraction, if there is an attraction, why the Polish community would go there. Instead they frequent the run of the mill pubs that run the length of the Perth Road. I have done some demographic research and I have discovered that most of the Polish community live on the periphery of the City Centre.' She took a deep intake of breath.

'I see a business opportunity. Well I think I see a business opportunity. When I was looking at the demographics of the Polish and other eastern European communities, I started looking for pubs that were up for sale, there seemed to be plenty pubs up for lease, but I don't think this is the way forward. I have been keeping my eye on a certain pub; the owners have tried to lease it for as little as one hundred pounds a week.

'This obviously hasn't worked, they have put it up for sale for offers over one hundred and seventy five thousand, this jumped out of the computer screen at me. There are flats above the premises but I don't know if they are part of the premises. If not then there would be a problem with noise. They look rundown and uninhabited, but you never can tell.

'The information on the website was scant, if you want more information I would have to email them for a full schedule. The pub would need a full refurbishment, that I am certain, the same for the flats. This is the reason that I'm coming to you Ian, my plan is to turn this rundown pub into a vibrant Polish stroke Scottish bar. Young people can meet and make friends, I would have Polish and Dundee door security as well as Polish and Dundee bar staff. I have even thought of inviting the Celtic goalkeeper Artur Boruc to pull the inaugural pint. I'm sure the local newspapers as well as The Sun and Daily Record would run this as a good story. The pub would have large screens showing Polish, English and Scottish football. Polish and Scottish beer would be stocked. However, my biggest fears are if I requested a schedule the price maybe out of my reach because of the refurbishment cost of the pub and the flats above; and if I went to a bank and gave them my business plan, this would leak out and some established businessman would turn my dream into their reality. So what do you think... am I a dreamer?'

Ian stared at her; she had been his ideal candidate for Spain not because of her linguistic skills but there was something latent within her that would bring growth to his business, he had heard and saw her vision, which was anything but a pipe dream. If the pub was in the right location... he had to ask where the pub was so he could personally inspect it. The negotiations with the owners he couldn't envisage any insurmountable problems; had Mary told anyone else about her plans?

'More coffee?' He was impatient to tell her one step at a time, but he knew this would have inhibited any further ideas she had on the back burner, she nodded.

'Your business plan is flawless, your research couldn't be faulted, your plan for this being a focal point for the Polish community... fantastic. And what you said if you went to a bank or business advisor is one hundred per cent correct; your idea would be in the hands of a number of businessmen and women within hours, as a result of this a bidding war would start and the premises would be out with your financial reach, then it would be a pipedream. The big question is; where is this El Dorado?'

Mary looked tentative and removed the coffee cup from her lips. She was hesitant. 'The Weavers Arms in Princess Street.'

Ian knew where it is; when it opened about twenty years ago it was one of the 'in' pubs. Since the early nineties it had deteriorated into a shebeen; hardened drinkers frequented and junkies done their deals there. They also left an array of needles in the filthy cubicles. But that was all in the past. Presently it is in area which is up and coming, Mary had not had a dream she had a vision, an optimistic vision.

Graham Ford was another Fintry boy. When his father died he was left a modest sum. But Graham had seen the Thatcherite policy of closing the State's old people's homes and transferring the residents' over to the private sector. He borrowed a substantial sum of capital and built these modern and pleasing 'retirement communities.' He never looked back.

The 'retirement communities' were later bought by an American company for many millions over and above the price he had built and kitted out these luxurious care homes. He purchased surplus Council land adjacent to the Olympia swimming complex commonly known as the Waterfront from the proceeds; on the advice of Linda Simpson. Graham Ford and his brother went on an acquisition spree snapping up thriving and not so thriving pubs in Dundee. If Graham had just heard what he had heard from Mary; he would not been able to contain himself.

'I know the place well Mary, if you said to me that you wanted my advice whether to buy it I would have said no it's a dump the clientele was unrefined to put it mildly; forget it. However, this plan for the Polish workers and students is a winner.' She let out a sigh of relief.

'But making it a Polish/Scots pub is thought of genius. The publicity you would be able to generate would be fantastic. A thought did come into my mind; you could have a website displaying everything from the usual welcome, to accommodation and a jobs service.'

Mary was so pleased that she was not being laughed at.

Ian continued. 'Have you mentioned this to anyone else?'

'No one. Absolutely no one.'

'You mentioned that you said something to the Polish priest from the Perth Road?'

'That was just a casual conversation; I said it would be great if the Polish people had somewhere to meet, I think he was thinking more of bingo nights in the Chapel.'

'That's what I hoped to hear... one thing at a time.' He turned round his computer so it could be seen by the both of them. He clicked the browser to bring up the website that gave the details of the pub. Joy was emanating from Mary's face; the strain that she had been under formulating her business venture had been palpable. She had been unable to sleep soundly. Though winter had laid its marker over the Fife hills she found herself going into a semi routine: two- am rise, place on dressing gown, go to kitchen boil kettle. When she poured the boiling water into her coffee mug her eyes would be drawn to the twinkling vista of Wormit. She would drift over to the French doors and press her nose against the cold glass for a clearer view, she would be unable to control the urge to venture out onto the balcony and sit at the table with her hands cupped around the coffee mug for warmth. Then her mind would start the unending quest to the Weavers Arms. She had had her flat re-valued she opened the valuer's report with dread; the property is in excellent order... one hundred and ninety thousand pounds, but an auction would surpass this price up due to excellent order and location.

The valuer had personally said that the property would be likely bought by buy-to - let investors from Edinburgh, Glasgow or Ireland. He would not be surprised if it went for over a quarter of a million. She was not intending to sell, she would be borrowing money from the bank, how much she didn't know, but she knew or hoped once the bank had this valuation of her flat, they would give her the loan with the flat as security.

The website came up Ian invited her to study the page with the details of the pub. She was right, not much details. Rather than send the email requesting information he decided to give the agent a call. Surprisingly the secretary managed to locate the individual concerned with the sale of the pub. Ian placed the call on speaker phone so Mary could hear. Ian was told there had been a lot of interest, at this Ian told the agent that if that was the case he would not require any further details. This brought a change of attitude from the agent, Ian continued to press him, 'how much genuine interest had there been, and had this interest firmed up into an offer?'

'At this moment in time no offer had been received, but it was early days yet.'

Mary watched and listened in awe at the skill that Ian had brought out a more conciliatory response from the agent. Ian was able to elicit more information from the agent effortlessly; there were two, two bedroom flats above the pub they were included in the sale of the pub that would benefit from refurbishment and they were unoccupied. Ian had calculated that the flats couldn't be sold separately from the bar due to the bar being below the flats and vice-versa. Even in an overheated property market no one would touch the flats whether they were refurbished or not; the bar would be the fly in the ointment whether they were being sold to owner occupiers or to buy-to-let investors, no professional or student would want to live in the flats when they were hundreds of hi - spec apartments in Dundee in a better locale.

Ian had politely pointed out to the agent that he had the potential buyer waiting outside his office, the buyer had money ready available, if they could meet at the pub tomorrow morning say about ten am, the agent would receive an offer the same day if the buyer saw potential. He confided that the buyer wanted to turn the pub into accommodation as well.

'But you would appreciate that the planning regulation for Change of Use could be tricky as well as lengthy.

Moreover, the expense of the conversion of the pub and the refurbishment of the two flats, we are talking a lot of money.'
The agent concurred. Ian went on to enquire if in the agent's opinion the price over one hundred and seventy five thousand was optimistic? The agent was smart; he never came out and said either yes or no, but he emphasised the sellers were keen to sell quickly. Ian politely brought the conversation to a close.
'The potential buyer's appointment was due in five minutes; I look forward to meeting you tomorrow at ten.' He ended the call and looked at Mary with a smile.
   'That's the appointment made as you heard, it looks to me that there has been no credible interest; and they are keen to sell. Tomorrow you will be accompanying me to the pub and all will be revealed. I'll bring along my brother he's a chartered surveyor, he'll be able to give us a rough idea how much it will cost to refurbish; and check to see if the fabric of building is in reasonable good order. As we are going to be business partners we are better to see things together.'
   Business partners? She repeated again and again in her head.
She coughed. 'Without being premature Ian, I have had my flat valued. I was pleased to put it mildly at the valuation.' She hands the report to him
   He peruses the report.
   'After mortgage costs and legal costs are taking into consideration I will have over a hundred thousand pounds in equity, plus I have an endowment policy that is due to mature in seven years' time that will be worth sixty thousand plus the terminal bonus which I estimate to be thirty-thousand. I hope that I have enough to secure a fifty- fifty per cent of the pub and property.'
   Ian looked at the valuation report and disagreed with it; it was worth much more than the sum on the page. He was pleased that she had done her homework and had the cursory things done such as having her flat valued, and the much maligned endowment policy would be another level of security, the bank would appreciate her due diligence on her finances.
   Ian had lost count of the many professional people he had seen cash in or sell their endowment policies because of the misselling scandal. He set up a subsidiary company and blitzed the local radio station and Press with advertisements with promises of paying the best rate for the endowments with no selling fees that national companies were charging. The long-term profit margin he was accumulating was phenomenal.
   'Once again Mary, you are one step ahead, everything that the banks' would require for security is in place, your home as well as your endowment, which I would bet that you are glad that you never sold. However, as it was your idea about the pub and the Polish and Scottish theme, and you came to me, I would like to put this offer to you; I will finance your share of the purchase price and the refurbishment, but I will put a charge on your flat as security, just as a business measure, I won't take your endowment into the financial equation. The interest that my company will offer you will be at less than the commercial interest charged, and there will be no other charges for setting up the company. It will be a straight fifty-fifty deal; my company will own fifty per cent and your company the other fifty per cent. You can go to the High Street banks' if you wish, that is your choice.'
   Now she was elated. He continued. 'But I'll wait till we see the Weavers Arms tomorrow, then we both will see whether we are looking at gold or lead.'
Mary was delighted, 'I understand that.'
   'The legal work for the business partnership will be done by an independent solicitor, he will act for you, I know one who is very good; he sometimes does work for me, as I said I won't charge you any fees for you setting up your company, he will invoice me for the legal work, if you want I can give him a call, if we go ahead with the purchase of the pub and the flats.'
   She felt faint, everything has moved so quickly. She felt the tears well up in her eyes; please God let this dream come true.

Ian noticed she was getting emotional, that brought back memories of his mother at the end of her tether, 'Why did we let ourselves go,' she would often shout at William as he lay in a drunken stupor in his chair.

Mary was on the verge of crying. 'I'll go into the other office and contact my brother to arrange the appointment for tomorrow. I realise the speed of events have come as a shock to you, but have another coffee and think about the finance, if you want to go to another bank rather than my company I won't be offended. See you in ten minutes.'

He left the office. She poured herself another coffee. The tears did not arrive, euphoria kicked in. She grabbed her newly purchased blank notebook and grabbed one of the pens that were neatly stacked on his desk. She wrote furiously on the notepad, two flats, and then crossed it out. She wrote two-two bedroom flats. They could be rented out to the Polish bar staff, that would be an incentive for good bar staff, rent them out at a discounted rent, if there were any problems with theft or shortfall in stock, not only would they lose their jobs but also their homes, which would be furnished to a good standard. Insurance costs would be reduced because of staff living on the premises. A donation to help the Polish community who were suffering penury; that would appear in the papers, the first donation would be handed over to the Polish priest one month after trading had commenced. He would have the knowledge where the money would be best spent. She then wrote on another page in huge capital letters: name of bar. It would have to reflect some common link with Poland and Dundee if not Scotland. She could ask the priest, then again perhaps not.

She would simply type in an English word into google and translate it into Polish. She was pleased that problem was solved. She turned to another fresh page and again in huge capitals she wrote Special Events; The third of May is Polish Day; she remembered that from the time she worked for the EU in Strasbourg, she laughed out loud at this thought; that was some party. That would be another event that the pub could celebrate and it would also generate massive Press interest. She would invite the local politicians, war veterans' et al.

A football team would be started and sponsored by the pub; she wishes she could think of a name, she hated calling it the pub. Then she placed the pen back into the correct position on Ian's desk and let out a relieved sigh. She looked around the office; everything seemed to be in its place as though it had been there for over a hundred years. Apart from the office chair, modern telephone and computer, it was like an office from 'A Christmas Carol.' She felt less teary now; she had the projected figures for a loan of one hundred and fifty thousand pounds over twenty five years, they were coming in at eight hundred and thirty eight pounds, plus insurance costs etc. The estimated costs overall would come in at thirteen hundred pounds a month. But she also had to pay her mortgage on her flat as well as live. The pub would be up and running in eight months' time, hopefully less. When the pub is opened money would be generated, helping to offset some of these crippling costs. But all these figures meant nothing until they see the pub and if they can refurbish it within a reasonable budget.

With Ian owning properties and working with builders' that was one thing less to worry about. The savings she had were modest; however they would cover her mortgage costs on her flat and living expenses for six months. Maybe she was getting a little bit ahead of herself? To temper her aspirational side with cold pessimistic reasoning she went over the downsides of her plan, yes everything could be stopped at the first viewing of the pub, maybe it was structurally unsound or unsafe? The cost of bringing it up to an acceptable standard could be prohibitive.

However, the building could be in sound condition and the costs to bring it up to a good or acceptable standard could be in line with Ian's expectations. The warmth of contentment was accumulating at a pleasing and accelerating rate. Optimism was winning. She had experienced enough depressed events in her life. Pessimism was banished.

***

The Hilton is busier than Eddings had anticipated. Linda obviously is a regular here.

As soon as they walked in they were guided to a table away from the cacophony of the numerous sales delegates who were wearing their ID badges around their necks like they were proud recipients of the Victoria Cross. Within a minute of them taking off their jackets a waitress had placed coffee and croissants on their table. It certainly wasn't like this in the police cafeteria.

Linda started to pour the coffee.' Milk and sugar?' she enquired
'Two sugars and plenty of milk please.' I wonder how much this is going to cost me he thought.
She opened the conversation so naturally. 'So where do you think Raymond is?'
'That's why I need to talk to you; I'm hoping I can jog your memory.'
She sat back in the high backed chair and sipped her coffee. 'Go ahead; feel free to ask...anything.'
'Has he been in contact you since the phone call?'
She continued sipping her coffee, a slight shake of the head indicated no.
'Did you and he go to a special place... something like a country hotel or a lodge for a weekend break?' She placed her coffee down and leant across the table.
'He liked to go hill walking in Cumbria; I am not too keen on outdoor pursuits, but he is.'
'Where did he stay when he went hill walking?'
'I never really asked... I'm sorry if I'm not much help.'
'Don't worry; things might come back to you... how is your jaw?'
'My jaw is healing nicely; ice cream seems to help, when I am watching television I indulge in this treat, but it certainly dulls the pain, thanks for asking... and if anything comes to mind I will be in touch.'
'There is some concern that he has not been seen in Dundee or Edinburgh, maybe he is going through some mental anguish?'
Her posture changed at this assessment. 'Mental anguish?'
'I was thinking his political life maybe was getting too much for him, his break-up with you, maybe he had money worries? Something must have sent him over the edge that's for sure.'
'Something definitely made him snap. But for the life of me I can't think of one single reason, again I'm sorry for the lack of theories.'
'Drugs?' Eddings spat out the question hoping she would be flummoxed at this curved ball.
'Drugs... what do you mean by that?' Her throat became arid.
'Was he a user of any other drugs apart from cocaine?' He watched her intently.
'He could have been using other drugs when he was not with me... when we were being intimate he practically forced me to use cocaine, unknown to me he was filming the whole episode, which I would rather not talk about.' She was genuinely embarrassed.
Eddings was unnerved by this type of questioning but he had to see her reaction.
'If it's any comfort to you the DVD has not surfaced... yet. Once we locate the elusive Mr Andrews the DVD might emerge and if it does we will let you know, that I promise you.'
'May I ask you a question of another matter, the money that was thrust into Brian, the Union Official, which was tainted with cocaine, has someone's fingerprints shown up on the money?'
'I have not heard anything significant on that case, but it wouldn't be much of an issue even if your fingerprints were on the money or mine for that matter, there are probably innocent members of the public fingerprints on that money, it would be hard to say if X's fingerprints were on some notes. But it would be serious if someone's fingerprints were on the majority of the bank notes, but I have not heard that.'
'The reason I asked, I just want to put Brian's mind at rest. Originally he said he didn't touch it when he was given it, but later confessed he did count it out of curiosity.'
'I would advise him to contact the officer in charge of that case; and to tell him that he did count the money, that's why his fingerprints will be on the notes.'
'I hope to speak to him later, but because of this jaw, I have to ration my speech.'
'Tell him not to worry, that will clear up any questions that his prints will throw up. How does it feel to be the saviour of the factory?'

'Now steady on, it was a team effort, it was the Council, the Scottish Executive, the Unions, Pension Funds and a very small part played by myself.'
'Are you not being modest?'
'Definitely not… it was a team effort.'
'Are you not forgetting someone else who helped or was part of the team?
She looked genuinely perplexed at this question. 'Who did I leave out?'
'The esteemed Mr Anderson, the manager of Romans.'
'I can recall Mr Anderson playing an active role... to close the factory, but no, I can't recall him formulating a plan to keep the factory open.'
'I was just teasing... Raymond Andrews was in the team as well wasn't he?'
'Yes, let's just say he was an unused substitute who wasn't required.'
'Is there anything else I can help you with?' She again didn't wait for the answer; she had risen and placed her coat on. Eddings was flabbergasted she had outmanoeuvred him by bringing the conversation to an end on her terms, and he still had to pay for the coffee.

He rose from his chair he didn't know whether to shake her hand or bow; the waitress on cue came and cleared the tray away. 'Just put this on my account Lucy,' the waitress acknowledged this order, 'and no doubt I will see you again,' she held out her hand, he met it.
'No doubt, no doubt,' he replied and she was on her way out of the hotel.

Linda was in the pre ordered taxi: she was relieved that Andrews's fingerprints were not on the notes. Eddings had watched her leave the hotel, and was struck at the many conversations that ground to a halt. Most of the people had eyes only for Linda as she elegantly walked to the lobby then out of the hotel.

Eddings mobile rang: it was Feeney throwing a strop; he was annoyed that Eddings had failed to tell him where he was going. He was further annoyed when Eddings told him that he was in the Hilton enjoying coffee and croissants with Linda Simpson.

'Is there a problem?' he enquired.
'No, but you could have shown some courtesy by saying where you were going, as we are partners…remember?'
Eddings continued to tease him. 'Do you want to come down to the Hilton? The coffee and croissants are delicious.' He went to further explain he was hoping to go with Linda for a swim then a massage; did he really need him back at the office that urgently? The response was predictable.
'You bet, get your arse back to the office pronto.'

Eddings placed the mobile back inside his jacket. Feeney was so predictable. He drained the last drop of coffee from the cup and casually gazed around him, he was envious of the clientele for some unknown reason, he was entering a period of his working life with a more cynical view of his job description, things were changing in the world of forensics, intuition which was an asset was now looked on as an anachronistic foible, if he started to doubt his innate radar, maybe it was time to retire. He chased away this depressing thought quickly. He was making his way out of the hotel no one gave him a second look, his ego was momentarily crushed at this. Obviously no one was curious who this gentleman was having coffee with Linda Simpson. His mind automatically cruised back to the matter in hand; Raymond Andrews where art thou?

'Enjoy your liaison with the black widow then?' Eddings smiled, took his overcoat off and moved to hang it up. 'Couldn't have went any better than if I planned it myself, pity I missed the swim with her and the massage, funnily enough my back is hurting, maybe it's because I have been carrying a dead-weight on this case.' He hung up his overcoat.
Feeney was stunned at this dig at him. 'Sorry..? And what do you mean by that?'
Eddings turned around with a stern look on his face. 'You're the alleged top detective, go figure as our American colleagues would say... any coffee going about?'
'Now you listen hear, to the untutored eye, I have been building up a rapport with the uniform guys, and you know why?' Eddings held up his hand to stop him expounding.

'You listen to me you have taken your eye off the ball, you're convinced that Andrews is not just a suspect he is the murderer, that's lazy logic.'
Feeney claps his hands sarcastically. 'Bravo... at long fucking last the penny has just dropped; he is the murderer, I'm convinced of that, when he surfaces we will take him in, don't worry; he is our man without a doubt.'
   Eddings just smiles. 'Is there any coffee?'
'Over in that jar beside the kettle... go figure.'
Eddings has achieved what he set out to accomplish, get Feeney's heart, soul and increasingly prosaic mind back on the case. He walks over and switches on the kettle, he deliberately keeps his back to Feeney, which Feeney hates. 'Where's the evidence then... that points to Andrews?'
'Are you for real! The golf club is the main piece of evidence which has his DNA and fingerprints, and when we have him in here, he'll talk, I just know it.'
'What if he fails to turn up, what do we do?' He pours the water into one cup only.
'He will turn up, why wouldn't he?'
'Hmm, let me think because he is the murderer?'
'Exactly! He will turn up eventually, they always do… the stats show this.'
   Eddings is pouring milk into his coffee. 'Is this how the Scottish Crime and Drug Enforcement Agency, the elite of law enforcement operate; on the dubious premise 'they' turn up eventually.' He is mocking Feeney with laughter. 'Ah, now I get it! You are jealous of me because I'm a younger man that has overtaken you on the highway to success, that's the real reason isn't it?' Eddings looks at him with a degree of pity.
   'Not really, and I'll give you some evidence to suggest that the SCDEA are just a politician's way to say via the Press that they take crime and especially drug crime seriously; Martin Johnston served three prison sentences, the first fifteen years ago, seven years in jail for heroin, he was released after four, and then two years later he gets caught again with heroin, sentenced to four years, after he is released he gets caught again, he gets four years again no increase in sentence you'll note… out in two.'
'It's the judges' fault, not the SCDEA, we are catching the dealers, and the judges' are jailing them.'
'Oh really? It was in the Sunday papers last year that the Head of the SCDEA was on holiday in the Algarve staying in a million pound villa owned by... Martin Johnston.'
Feeney feels sick at this news being brought up. 'No that was pure coincidence; the Chief hired the villa through an agency. He didn't know the villa was owned by Johnston.'
'Of course he didn't, that was just an honest mistake wasn't it? Who are you are you trying to convince me or yourself?'
'Look it's a pointless exercise discussing Martin Johnston, anyway he's dead now.'
'Yeah, he killed himself, strange case; it went all quiet, did it?'
'I know you're upset, but I am willing to listen to you, any suggestions that will bring this case to a conclusion? Feeney was more conciliatory now, he bitterly regretted saying Eddings was jealous of him.
'Is that your way of apologising?'
'Yes I'm sorry, now back to the case, what's on your mind?'
'I accept your apology, if we are not cooperating with each other the only beneficiary is Andrews. We have made very little progress on this case, we have to go to Andrews flat and search it for anything that could lead us to him, is his passport still in the flat, or if not has he taken flight? Feeney agreed. 'I will get the warrant to search his place, but I would prefer a locksmith and the alarm company to open the door rather than the big baton crashing in the door.'
Eddings was pleased that his partner was once more onside; he felt that once in the flat, it would give up some clue or clues however reluctant.
'You go and organise the warrant, locksmith and the alarm company, I'll make you a coffee.'

Feeney felt embarrassed and a lit bit ashamed he had spoken to his older partner in a spiteful and disrespectful way. Before he got to the door he apologised again, Eddings just smiled.
Once he had left the office Eddings reflected on what he had said about the SCDEA, he examined every word; he had no need to search his conscience and recant.

One thing was troubling him was Feeney's reticence in looking for Andrews; no rants as per usual, not even 'I'll get the bastard,' he was relaxed, he would be caught, charged and convicted.
He didn't share this open and shut case that Feeney not only embraced but was waltzing with.
It was just too simple; the assault on Linda Simpson was a planned and vicious assault; Lotus's club 'accidentally' left behind with Andrews 'prints and his DNA. It was verging on implausible in his mind.

***

'These are my brothers, James and Peter, James is an architect and Peter is the chartered surveyor I was telling you about... and this is Mary my potential business partner.'
The agent introduced himself with the formalities. 'Let's hope the key fits,' the lock is not being cooperative, and the agent is somewhat embarrassed, he tries again, this time with success.
He offers Ian a large torch, there is no electricity connection into the pub; vandals had dug up the cable for the copper content.

'Follow me,' he says as he carefully enters the pub, the smell of damp is evident. Mary is aghast at the state of the pub, not the damp or the dated decor but that the bar is still strewn with glasses, on the tables and the bar itself. Mary is shining her torch on the numerous glasses.

'The previous leaseholder was not so house proud,' the agent said slightly embarrassed. Peter and James have moved away from the others and are shining their torches into every nook and cranny then they go into an animated conversation, much shaking of heads then they write in their respective note books. Damp meters are pressed into the walls with regularity, and then the high pitched sound of the meter screams out. At every high pitched sound Mary is feeling less and less confident. The agent seems to ignore this activity going all around him and continues to pepper the conversation with 'potential' with alarming monotony. Her eyes were at odds with her ears. Peter and James bring their cursory inspection to a premature halt; 'Ian, we have seen enough...'
The agent is witnessing his fat commission disappear in front of him. 'You have still to see the function room downstairs.'

James turns to Ian as if the agent does not exist. 'This place is practically a swimming pool. The place is full of damp, every piece of porous material needs replaced, as the function room is downstairs that will be in a more perilous condition, based on that I have to use the acronym; C.R.A.P. Can't Recommend A Purchase.'
Mary tries hard to control her feelings but the sickening feeling has returned to her stomach.
'So it's pointless even having a cursory look downstairs?' Ian asked
James joins the conversation. 'Damp travels upwards... if the upstairs is like this, I would hate to see the condition downstairs.'
The agent tries to bring the conversation into positive territory. 'I think you are being too negative... no one present here this morning has seen down stairs, let's all go down with an open mind, even for my sake, I may have to update the report which will affect the price southwards, what do you say?' Ian stares at his watch.

'I don't see the point of having a look, we are very busy Ian.' Peter said.
The agent knows he is facing a losing battle. 'Look I'm not asking you to give a detailed report, just give it a quick look at least.' The agent is cutting a sorry figure.

'Okay, Peter and James give it a quick look, five minutes maximum; we have a busy schedule, Mary and I will stay here.' 'Thanks a lot,' the agent said. They make their wearily way downstairs to the function room, Mary and Ian are left in the damp and desolate surroundings.

'It looks as though we will not be partners after all; I knew I shouldn't build myself up for this fall'. Ian is just observing the pub. 'This was a good pub in its day; how things change... it does need plenty of work done to it.' He walks over to the glass strewn bar and rubs his hand over the scarred surface. 'They even stubbed their fags out on the bar!' Ian let out a laugh.

'The clientele must have been quite rough,' he continues to walk the length of the large bar, he stops and looks in each corner.' Four large screen TVs wouldn't engulf this pub, one showing, Polish football, one showing English, one showing Scottish and the other golf or some other sport, do you agree?'

Mary has missed most of what Ian has said; she has been lost in her what might have been world.

'Mary did you hear what I said?'

'I'm sorry I was just thinking... what we could have done if this place was in good condition.'

The heavy sound of feet pounding can be heard on the stairs, they emerge from the function suite. The agent's face said it all; James and Peter had failed to be won over.

'Are we all finished here then?' said Ian

'Yes, just as we said, damp is present everywhere.' The agent is determined to have a last hurrah. 'You have still to see the two flats, there in decent condition, and have massive potential.'

'Thanks anyway, but we have to get going.' They start moving towards the door. Mary can't resist looking back one more time at her forlorn dream. The agent is looking around the bar with massive potential, he is analysing his sales pitch; must stop using potential in sales pitch.

He knew that the building had serious damp problems; that was stated in the report two years ago, but now the damp was rampant. He will have to market the premises in another realistic price bracket; Ian was only the second serious businessman to have professional personnel with him. The others were 'wall tappers' who were avid watchers of property programmes on television.

Ian had the courtesy to wait on him; the others were in their respective cars. The agent pulls the door closed and turns the key; he wonders how many months it will be before he shows interested parties again. The agent still does not give up.

'If the property is re-marketed at a more acceptable price would you like be kept informed?'

'I admire your resilience, but it would not be cost effective in converting the pub into flats.'

'But if I come back to you with a more realistic price band, would you be interested?'

'To be honest, and I can see that you are thoroughly professional and diligent in your manner; but the premises would have to be on offer at less than one hundred thousand, and I mean about ninety thousand.' The agent was shocked at this derisory valuation.

'The owner wouldn't take that as a serious offer, he was looking for near the two hundred thousand, minimum...'

James is impatient and sounds his horn repeatedly and points at his watch, his face showing annoyance. 'I understand the owner's position but he should come and see the premises himself then he might agree with my estimation of the value... thanks anyway I have to go, have a safe journey back to Glasgow.'

The agent watched the three cars move away from the pub. He turns around and makes his way back to his BMW resigned that this pub will be extremely difficult to sell. On the windscreen is a parking notice that's all he needed he looks at the pub again; the pub should be called The Ugly Duckling. But he refused to give up on this pub, the owner needed a reality check that was certain, however, the price Ian mentioned was too low, he knew it and so did Ian.

Ian looked in the rear view mirror at the thoroughly dejected agent; a smirk ran across his face. 'He's not had a good morning has he?'

No response. Mary is looking straight ahead thoroughly disconsolate.

'Disappointed then Mary?'

'That doesn't come close to how I feel, and it's my fault for building up optimism, instead of being realistic but that's life I suppose.'

Ian turns the radio's volume down. 'It's always good to be optimistic; you must always have hope, without hope negativity can set in and that can have a corrosive effect on the human spirit, anyway you saw the building today, what has made you feel melancholic?'
'The building is in a terrible state, I heard the conversation with the agent...'
'You didn't hear me say that we didn't want it, did you?'
'No...But I heard you say a lot more than that, have I missed something here?'
'That's the first meeting; there will be another of that I'm certain, everything will become clearer you just have to temper your impatience and top up your hope.'
She stops looking straight ahead and turns to Ian. 'Are you saying you are interested?'
'Very much so, we have to play this without any enthusiasm and plenty of pessimism to bring the valuation down. He hasn't had a real offer of that I'm certain, he'll tell the seller that the client this morning is only interested in turning the bar into flats, but the cost of the bar and the conversion costs prohibit the deal being struck. He'll suggest that the property be re-marketed at a more realistic price. The seller in his heart of hearts will know this already. He might and I emphasise might suggest that the agent comes back to us and suggests I make an offer. The agent will welcome this change of heart. And then I'll massage his ego and I will ask his personal view of what price the seller will be comfortable of accepting, then we'll see where we end up; after all no sale; no commission for the agent.'

'You convinced me that you weren't interested, I hope the agent will be in touch with us again, I don't feel so bad now.'
'Don't worry he'll be in touch, he's got the gift of the gab he'll talk the seller round, I know the price will become negotiable.'

***

The old lady is watching the locksmith at work. 'Everything is alright here you can go back into your flat,' Eddings says smiling. The old lady continues to watch without reply.
'Just ignore her, she is harmless,' said Feeney.
'Harmless but not deaf,' replied the old lady.
'You're welcome to watch, but there is nothing to see, any chance of some coffee and sandwiches?'
The old lady has seen enough and returns to her flat and closes the door.
'Did you have to say that to her?
Feeney doesn't bat an eye-lid. 'It got rid of her, didn't it?'
The locksmith has completed his task he opens the door no alarm has been activated. Eddings advises the locksmith and the alarm technician to remain outside the door and not to let anyone enter the premises. He nods the four forensic officers into the flat.
He and Feeney place their latex gloves on and follow the forensic team in. Feeney harboured his suspicion that Raymond Andrews would be found with no sign of life about him, the only thing he is concerned was how he had died. The forensic team went into the flat with their tried and trusted methodical approach. After each room had been given a visual search Feeney's theory was well wide of the mark, instead of the smell of a decaying corpse they were met by a pleasant and welcoming fragrance of orange blossom. Every cupboard, wardrobe and drawer was thoroughly searched.
Bank statements and other financial documents are placed in various boxes and labelled; the laptop computer is placed in a plastic container then sealed. Eddings called one of the forensic team into the bathroom and asked her to remove the tiled bath panel. When it was removed Eddings asked her to shine her torch into the dark space. 'Nothing in there,' she advised. Eddings asked if he could look, she shrugged her shoulders and handed him the torch, he went on his knees and shone the torch back and forth, she was right nothing there except pipe cuttings and plumbers tape.
'Satisfied?' He was not impressed by her sarcastic tone. He stuck his head in further into the cavernous space. He moved his free hand onto the floor boards and tapped them individually.

One floor board didn't make the expected hollow sound; a more dense sound came back. He asked her to hold the torch. 'Have you found something? He ignored the question, he pulled at the floorboard, it was not budging. 'I need a thin screwdriver.'

She returned to the bathroom with the screwdriver; Feeney and the rest of the forensic team crowded into the bathroom. One of the team that had been in charge of videoing the operation nodded for Eddings to continue and prise the floor board clear of the other floorboards. Eddings placed the screwdriver into the adjoining floorboard and eased the floorboard up. The forensic officer beckoned him back when he videoed the floorboard being taken from its original location and being temporarily placed adjacent to the toilet cistern, Eddings shone the torch into the space but nothing was seen apart from discarded grey electrical wire. He eased his fingers further into the gap.

'There's something here, it's a bag of some kind, but it's jammed, it's coming loose... got it!' He pulls out a Sainsbury plastic bag and places it on the floor. The forensic officer asks everyone to move out of the way, he invites Eddings to open the bag which he does like a child reluctantly opening a Christmas present. The bag contains a hand gun.

Feeney is smiling maniacally, he is careful not to let any expletive out. He steps away from the bag. He beckons Eddings to move into the lounge.

'I was expecting to find Andrews dead in here, the gun I wasn't expecting that, what about you?' He sits down on the Queen Anne leather chair. His eyes move from left to right examining the lounge. 'This place is too clean for a bachelor pad, don't you think?'

Feeney is puzzled. 'You've lost me there?'

'This place is too clean, too sterile; I know the forensics have been shining their lamps looking for microscopic splashes of blood, but they have found nothing ...that's what worries me.'

Feeney is desperately trying to refrain from berating his colleague.

'The place is spotless because the cleaners have been in after the flood... what about that gun... the hand gun? *You,* not me have just pulled it from the floorboards under the bath... you know what I'm driving? It could be the gun that killed the two junkies and Swithers.'

Eddings is uneasy he looks over to Feeney. 'This is going to sound stupid; we are turning up more and more evidence but instead of progressing I feel we are regressing, until we speak to Andrews, I can't relax evidence or no evidence.'

Feeney is exasperated. 'When this gun is tested, it will either confirm my theory or it will ridicule it, Andrews is our man I'm sure of that. The golf club with his fingerprint *and* his DNA, and if the gun which was found in *his* flat has his prints or DNA; it's a slam dunk as far as I am concerned.'

Eddings looked at him but offered no comment.

'Surely, you agree?'

Eddings rose from the seat and walked over to the huge window and looked over to the Tay Rail Bridge. 'I suppose you're right. Andrews has done a runner. But only he knows why he killed those poor bastards; that's what's troubling me. If he doesn't turn up, we will never know, will we?'

'Why worry; as long as we nail him. His defence team will come up with some bullshit, his mummy didn't kiss him goodnight, or he was bullied at nursery or in the maternity ward. We have the gun and golf club; there is no way his legal team can talk their way out of this. And he is a coke-head. Our job is done.'

Eddings moves slowly away from the window. 'I suppose you're correct. Interpol will be handed the baton now. He will be abroad somewhere; he won't be in Dundee, that's for sure. We will have to wait on the forensic report; before we crack open the bubbly.'

'Well, I'm not waiting; Andrews is our man, there is no doubt in my mind and I am sure no doubt in yours. You are just being cautious; that was the way you were trained decades ago, we now have forensic science... we are going for a pint.'

The man who knew the whereabouts of Raymond Andrews is enjoying an alcohol free beer watching the glorious sunset from his balcony.

All his assets had been sold to his business associates for a price that exceeded his accountant's expectation. He was expecting lower than the commercial price but was surprised when it turned into a frenzied auction. He was enriched by an additional two million euros that was the currency that he would be now trading. All those Eastern European countries that would be joining the European Union would be the perfect locations for his bountiful fortune.

Tenerife would be another chapter in his life. Once he had the hotel up and running he would venture into these fledgling new members of the European Union. He was spending thirty- million euros to capitalise and secure twenty per cent of a new bank that was to be set up in Bulgaria; his other partners were from Ireland. Now that the armed struggle was over and weapons had been rendered inoperable, there were money dumps to be taken out of active service.

Forensic accountants would be crawling over each and every suspicious bank account, the money had to be placed into a less vigilant and rigorous banking system: Bulgaria. The money that had been collected from sympathisers in the United States; had to be seen and appropriated for educational purposes for the young. Hundreds of hand- picked students from a Republican background with no criminal convictions were financed through the University system in Britain.

Many towns and cities had a large influx of Irish students in Scotland; Edinburgh, Glasgow and Dundee. The students would become lawyers in Commercial as well as Criminal law. Others would become first class accountants and placed within well respected companies.

The armed struggle would need these white collar republicans as well as green collar volunteers' for years to come when the republican movement achieved its aim; to be the de facto Government, that day had come. Ramage had known friends from across the water for over two decades; he had assisted them with money and 'hard goods.'

He was welcomed with open cheque book into the new bank as a trusted investor that shared the same values and aspirations as the other investors. The other investors' had courted the much respected members of the financial and banking community in the early nineties when the republican movement edged away from the armed struggle and became active in politics.

When they were finally seen to be putting criminality behind them the British Government assigned millions of pounds into new building projects. Which consisted of new social housing, new private estates and modernisation of old dilapidated buildings. These were all put out to tender. The republican front building contractors were successful in the tender process and they carried out the work to a more than satisfactory level. However, millions had to be spirited out of the North of Ireland along with the legitimate profits from the building firms. There were many other businesses that were not one hundred per cent legitimate; clubs and security firms.

The British Government had warned the republican movement that when there was sustained peace these quasi legal clubs and security firms would be required to pay Corporation Taxes.
By the time peace came on a permanent basis the students that had been educated and farmed out to top City firms where they were taught the art of finding loopholes in the Government Tax Laws and thus avoiding paying as much tax or even better no tax on certain investment strategies

They returned to Ireland or went to other subsidiary offices of the financial and tax planning offices throughout Europe. Dotted throughout Bulgaria were such offices they had been trading for over three years. British and Irish buy-to-let investors were arriving daily by the plane load. Having a new established bank that was owned by much respected Irish businessmen created an air of trust to the buy-to-let investors, the bank's non- executive directors' were the cream of semi- retired businessmen and ex –Dail Eirann officials.

Much speculation in the British press questioning if Bulgaria would be allowed to join the EU, the Shareholders' in the bank had the ear of the higher echelons of the EU Commission; the Bank's directors had been advised that Bulgaria would have the full membership and benefits of the EU. Billions of Euros would be pumped into public services, the EU had a caveat; no Bulgarian bank would be considered to administer any EU funds because of endemic corruption.

Fortunately for Ramage and his investors their bank had been chosen to vet projects whether they were beneficial to the indigenous population or whether they were scam companies. The bank had negotiated a twenty-per cent administration fee to manage the EU funds. The bank would be going public after five years trading but a percentage of shares would be set aside for hedge funds. Ramage and his wealthy cohorts would see their investment quadruple.

Ramage was so pleased that he maintained a close and personal relationship with the republican movement through intermediaries. His erstwhile business associates were keen to buy his many assets and they accepted he would not set up any business in their fiefdom whether that was in Spain or Glasgow. They were blissfully unaware that he had a lucrative drugs business operating from Dundee and distributed drugs up the east coast and as far north to the fishing town of Fraserburgh; however, he was in the process of relinquishing from this business also. The money from his sale of his various businesses went through the tried and trusted methods of electronic bank transfer, through a myriad of names and companies where it would end up in his Law firm. Then it would be invested in the new bank in Bulgaria. Everything above board or so it seemed. Who would have thought that he was the real owner behind the respected Law firm, the one and only person who knew this was his childhood friend who left with his family and emigrated from Glasgow to America and settled in Kearney, New Jersey.

His mind effortlessly drifted back to Raymond Andrews. Before any drug deals had been set up he had as usual done the background check.

A relative of Andrews had approached a friend of his with the news that someone in Dundee was wanting in on the act and he had plenty of money to burn. They checked him out and did a dummy run; it wasn't a set up. They were in business. Eighteen months' down the line information came to him that Linda Simpson was the money behind the deal, this was Andrews protecting himself; he was the boyfriend of the multi-millionaire Linda Simpson.

She no doubt gave him money for legitimate business dealings unknown to her he was using her money to give to his relative to buy heroin. He was getting carried away, he approached one of Ramage's associate's with the news that if Romans closed he would guarantee that he could obtain planning permission for executive style housing even though it was an industrial estate. He was paid a one hundred thousand pound introductory fee to befriend the Romans son, and it looked certain the factory would close. However, that was before the indefatigable Linda Simpson came to the rescue of the workforce.

Andrews on numerous occasions said Linda was doing this as a public relations exercise, after an initial meeting of defiance she would slowly fade into the background. When the workforce had accepted their fate, she would return with the welcome news that she had managed to extract from the management an enhanced redundancy package. Andrews had been advising the manager on the tempting redundancy package, this would ensure that when it went to the vote to accept closure it would be a sure thing. Ramage was impressed at the careful and meticulous planning that Andrews had choreographed.

The houses that were to be built would be of the highest order with a village pond and ducks to add to the ambience, but it was now a pipe dream. When the wind turbines came into the argument from Linda Simpson of all people, hope started to flicker in the workers hearts. Andrews was still reiterating that Linda was playing the public relations card; it was an act he told Ramage's associate, relax it was all an act. Ramage watching her on television concluded she was full of passion for the factory to remain open, but if it was an act her thespian skills were a wonder to watch. But it wasn't an act, Andrews was unable to persuade her to drop her campaign, he couldn't tell her that he would be making money from the closure of the factory.

He couldn't confide in her that he was the one who thought up the idea to close the factory even though he was going through the motions of given statements to the Press regarding the economic impact on Dundee. If Linda knew that he was the catalyst for the demise of the factory, their other 'business' would end; and she had the profits from the business.

That's when panic set in and he started abusing cocaine on a daily use, nerves and the repercussions from the West Coast building firm that he promised the land to. Andrews was spot on in his assessment of the situation, Linda would end their romantic and business relationship and he would not see a penny of the profits, and as for the 'executives' of the building firm, they could become his executioners.

He had to disappear and quickly. Andrews was in a desperate state physically and mentally, he knew what the end game would be. He offered the hundred thousand pound fee back to them, this was accepted. Arrangements would be made to pick up the money; in cash, Andrews believed he was off the hook; however he was not naive to meet them in a darkened car park or other sparsely populated location even in daylight. He accepted his relationship with Linda was over, he was glad that he skimmed off some of the drug profits for himself for a rainy day, that day had arrived but it wasn't raining it was a deluge.

He knew that Linda had been meeting Ian on a regular basis, together with the cocaine and the end of their romance; he irrationally attached some of the blame to Ian for the factory remaining open. He assumed that Ian maybe had been tipped of about the plan for executive houses, and he and Linda cooked up this facile 'save the factory campaign' for their own self- aggrandisement, keep the factory open for a few years then when it does close they can benefit by buying the land and building new houses on the site. Ian had an abundance of experience of building houses on industrial land. The development down at the docks proved his point with precise clarity.

Linda was well aware of whom to talk to regarding planning permission, she could run rings round any objectors, she had learnt from Ian. His housing was embracing the latest technology and green issues, solar power panels, heat retaining materials etc. He knew what he was doing when he bought that land at the docks from under the nose of Linda Simpson. Now they were allies; he was the outsider and his life was under threat. The instant he hands over the money he'll tell all about their cosy business relationship and their plans for the Romans site in years to come.

He had been doubled crossed, and his political career was finished, he'll move abroad he had plenty of money in various banks in Europe, he just wanted a safe passage out of Scotland and he was confident that the return of the hundred thousand would guarantee this. He made the contact and the response was favourable someone would be at his door at eleven am dressed in a dark suit carrying a clip board; have the money there.

True to their word the bell ran out a welcoming tone. He launched into calming breathing techniques. He studied himself in the mirror. He had rehearsed this moment many times. Before he hands over the holdall he'll make sure that they know it was Linda Simpson and Ian Williams who had conspired to keep the factory open and when it did close they would develop the land for their benefit. The doorbell rang, it rang again he looked again in the mirror practising the politician's warm smile, content he made his way up the long hall, he made sure that the holdall was in full view from the front door; that should defuse any potential tension. The door opened and the man with the clipboard went into a professional monologue about the benefits of switching power companies, he was invited in. He followed Andrews down the hall; he saw the holdall sitting on the table. He looked into the holdall and was pleased to see Her Majesty looking resplendent, he counted out four random bundles of one thousand pounds neatly bound he was confident that the other ninety six would be of equal worth.

Andrews went into his well-rehearsed tale about the conspiracy; Linda Simpson and Ian Williams and of course he was the fall guy. When he had told his tale of woe he felt much better, a heavy burden had been lifted he smiled and was delighted to be told 'not to worry, it was better for him to make a clean breast of things, my taxi will be here in ten minutes, could he trouble him for a cup of tea?' Andrews was relieved for the first time in months,' he was very obliging, he was still talking as he made his way over to the open plan kitchen fitted with Smeg appliances, as he switched on the kettle a green plastic bag came over and engulfed his head.

Panic set in, he felt himself go light headed he was now on his knees being held down, a sense of hopelessness set in, then calmness came then he was not in this world. He was lifted on to the Queen Anne chair, the holdall was placed in the centre of the hall, and then he went into the bathroom removed the bath panel and prised up the fourth floorboard, he returned to the lounge and removed the green plastic bag from Andrews's head, took the gun out of his pocket and placed it in the right hand of the silent Andrews and expertly curled the finger around the trigger. After this was done he placed the gun in a Sainsbury bag that was found in the kitchen cupboard below the sink. He then went into the bathroom and secreted the plastic bag forcefully into the recess of the floorboard, replaced the floorboard and finally the bath panel. He made a call on his mobile and left with the holdall.
    He left as he came into the building nondescript. He returned to his car parked in Scrimgeour Place a haven for students who parked their cars that irritated the owner -occupiers on a daily basis. He watched the grey Mercedes electrical appliance vehicle which displayed on its sides all the expensive brands Miele, Bosch and Smeg park five metres from his car. The two delivery men went to the rear of the van and took out a large American fridge that was well -protected with polystyrene foam to prevent accidental scrapes and bangs, they went into the building.
    They entered Andrews flat and placed him into the bespoke box that looked similar to a large American fridge and returned to the van then left. This was poetry in motion, the mundane sight of seeing a fridge being delivered would not attract anyone's attention. He moved off and drove back to Glasgow, where the car would be taken to a scrap yard, left and crushed.
    He would call Ramage from a public phone box and tell him that the 'Fridge was collected' he didn't wait for a reply. Ramage raised a contented smile, the unknown assassin was expensive but ingenious in his methods and it would be clean hit, no one knew who he was, rumours he was an ex-Provo was just subterfuge. Ramage preferred no physical meeting, no contact or other incriminating evidence linking him with any suspect. Two days later one of Ramage's men spoke to the assassin by mobile phone; the assassin used a convincing Dublin accent. He told him what Andrews had said about Linda Simpson and Ian Williams, and then abruptly ended the call.   Ramage ruminated that it had some merit to it, Ian Williams had connections in local and national politics; he had stopped Ramage from constructing luxury student accommodation near Dundee University, the council was flooded with objections from prominent people as well as the local residents, he was assured that the plans that he submitted would be approved but they were defeated by two votes. One year later one of Williams's companies submitted similar plans for luxury student accommodation this time they were passed. Council officials explained that these plans were passed because they were innovative and embraced environmental technology. They ticked all the green issue boxes, solar panel energy, heat retaining materials etc.
    He was now letting out these en-suite rooms for fifty -pounds a week there were communal lounges with Sky television, and even an extensive library.   The accommodation had gained a very favourable reputation by word of mouth; other families whose off-spring were intending to study in Dundee the following year visited the accommodation and adored what they saw, they booked the accommodation there and then.
    Ian Williams Legal Services were subject to a hostile take-over from Ramage's Law Company five years previously but was rebuffed. Far from agreeing to being taken over or incorporated Ian left the smug and supercilious Acquisition Manager with a polite refusal, Ian also mentioned that he was also acquiring companies in the legal and accounting sector, Ian would be very interested in *acquiring* his Company subject to a thorough and forensic account examination. There was no love lost after this riposte. When Ramage was informed of this he felt his masculinity had been challenged. Losing to Ian Williams once was unfortunate, being insulted by a counter offer for his Law Company was tantamount of being slapped in the face by a gauntlet. Of course Ramage could not take the normal appropriate action against an upstart; his involvement in the Law Company had to remain in the shadows. He would neither forget nor forgive Ian Williams.

Linda Simpson on the other hand was a dippy blond as far as Ramage was concerned he wanted to cultivate a professional relationship with her so she could introduce him on a regular basis to her influential friends. The invitation he had offered to Linda to come over to Tenerife for some sun and relaxation was neither declined nor accepted, she never replied, he didn't pursue it. Like most of the women he had encountered, if he was rebuffed it did not cause him any angst. He moved on.

He enjoyed the serenity of his villa in the sun; he was missing Glasgow not a jot. He picked up the previous day's Daily Record and the headline filled him with glee. Another drug baron gunned down in broad daylight. That made it four gangland style executions in ten days. When he had to remove rivals he never went down this ludicrous route. It was too brazen and the likelihood of the gunmen getting caught was increased by the proliferation of CCTV cameras. Then someone might talk, the risks were increasing every day, someone from this family is shot, and retaliation was always returned and so it went on. He preferred the tried and trusted method; an associate would make contact with the UA (unknown assassin)

He would explain who the problem was and then that would be it; money was paid into the requested bank account. The money would go on a convoluted odyssey in and out of various banks' accounts around the world. Sometimes the UA would decline some work, Ramage had used him sparingly over the years; Andrews would have been the last, but things had changed, one more job needed to be done then that would be it. He felt as though he had done Linda Simpson a massive favour by removing Raymond Andrews from her personal and business life.

Being duped by Andrews investing her money into drugs instead of legitimate ventures would be embarrassing for her. If Andrews had been caught he would have implicated her saying she was the brains behind the operation; she owed him. That invoice would be paid not in cash but in kind.

Raymond Andrews had decided to remove himself from society had been the theme behind the headlines in the local newspapers then it made news in the national newspapers. Various sources from within the Scottish Parliament had said he had a crisis of confidence that started to affect his parliamentary duties and he had set backs in his personal life. Various rumours began to circulate that he was having difficulty with money, his sexuality or gambling debts. Rather than play this down, the local and opportunistic MSP sought to brief the Press about him, even though she had rarely met him.

Some of the MSPs had suggested that he had talked of going to the Swiss Alps to start a new life but this was never confirmed. Sometime later 'sources' close to the investigation of the murder of the two police officers said that they were anxious to speak to Raymond Andrews as a matter of urgency. This raised the public's eyebrows they saw plenty of smoke but no fire. Reading between the lines Raymond Andrews's disappearance and the murder of the police officers were linked, then the conspiracy theories started to trickle out; sexually outrageous threesomes, people trafficking from Poland, and of course drugs. All these theories had to be investigated which took time, resources and money. Impatience was flowing down to Feeney from the Chief Constable. Eddings did not ponder over the Chief Constable's demand for an arrest. He exploded into the office where Feeney was holding court with his fan club from the uniform branch.

'Out the lot of you... now!'

The police officers swiftly moved out.

'Are you behind this?' Eddings threw the newspaper with the story on the desk.

Feeney gives the headline a cursory glance. 'Why... is there a problem?'

'You just can't help it can you, you are like these nobodies on X-Factor you smell fame and crave to be in the spotlight.'

Feeney is still calm and still has his feet on the desk, a pet hate of Eddings, he notices Eddings stare at his feet. He casually removes them from the desk.

'I had approval from upstairs so you can dump the outrage, it's been approved.'

'Are you telling me you went upstairs and asked for permission to leak information to the Press?'

Feeney nods.

'What is the problem... this will smoke Andrews out, and once we have him he'll confess, look I don't want to sound arrogant, but I do have a degree in Criminal Psychology.'
'Oh I didn't realise that... and has anyone called in to say where the fuck he is?'
'Its early days, look you have to relax, c'mon let's get out of here, we'll go to the Law Hill it will be cold but it might calm you down.'
'It's the Law, not the Law hill, that's equivalent of saying lets go to the Hilltown on the Hill.'
Feeney grabs his coat and throws it at him, then takes his own coat off the hanger.
'Really, that's really interesting...I think.'
'Don't you know anything about Dundee?'
'I'm interested in the future not the past.'

Eddings has calmed down a little but he is still angry that Feeney didn't run the plan by him about leaking information to the Press. Paradoxically he could understand why he didn't, because he would have said no. Since he told him about being in the SCDEA and he hadn't shown any admiration, he knew he was looking for brownie points by solving the murders. They drove up to the Law; Feeney did all the talking he was keeping his own counsel to a certain degree. The both of them walked over to view the Tay Rail Bridge.

Feeney felt he had to get Eddings back onside he knew he had marginalised him to some degree but he felt Eddings was ignoring glaring evidence.
'Some engineering feat that.'
'I wonder how many poor buggers died building that?' replied Eddings
'And what about the working conditions they endured, it must have been a nightmare, but that was then.'
Eddings walks over to view the skyline of the docks. 'It is taking shape now, but still lacks something, all those flats look so boxy... and I bet they aren't cheap. 'I was thinking of maybe putting money down on one of the next phase...'
'Are you a detective or a property developer?' Feeney is annoyed at this.
'That's uncalled for, my mind is totally on this case, so don't have any worries there.'
'Property in Bulgaria, property up at the DRI and now at the docks, you can certainly multi-task.'
Feeney refuses to respond to this jibe. 'What do you suggest we do about Andrews, then?'
'Try to find him for a start; I spoke to the IT boys nothing on his computer, all information on it mostly mundane Scottish Parliament business. Have you thought where he could be?'
Feeney shakes his head. 'Bank accounts and visa cards have not been used for over two weeks, trail has gone cold. You didn't get anywhere with Linda Simpson... I'll have a go at her; she might be more open with me.'
'And what is that meant to mean?'
'I think she finds me attractive. All women fancy me, that's a fact and you know it.'
Eddings bursts out laughing. 'Really, how come you're single then?'
'Ah, getting jealous now, because you're getting old.'
'No, I'm not jealous of you going home to a freezing flat and living on Pot Noodles.'
'I can't argue I like the odd Pot Noodle, but my flat is not freezing. Anyway, back to Linda Simpson, I'll try a more experimental mode of questioning, she won't realise she is being interrogated, I know which phrases to use.'
'Do you want me to accompany you or do you think you'll be better on your own?'
'Better on my own, that's no reflection on your interviewing technique.'
'Oh, of course not, I just thought it I would benefit to see an expert like you have a different method of questioning, but in saying that every murder case that I have investigated in Dundee for the last ten years, me and my team have solved them. And funnily enough none of us have a Degree, how lucky is that?'
'I know, I know, but this case is different I don't want to bore you with psychology.'
'That's very kind of you. Do you care to explain why this is different?'

Eddings is starting to feel that he is not been fully appreciated.

'This is political or it seems to be a political matter; and once politics comes into the equation, that is why it's different, someone high up the greasy pole of politics could be involved and if there is, we don't want leaks to newspapers...'

Eddings is incredulous at this comment. 'And who leaked that Andrews could be involved in the murders of the police officers not forgetting the two young lads or do they not matter?'

'They matter, but being brutally honest, they don't matter a lot, but the two police officers matter more, they had a tale to tell but they were silenced. As for the leaking of the Andrews story I make no apology we have to smoke him out, the case has stalled.'

'That's what I have been telling you! But you are more interested in being chummy with the plods.'

'I've told you before the information I have is that there are two police officers under the influence of Ramage, and I'm making progress in identifying them, you'll have to trust me on that one.'

'You mean taking money from Ramage, forget this influence bollocks.'

'I can't say anymore on this subject, but I have a good idea who one of them is.'

Eddings knew that if he asked he would be stonewalled, and he wouldn't give his partner the satisfaction of rebuffing him. He came to the conclusion that this would be the last case that he would be working with Feeney. He was a vanity detective. Feeney would gather all the information that *he* had mined and Feeney would walk into the Chief Constables office giving the impression that he was the engine of the enquiry and it was him that wrapped up the case.

Eddings would be described as a Luddite and would be perceived as Feeney's little helper rather than the innovator in pursuing leads. He would be seen not as a wallflower but as a weed. Eddings had giving some thought about retiring after this case but there is a caveat; only if he solved it. The evidence gathered pushed his days in the sun further from his mind, now he had to watch what he said to Feeney, he was more devious than cunning. He had more faces than Big Ben.

If any new information came to light he would log it and take someone else to make the arrest, Feeney would be side lined. Perhaps he had been too outspoken as he progressed through the ranks. In the early 'eighties he was dismayed at the corruption that flowed from the higher echelons to the lowly constables. Anybody who wanted to be promoted in the future was encouraged to join the Brotherhood. He joined not because he wanted too, but he wanted to see who pulled the strings in the Lodge. He learnt to keep quiet, and watch closely. In the Lodge he was astonished to see career criminals, solicitors, council officials and town councillors mix freely with serving police officers. This was where all business was done; contracts and tenders were fixed in advance. After he had been accepted as a Brother and was trusted, he contacted the Sunday Times, and laid bare the institutional corruption.

The consequences of the Sunday Times investigation were dire. Two councillors were jailed for corruption, four detectives resigned and one official from the planning department hung himself. The Lodge was in turmoil, they had their suspicions who was the mole, but the suspicions never fell on him, the suspect was a soon to be retired detective who was too frequently telling certain salacious tales to other Brothers. Eddings saw the same insidious trait run through Feeney, ambitious and avaricious he would place his grandmother on EBay to achieve his aim.

Feeney coughed. 'I don't feel comfortable with your silence and just staring into space.'

'I was just thinking to myself how intelligent you are, and how you can juggle so many balls in the air but still keep your attention intact on this case.'

Feeney's ego was been stroked and he was enjoying it; the tension headache that he had disappeared.

Eddings continued. 'On reflection, that's a great idea about you going to interview Linda Simpson, she may let slip something, you are more her type of person, early forties well- educated with an entrepreneurs brain. You have your property to discuss with her; that could break the ice.'

Feeney would be pumping information from her, but he would also ask her about the DRI development and the new phase of building taking place at the City Quay.

'Have you been reading my mind? That's the course I'm going to take, something in common with her, then back to the thrust of the meeting with her; Andrews. I'll ask if they went clay shooting, then ask if he had a handgun.'

Eddings couldn't over praise him, small doses would be suffice.

'No time like the present, she often goes into the Hilton for coffee, lunch and dinner, she might be more forthcoming if she is in familiar surroundings. My meeting with her was brief and I mean brief, some questions and she was off. But you on the other hand you could prolong the questioning by mentioning even Bulgaria.'

Feeney was anticipating negativity from Eddings, who said you can't teach an old dog new tricks?

'While I'm interviewing her on what she thinks is an informal basis, what will you do to locate and bring Andrews in?'

'Same old same old, hammer the phones, chase up forensics that old and trusted method.'

'When you hear from forensics phone me right away...'

'Why? Where are you going?'

Feeney starts fiddling with his tie. 'To locate the ice queen, if she is not at the Hilton I'll try her house.'

'Why don't you just call her on her mobile?'

'I don't want to give her an excuse to say she is busy, it's not convenient I want to doorstep her, give her no wriggle room.'

'She is still a frequent visitor to the Lord Provost's office, I know that.'

'No time like the present, I'll drop you off at Bell Street, and then see if I can catch her?'

'Don't bother you go ahead, I'll walk down its only fifteen minutes away.'

'Are you sure, its freezing?'

'No, you go ahead, keep me informed of any developments.'

'Ok, no problem; will do.' Feeney walked over to the car.

Eddings had no intention of returning to the office, Feeney had inadvertently given him an idea. He would now conduct a parallel under the radar inquiry alongside the official inquiry; he would not log anything or mention certain aspects of the case unless he had to, but he would work on the paradox; less is more. Feeney was now out of sight, Eddings looked at the memorial to the War Dead, this was where the Sunday Times sting happened with the councillors all those years ago. Those venal councillors' were the fall guys in their own devious twisted minds. This was the normal practice for those Dundee Corporation officials, councillors' and their friends in the construction industry operated. He who slipped the councillors' the fattest envelope 'won' the contract. The councillors' did not name names; they would be looked after when they were released from prison. The son was effortlessly whisked into university to study Law, even though he lacked the required qualifications. The son is now an eminent and much respected QC practicing in London. That stuck in Eddings craw. Crime doesn't pay? Really? The son would beg to differ.

***

Mary anxiously stared at the door of Ian's office door which was not fully closed, she was straining to hear the telephone conversation, she could only hear snippets of it; her imagination was filling in the gaps in the conversation. The phone rang on her desk she momentarily concentrated on making the appointment with the client and logged it on the computer. Her eyes were fixed firmly on the door, she heard his footsteps go back and forth in the office, and then the door closed firmly.

Deflated, she decided she was going into the office, she just needed an excuse. She made a cup of coffee for herself and unselfishly knocked on the office door and entered.

'Would you like a cup of coffee Ian?'

'I was hoping you would suggest that, thanks... oh, and that was the agent for the Weavers Arms, I have made the final offer of one- hundred and twenty- thousand, we'll see how that sits with the vendor.' Mary looked for any signs on his face whether he was confident of the sale going through, there were none. She brought in his coffee.

'Do you think he'll accept the offer?'

'I would hope so, there have been no other offers, and that would worry me if I couldn't shift it in a rising market... don't worry everything is in our favour.'

'Let's hope so... I have had difficulty sleeping at night, but that's business I suppose.'

She left the office and returned to her desk. I wonder when they will get back to say if the final offer was accepted. She hadn't had long to wait, Ian's direct telephone rang, the mumbled conversation was heard then footsteps becoming clearer. He opened the door and invited her in.

'They have accepted the offer, so we will be business partners, what do you have to say?'

'I don't know? I'm pleased obviously but what about the cost of refurbishment?'

'We have an absolute bargain that I can definitely tell you, the building is far from perfect but it will be a straightforward process to update the bar and the flats, the hardest obstacle was convincing the agent that the building was beyond repair at the price the vendor wanted, we achieved this. Go back and finish your work, Christmas is just round the corner.'

She returned to her desk thinking this would be the best Christmas ever; and she really meant that. She hadn't even thought about Christmas but Ian was right it was just over two weeks away. Her desk faced onto Reform Street which was thriving with Christmas shoppers, the heavy snow that had fell overnight gave a sense of Christmas, global warming had by-passed Dundee again.

She rarely enjoyed working as the receptionist or secretary she couldn't differentiate which was which, but was glad she was only a stand in. In the summer she hoped that one year she would spend Christmas in Spain; her plan was too attend Midnight Mass in the small village of Sant Jorde, she wanted to recapture the true meaning of Christmas. However, she would be attending Midnight Mass at her church this year with much more optimism, firstly because of the upturn in her own life; and; secondly the influx of Polish students and workers' who had swelled the congregation on a weekly basis. Midnight Mass had now been deemed a ticket only event; such was the impact that the Polish community had on expanding and reinvigorating the falling aging congregation.

A Polish Television Company would be coming over to film a documentary on how the Polish community were perceived by the indigenous population of Dundee, and how they were coping with the demands of their studies and work. The Polish priest was instrumental in encouraging the television company to come over to Dundee to see how the people of Dundee had been very welcoming of the influx of the Polish community. The producer of the documentary had been intrigued of the tale of the Christmas tree on the Perth Road that had become the focal point for different nationalities and how they gathered around the tree and sang hymns.

The priest had told him that the Christmas tree was a symbol of hope for humanity and that was why some people spontaneously gathered round it one year and had videoed the gathering via their mobiles home. It had been uploaded onto Youtube and it had become an Internet sensation. Some people who had viewed the footage had to be there themselves at Christmas time.

Mary enjoyed thinking about the Christmas tree she hoped for snow again this year. Last year the forecaster apologised for the lack of snow but as soon as the carol singing began at the Christmas tree at eleven pm the snow fell heavily, the singers looked up to the heavens and sang the hymns in one language then another then lastly in English more lustily.

Mary had viewed this from across the road with other people, who had stopped to watch and listen, one comment from the throng remained in her mind. A woman behind her had whispered to her partner, 'this is hallowed ground.' Additionally a small throng of people who were on their way to Midnight Mass stopped and stood behind Mary to watch with intense interest the carol singers around the Christmas tree, Fife was a magnificent backdrop to the serene scene. They were in their sixties two by two they crossed the road to join the young people gathered at the Christmas tree.

But that was last year, this year she would sing under the tree rather than watching from the other side of the road. Mary offered up a silent prayer for her dream to come true, of turning that run down bar into a thriving, busy and profitable meeting place for the young Polish and Dundee communities.

Even before Ian had the encouraging phone call from the agent, she had been on the Internet pricing and locating the popular Polish beers. The most cost effective way of securing these beers were direct from Poland; that gave Mary another genesis of an idea, why can't she be the conduit or middleman for the other pubs that surely will one day cotton on to the Polish population that is on their doorstep? She never saw the downstairs function room at the Weavers Arms, but she did hear from the conversation that it was expansive and it had also a cellar with plenty of storage space, could that be the area to store the beer that would be delivered to other pubs? She would mention this only when the plans and the builder's costs were agreed and she had seen the size of the function room. If the function room were to be used fair enough; she wouldn't mention it, on the other hand if it is going to be used for storage she will outline her business plan to him.

Then her mind drifted to the flats above the pub, would the cost of refurbishment be prohibitive? That sinking feeling came to haunt her again; maybe the Council would deem them structurally dangerous? Ian would overcome any problem; he was familiar with building problems. She would not worry anymore, what lay in store for her, lay in store for her. It would be a harrowing exercise to try to second guess the future. Presently things were going well, she had her health, a rewarding and interesting job; and her family were happy. Her mind returned to the function room.

She was more at ease when she had been sourcing the Polish beers, surely the young Dundee people would be interested in tasting the Polish beers? Of course they would, and so would the Polish contingent who were living and working in Angus. If they managed to secure the pub, she would be delivering the Polish beer to pubs and hotels in Angus, she was surprised how many of them there are.

With her mind tightly focused on the Weavers Arms, in the office on Monday she forgot to mention to Ian that the builder had called and would be coming in that afternoon to confirm the alterations to the office with him personally and the time they would start, they would be working twenty fours a day up till Christmas Eve. They were fully aware that Ian had exacting standards and never accepted delays. She decided to wait ten minutes, bring in Ian a coffee and mention that the builder was coming in to see him. The builder could not give an exact time in when he would arrive to discuss the refurbishment.

***

Planning permission had been sought and approved for the wind turbines, very few people objected, the incentive of cheap electricity for homeowners and businesses alike put paid to any organised protest. The Lord Provost had had coffee with Linda at the Hilton at her request she wanted to give the workforce at Romans a psychological boost before the factory closed for the Christmas break, she wondered if the Lord Provost could use his persuasive powers to allow the foundations for the wind turbines to be dug and the concrete poured before the workforce started their Christmas and New Year break?

This would generate a sense of security for the workforce seeing that the wind turbines would be built and if this could be done with some kind of ceremony with the Lord Provost laying the first brick on the foundation they would return from the Christmas break in a positive frame of mind. The newspapers and television would cover the ceremony she could guarantee that.

The Lord Provost did not recoil from this suggestion neither did he have to ruminate, the local elections were to be held next year and he enjoyed the trappings of power as well as the fact-finding soirees abroad. He couldn't see any obstacles to prevent the foundations being dug for at least one of the wind turbines and the symbolic gesture of laying the first brick didn't pass him by.

Of course, he would only do this if she would join him on the foundation block which would be a considerable size, it could hold an articulated lorry with room to spare, after much cajoling Linda agreed. The Lord Provost assured her that the building contractor would accede to this request. The building contractor would have strategically placed signs around the foundation block that would be picked up by the television cameras. Linda suggested that having Brian the union convenor on the foundation block as well would be a good thing as he was an active part of the team. Again, the Lord Provost warmed to this suggestion, votes from the union members would naturally be cast for his political party if the union convenor was to be seen side by side with the Lord Provost, a few kind words about the active role that Brian had played in the retention of Romans wouldn't be understated. The surrounding residents would surely vote for his Party when they received their cut price electricity? He excused himself and then made the calls to the building contractor and Planning Office.

***

 Ten am in the office and Eddings is awaiting the arrival of Feeney; he is going to call him on his mobile then decided against it. The forensic report lay wide open on his desk, the gun was used in the murders of the two young junkies and Swithers, Raymond Andrews' fingerprints were on the gun, the bullets that remained in the gun chamber matched the bullets that were removed from the bodies of the junkies and Swithers; his fingerprints as well as his DNA were on the bullets.
 This coupled with the golf club that was used to bludgeon the other police officer Robert Lotus also had his fingerprints and DNA, why did he not feel elated? Maybe he was losing his analytical judgement? The evidence was overwhelming. Examine all the salient facts he said to himself. The suspect is missing, his fingerprints are on two murder weapons, and he was a frequent user of cocaine oh, and he beat his partner up, and he still thinks he isn't the murderer?
 Then he accepted the fear that he had not discussed with his wife never mind Feeney, for obvious reasons. His father was in a care home he had dementia; might he be succumbing to it as well? He had forgot simple things, the digits for the alarm, leaving lights on before going to bed, placing down keys then forgetting where they were. A chill ran down his spine. It all made perfect sense now. He would make an appointment with his GP and get some tests.
 When Feeney turned up and saw the forensic report he would need to be prised off the ceiling and then he would go upstairs to the Chief Constable with his findings. A knock comes to the door. He beckons the person in, a young uniformed officer no doubt looking for the 'hero.'
 'He's not here yet, try coming back in an hour.'
'It's you I want a word with... if you have a spare minute?' The young officer is a fresh faced twenty-something.
'Would you like a tea or a coffee or doesn't your mum allow you hot drinks yet?'
'No thanks,' he replied with a red hue that quickly appeared on his face.
This broke the ice, he sat down without an invitation and he removed his hat and held it in both hands and started to turn it slowly.
'What's on your mind son?'
He looked around him. Then whispered, 'It's your partner; I think he is on the take... as well as being involved in drugs.'
Eddings was flabbergasted at this but quickly regained his composure.
'I'm here to listen... start the story.'
'I need assurances that you didn't hear this from me.'
'Be assured. Go on, but speak up I can hardly hear you.'
'Okay. I'm just worried that someone will hear me. I don't know where to start, bear with me; I know that the two uniformed officers were dealing, I was brought up in Kirkton so I know what's what, three months ago I was visiting my mum in Kirkton and I went into Asda for petrol, I saw the two officers in civvy clothes sitting in their car in the car park.

' I was going to give them a wave, but they were looking all about them they seemed agitated and nervous, anyway a youth climbs in the back seat of their car, I'm only twenty- feet away filling up with petrol, I see one of them hand over small packets to the youth, he in turn hands over a wad of notes he leaves the car and walks away.

My car is filled with petrol and there is someone wanting to use the pump, I don't want him to be pissed off at me and start blowing his horn, which would make the two officers look in my direction so I slowly replace the pump still watching their car, then I see Feeney walk up to their car and one of them handed over a plastic bag to him he doesn't stop or talk and placed the bag inside his jacket then he walked back to his car.'

Eddings stares at him, his mouth is dry he is incredulous, he hands him his card.
'Keep this to yourself tell no one. This is my mobile number, don't come in here again, meet me tonight at the Law at eight, we'll be able to talk further.'
The young officer rises from the seat. 'Thanks that's a lot off my mind... I wasn't sure you would believe me... if anybody asks why I was here say I was looking for Feeney.'
'I figured that one out for myself son, but thanks for the lesson.'
'Sorry, I'm just nervous; I didn't mean to sound like an old timer like you.'
'Some flatterer you are, just walk out casually, Feeney will be told by some of his fan club you were in here.'
'That's why I mentioned that to you about looking for him.'
Eddings smiled at him. 'I can see you have your wits about you, I'll see you tonight.'
'Before I go can I ask a personal question?'
'Be my guest.'
'Did you have any suspicions about him?'
'We'll talk about that later... I'll ask you a question, what colour of hair did one of the officers have? ...was it ginger?'
'Yes... the two officers in the car were the ones who were murdered, didn't I mention that?'
'Don't worry, and don't be late.' He leaves the office and Eddings returns to his desk, he watches him through the slits in the blinds and he is stopped by another officer, the young officer retains his composure and chats briefly with his colleague then makes his way along the corridor.

He sits down at his desk and places his hands on his head. 'What is going on here?' he says out loud. His mind is going through the all evidence again and again, but what if the young plod said is true? Feeney must be involved. He has to locate Andrews that is a must, when Feeney returns to the office he might have some information but he doubts it, and if he does will he share it with him? This is going to be a long day and it would be torture to stay here all day brooding. He would try and locate Feeney; first he would try the Hilton, if he was there with Linda Simpson he would probably be talking about property investment.

Then a thought struck him, property purchase would be the ideal way to dispose or clean his ill-gotten gains. Everybody in Police Headquarters knew he was obsessed about his pension and he saw property as a top up for this. He had the perfect alibi; his colleagues, they would come to him with financial queries, where is the best deal to get a mortgage, interest only or repayment? The same with personal loans he knew it all. He would call him or leave a message and say that he would be out the office for the whole day he had a few things to do; if anything came up to call him. He did this the mobile went straight to voice mail, he was pleased with this, he left the brief message.

Today would be the catalyst of the parallel investigation; and Feeney would be the focus of his attention. He would delay making the appointment with his doctor; that could wait for another day; it was probably lack of sleep that caused his forgetfulness.

He left his office and told the other detectives that Feeney had not shown up and was not answering his mobile; if he turns up today tell him to give me a call. They looked totally disinterested; he made up his mind he would be retiring next year.

If only the public could see these university educated detectives now scouring for information on the Internet not for some obscure habits of the prime suspect; Raymond Andrews; no they were surfing E-Bay. He was disgusted at this and let the detective know this, he said to him, 'how much for four hardly- used detectives?' Not one lifted up their heads from their computers

**

True to his word the Lord Provost had accelerated the planning proposals; the ground was being gouged for the foundations. Linda was feeling more confident seeing the bulldozers hard at work in the area where the first wind turbine would be built. The bulldozers seemed to be similar to the dodgem cars at a fair ground the way they criss-crossed the vast empty space adjacent to the factory. She often appeared at the factory grounds unannounced, today she would bear witness to seeing the first sod of earth being removed. The workforce coming off the twelve hour nightshift could not fail to be impressed. And when they saw the army of bulldozers lined up in the area where the wind turbines were to be built, this raised morale as Linda had envisaged.

This experience imbued the early shift workforce. A perfect tonic now that they were nearing Christmas. Every year Linda always took herself and friends over to Austria for skiing for the Christmas period, this year she would postpone the holiday until the workforce returned from their Christmas break. Nothing would be left to chance; the Lord Provost had even arranged a school choir and musicians for the foundation ceremony, he was a meticulous planner as well as a shrewd political operator, this ceremony would also raise his political profile. She viewed the noise and controlled chaos of the building site as a triumph over hopelessness and apathy.

She had imbued the workforce who had accepted the closure with hope and resilience; she knew she was lampooned by the majority of the workforce as a businesswoman with a heart of granite. However, through sheer perseverance and economic arguments she had convinced even the most sceptical employee that there were no economic reasons for the factory to close, there had to be other reasons. She stepped back from the chain link fence pleased that she had at least contributed something positive to the campaign to keep the factory open, history would judge her well unlike Walter Simpson who had built the fine hospital, but even though he was long gone there was still visceral hatred when his name was mentioned.

She turned around and faced the scene of the hive of activity and the deafening roar of the JCB tearing at the snow covered frozen earth. This was a more welcoming noise than the deathly silence of a closed factory. She took the sunglasses off the top of her head and carefully positioned them on her still tender nose, and then made her way to her car. She looked at her watch just past nine o clock, time to visit her two flats under construction at Carnoustie golf course. These two flats would be another welcome addition to her property portfolio and another income tributary that added to the river of money that was pouring into her numerous bank accounts. A mutual friend had tipped her off that a well- heeled ex sports person was intending to purchase the whole block of flats.

The flats were due to be finished before the start of the Open 2007. The intention was to market the flats to the players' or to wealthy golf aficionados. Linda visited the builders head office before the marketing suite was opened and placed a fifty-thousand deposit down on the two hundred thousand pound flats. This did not go down well with the proposed owner of the whole block of flats. Timing is everything; Linda's solicitor had everything faxed to her office in a matter of days. Linda would be formulating the interior design herself, she rejected the builder's designers; she would choose Italian marble for the bathroom and floor tiles, real oak flooring for all other areas, the hi-spec kitchen was not to her taste this would need to be upgraded at no extra cost to her.

The new road that ran from Claypotts Junction to Arbroath was a vast improvement than its predecessor which was a narrow and twisting road that was used frequently by slow moving farm traffic, which caused impatient commuters to take risks and attempt to overtake, resulting in numerous injuries and sometime deaths.

Linda had campaigned for a new road which was long overdue and had mobilised the public; eventually an array of Road Traffic Management Consultants came up with a design for a new road. Simultaneously, Linda was instrumental in lobbying the Scottish Executive for much needed funds to complement and enhance the Consultants' proposal; she wanted the road to be widened on each side by one metre to prevent the new road flooding from the natural flood plains that intermittently ran the length of the road between Dundee and Arbroath. After four years her efforts were fruitful. When she had a preview of the plan for the road she noticed that it would slew across agriculture land, she noted this firmly in her mind. One of her business associate's formed a company and purchased up surplus land from one avaricious farmer. The young man was gambling that planning permission would be granted for building houses sometime in the future. The young man left his card with the farmer and mentioned he was looking for more surplus land.

After the gullible young man purchased the first hectares of useless land the farmer telephoned his friends telling them that he had left his business card informing him, 'if you know of any other farmer looking to sell land I would be interested.' He was inundated with offers from farmers who are selling 'surplus land.' The beauty of this business plan was that the farmers were coming to him; they were offering 'surplus land' to him. The farmers were ecstatic about the price he had paid for the land.

When the news came out about the new road, everyone assumed the new road would follow the same course as the old road; how wrong they were. The plan for the new road would be straight as economically possible, thus cutting across the 'arable land' which was fortunately owned by the young man. He made millions' from the sale of the land to the Scottish Executive; he believed in progress and did not wish to be an impediment to progress. The general public and commuters benefited most of all; the new safe road reduced the accident rate by ninety –percent and it only took fifteen minutes from Arbroath to Dundee.

Linda profited as she supplied the money to set up the young man's company, the farmers' profited by selling the poor arable land at extortionate prices to the seemingly gullible young man. Some of the farmers claimed they were duped and went to the police, the police pointed out to the irate farmers' they had called the young man and offered to sell their surplus land, moreover they had been paid more than treble the market value.

Linda saw another benefit of the road in another sense. The property market in Dundee was overheating at an alarming rate, she purchased land in Arbroath knowing that people would sell their houses in Dundee and move to Arbroath now a mere fifteen minutes away, if there were good quality houses and flats. She would build them and they would come she had no doubt about that.

She enjoyed the short drive to Carnoustie and spoke to the sales rep; everything was going to plan, they had received the letter from her solicitor and she had spoken to the Directors' they would upgrade all the appliances, change the tiles and use real oak on the floor, at no cost to her.

She meandered around the area where the proposed car park would be. She took a few steps back and photographed her two half built apartments, she did this not for posterity, but for future reference, she had a reputation for suing companies that did not comply too her wishes. The sales rep saw her take the photographs and strolled over to talk to her, she engaged Linda in small talk.

She deferentially enquired if she was pleased that the building was ahead of schedule?
Linda as usual, was sharp with her, as long as corners would not be cut, then of course she would be pleased. Linda had taken enough photographs she had an hour to kill; she would have coffee and croissants at the Carnoustie Hotel. Although snow lay on the ground golfers' were still waiting to tee off from the first tee. As she passed the golfers she heard the unmistakable drawl of American accents as the golfers took practice swings, waiting politely behind them were four Japanese golfers smiling at the brash antics of the Americans. Not bad the hotel being busy at this time of year, her thoughts were interrupted by the wailing sound of a horn from a passing train, the four Americans waved at the train, unknown to them the driver blew the horn as he approached the public crossing that ran from the road over the railway to the path that ran along the golf course.

The Americans thought the driver was given them a friendly toot.

Linda walked into the lobby of the hotel, she was disappointed at the design of the lobby, disappointed; was the most charitable description she could muster. In her opinion corners had been cut. It was unimaginative; it was obvious the architect's mind had not been exercised. Very few sleepless nights would have been lost on this project, but at least the waiter was courteous and pleasant. One escorted her to a table overlooking the course. She took her coat off and threw it over the empty chair that was directly across from her. She ordered her coffee and croissants and people watched as she nibbled the croissant. The number of foreign accents she heard was encouraging; her apartments would exceed the hotel's best rooms for style and comfort, after she had finished her breakfast she made her way to the check in desk.

The young Polish clerk saw her approaching; he fixed her with a synthetic smile. Linda asked if it was possible to block book his best rooms for the forthcoming Open. His smile grew wider he was so sorry but every room had been booked months before by the P.G.A. But if she cared to leave her number he would call around and try to locate the rooms she required. She declined the polite request and made her way to her car. The sun was low but bright; she carefully placed her glasses on her nose to avoid the pain. The hotel being fully booked was no surprise to her. She just wanted to confirm this; she would be marketing her apartments this week on the Internet to meet the unprecedented demand that would be accumulating. With her soiree over, her next port of call would be Arbroath to check the progress of the block of flats and townhouses that were under construction. No price had been allocated to any of the properties; the public would be invited to participate in a sealed bid system that way her properties would attract maximum publicity as well as a perceived higher price when the show house and the show flat were complete.

They would sell quickly as they were more luxurious than any other development from Dundee to Montrose. Her office had been snowed under with enquires about the development, she knew the demand was there. As she walked across the hotel's car park she was met by the ex-sport person's solicitor who after the niceties, asked her to name her price to sell the two apartments under construction at the hotel. Linda said she was pleased to see him and that coincidently she was about to ask him what price they wanted for the six flats they owned. The solicitor made it very clear that they were not selling.

Linda told him if they change their mind he had her number, she had other business to attend to goodbye. She knew the ex-sports person was in the BMW with blacked out windows, she waved at the rear window of the BMW and continued on to her car. Big deal; that the sports person was now a millionaire, but he was playing the 'I want to be alone' card a little bit too conspicuous. That was the problem with the nouveau riche they had sheds full of money but no class; that could not be bought, you had to be born with it.

***

Eddings was riddled with doubt, maybe he won't turn up. He looked again at his watch it is ten past eight he would give him another five minutes then he was off. No other person or car is at the Law he is all alone apart from the howling bitter wind. He had parked his car outside a house on Law Road and walked up the steep road that led to the summit of the Law.

Only the exquisite vista from the Law stopped him from stomping back to his car in a foul mood. The night sky was clear and an abundance of stars met his wondrous eyes. His silent mobile vibrated in his pocket he took off his thick gloves and his fingers felt for the tiny mobile. It's Feeney; he is asking where he is? He replied he is walking the dog at Baxter Park; he turned the question back to him, 'where have you been, you didn't turn up at the office this morning'?

He is temporarily blinded by the car turning into the small car park; the occupant of the car came towards him, he is carrying something. He abruptly ended the call, and concentrated on the figure moving towards him, when he got nearer he saw his features it is the young police officer. 'Where have you been?'

'My washing machine flooded the kitchen, sorry I'm late.' Eddings looked all about him no sign of any humanity. Eddings quickly quizzed him what he had seen at the Asda car park, the officer repeated it again and again; he was in no doubt that the occupants of the car were the two police officers who were murdered. He was impatient to tell Eddings other news. Other police officers were still dealing; he knew that for sure he had seen large tranches of money changing hands in the locker room, he gave Eddings their names.

Eddings couldn't tell the inexperienced officer that Feeney is working undercover to catch corrupt officers, he would go along with the information that the young officer told him. He wrote the names of the two alleged corrupt officers in his notebook and told him to observe and listen from a safe distance; don't mention anything to any other officer including any senior officers. Any further contact would be by mobile and they would meet up here again. The young officer was shaking is it the bitter cold or nerves? Eddings told him he is doing a great job, now go home.

He watched him drive slowly down the narrow road; but then near the bottom of the winding road the brake lights came on and the car came to a halt. His heart started beating too rapidly for his liking; he was at the dangerous age when heart attacks had become quite common. He said a swift silent prayer begging not to have a heart attack here, at least if he had it at home his wife could phone an ambulance or she could call on the neighbours where numerous doctors resided.

He took deep breaths trying to reduce his rapid heart rate. He opened up his heavy jacket hoping that the cold night air would aid his recovery, but his full attention is the stationary car. The passenger side door is opened he could see the telling red light; his heart rate seemed to speed up again.

He quickly surmised that the mystery persons talking to the officer were on foot, there are no other cars parked in the road. A moment of sheer terror invaded his head; they could be making their way up to the Law to confront him, he decided if that was the case he would descend from the Law via the rabbit paths instead of the road. He watched the car intently; the cold night air is disturbed by the hushed voices that elevated up to the Law, he was sure that there were three voices. He descended down the Law, he checked his mobile to ascertain it was still on silent, thankfully it was. He gazed down at the car for the last time it is still stationary, his descent started he would make his way down as quickly and silently as possible he hoped to identify the unholy trinity still in animated conversation, he is convinced one of them is Feeney. The phone call was just a ruse to make him tell a lie.

His heart rate started to stabilise or so he hoped. He is approximately fifty metres away from them; it was still difficult to identify the two individuals who were engaged in conversation with the officer. Against his better judgement he decided to creep nearer for clarification of the individuals, gorse bushes were thick and plentiful, if he didn't cough or have a heart attack his presence would remain secret. The car's engine grew louder he watched it move off then park on the right- hand side near to the houses at the bottom of the road. He identified one of them as Glaswegian their conversation became hushed tones. One of them held up his finger and placed it across his lips, he took out his mobile then dialled, Eddings mobile vibrated; they looked up expectantly towards the Law.

***

She was sitting at the breakfast table checking her emails on her laptop, nothing to raise her blood pressure or conjure up a smile. She would miss the cut and thrust of her campaign to retain Romans but now she would be able to fully concentrate on her businesses.

Tomorrow she would at the factory for the ceremonial laying of the first brick by the Lord Provost, she would have a facial and her hair coloured to hide the silver threads that were now becoming more prominent. She gazed at the pile of letters on the table she placed the brown envelopes to one side and opened the white and variously coloured envelopes. Most were Christmas cards; one is a hand written letter it is from Brian the trade union official. He thanked her for all the help that she had given him.

And had persuaded the workforce that they had to fight for their jobs as other companies were watching the situation in Dundee; if Romans closed a copycat strategy would take place not just in Dundee but throughout Britain. They had a future to look forward thanks to her; the workforce would be making a presentation to her tomorrow. Linda is quite moved by this and is glad that she had been forewarned as her words of thanks could maybe sound indifferent; she would stay home tonight and work on an Oscar type speech without the tears.

Maybe she would be fondly remembered by future historians after all? She would have one more cup of coffee then shower. This would still give her ample time to make her appointment at the beauticians in Broughty Ferry; she would be brought up to speed with all the gossip from the nail technicians to the hair sculptor, who did not take kindly to being addressed as a hairdresser.

The coffee is still percolating merrily; the six pm news bulletin is imminent, the ceremony tomorrow should be the first news item or so she hoped; she enjoyed her name being mentioned on the radio as this would lead onto her as the descendent of the philanthropist Walter Simpson. The jingle came on, the ceremony was not the first news story it was Raymond Andrews; developments were expected in the case, a police source had indicated that they were following up leads regarding the reported of his sighting in Paris. Dread filled her thoughts.

***

The noise was deafening, dust was rising and obscuring her vision. Mary was the midwife to the birth of her dream. Old chairs and tables were being removed and thrown into the massive skip in Princess Street. Even with the lighting from the generators the pub still retained partly its depressing demeanour. The army of workers, most of whom were Polish, made light of the laborious work. The bar area seemed to grow in size, she compared the now empty area with the new seating arrangements positioned on the plans that had been sent to the Planning Department, Ian had given one of the Planning officials a first draft of the plans for his opinion, the reaction was positive, nothing would need to be altered and the Council wanted to bring new life into the area; the refurbished pub would be the focal point.

Plans were being prepared by the Council for further regeneration of the area, the new housing and small independent retailers, the pub would seamlessly dovetail into the Council's plans. Mary thought the six week deadline for the pub and flats to be refurbished were optimistic. Ian had no doubts whatsoever that the work would be completed, moreover he had a secretly hoped it would be done in five weeks. Ian couldn't understand her pessimism.

When the sale was completed he had the paperwork for the liquor licence in Mary's name delivered by hand to the relevant Council Department, that had been approved furthermore the refurbishment was being encouraged, albeit in a nod and a wink fashion. The pub should be pouring its inaugural pint before the end of January. Ian could see that Mary was seeking the cloud to obscure the silver lining, but he hoped that the imagined cloud had been blown away. It was time to return to the office he had to clarify with the builders where some wall lights would be repositioned, the builders were due to start remodelling his office the following week.

Mary was obviously bored working in the capacity as his temporary secretary; she segued subtly into the conversation if there was progress on the injury sustained to the permanent secretary, and when did he expect her back? Before the end of January was his stock reply. She asked if she didn't return, what were his plans?

Did he intend to employ another secretary? She was told she would be back in January. Mary's biggest fear was, that Ian was delighted with her office administration skills she would be asked to combine these newly acquired skills with her sales executive role in Spain. Although she loved her sales executive job, she had a smouldering ambitious iron in the fire.

When the pub is established and her dream of creating a subsidiary company that imported and distributed Polish and other foreign beers were a reality; she would be running these companies.

If that were the case then her fledging career as the sales executive in Spain would come to a premature end. The children would be devastated. They loved Panoramica and the Spanish lifestyle. Then her imagination cranked up into overdrive, if these businesses were successful and more important profitable, perhaps she could purchase a property on Panoramica? Ian would surely offer her a generous discount when she brought the subject up?

The thought of returning to the office administration filled her with dread, even though it was on a temporary basis. She would rather do a nightshift clearing the detritus from the basement of the pub, and had no objection to getting her hands dirty clearing the pub, whether it was long-discarded needles and knives secreted in various ingenious niches in ceilings. She stopped and stared through the choking dust that rose and engulfed the bar area, to others it was a stinking mess, to her it would be one day, not long after Christmas one of the best pubs in Dundee.

The area was already served with a natural customer base, however, when the new houses in the Council's regeneration plan came on stream; this would provide the pub with more potential customers. The pub was attracting curious salesman who had wares to be sold, bar equipment to security alarm systems. Ian was the centre of their attention.

***

Feeney turned up at the office he is in an ebullient mood. 'I spoke to Linda Simpson but she wasn't able to add to her statement about Andrews... but she gave me some knowledgeable insight into the property game. Anything interesting happen while I was interviewing Linda Simpson?'

Eddings is sitting at his desk; he has reams of paper strewn on his desk he looks up at Feeney. 'Nothing I can think of, it seems we have come to a cul-de-sac in our pursuit of Raymond Andrews.' Feeney is watching him more intently as though he is going to correct him.

'It's still early days, he'll resurface don't worry, have you spoke to your wife about buying in Bulgaria?' Eddings removes his hands from the desk and squeezes them together under the desk. 'Not really, I'm working on a murder inquiry it might seem daft to you regarding your property dealings, but the murders of two police officers and two youths take precedence.'
Feeney is outraged at this slur on his detective skills again.
'Are you trying to suggest that I don't care?'
'Is that what you think I meant, I'm sorry to offend you, do you want me to arrange counselling for you?'
'Just because I have a business brain doesn't mean to say that my mind is being diverted from the case, what do you think I went to see Linda Simpson for...?'
'Property information, interior design, what's in, what's out, Eurozone mortgages, anything it seems but murders.' Feeney has gone white at the invective and ferocity of this response. He takes a deep breath, this has been troubling him for some time, he can't hold it in any longer, he has to mention this. Here goes. 'Are you suffering from depression?'
'Now he's a fucking doctor now! Anything but a detective, can you not see what's happening here?'
'Is everything all right, at home?'
'Absolutely spiffing, how are you making progress in this case, Doctor Freud?'
'How many times do I have to tell you? Andrews is our man once he turns up the case is closed.'
'When or if he turns up, seemingly he was seen in Paris, next week it will be on the beach at Rio de Janeiro.'
'Patience is a virtue; everything comes to those who wait...'
Eddings bursts out laughing, 'What did you get last Christmas, the Hallmark book of quotations?'
The door opens, a detective enquires,' is everything alright?'
Feeney walks over and pushes him away and closes the door. He turns to Eddings.
'You need to get out more socially; this case is having a corrosive effect on your mental well-being, I'm talking as a professional and as a friend.'

Eddings brings up his former clenched fists from under the desk and places them on the desk. He is less agitated. 'Look, I have to tell you in the strictest confidence do you understand?'
Feeney moves away from the door and sits on his desk. 'Go ahead, what is said in here stays in here, what's troubling you?'
'I have not had it confirmed, but I think I have the first signs of dementia, I'm forgetting things, simple things, I don't want to go into it, but I'm convinced I have got it. My dad is in a care home he can't look after himself, he's got dementia bad, I know dementia is inherited. I think that's the reason I'm flying off the handle, I never used to before.'
'Wow, what age are you fifty- eight?'
'Not quite, fifty-eight this year in December. After this case is done, I will go to the doctor then I will retire voluntarily, rather than been retired compulsory. I really appreciate your concern for me; just show some concern and compassion for the victims, all the victims not just the police officers.'
'I knew something was wrong, it might not be dementia, just might be paranoia.'
'Oh, thanks, think I would rather have dementia.'
'Or it could just be depression.'
'Just depression? What have I got to worry about then?'
'Or it could be just that time of life when everyone your age questions their own mortality, nothing wrong with that mate. You underestimate my concerns; just because I have an active life outside this place doesn't mean I don't care.'
'Well, as soon as we get Andrews, I can get to the doctor get the verdict and then retire.'
'I think that's a good idea, when Andrews is found and charged, you can retire on a high.'
'Right that's my medical dilemma solved; could you place your property business on hold for now and fully focus on Andrews?'
'Didn't take you too long to being sarcastic again did it? Oh, I was told you had a visitor to your office what was that all about?'
'It was one of the young plods' he was in to see you not me, he asked where you were.'
'Oh, really, and what did you say?'
'I don't know where he is, he is never here... then I told him to fuck off as I was busy.'
'No wonder the junior ranks are pessimistic, it's time you dinosaurs were put out to grass; the world is moving rapidly, including technologically and in forensic fields, old fashion detectives like you are seen as an impediment to progress.'
'Oh is that right? How come a state of the art high- tech detective with his own fan club had to ask an impediment to progress dinosaur detective like myself, show you how to delete an unopened email?'
'I'll give you that, you helped me delete an email, doesn't make you out to be a computer expert does it?'
'I never said I was. And the time your car wouldn't start, do you recall that so embarrassing incident?'
'You changed the battery for me, big deal.'
'No, that's the part truth, before you called me you went to a garage and they sent out their mobile mechanic and he diagnosed via his laptop computer that it was the starting motor and the alternator, the cost would have been about four to five hundred depending how quick you wanted it back and they would throw in a free top of the range service because you were a valued customer.'
Feeney went crimson at this memory. 'Yes, yes, you saved me a few pounds, I grant you that.'
Eddings is enjoying reminding his younger colleague that he possesses other life skills as well as excellent detective skills.
'Your generation is the brown nose generation; you go on all these courses and innovative lectures about detection methods in the twenty -first century and come back and dismiss tried and trusted methods. All you had to do is ask the dinosaurs about certain things and they would willingly tell you but you and your acolytes dismiss us.

'Unless it comes to opening emails and solving obvious car problems. You might know the volume content of a jam jar, but you don't know how to open it.'
'You have a good conceit of yourself don't you?'
Eddings erupts into laughter again. 'Are you serious?' All the young plods call you 'Humpty Dumpty' because of the size of your head.'

The door bursts open. 'Will you two keep the noise down; everyone can hear your conversation,' the Inspector closed the door.
'Well you don't seem to be suffering from dementia now, maybe you are using me to get early retirement, that's it, you're using me, I bet your dad is not in a care home.'
Feeney moves away from the desk; he can see that he has struck a raw nerve. Eddings rises from the chair; he grabs Feeney and marches him to the door. 'Get out, and if I hear you have mentioned anything about me, I'll…'
'Get your hands off me now, if you don't remove them I will.'
Eddings removes his hands.
Feeney regains his calm. 'Don't threaten me in any way; I am here to help you, but anymore outbursts like this, and I will have you thrown off this case and have a garden hoe thrown in your hands. ' He then leaves the office, but leaves open the door. Eddings closes the door, and leans hard against it. Think. Think, he said to himself. He has to follow his instinct, listen to the gossip and cultivate the young officer. Why has he not called him regarding his car coming to a halt after their meeting on the Law? Who were conversing with him, was Feeney one of them? He went over and over in his mind what the young officer had told him. Then doubts start to drip into his confidence, was it really a definitive Glasgow accent he heard when he was descending the Law?
It was windy that bitter cold night; could the wind have tricked his ears?

***

The workforce and their families were listening to the Lord Provost giving them platitudes; he was a wily old politician who knew which clichés to use. Snow was starting to fall and the bitter wind grew stronger, but it could have been a warm sunny day in July as far as they were concerned. Their jobs were secure and they could look to the future with some degree of optimism. True, over a hundred workers had taking up the offer of voluntary redundancy, but they were not complaining about the generous terms.

The foundation concrete block on which they were standing is elevated high above ground level. Linda is taken aback at the height and huge area that the foundation block covers. She is there with the Lord Provost, various MSP's and the manager of Romans. After the Lord Provost had given his speech he would introduce Linda, the Lord Provost had advised the manager of Romans that it would be not in the interest of his safety to address the workforce, the manager did not reply.

'And so I hand you over to Linda Simpson, who has a few words to say to you, I am sure of that.' The Lord Provost walked back from the microphone and Linda elegantly took her place. She had no notes; she would talk from the heart. The workforce gave her an enthusiastic welcome, she was surprised at the depth of feeling that they had for her. 'Thanks for that, I'm sure I didn't deserve that much applause. The people that deserve to be up here on this monster block of concrete are you and your families. You were the ones who challenged the management to consider the economics of this closure, the redundancy terms were very tempting and no one would have been surprised if the majority had accepted them. But all of you have shown great foresight at the implications if you had accepted redundancy, not only would have it affected yourselves but it would have trickled down to the butcher, baker and candlestick maker. Dundee would have been cast into a deep and catastrophic economic depression.

'Marriages would have been under tremendous pressure, some would have survived others would not. Be under no illusion a housing crash would have visited this great city of ours.

'The affluent suburb of Broughty Ferry would have been severely affected. Some of you will be aware I own several licensed establishments in Broughty Ferry they would have seen a significant downturn in trade. The restaurants would have been especially hit hard; waiters and waitresses would have been laid off. Although they are young students, some would have to give up their studies due to their employment being curtailed. The Chef that I employ has just bought a three bedroom house, he still has to sell his two bedroomed flat, the people who have sold their house to him are moving to a new build. Believe me if this factory closed none of these moves would have been completed, students from modest backgrounds would have their dreams shattered. From accountants, solicitors to taxi drivers, if Romans closed all would have been affected. The people standing before me are the ones who should be up here and all we up here should be applauding you.'

Rapturous applause rings out the media turn their cameras to the crowd, Linda continues.

'The Lord Provost told me of your invitation for me to be present at this inauguration and the symbol of laying the first brick; it is a very humbling experience. Brian your Union Convenor declined to be up here with us, but he declined not out of rudeness but he felt that he should be amongst his own people… I can see you Brian, history will judge you well and others less well.'

The crowd applaud Brian who is looking leaner and fitter. 'I have taken up too much time already, but I will end with this: Future generations will look back at the fortitude and the resilience of all of you, they will marvel at the way you all conducted yourselves with dignity; the old maxim the pen is mightier than the sword has never been so pertinent; this is your day.'

Linda steps back, the crowd are calling her name but she declines to take any encore. The opportunistic MSP takes Linda's place at the microphone; the crowd are still cheering Linda. Much to the annoyance of the Lord Provost, she was not scheduled to address the workforce.

'Thanks for that welcome, I have been a believer in workers' rights all of my life, I am also a believer in green renewable energy, I played a small part in securing funding for the wind turbines at the Scottish Parliament…' Some jeering is coming from the crowd. The MSP has a neck that would not have been marked by a blow torch. The Lord Provost has heard enough; he cuts the power to the microphone and signals the brass band to strike up. Linda is tapping her foot to the stirring sound of the brass band. She is unaware she is literally dancing on Raymond Andrews grave.

***

Only one more appointment and that will be that for another day. Her mind refused to budge from her and Ian's pub, however hard she tried. The office would be closing after today; the builders would be tearing this place apart as soon as he had left. Here he was at last, white track suit with baseball cap, the shoplifter, alleged shoplifter.

He is carrying a bulging Primark bag; I wonder if he had paid for the contents she thought. She hoped the consultation would not last too long as she wanted to drive to the pub and see if the difficult old bar fixtures have been removed successfully.

She rose from her chair to show the client into Ian's office she only took one step when she was grabbed from behind and lifted off the ground, his forearm was around her neck and his gloved hand around her mouth, life was being sucked out of her, she first felt dizzy then it all went black.

He carried her into the small toilet and laid her on the floor. He moved silently towards Ian's office and placed his ear to the door, only the shuffling of papers could be heard. He opened the door and saw the solicitor as he expected eyes down examining a file; he looked up their eyes locked, two bullets were embedded in his brain before he had invited the client to sit down. He looked around, a perfect operation, he confidently moved from the office to the stairs that led to the front entrance on to Reform Street, he went to the rear door that led in to the old Howff graveyard; he walked through the old graveyard then exited out on to Barrack Road, where he took a left that took him into the Overgate Shopping Centre which was bursting at the seams with Christmas shoppers.

He went into the toilets and located an empty cubicle. He took the laptop and Hugo Boss dark suit out of the Primark bag and replaced it with the Lacoste shell suit, baseball cap and trainers. He waited five minutes placed fashionable spectacles on, and then left the cubicle with the Primark bag tucked into his jacket. He made no eye contact with anyone and walked out into the mass of shoppers, cleaners are chatting and walking picking up wrappers of every kind imaginable, they were throwing massive plastic bags into large moveable containers; he expertly threw the Primark bag into one. He had seven minutes to catch his London bound train. From the Overgate Centre to the train station platform it took two minutes thirty seconds, he had plenty of time.

His First Class ticket had been purchased via the Internet by one of his numerous aliases' credit cards. Tonight he would stay the night in London at the Savoy, and then fly out to Madrid in the morning. As he walked down Union Street he glanced over to the shop that sold people their dream homes in Bulgaria. Nothing looked untoward the shop was closed for the Christmas holiday.

He crossed the busy road to the train station; commuters had been out to celebrate the Christmas break they were in a boisterous mood. One young woman was nearly run down as she stepped on to the road oblivious to the thunderous roar of traffic. The green man came on and he followed the rest of the commuters and day trippers to the station. He descended the stairs to the ticket barriers and handed over his ticket to the young lady on the barrier. He is told the train was on time and it is leaving from Platform One, First Class accommodation is at the front of the train. She handed his ticket back to him; two drunken women were behind him they were politely told they had to place their ticket in the slot on the barrier.

He made his way to the platform heading up to the south end, studying the people on the platform, everything seemed in order, weary people anxious to get home, and people going to London. The train came through the tunnel and incrementally made its way up to the south end of the platform, he noticed that the First Class accommodation was sparsely occupied, that was an added bonus. He was on his own at the top end of the platform; it seemed he was the only one travelling First Class; he would mix in amongst the other travellers then make his way to First Class when he was on the train, he didn't want to be the man in the suit standing on his own, people may remember him. He boarded the train with the other travellers then easily made his way to the First Class carriage his reserved seat had been allocated two tables from the end of the carriage. Only four people are in the carriage all men in their fifties. He took his jacket off and hung it up; he placed the laptop on the table. A steward is making his way towards his table. He would open his laptop when the steward had departed. He ordered a cup of coffee; the steward brought it to his table accompanied by a small plate of biscuits. The train made its way onto the Tay Bridge it was moving slowly, he had six -minutes before the train reached Fife.

He had enjoyed his time in Dundee; it had been very profitable. The other side of his stay had been the merciless bloodletting never seen before in Dundee; he had not a modicum of an attack on his conscience; the people that he had sent into the next world were not assets and would not been missed, there would not have been a spike in the sales of Kleenex. He had done society a favour. This was business mixed with the unequal partner pleasure. He knew his paymaster was an odious individual; he would rid the world of him in the bat of an eye lid; if someone requested and took care of his 'expenses.'

The laptop sprung into life after a myriad of complicated passwords and numbers (he had installed the laptop with sophisticated software that would destroy important information if ever it came into the hands of someone else) He Googled and brought up three websites; The Evening Telegraph, Radio Tay and BBC Scotland News. Nothing about the shooting of Ian Williams, he checked his watch; it was only twenty -minutes ago since he entered his office. The secretary should have come around by now he had only induced a fainting turn on her. The coffee was excellent; in fact it was the best he had tasted in months, he looked along the corridor and caught the steward's eye, he held up his coffee cup, the steward moved towards him with the coffee pot, he went to the toilet in the rear of the carriage; he didn't want the steward to initiate a conversation.

In the toilet he looked in the mirror he was calmness personified, the clear lens glasses made him look at least five years older. He splashed his face with the ice cold water through habit not for any other reason, there were no doubts or signs of panic, another first class operation completed; he smiled at himself in the mirror. Tomorrow afternoon he would be in Madrid, sunny but still chilly.

He opened the toilet door slowly, there is no one in the corridor he could see the train is half- way over the Tay Bridge by the high girders. He stepped out of the toilet and made his way to the window in the corridor, he slid the window down and he felt the night air rush in. He leaned slightly out of the window the train would be beyond the last of the girders any second now.

He casually removed the small gun from his pocket and waited till the train was clear of the high girders, then threw the pistol into the depths of the Tay. He then discarded the remaining two bullets that he had removed from the pistol and they joined the gun in the murky depths. The latex gloves were disposed of in the same meticulous and expedient manner. He closed the window and returned to his seat, the coffee was on the table. After he consumed the coffee, he refreshed the websites.

Is there any news of the shooting? He had no doubt that Ian Williams was dead; he just wanted it confirmed by various news channels, he was overcome by tiredness and wanted to have some semblance of sleep for a couple of hours. The BBC and Evening Telegraph's websites showed no details of the shooting. He went to the Radio Tay website; 'Solicitor shot in office... mistaken identity theory... more reports later.' He stared at the laptop with a wry smile, 'mistaken identity theory,' once again the media were wrong; there was no mistaken identity. He would keep the laptop open for another five minutes more updates would be forthcoming. He went back to the BBC website; 'Solicitor shot dead in City Centre office' screamed the headline.

He clicked on the story and read quickly through it, and then shock overcame him, the story explained the solicitor shot dead was Grant McEwan; who the fuck is Grant McEwan?'

He read the more detailed story. It said that the solicitor carrying out the work was a last minute replacement; because the well- known and controversial solicitor, Ian Williams was attending an event at a local factory. He went back to the other websites and they replicated the story. He had killed an innocent man. He was in the wrong place at the wrong time; what could he have done?

His thoughts turned to Ramage he had paid him his fee upfront. He would not be returning it. He quickly realised that this was the last contract he had completed for Ramage, and Ramage would do everything and anything to retrieve his fee back and dispose of him. He instantly shrugged off the remorse of the innocent solicitor. He would not set foot in the UK again after tonight.

Grant McEwan's unfortunate death was confined to history. His thoughts concentrated on the positive; the Bulgarian scam he had operated from the Dundee office had ran smoothly without any complications. In January the scam about Bulgaria would break, but not one of the employees would be able to shed any light on the proprietor of the business.

Ramage would be livid that was certain, he hated Ian Williams with a passion; he didn't see any irony when he called him corrupt and a crook. He had been 'cheated' out of land in Dundee; Ian Williams had managed to secure the land then gain planning permission without too much difficulty. The Legal opinion at the time was he had less than no chance in gaining planning permission for student accommodation or any other accommodation for that matter. But because Ramage's Legal firm had not been innovative or devious about jumping on the Green renewable energy bandwagon, the Council were persuaded by his persuasive arguments that Dundee could be at the forefront in Green renewable and sustainable energy. Ramage through his widely respected Legal firm tried to buy Ian out but had been rebuffed; Ian had leaked the details of the proposal to the Press. That was the reason Ramage gave up on the Legal route to eliminate Ian Williams, he would go for the more traditional method. With the bungled assassination now known, he could not attempt another attack on his life. Ramage had invested millions on recruiting the finest established Legal brains and the potentially brightest young trainee solicitors to sew up the Legal work in Dundee then move into the more lucrative city of Aberdeen.

He had important contacts in the police they were not inexpensive. They had looked and listened for wrong doing on Ian Williams's part, but found nothing. Ramage had been outfoxed again not by Ian, but by fate and it had cost him a substantial sum.

***

The atmosphere in the Chief Constable's office is tense. Squeezed in the office are the high echelons of the Serious Crime department and two ex- detectives; David Floyd and David Towers. When they were detectives they were imaginatively called 'the two Dave's', they were all standing including the Chief Constable. Sitting at his massive desk is Feeney and the young officer who had spoken to Eddings in his office. The shooting of Grant McEwen had added to the woes of the soon retiring Chief Constable, he was showing impatience with the lack of arrests on the previous murders. That was until Feeney showed up and requested today's meeting. Feeney had told him that he suspected Eddings was ill. Mentally ill and unstable. He was suffering from a nervous breakdown he had accused him (Feeney) of working for the Scottish Crime and Drug Enforcement Agency.

Moreover, he had asked the young police officer to spy on him and report anything that he thinks is 'unusual.' He had requested that the young officer meet him late at night at the Law Hill. He was so concerned about the young officer's safety; he and the two Dave's went to the Law Hill with him, they waited at the bottom of the Law while the young officer kept the rendezvous. The Chief Constable was fearful of this unstable detective causing a side-show, rather than bringing in the murderer.

Feeney went on to explain that Raymond Andrews is the killer of the police officers. And the young junkies and Grant McEwen, the two bullets from his brain were from the same batch that killed the police officers and the two junkies.

'Eddings would not allow me to arrest Andrews if we could locate him, because he insists there is not enough evidence; he is protecting Andrews for some reason I do not know.'
He is asking the Chief Constable to organise a Press Conference to indicate they were looking for Raymond Andrews for questioning in relation to all the murders recently committed in the area, including Grant McEwan.

The Chief Constable studied the faces in the room. There were no sign of dissention. They unanimously agreed with Feeney. He picked up the phone and told his secretary to contact the local and national news organisations about the impending developments in the case. Feeney felt exhilaration rush through his body.

If a total stranger was present in the room, he would have been forgiven if he had the impression that Feeney is the main man and the Chief Constable is his underling. Feeney had shown the ruthless side of his character now it was the perfect opportunity to show his caring side. He suggested that Eddings should be let go from the case or cases immediately with a lucrative financial package, the two Dave's were prepared to give him a meaningful job in Dubai as a security consultant. The Chief Constable didn't need any encouragement to rid himself of this troublesome detective, the money side of the settlement would cause no concern and it would allow him to retire with a last hurrah, and more importantly no unsolved murders in his tenure. There could also be a gong in it for him as well. The young officer was thanked and excused from the meeting. Everyone else sat down.

The Chief Constable was pleased that Eddings would receive an enticing change of career abroad in addition to his financial settlement; any guilt was extinguished by this career opportunity. This was the sole reason two Dave's were present to persuade Eddings to go to Dubai, they wouldn't mention about his unusual behaviour and clandestine meetings at night, this was a job offer from Allah; after all he was thinking about retiring next year, they were just bringing forward his departure date.

The two Dave's had a reputation of talking anyone round to their point of view, with the recipient of their persuasive powers understanding that they themselves had come to this point of view. They were great friends with Valentine Eddings and they worked together on some heinous and disturbing cases. But the two Dave's had seen that they were being treated as irritants and started looking further afield for a career that matched their job skills and personalities. They were too young (in their middle fifties) to play golf in the damp wet climate of Dundee. Their Masonic tentacles stretched over many continents, thus the offer from Dubai fell into their respective laps. They sincerely hoped that Eddings would seize this manna from Allah, that way *he* could approach the Chief Constable about early retirement.

***

He sat in his spacious kitchen overlooking the Tay, it was freezing outside but the Tay looked magnificent. He was encouraging his mind to veer away from the slaying of Grant McEwan, Feeney had telephoned him informing him that the bullets were from the same batch that had killed Swithers and the two junkies. They had to go on television to say that Raymond Andrews is requested to come forward for questioning regarding the murders in Dundee. Eddings accepted that Andrews was being set up as fanciful now, Andrews was undoubtedly the killer, for what reason God knows. Feeney told him that he was going to see the Chief Constable with the proposal of a Press Conference; did he wish to be present? Feeney knew that Eddings was not remotely interested in the bright lights the cameras of the Press Corps. Feeney told him to stay at home it would be pointless of him to come in to the office. He then casually mentioned that the two Dave's were home for Christmas and had popped into the office to see him, they asked to see Valentine. Feeney knew that he hated his Christian name and never used it nor did others, he went on to say that they looked lean, tanned and fit, playfully suggesting everything he was not.
'Don't be surprised if they give you a home visit.'

Eddings mood was elevated at hearing his two best friends were in Dundee; he would cancel his bracing walk to the nearby Baxter Park. He didn't want to tempt fate by leaving the house, he needn't have worried, they were on their way to see him, the double act and they would be trying to entice him to Dubai; they also wanted to see if he had changed. Eddings had underestimated Feeney he hated to admit it but to a certain extent he had also underestimated Raymond Andrews. Coming back to Dundee knowing his vanishing without a trace had caused a stir, but coming back and executing a solicitor in his office, which was either reckless or showed determination for revenge for some perceived slight against him. Raymond Andrews must have known that the area around Reform Street was awash with cameras he would be identified without too much trouble.

The secretary was relatively unharmed she would be able to make a positive identification; Feeney would call him after the Press Conference with the nuts and bolts of the McEwan murder.
His mobile which lay on the large circular breakfast table shattered the silence in the kitchen. He did not recognise the number but he recognised the voice, it was Dave Floyd they were on their way over, where exactly in Fairfield Grove is his house? At the bottom of the development, coming in from Banter Street, number eighty-four. He filled up the kettle and waited on his two friends, he missed them badly, if they were still detectives he was confident that they would have come to the conclusion that Andrews was being set up, then he thought again about McEwan being shot, that diminished the first theory. The kettle came to the boil he threw three tea bags into the pot and poured in the boiling water. Dave Floyd was a tea jenny; he would miss his Tetley tea over in Dubai. It would be good to hear how they were settling in in Dubai; he wished he could go out there for a long holiday without his wife.

She wasn't fond of oppressive heat. The doorbell echoed along the large Spartan hallway he moved quickly to the front door, the two Dave's were indeed tanned and they had lost weight, he invited them in and led them into the kitchen.

They walked past him and went to kitchen windows through the large French doors.
'What a view!' 'This is what I miss about Dundee, the Tay.'
Dave Floyd moved away from the French doors and sat at the table. 'Are you not going to offer your guests a drink then?'
'The tea is infusing just now; I know how you like it strong... are you not going to take your coat off?'
He rises and takes his coat off and places it on an empty chair, Dave Towers hands Floyd his coat.
'No tea for me please, something musical would fit the bill,' he winks at Eddings. 'Bells coming up, do you want water or ice?'
'A wee drop of water thanks... so how is things?'
'Can't complain... actually I will complain, even though I am not a geriatric, I feel like one, I am going to ask to get away early, things are not the same, standards have slipped its all computers now.'
'Things can't have slipped that bad, you were confident using computers, and we weren't, are you not just fed up?' asked Towers
'I'm just losing the appetite for it, and I think I'm too long in the tooth, nobody wants to go and interview people for longer than ten minutes, they all want back to the office.'
'But that was coming, everybody saw that when they started recruiting from the Universities and putting them on courses then straight into the field, most of the new lot thought they knew it all,' added Floyd.
   Eddings brought over him his tea. 'Do you want a bacon roll with that?'
Towers nodded. 'I'll have two please.'
'He wasn't talking to you... I'll have one,' said Floyd.
Eddings went to the large American style fridge and took out a packet of bacon; he moved towards the George Foreman grill and switched it on. He took the bottle of Bells Whisky out of the overhead cupboard; and poured the drink and added a small amount of water and gave it to Towers.
   'How do you get on with your partner Feeney?' asked Floyd
'He is a high flyer, I think he thinks I am too cautious, maybe I am,' he walks over to the heated grill and places four pieces of bacon in. 'I thought this Raymond Andrews was being set up, but that seems not to be the case, that's finally convinced me to leave next year, I suppose it comes to us all.'
He turns the crackling bacon over then takes out the rolls and butters them.
'We spoke to Feeney he told us that this Andrews was dressed as a young ned; he certainly fooled the secretary and the CCTV.'
'Fooled? How?'
'The CCTV picked up someone dressed like him going into the Overgate Shopping Centre, but not coming out, they knew that he was carrying a Primark bag, but so were other neds, they still have to go through all the CCTV footage, but the quality is not good.'
   Eddings takes the rolls over to the grill and throws the bacon into them and gives it to his friends. He pours himself a mug of tea. Floyd gives his unasked opinion.
'All the evidence points towards Andrews the gun found in his flat; his fingerprints on the golf club and the bullets from McEwan etc.'
'I know, I know, I just don't feel right about this case, a gut feeling, the evidence points to Andrews, but... it doesn't matter.'
Towers stands up and goes walkabout in the kitchen. 'The two murdered policemen, am I allowed to call them that? Eddings laughed. Towers continues, 'they were involved in drugs, that's not disputed, and if Andrews did murder them, the two young lads and McEwan instead of Williams he was silencing them but why? They all must have knew something about him that bad that he kills them, now what did he do that was so bad he would kill all those individuals?'
'He could have been involved in the drug financing?' said Floyd
'Or he could have just went mad, because he was taking coke too frequently, that made him paranoid so he acts without fear or caution,' added Towers who walks to the cupboard and takes out the Bells and pours himself a generous measure.

'Feeney is convinced it's him and I agree,' said Floyd.
Floyd looks at Eddings. 'Do you think Feeney sees you as a hindrance?'
'He's young ambitious and wants to climb up the tree as high as possible, does that answer your question?' Towers walks over to the table and takes a bacon roll, he moves over to the window and takes in the view. 'I don't trust Feeney one inch, if you have any suspicions about him, dump them, he's the type to make people forget what they saw or heard. You are retiring.'
Eddings guilt about the young officer evaporates. Towers returns to the table and sits down.
'If you are serious about leaving the force, we know there's a job coming up in Dubai, pays double the money that you are on now, we can secure it for you, but you would have to let us know by next week. The job comes with a four bedroom villa with swimming pool and maids...'
Floyd jumps in. 'The salary is tax free; do you really have to think about it?'
'I would have to speak to the wife; she doesn't like the heat, would they let me go so soon, at this short notice I don't want to lose money by resigning?'
'I can sort that out,' he winks at Eddings.

***

Ian leaves Bell Street where he has giving a statement to Feeney and another detective, Feeney was trying to establish whether Ian was the real target or not. The statement Ian gives is straightforward he was at the Romans factory as a guest of Linda Simpson; she called him the night before and asked him to accompany her. He called Grant McEwan the same evening and asked him if he could stand in for him as he had been persuaded by Linda Simpson to go to the Romans factory. Grant said he had four appointments in the morning and nothing pencilled in for the afternoon, he told Ian to enjoy himself in the freezing conditions up at the factory. He ended with the chilling prophetic words; better you than me. Feeney asked if he had any threats or business worries. Ian answered all his questions with a resounding no. He was more concerned about his dead colleague's family and their financial plight. Grant was no financial genius.

Feeney was going through the motions he knew he would receive stock answers from Ian. He had interviewed Linda Simpson and she had corroborated what Ian had said in his statement. Ian left Bell Street an hour after he had arrived there. Feeney did not let his guard drop, Ian was sure who the police were looking for but he didn't offer up his theory.

Mary's statement was laconic, youth, medium height and wearing white shell suit, he was wearing spectacles and a baseball hat, she was grabbed from behind; she woke up in the staff toilet on the floor. She came to herself and went to see Grant, she found him upright in his chair she could see the two bullet entry wounds, his eyes were open. She called the police and an ambulance, although she knew this was futile; he was dead. She then called Ian on his mobile to tell him the sequence of events; he in turn took Linda aside and told her the bad news. Linda like the true professional that she was went through with the acceptance of a print by McIntosh Patrick from the workforce in their canteen; she thanked them profusely but said she had to go as she had an urgent appointment. She accompanied Ian to his office in Reform Street.

***

Dave Towers had removed the whisky from the overhead cupboard to the kitchen table; they are doing an excellent job persuading Eddings that his future lay in sunnier climes.
They were relaxed about time off, they could not foresee any problems if he needed to return to Dundee for a holiday. They ran the show. Eddings tried to keep his excitement intact, but the smirk turned into a wide smile. Towers knew if they had the contract there on the breakfast table he would have signed it there and then.
'Are you sure the Chief Constable would agree to me leaving at short notice?'

'He's leaving himself soon; he knows that you have been at the forefront in solving serious crimes, he thinks you deserve your place in the sun, that was his exact words,' not a flicker of remorse as he uttered this lie. Eddings felt reassured at this testimony from the Chief Constable.

   A quick calculation done in his head meant that his retirement package could clear the modest mortgage on the house. Jean would like that; she could mention that they hadn't a mortgage, no doubt she would exaggerate and say they bought this house outright years ago; she would agree he should go to Dubai. He left the table and went to the overhead cupboard and took out a small glass, he returned to the table and poured Towers a drink and then one for him.
'Here's to Dubai.'
Towers and Floyd looked at each other and stood up to clink their glass and mug with him.
 'Mission accomplished,' said Floyd to Towers, who downed the whisky in one go.
 'Where's your phone?' asked Floyd
'Through there in the family area, on the coffee table, why can't you use your mobile?'
'I have to go easy on my minutes... do me a favour and make another pot of tea.'
Floyd opens the large French doors and sits down on the leather sofa; he can smell the freshness of it, he calls the Chief Constable with the news that Eddings requires to resign today.
  'Could you have the paperwork brought over to his house in the next couple of hours?'
The Chief Constable opens his desk and pulls out Eddings resignation letter and medical report due to ill health, he had been examined by the police doctor and that he is suffering from exhaustion and work -related stress, he wishes to be considered for early retirement. He reads this out to Floyd.
'How does that sound to you?'
'Perfect, couldn't have written that any better, nothing sounding too indelicate how much of a lump sum will he receive and how much will his pension be each month?'
'I have managed to manipulate some conditions of the ill health programme to his advantage, the lump sum will be, one hundred and two thousand and his pension each month will be fifteen hundred, subject to tax, I think you'll agree that the figures are generous.'
Floyd is delighted at hearing this, 'I can't see him turning this down, hold on a minute I'll tell him the figures.'
   He returns to the kitchen, and explains the figures. 'I'll take it now.' Eddings feels happiness has come to visit him again; he has not felt like this for years.
Floyd returns to the phone and tells the Chief Constable Eddings has agreed to the financial package, as he thought he would. The Chief Constable is relieved at this; now he could look forward to the Press Conference. He will send over the papers by courier to be signed, the lump sum will be in his account by the end of the week, four weeks from today his pension will be in his account, he needed to ask this, but did he want counselling?'
'He's okay, he doesn't need that, thanks for all the help Chief; try and get the paperwork over in the next hour, we don't want him changing his mind do we?'
The Chief Constable's blood ran cold for a second at this, 'It will be over in the next twenty-minutes, make sure he signs it. Thanks for all the help you and Towers have given me; it could have been embarrassing, bye.'
Eddings looks up expectantly at the return of Floyd.
'The paperwork's is on its way, all you need to do is sign it; your lump sum will be in by the end of the week, pension in four weeks.'
'I need another drink,' Towers pours him a large drink.
'Is the tea made then?'
'Sorry, I can't remember... yes I did make it but I've not poured it out.'
Floyd walks over and refills his mug then returns to the table. 'Well, how does it feel to be retired... and rich?'
'It's still sinking in, I feel like I'm dreaming, oh, I'm sorry, I didn't thank you two did I? Thanks for everything. '

He sipped the whisky and stared into space. 'But, I need to say goodbye to my friends... who the fuck am I kidding I have no friends, they can empty my locker, I have nothing valuable in it apart from toiletries, and they can keep them.'

Towers and Floyd are pleased to see this belligerence and hostility towards his colleagues, there is not a chance that Eddings would have second thoughts about retiring.

'Send in a card to them saying sorry couldn't get down because of the speed of events, going to Dubai, they'll fall for that.'
'Or they won't care,' Eddings interjected.
'Who cares about them, you're well out of it and you have the rest of your life to look forward to, fuck the lot of them.' Floyd agreed with the sentiment of his colleague, but wouldn't have used that type of language.
'So, what's it like living here then?' asked Towers
'Fine nothing spectacular, I was looking forward to getting stuck into that garden, but I have other things to look forward to, don't I?'
'You'll love it over there. The sun, the lifestyle and not forgetting the generous salary, there is a large ex-pat community over here, mega- rich individuals; you'll have to start playing golf again, we are on the course at least three times a week; and the night life is something else.'

***

'Send him in now,' the Chief Constable boomed into the telephone. Feeney walks into the office and takes a seat. 'The two Dave's have worked their magic again, Eddings is no more. He has taken early retirement; take a look at the paperwork it just arrived ten minutes ago.
'That was good advice you gave me about having the doctors report about him suffering from work related stress among other things, these doctors we have here are magnificent, they don't even have to see you to diagnose the problem.'
'Things have moved more quickly than I anticipated the two Dave's must have held a gun at his head to make him sign...'
'No, no, I had the paperwork sent over to Eddings house, he signed it, and it was brought back to me, which I have accepted. Once he had signed the paperwork that was it.'

He was given a letter from me thanking him for his service to the people of Dundee, and how he had an excellent detection rate, he had sent many evil people behind bars, and then went on to praise him for his help in developing the careers of other young detectives.' The letter had eased the Chief Constable's conscience.

Feeney feigned sadness, 'Hard to believe he is not here anymore is it?'
'All's well that ends well... now we can concentrate on this Press Conference, then follow up the latest sighting of Andrews in Paris.'
'It would be better if we send over a couple of the female detectives, personally I think he is hiding in a more rural climate, he is a keen hill walker, I would rather stay here and see what turns up, if that is okay with you?'
'It's up to your superior how you go about trying to find Andrews, but now we can tell the Press. We need to question him about the recent loss of life of certain individuals, or should I say for the murders of...'
'We need to question him about the murders of... and then name the victims one by one in a slow measured tone. The public will be in no doubt that we think he is the killer, but we have not actually said that.'
'But the public will make up their minds; he's the killer,' the Chief Constable added.
'He's the one; that is certain; we couldn't have more evidence if we wished for it's just getting him here in an interview room,' Feeney said with frustration in his voice.

'At least Eddings is going out the door on his terms with a decent settlement it's sad when you hear of a good man succumbing to mental illness.

'I'm glad you came to me when you did, the new Chief Constable might not take the same humanitarian view as me. Luckily for Eddings I was able to call in a few favours from the medical side to say they had examined him, these favours will not be available in the future, I'm sure of that, you should be proud of what you have done, if only Eddings knew how much you cared and looked out for him.' Feeney shifted uncomfortably in the seat.

'You have done him proud as well Chief Constable; very few senior officers would stick their necks out for one of their men,' Feeney added.

'That's true… but after this Press Conference; let's hope this maniac hand's himself in, or someone informs us where he is, I take it for granted that his flat is still under surveillance?'

'Yes, but I can't see him returning to his flat. We have got Linda Simpson still under surveillance, just in case Andrews has another go at her, which is unlikely but we can't relax with Andrews still in Dundee,' Feeney replied.

'We just have to keep an eye on her, Andrews is facing a life in prison for a long, long time, he might want to die by suicide by cop, that's common practice by mentally ill criminals in America, I was told that at a conference in New York last year, and you know what the British are like if the Americans are doing things we slavishly ape them. But that is just my opinion; I'll be finished soon like Eddings.'

Feeney had to dispose of his smile as he left the Chief Constable's office, he could feel everyone's eyes on him, they wanted to ask how Eddings was, he had told a couple of officers' that Eddings was seeking psychiatric help; and it would be unlikely that he would return. Just as he anticipated the story was around the Headquarters before he had reached his car. He continued his walk along the long corridor passing the small cubicles that were occupied by a man and a computer, each one stopped as he passed them. He was metres from the door now he stopped and turned around and shook his head slowly, then turned and strode through the door.

The jungle drums had started Eddings was finished, emails spun through the ether, others added more to this, he has been admitted to hospital, he could be in for a long, long time. Feeney was pleased to say the least that his course of action had worked superbly, Eddings was out of the way, aided and abetted by the two Dave's, the smartest detectives there had ever been, so legend had had it. If they were the smartest he would be curious to see the dumbest. He walked to his car, he had an appointment to keep; he was looking forward to this. He never met the same person twice and he never spoke directly to them, even by landline or mobile and definitely not by email. He would park in the Overgate Centre then go for a coffee at Starbucks; he would take his coffee to the furthest table from the door and start reading the Private Eye satirical magazine.

He would be told where and when this meeting would take place and from the most unlikely and innocent sources; 'the estate agent phoned about…' would mean the meeting would take place in the Tayside Solicitors Property Centre, 'the garage called…'would mean in Asda's car park in Kirkton. He envied the way they operated; nothing was left to chance to compromise his position. He carried the coffee and sat at the table.

He took out the magazine and gave the impression that he was engrossed in its contents. Out of the corner of his eye he saw the figure approaching. He didn't feel alarmed; he had seen this subtle approach many times. The male in his forties placed his coffee on his table; he then placed a Euro coin next to his coffee then picked it up again and placed it in his pocket. This was the contact: Feeney took out his mobile he pressed the keypad and then spoke into the mobile. 'My friend has retired due to illness, Andrews is prime suspect.'

When he heard this innocent conversation, he drank part of his coffee then left. Feeney would stay in Starbucks for at least fifteen minutes. The contact used the public phone in the Overgate; he dialled the Glasgow travel agents and asked for any cancellation holidays to Tenerife for that day?' He was giving the terse reply, 'Sorry, could I interest you in Spain?' 'No thanks, I'll try somewhere else.' This was relayed to Ramage; he was delighted that Raymond Andrews was now the number one suspect for all the murders and he knew that he could not talk.

If he was honest with himself he was disappointed that Ian Williams was still alive, due to the twist of fate of his colleague standing in for him. Feeney had been more than helpful, he had convinced the Chief Constable that his partner was having a nervous breakdown, Eddings would never realise how close he came to unravelling the evidence that implicated Raymond Andrews, if he had done so Feeney's other extra - curricular activities with unsavoury characters might have come to light. He conceded he had paid the UA for not completing the job, he would be aware he had eliminated the wrong man, a refund would not be coming through the post by Federal Express anytime soon, with a note offering an apology. He liked doing business with him, but because of operational difficulties their relationship was no more.

Ian Williams had been sent a warning, whether he heeded it or not was up to him. He accepted that any wishful relationship with Linda Simpson didn't get out of the starting block; he was rich and without sounding immodest was good looking, but the class system still operated he convinced himself, hence Linda Simpson rejecting his subtle invitation to join him in Tenerife. He had done an inventory on his life, he had to relocate to Tenerife, businessmen; of his type were killing each other on the streets of Glasgow.

He had sound advice from his legal firm, sell your assets then move out of Britain, the money realised from these assets could be made to work more productively and more important legally. His prize asset had been Raymond Andrews; the information passed from him made him millions, from leaked plans for new railways to regeneration of waterfronts. The land was bought then sold to the Scottish Executive; all legally. But Andrews' using Linda Simpson's money to enter the drug trade was reckless stupidity. If he had been caught he would have blamed Linda Simpson, he had bestowed on his constituents and Linda a favour by having him disappear.

He would watch the Press Conference on television that night; the heat was on Raymond Andrews which was an oxymoron; he was stone cold in the concrete grave. The vista from the balcony was inspiring as well as comforting, he kept repeating to himself he could see anyone drive up the road to his villa, he was safe and secure. I bet Ian Williams could not say the same thing. But that was all behind him, his legal firm had made tentative enquiries in Aberdeen about any impending early retirements, or any legal firm that would welcome a take-over. He would make as much money legally as doing drugs; he is older and slightly wiser. He had an abundance of capital scattered around Europe's banks'. Eastern Europe is awaiting his cash, opportunities were omnipresent. Grants from the European Union were groaning in the vaults of Brussels, his Legal firm would relinquish some of the pressure.

The local difficulty in Dundee had been dealt with harshly but quickly. Some stories emanating in the Press stating Dundee was in the grip of an organised crime war between the Poles and Romanian gypsies who were marking out a turf war. This was the big news and an exclusive so the journalist told his readers. This nonsense was given to him from Feeney. The journalist said it came from 'a senior police source,' Eddings was the source according to Feeney when police officers asked him who the source was. This helped muddy the waters and stir up local hysteria against the economic migrants. Ramage opened a bottle of beer and raised it to the sky. 'To my absent friend… Raymond Andrews.'

The End

Made in the USA
Charleston, SC
15 July 2015